Praise for *Quartet for the End of Time*

"[It] is exhilarating to join a novelist working at these bracing heights, where no abstraction—not God, not time, not death, not art, not the meaning of life—is out of bounds, yet where all philosophical searching is rooted in human experience, whether sickening or sublime, and rendered with clarity and sympathy." — *The Washington Post*

"Deeply compassionate and beautiful … Like *The Sentimentalists*, *Quartet* explores the limits of moral freedom and the mutability of human perceptions. But its characters are less important in themselves than as notes in an all-encompassing, eternal music." — *The Globe and Mail*

"[*Quartet*] is at once a sweeping tale and a deeply layered meditation on the nature of time, justice and agency … A unique work of literature; Skibsrud … has embedded meaning in terrific turns of plot."—*Maclean's*

"A sweeping, ambitious work, *Quartet* gives evidence of the author's prodigious talent and a vision that's beyond her years … Skibsrud is a writer of profound intelligence whose talent deserves applause." — *The Chronicle-Herald*

"A spellbinding story of epic scope." —CBC Books

"Skibsrud's background as a poet is clear in her writing style, which flows in an almost dream-like narrative. The story unfolds beautifully … Intensely engrossing." — *Winnipeg Free Press*

"Intricate [and] ambitious … a haunting meditation on responsibility with vivid glimpses of history, and a distinctive and nuanced voice." —*Publishers Weekly*

"Elegant, intricately woven … [Skibsrud's] unique voice and eye for historical detail lend the book a satisfying richness." —*Kirkus Reviews*

"*Quartet for the End of Time* is a brilliant work of art, and it is brilliant in so many ways—its dense, rich, and immaculate prose, its vivid evocation of a watershed period in American history, its high-stakes political and personal drama, and, above all, its intimate and completely compelling portraits of human beings struggling to do the right thing under ambiguous moral circumstances. This wholly realized book has everything I crave in a work of fiction." —Tim O'Brien, author of *The Things They Carried*

"This is that rare novel which brilliantly weaves together a stunning sweep of historical events with an intimate exploration of human bonds, betrayals, and quiet subterfuges. Working with a deep and intricate attention to the convolutions both of the individual heart and of World War I and its aftermath, Skibsrud delivers a tale that is as powerful as it is satisfying." —Vincent Lam, author of *Bloodletting & Miraculous Cures*

"Skibsrud reminds us how family members treat each other during political upheaval—and how war is an extension of domestic policy by other means." —Michael Winter, author of *Minister Without Portfolio*

"Mysterious, richly detailed, and wholly original, this symphonic fiction makes emotion palpable, weaving the consequences of acts and emotions into its very structure." —Andrea Barrett, author of *Ship Fever*

"This is a wonderfully original novel. Scenes of extraordinary high drama take place in a realm drawn with great historical accuracy—in prose that marks this fiction with its own unexpected ethereal tint. Skibsrud has talent to burn." —Joan Silber, author of *Fools*

"*Quartet for the End of Time* is a searingly beautiful book, at once a sweeping historical epic and an intimate meditation on faith and memory. Johanna Skibsrud's newest novel is so intelligent, so compassionate, so moving—and above all so gorgeously written—that it's impossible to put down. She is an astonishingly good writer." —Molly Antopol, author of *The UnAmericans*

PENGUIN

QUARTET FOR THE END OF TIME

JOHANNA SKIBSRUD is the Scotiabank Giller Prize–winning author of *The Sentimentalists* as well as the short story collection *This Will Be Difficult to Explain and Other Stories*. Originally from Pictou County, Nova Scotia, she currently resides in Tucson, Arizona.

ALSO BY
JOHANNA SKIBSRUD

———

This Will Be Difficult to Explain and Other Stories

The Sentimentalists

Sometimes We Think You Are a Monkey

Quartet

for the

End of

Time

A NOVEL

JOHANNA
SKIBSRUD

PENGUIN

an imprint of Penguin Canada Books Inc., a Penguin Random House Company

Published by the Penguin Group
Penguin Canada Books Inc., 90 Eglinton Avenue East, Suite 700, Toronto, Ontario, Canada M4P 2Y3

Penguin Group (USA) LLC, 375 Hudson Street, New York, New York 10014, U.S.A.
Penguin Books Ltd, 80 Strand, London WC2R 0RL, England
Penguin Ireland, 25 St Stephen's Green, Dublin 2, Ireland (a division of Penguin Books Ltd)
Penguin Group (Australia), 707 Collins Street, Melbourne, Victoria 3008, Australia
(a division of Pearson Australia Group Pty Ltd)
Penguin Books India Pvt Ltd, 11 Community Centre, Panchsheel Park, New Delhi – 110 017, India
Penguin Group (NZ), 67 Apollo Drive, Rosedale, Auckland 0632, New Zealand
(a division of Pearson New Zealand Ltd)
Penguin Books (South Africa) (Pty) Ltd, 24 Sturdee Avenue, Rosebank, Johannesburg 2196, South Africa

Penguin Books Ltd, Registered Offices: 80 Strand, London WC2R 0RL, England

First published in Hamish Hamilton hardcover by Penguin Canada Books Inc., 2014
Published in this edition, 2015

1 2 3 4 5 6 7 8 9 10 (RRD)

Copyright © Johanna Skibsrud, 2014

Manufactured in the U.S.A.

Book design by Barbara M. Bachman

LIBRARY AND ARCHIVES CANADA CATALOGUING IN PUBLICATION

Skibsrud, Johanna, 1980-, author
Quartet for the end of time / Johanna Skibsrud.
Originally published by Hamish Hamilton, 2014.
ISBN 978-0-14-318196-5 (pbk.)

I. Title.

PS8587.K46Q37 2015   C813'.54   C2015-900690-2

eBook ISBN 978-0-14-319322-7

Visit the Penguin Canada website at **www.penguin.ca**

Special and corporate bulk purchase rates available; please see
www.penguin.ca/corporatesales or call 1-800-810-3104.

CONTENTS

.
.

As a musician I studied rhythm. Rhythm is, in essence, alteration and division. To study alteration and division is to study Time. Time—measured, relative, physiological, psychological—is divided in a thousand ways, of which the most immediate for us is a perpetual conversion of the future into the past. In eternity, these things no longer exist. So many questions! I have posed these questions in my *Quartet for the End of Time*.

—OLIVIER MESSIAEN

QUARTET FOR THE END OF TIME

I.

Sutton

RIOT ON THE MALL. THE JUDGE'S HOUSE, DISTRICT OF
COLUMBIA COURTHOUSE, CAMP MARKS, WASHINGTON, D.C.,
JUNE–JULY, 1932—WITH A BRIEF DETOUR TO THE
DISTRICT OF COLUMBIA COURTHOUSE, 1928.

I t was her mother who accompanied Sutton to her father's door. Who
stood beside her, hand raised and trembling, before she finally
brought it down: knocking, sharply, twice. Who, in response to her husband's voice, which echoed from inside, touched her daughter lightly on
the shoulder, as though in sympathy for something that she couldn't
name, then stepped aside to let her pass.

It was the afternoon following the riots; Alden had not yet returned,
and the household had been thrown into turmoil of a rare sort—her
mother's incursion beyond the limit of her own quarters was certain evidence of this. And now, inexplicably, the Judge wished to speak to *her*.
She was to listen very carefully, her mother warned, and do as she was
told. This was counsel that could, in itself, have hardly been deemed
unusual—except that it went without saying in the Kelly house. When

the Judge spoke, there was never any choice but to listen. Of all people, it was her mother who should have known that. Sutton had, therefore, no idea what sort of man to expect in her father's room, now that the remarkable idea had been introduced—if in the negative—that her father was a man whom she conceivably *might not* listen to or obey.

What drew her attention immediately, however, upon first entering, was not anything out of the ordinary with her father himself (he appeared very much as he always had, sitting upright behind his desk in his straight-backed chair), but a hat. A man's hat. Rather sad and misshapen-looking, it sat, incongruously, on her father's desk. A hat on the table, as the Judge himself had taught her, was a very definite sign of bad luck. It was an old cowboy code, a tradition the Judge prided himself in having inherited—though, truth be told, the Kellys themselves had never been actual cowboys. They were wheat farmers from Indiana. The Judge kept an old riding whip anyway as proof of his midwestern pedigree. It lay coiled in his desk's thin middle drawer, and from time to time he would take it out and flick it back and forth with a repetitive twist of his wrist, making, as he did so, a swishing sound that could be heard through the house. They always knew when the Judge was in a meditative mood because of it. It never failed, he said—that particular rhythm, and the accompanying sound the whip made as it cut through the air—to soothe him, and help him to think. Perhaps, as he reflected on more than one occasion, it was due to being reminded through the object's weight and the steady rhythm of it in his hand, of its great and complicated history—which, by extension, was also his own. As a child, Sutton had marveled over the multitude of various conflicting details that surrounded the object, and it had taken her many years to realize what it meant that—on the subject of the whip—her father never told the same story twice.

Now, however, though the Judge had taken the whip from its drawer, he merely fingered its rough leather absently. Only occasionally did he allow it to twitch, restlessly, as if more or less of its own accord, in his hand.

In any case, it was not her father's whip, but the hat, which held Sutton's attention as she entered her father's room.

Why on earth, she wondered, had he not only let it remain on the table, but seemed to have deliberately placed it there? It seemed quite pointless, she reflected (and she could only assume that, on this count, the Judge himself would agree—it was only according to his "code," after all, that she considered the matter), to go about knowingly courting ill fortune in this or any other way—even if one was (as the Judge himself, despite any Romantic allusions, surely was) the very opposite of a superstitious man. Things *don't just happen*, he had told her and Alden on she didn't know how many countless occasions. *You make them happen.*

BEHIND HIS DESK, JUDGE KELLY was sitting very upright, indeed. It was the same posture he assumed while marching in the parade every Fourth of July. (A former colonel, the Judge had been heavily decorated for his service—particularly during the Banana Wars, where he had helped to quell the March riots back in 1911.) As Sutton entered, he cleared his throat and sat more upright still.

He hoped—he said quickly, waving her toward the empty chair opposite his large, low desk, where she was to sit—she had not been too much disturbed by recent events.

Sutton sat. She shook her head.

No, she had not.

But the Judge had hardly paused long enough for a reply.

Now, look, he was saying. Your brother. He's gone ahead and gotten himself tangled up with all of this somehow. As usual with him, it's just a case of having found himself in the wrong place at the wrong time—something that's become almost like a habit with him. But see now, if we aren't careful in this particular case . . .

Here the Judge paused. He cleared his throat, and—distracted suddenly—looked up to where an empty chandelier hook, upon which nothing, as far as Sutton was aware, had ever hung, marked the exact center of the high ceiling. Almost absently, as he did so, he extended a hand toward the hat. Then his eyes descended, meeting—for the briefest of moments—Sutton's own.

A great many things, he said, his eyes fixed firmly now on the hat between them (as though, indeed, it were to the hat, and not to his daughter, he spoke), are held in balance by a very few. This is something that may be difficult for someone of your age to understand—but that is not the most important thing. The more important thing now, he said (still as though to the hat), is to establish that you and I both have in this case . . . a certain . . . *responsibility*.

He looked up now, flickeringly, this time without meeting his daughter's eye.

Let's go back, he said. To just around this time yesterday afternoon—

But Sutton's heart had begun to beat here so unnaturally fast that—though it was a very simple one—the Judge was forced to repeat his question twice before she heard.

Sutton, the Judge said again. I'm asking you. Where were you? Yesterday afternoon?

It was only according to a tremendous effort that she was able to reply.

Here, she said, finally. In a small voice, hardly her own.

IT WAS TRUE. As the noise had drifted from the Mall, Sutton had remained with her mother indoors—only once venturing out to the yard, where she heard the scream of sirens and exchanged a few words with the neighbor, who was just at that moment passing in front of their house to his own. Everything had just "gone wild," Mr. Heller had said—taking unconcealed pleasure in being able to pass on the news. The veterans had stormed the White House, and he—Mr. Heller—would not be surprised if a Communist flag was flying there now. Anyone could have seen it coming, he concluded dolefully, shaking his head and continuing past.

Shortly after, the Judge telephoned. They shouldn't wait dinner, he said. But, no, no—everything was all right.

Sutton could hear his voice through the receiver, which her mother held at an angle, away from her ear. Everything would be cleared up in no time now, he said. Look at it this way. This may be just the break we need. They've called in the Army. Now the whole thing is certain to be over and done with—and soon.

A pause, then: Where's Alden? With you?

Alden had not been seen since late morning, when, after rising late as usual, he had eaten breakfast alone, then—giving his mother a kiss on the forehead—headed for the door. He hadn't said where he was going; he never did.

No, Alden was not with them, Mary Kelly said, her voice rising. They hadn't seen him, she said, but here she paused. She could hardly think. Her eyes flitted nervously about the room. Since—when?

Sometime just before noon, Sutton said. Mary repeated the information. Stephen's voice came back sounding flat and mechanical through the line.

Well, not to worry, he said. The Mall's almost clear. Even if he made it down that far, he'll be home before long.

Then, without signing off, as was his habit, the Judge hung up the phone.

SUTTON WATCHED AS HER mother set the receiver down.

Well, that's all right, then, Mary Kelly said loudly, as though someone might disagree. Then she went into the kitchen and fixed herself a pot of tea. By that time it had become very still and quiet. There was no noise to be heard from the direction of the Mall or anywhere else. All the houses in the neighborhood, including the Hellers' next door, were shut tight.

As they waited, the hours lengthened. Now and then—in order to interrupt what seemed their interminable flow—her mother would get up and turn in a slow circle. Was Sutton quite comfortable? she would ask. Did she need anything? When Sutton replied that she was quite all right, as she did every time, her mother would press a hand to her head. Oh, the *headache* of it, she would say. The very multipurposeness of this expression—which, for as long as Sutton could remember, had been employed by her mother just as readily in the most innocuous of circumstances as in the most acute—served to comfort them both. Once or twice its effect was augmented by something of a more material nature when Mary Kelly slipped away to the medicine cabinet at the back of the house, within which she kept a cure for just about anything you could think to complain of—and even some mysterious conditions you didn't know, until you were cured of them, you actually had. The bedroom, and its cabinet, was a further extension of her quarter of the house. It had been known as the "guest bedroom" until gradually Mary herself became its permanent "guest." Now they called it the "back room." Never "Mary's," or "Mother's" room—though she not only slept there nightly, but also spent most of the late afternoons there, up to four hours at a time, the door shut tight.

Now, after each disappearance, she would return, looking momentarily refreshed, and say, Well, that might be some help. Are you sure you're doing all right?

Each time, Sutton assured her she was. But not an hour would go by before her mother would disappear once more—to fix tea, though neither one of them required it, or to go look up in the telephone directory the number of the police dispatcher, or the family doctor, just to have them "on hand."

Finally, the telephone rang again. It was the Judge. Both Sutton and her mother got up and listened into the heavy handle of the phone, which the older woman once again held away from her ear.

Now—the Judge hesitated—I don't want you worrying over nothing, but, see, there's been some—slight—trouble, which I'll need to look into. Alden—now, look, he's *all right*. It's taken care of, see. Now, you just turn in—don't wait up. Alden's here. With me. Like I told you—everything's *all right*.

Well, the Judge said after Sutton had recounted all of this to him— her heart still beating wildly for some reason, though there was nothing in it the Judge would not have already known—that's good, very good.

Because—he gave her a quick, decisive nod—it's the truth. I've no doubt of it.

Sutton's cheeks were cooling now, her heart beginning to slow to its more regular pace.

It is best—the Judge went on—as I have always maintained, to tell the honest truth, whenever it is possible to do so.

There was something new, now, Sutton noticed, in her father's voice. At first she found it difficult to place, but then—she remembered. It was the same voice she had heard him use on the one occasion she had seen him preside in a court of law. Both Alden and she had been in attendance, accompanied by their mother. She herself could have been no more than ten—Alden, twelve or thirteen. They had sat at the back, and left as soon as the proceedings were over—their mother's hand ushering them out the door before anyone else had yet risen.

It had been a simple open-and-shut case, the Judge had told them—they knew even before it was over what the verdict would be. What else could it have been? A Negro, in the process of holding up a hardware store, had fired a gun and mortally wounded the wife of the store's proprietor. He had confessed to the deed without hesitation—pleading only that the crime had been unmeditated, resulting from the confusion of the holdup. The prosecution had argued, to the contrary, that the crime had been malicious in intent: that the young man in question was of "underdeveloped" character and would continue to prove a certain and perpetual danger to society.

Are these the sorts of "accidents" to which we would like our city streets prone? Accidents, ladies and gentlemen! the prosecutor had shouted. Nothing happens out of the blue—on its own, and for *no reason*!

Then an exhausted-looking woman, in whose house the young man had once been employed, testified that on several occasions she had feared for her virtue in the company of the young man. At the time, the word *virtue*, used in this particular context, had confused Sutton, but she knew enough not to ask her mother about it—that it was something that had, for good reason, been left undefined.

In the end, the maximum penalty was served: death by hanging. Sutton felt her blood thrill suddenly in her veins as the verdict was read. A murmur rippled through the crowd. There was no time to observe the reaction more closely, however—or assess her own. Her mother was already pulling her up by the hood of her spring coat and ushering her out the door. What was it within her that had thrilled at the mention of the accused man's demise? Now, as she listened to her father speak— that same note ringing out in his voice as the one she had heard all those many years before—she tried to recall it: the particular dimensions of the sensation she had felt at that moment as the verdict was read. It seemed it was almost possible—that it was a thing that might, after all, prove measurable. But still she could not ascertain the slightest thing about it—where it had come from, and what it meant to have found it so suddenly within her own body.

Later that evening she overheard her mother speaking sharply to her father.

That was *hardly* a suitable case for children, Stephen, her mother had said. If I'd known— But Sutton never was to find out what it was her mother might have, but had not known, because her father ended the conversation abruptly.

Mary, he had said. Justice is justice! There's never a time where that is not observable, even—or especially—by the very young.

SOMEHOW, THAT PHRASE—her father's voice, and those words, beginning with her mother's name—became inseparable for Sutton from the memory of the accused man's face, as he had stood quavering on the stand. It was perhaps the first time she had looked, for any extended period of time, into the face of a black man. She was fascinated by the way the whites of his eyes stood out in such sharp contrast against his dark skin. Even from that distance, in the back row, wedged between her mother and brother, she could see the way his eyes, when the verdict was read out loud in her father's voice, darkened slightly. They did not flash in alarm, or in fact move at all, but somehow there was a change—and she had witnessed it. It was that change to which the words her father spoke later, beginning with her mother's name, seemed, afterward, to cohere. An almost unseen darkening of a stranger's eye. And it was that which was somehow evoked for her again as her father pronounced those words—*the honest truth*—so many years later.

Never again after that was she to see her father preside in court. Not only because of her mother's sense that the case they'd observed had not been "suitable," but because, shortly afterward, her father was elected to Congress. From then on, he was a government man—the work that he did even more mysterious and difficult to understand.

THERE ARE, OF COURSE, her father was saying, exceptions to every rule. Times when it simply *is not possible* to tell the truth in the way we ordinarily would be expected—would, that is, expect *ourselves* to do. Times when, indeed, telling what might at first appear to be a *stretch* of the truth actually corresponds more accurately with the truth than the truth itself.

The Judge paused—only very slightly. Into this pause Sutton nodded slowly, her lips pressed into a tight line. She fixed her gaze, not on her father's face as he spoke, but again on the space between them— occupied by the hat.

The nod, though slight, sufficed; the Judge answered it with his own.

Sometimes, he continued, following her gaze and touching the hat gently, as if almost by accident, it is in fact the *exceptions* to the rule that constitute the strength of the rule itself. Because it is against these—but here, again, he paused. Abruptly, he withdrew his hand from the hat.

Is this something, he interrupted himself, you think you can understand? Because it is very important, he went on, that you do. Important for your brother, yes, but more . . . particularly . . . for your mother. You know—again he hesitated, peering at his daughter over his spectacles, which he had only recently begun to wear. She isn't always in the most . . . perfect health.

It was on account of certain—sensitive—*materials*, the Judge informed Sutton, a small but (here he cleared his throat and, once more, his fingers grazed absently over the brim of the hat on the table between them) rather powerful bomb found in Alden's position, that they now found themselves in the difficult position they did. Certainly it could be a lot worse, the Judge admitted. Had the explosive actually *reached* its intended target they would, all of them, be dealing with one hell of a bigger mess than they already were. Alden—the Judge explained—had failed to cooperate. Indeed—the Judge was sure—he had never *intended* to cooperate with those *rightful* proprietors of the explosive in question, and its devastating goal. And so you see the matter is indeed—the Judge concluded—a question (depending on which way you looked at it) of being at precisely the *wrong*, or precisely the *right* place—and at either precisely the wrong, or precisely the right time. But that did not, he added quickly, prevent all of it, no matter which way you looked at it, from appearing, from the outside, very bad indeed.

Now, look, he said. We know some of the fellows involved in this business already. Communists, all of them. With nothing—as this incident convincingly attests—but the destruction of this country and everything it stands for in view. I hope that is clear to you. I have no doubt it is to your brother, now! It's just a matter of . . . wrapping things up. Putting the fellows we *know* are behind all this away—and for good this time. That's how it is with the law, see—it's not always as literal as one might wish it to be, or suppose. Even sometimes when you *know* something, without a shadow of a doubt—you still might not have all the right cards in hand, so to speak, to shut the case. Or to make sure that the truth itself (which is not, perhaps, though it be quite certain, necessarily held in hand) does not just . . . slip away. I know you don't want— the Judge said—any more than I do, for the men guilty of this particular crime to slip away. Especially (here he coughed drily into a cupped hand) at your brother's expense.

Now, what this means—he continued, after only the briefest pause, in which Sutton only stared across the distance between them marked by the hat—is that both your brother and I are going to be counting on your help in identifying the man *truly* guilty of this crime, which will (here he laid his hands down flat and looked straight at Sutton—for the first time, without a doubt, meeting her eye) require, he said, a slight . . . *stretching* . . . of the truth. Not a lie, see, because it is quite certain who the guilty party is. If I tell you the earth is round, but you have not yet circumnavigated it yourself, does it stand that if you also should announce, *The earth is round*, that it is a lie? To punctuate his question, he reached out and once again laid a hand on the hat—this time squashing it slightly in the middle. In another moment, however, when he had lifted his hand again, the hat quickly regained its original form.

Hardly, the Judge said, in answer to his own question.

SEVERAL HOURS LATER, SUTTON found herself following her father down the long empty courthouse corridor, their footsteps—his low and hollow-sounding, her own sharp and high—ringing in her ears. At the end of the corridor, when the Judge drew up short, she—a pace behind—drew up, too. From that perspective, she could see only the Judge's set jaw, and beyond that a perfect rectangle of gray hair, where it had been cut above the ear with astonishing exactitude. A heavyset guard was seated behind a low table. Behind him, a long panel of glass reflected darkly. It was possible, therefore, from where Sutton stood, to observe her father undetected in the glass, as first he shook hands brusquely with the guard, then leaned down, and—with a furious gesture—signed his name in a book, which lay open between them. He turned, then, as if noticing Sutton for the first time, and motioned her to join them. The guard peered curiously at her as she approached—but when, a moment later, he saw her looking back, he blinked quickly and glanced away. She was handed the same heavy pen with which her father had signed his name, then asked to sign her own.

Beneath the illegible loop her father had made on the page, her own name appeared naïvely discernible.

Shortly after, the heavyset guard disappeared, only to reappear a moment later through an identical door into another room, separated by the dark wall of glass. It was only, indeed, after he had entered it that Sutton realized it was a room at all—and not just the reflection of the one they were in. Behind the guard, a long line of men—their hands fastened behind their backs, faces pointed straight ahead—followed slowly. Though she could see them very well, her father informed her then, they could neither see nor hear *her*.

It was difficult, however, to keep this in mind.

When the guard reached the far end of the room, and the men stood, twelve or fourteen in all, across the length of it, he stopped and pressed the short stick he carried against the first man's chest so that he stopped, and then all the men behind him, one after the other, stopped, too.

It was only then that she saw him. Toward the end of the line: Alden. And then, next to him—and now she wondered how she had failed to notice either one of them before—Arthur. His lip was cracked, she could see now, and there was a line of blood that ran from it to his chin, then spattered in a spray of lines across his torn white shirt. She looked around now for Douglas. For Chet, and John—imagining briefly that she might only have overlooked them somehow as she had, at first, overlooked both Arthur and Alden. But she did not see them there, and after all it would have been very difficult to miss the boy; let alone tall Chet, or the big Indian. That was good, she reminded herself. That they were not there meant, necessarily, they were somewhere else. But then, almost at once, the possibilities of where they might be if not immediately before her overwhelmed her, and she felt a sudden panic at all the possibilities that existed, both for them and everyone else. But that they existed, she reminded herself, was better than that they did not.

While she was lost in these thoughts, they had been joined by another man, who looked—she was struck by the resemblance almost immediately—very much like her father. They both had the same tall foreheads, closely cropped dark hair, gray at the edges, and were dressed smartly in dark suits, which fit snugly in exactly the same places. Perhaps because she was busy reflecting on this remarkable resemblance, it took several seconds before Sutton realized her father had been speaking to her—his voice followed by the nearly identical low bass of the second man.

Can you identify—the second man, who looked and sounded so very much like the first, was saying (and it was only then, with the sound of the second voice, that she recognized that the words had already been spoken). Now she heard what had been said not only once, but twice, and remembered the hat, which had lain, unluckily, between herself and her father earlier that day.

At first, though, she did not see the hat. She looked up and down the line again, her eye obstinately refusing to settle. But after several more moments, sensing the growing tension as her father, and the man who looked like her father, waited for her reply, she had no other choice, and saw that the hat that had perched incongruously on her father's desk that afternoon was now perched, just as incongruously, on the head of Arthur Sinclair.

It had, after all, been a very simple thing she'd agreed to. To point at a guilty man, wearing a hat, was not a lie, her father had said. And, after all, had she not taken everything she so far believed to be true on simple faith? How was this, then, any different? It had not occurred to Sutton, until that moment, to doubt that what her father had said was true.

Now her father had moved nearer; he had placed his hand firmly on her shoulder.

This was all a terrible mistake. Sutton looked at her father, about to speak—to alert him. She had never in her life seen Arthur wearing a hat, let alone this one. She was about to tell her father that—but then she stopped, realizing that she would then be required to inform her father, if not then, at some later point, how it was she had come to know this, or anything about the man at all. Detecting her alarm, the Judge looked at her sharply.

Is, he said (and again, with the word, she realized that it was being spoken for the second time), the man you *saw*—yesterday afternoon— any of these men that you *see now, before you?*

Sutton stared first at her father, then back at the line of men. Something shifted. The edges of the room seemed to dissolve, giving way to blankness. Her father had not let go of her shoulder and now his grip began to tighten.

Tell the truth, he warned, gritting the words between his teeth.

She shook her head. Not exactly in answer, but because she could think of nothing else to do. Her father's grip tightened reflexively. I will repeat the question a final time, he said. The man. You saw. And on which the report *you filed* is based. Is he among the men you see now, before you?

Look carefully, now, the man who looked like her father warned.

Look once more—carefully, her father said, his grip tightening still further on her arm.

Can you identify the man? the man who looked like her father said.

A further blankness descended. And in that blankness Sutton lifted her one free hand and pointed at the hat that had lain on the table, between herself and her father, earlier that day.

There, she said. In a voice hardly more than a whisper. There.

—

THE FIRST DAY SUTTON ACCOMPANIED ALDEN TO THE CAMPS, IT HAD been pouring rain. They had got soaked through before they were even halfway there, and Alden bought a newspaper and gave Sutton half and took half for himself and they continued with half a newspaper each over their heads. By the time the camps came into view, the newspaper was soaked through and had bled black ink all over their hands. They walked down a rutted path that had sprung up between two rows of tents. The mud was so thick that, after a while, it was difficult for Sutton to keep pace. She had to hop a little in order to keep up with her brother whenever she slipped and lost a step.

Finally, they drew up in front of one of the tents, and—after giving her a quick glance so that she would know to follow—Alden ducked inside.

THE TENT WAS LARGER than she had expected it to be. It was in fact, she saw now, two tents, which had been joined as one—the center marked by a makeshift table, constructed out of a slab door and two half barrels. Around this table, three men and a girl of roughly Sutton's own age were seated on overturned crates. One of the men, very tall, with a long sad face, waved them over. Another shifted in his seat, indicating a space on the bench where Sutton could join them. She sat down and only then realized that it wasn't a man at all she sat next to, but a boy—two or three years younger than herself, she guessed. His eyes, even in the dim tent, appeared very blue, and his light brown hair, which needed cutting, was thin and soft-looking, like a child's. It fell a little in front of his eyes when he turned to look at her.

Douglas, he said.

Sutton nodded, and the boy looked away. It was not until then that she realized—when it seemed, suddenly, too late—she should have responded with her own name.

In the meantime, Alden had fallen into a heated discussion with the tall man with the long face, and another man Sutton understood at once to be Douglas's father. He had the same eyes and light brown hair—though the older man's had thinned, slightly, at the top. From time to time the girl joined in the conversation, but the boy—Douglas—did not. Several minutes passed this way before Alden paused, and—remembering himself—introduced Sutton to the rest. The man with the long face, whose name was Chet, nodded solemnly. Douglas's father's name was Arthur.

Pleased to meet you, he said.

The girl, Aida, leaned around to look at her.

Didn't you get her good and soaked, she said to Alden. Now Sutton could see she held a child in her arms. The girl saw her looking, and grinned.

Felicity, she said, indicating the child.

By then Alden had placed his heavy canvas bag in the middle of the table, and was extracting from it the remains of their own family's recent Sunday meal. Some fresh rolls, only a little squashed on top, a quarter of a roast, and some stewed potatoes, which he had left in their pot. The juice from the stew had leaked a little at the edges, and as Alden set it down it got on his fingers, which he licked clean. There was a jug of milk, too, and another loaf of bread and a thick slab of butter. All of this Alden took out, one item at a time—not slowly, exactly, but allowing time for a low murmur of approval to swell between each. When the bag had been emptied, everyone began at once to eat. Even the child, who had woken by then, eagerly accepted the little bites of bread and potato Aida offered her. Sutton saw now that the baby was dark like a Chinese, with slanted eyes.

Remember to save some for John, Arthur said, and everyone nodded and kept eating, but after a while they slowed down and there was still a portion left in every bowl, and Chet nodded in approval and said, Good, there's more than enough, and Arthur put his hands contentedly on his sides. Then he reached for the jug of milk and took a long swallow of it before he passed it on to Douglas. Then Douglas took a swallow, and passed it to Aida, who passed it to Chet, and so on, and when there were only a few swallows left, it was placed in the middle of the table for the absent guest. Then everyone was quiet, and the rain, which had tapered to a drizzle during the meal, stopped, too, so that the only sounds from outside were of people talking and shouting in the near distance, and after a while even that began to seem far away.

Aida asked Sutton if she liked babies very much. Felicity didn't mind strangers, she said, if she'd like to take a turn and hold her. Sutton said yes, she liked babies, so Aida passed her over. The child was surprisingly heavy, but Sutton found she liked the weight, and felt proud to be holding her. Her slanted eyes were as black as Douglas's eyes were blue and the child regarded her with them steadily but did not cry, and after a while settled herself just as she had in Aida's arms, and Aida said, Sure, she likes you.

Then Alden and Chet and Arthur began to talk among themselves again. Arthur was hopeful an agreement between the self-proclaimed leader of the Bonus Army, Walter Waters, and the government, could still be reached. But Chet shook his head.

Naw, he said. Even Glassford's keeping his mouth shut now.

The city's police chief, Pelham Glassford, was a known sympathizer to the Bonus cause, and Sutton noticed that everyone—Arthur in particular—looked uncomfortable now, hearing him slighted.

It's true, Chet said. I don't believe when it comes down to it he'll have anything more than his own best interest in mind—and, well, why should he? You can't trust the one's already got what he needs to do the work for the ones who don't.

Arthur shook his head. Glassford knows he's got to play nice, sure, he said. That's just the way it *is*, Chet—and he knows it. We start playing rough—we're sure to lose. But if we're careful, see, play fair—

Chet slapped a hand on the table. Fair! he said.

Again, Arthur shook his head. For a moment he seemed about to say more—but then he didn't. Chet and Alden carried on without him, and no one interrupted for a while.

There simply isn't any more time, Alden was saying. If we don't get things settled and every man's bonus in hand by July, there won't be any way to get things moving again for six months or more. And wouldn't it—he paused slightly, looking around him at the assembled company, all of whom, he was pleased to notice, were listening intently—be a shame, he said, to waste the efforts of everyone, like yourselves, who've come so far, and from every state in the Union!

Washington's poised—he continued, his voice rising now, gaining confidence with every word—on the very brink, see. And that's not something you can just . . . set aside. Something you can pick up later. If something's going to change—he concluded, scanning the small company; meeting and, if briefly, each in turn, holding their eyes—*it's got to change now.*

In his big overcoat, and in the company of full-grown men, Alden looked even smaller and slighter of frame than he was—almost like a child. His dark hair—which fell, like Douglas's, a little long in front—made his face, especially in the dim light, appear exceptionally pale. Their mother had often lamented the fact that it had been Alden, not Sutton, to inherit her own delicate skin, her slight frame. By contrast, Sutton had always been what her mother called "big-boned." Her features, too, had been inherited, rather unfortunately, from her father rather than her mother's side: a pronounced chin, a broad nose, and a high forehead—unsuccessfully shortened by a thick fringe of practical, nearly colorless, hair. Though she was more than two full years younger than Alden, she had always been, or very nearly, his equal in size; growing up they had often been mistaken for the same age. Now, however—despite Alden's youthful appearance—she felt the difference in their ages acutely. His voice, Sutton realized with some surprise—as she listened, along with the Chet and Arthur and the rest, and Alden continued to speak—was a man's.

She had just been thinking this—Alden had just paused, taken a deep breath, evidently aware of the impact his words had made—when the tent door was rolled back and an Indian stood framed in the entrance. An Indian so large that he blocked any light that might have otherwise entered, and made everything else—even Arthur and Chet, who a moment ago had seemed overlarge in their makeshift chairs—seem small by comparison. A shout went up, and everything else—Alden, and Alden's words, which had held them riveted only a short time before— were forgotten. But the Indian, oblivious, did not retreat. Instead, he ducked inside and began to make his way (no, there could be no doubt about it now, Sutton realized, a choking panic growing in her throat) directly toward her.

Before she could think of anything to do or to say, or find some way of protecting either herself or the child she still held in her arms, the Indian had knelt in front of her, smiled crookedly, and lifted the child from her grasp. And still, though a general commotion had erupted in the tent since the arrival of the Indian, no one said anything to him directly, or tried to stop him. The men, and Aida along with them, only continued to sit—chatting casually now among themselves—as the Indian, laughing, swung the child at a dangerous angle above his head.

Perhaps it was not such a long time as it seemed before Sutton understood. The Indian was the man, John, whose company they had for some time been anticipating, and whose dinner still remained on the table, in discrete portions. It was he who was the father of the child, and husband to small, pale Aida. It might have only been a few moments—just the span of time it took for John to settle at the table, and begin to scoop the portions of the meal, and scrape the meat that remained—still clinging to its bone—from her mother's flowered serving bowl. It was so incongruous a sight that, as Sutton's alarm diminished, she nearly laughed out loud. To think of what her mother or her father might say if they knew! She felt a distinct pleasure at the thought of it. There was nothing to be afraid of! She was sharing a table with an Indian whose child she had held just moments before in her own arms—whose plate she had eaten from on countless occasions, and would (if it managed to return itself to her mother's kitchen) eat from on countless occasions again. What was there in that to be frightened of? What in the world could, after this, remain extraordinary or unknown?

All of this over the course of mere seconds, during which time John settled himself, chewing thoughtfully. From time to time, he presented a small morsel to the child, whom he still held crookedly in one arm.

Only after he had finished his meal did he begin to speak.

It was true what they'd heard about Waters, the Indian told them. He'd disappeared again. Third time that month.

Chet raised his arms toward the ceiling in an unreadable gesture, and looked pointedly at Arthur, who sat across from him.

It had been Waters who had rallied the first "troops" in Portland, Oregon, nearly six months before. His countless adventures between there and the Capitol—both rumored and true—had been regular currency for some time in the camp. Everyone traded in stories—their own and others'—and if you ever ran into the same one twice, it would be a wonder if you recognized it. An especially popular one was how the Waters gang had got hung up in Illinois, where the rail companies had been forbidden by law to give any more "free rides." Trying to strike a deal to suit everyone, an engineer suggested the group might ride on top. Waters refused. It would be dangerous, he said, and besides, they wouldn't have any way to bring their supplies. He organized his troops, instead, to unhook the train cars, so that no sooner had the train pulled out of the yard than it had to stop in order that the railway men could go and hook all the cars back together again. But by the time the train made to pull out once more, the cars had once more been unhooked by Waters and his men. It went on like that for some time. Finally the train master got down and made several telephone calls. (I called the police but they won't come down, the cowards, Waters had heard him growl.) Then he turned and, begrudgingly, led Waters and his men to four empty cars at the back of the train, and they clambered aboard.

There were rumors Waters had fled as far away as Florida. Most suspected, though, he'd simply locked himself up in the well-appointed apartment provided for him by a certain Mrs. Evalyn Walsh McLean—who, as it was well known, had adopted Waters as her latest charity project. She had also provided, out of her own pocket money, sandwiches and coffee for every veteran and his family, on at least half a dozen occasions. It was for this, more than anything else—the beds, and expensive cast-off clothing for the children in the camps (her own children having already grown)—that Mrs. Evalyn Walsh McLean was much revered by most of the Bonus Army. There were some, though (due in no small part to the inevitable rapidity with which the sandwiches and the coffee disappeared), who remained less than satisfied.

Wasn't that just like a woman, Chet had said, for example, when the conversation came around to it, to think that a round of tea sandwiches and a few hand-me-down clothes could fix everything?

Aida threw him a hard glare.

I mean, of course, Chet said, women of a *certain type*.

Says he's sick, John said.

Sick! Chet said.

Are you only going to go on repeating everything that gets said? asked Arthur.

It's the health departments and not the government threatening to close us down, John said. Glassford's working hard—I do believe he's got our best interests at heart—but everything else seems to be lining up against us. There's the health reports—

It's not the camps they're worried about, Alden cut in. You know that! It's the rest of the neighborhood. There's been complaints—the camp is spreading out too far, they say. Out to the more . . . well-established neighborhoods. The "health reports" are just an excuse—

Either way, put in Arthur, it's not good news if the result is the same.

There's no result yet, Chet said. Nobody's moving anywhere yet. This is all just talk.

Then again, under his breath: Sick, he said.

JOHN—ALDEN INFORMED SUTTON later, as they walked home together through the wet streets—had worked as a "code talker" during the war.

In the summer of 1918, he (Alden said), along with twenty or so other young Choctaw Indians from southern Oklahoma, had been shipped to France as part of the 142nd Infantry. Shortly afterward, and almost by accident, it had been discovered that transmitting messages in Choctaw (a language unrepresentable in English or German, or any other written tongue) rendered Allied military communication virtually unbreakable.

After the war ended, John had been kept on—transferred to a government division and employed for several years in developing a new military code, which, though still based on the Choctaw language, would no longer be dependent, solely, on the availability of native speakers.

Now, like everyone else, the Indian was out of work, but he still had his connections in Washington, and, once more, his services had—if unofficially—been enlisted. For a small remuneration, the Indian supplied the War Office with regular reports on the "climate" of both the Anacostia and Penn Ave. camps—information that was then passed directly to General MacArthur, the Army chief of staff.

DESPITE THE CLOSE EYE Washington was keeping on things, however —and how hard Waters himself worked to enforce his All-American Agenda—the camp's reputation as a hotbed of Communist sympathizers and potential unrest only continued to grow. It was perceived, for example, that, by and large, the veterans were not really *veterans* at all—that they had another agenda above and beyond the passing of any Bonus Bill. In response, Waters had the camps "swept" routinely of possible Communist infiltrators, and tirelessly promoted himself for what he was: a committed anti-Communist. This inspired broad support from the veterans, who—on the whole, and despite the rumors— were a conservative crowd. They'd elected Waters for a reason—they appreciated the strict code of conduct he had introduced and now enforced in the camps. Many of the men (and Arthur was especially particular in this regard) dressed each day in a formal suit and tie, a sort of testament to the "all-American" integrity of their intentions, and those of the rest of the army. The suit Arthur wore was of a cheap quality, and because he washed it nightly as a point of pride, it had quickly become threadbare. Still, he took an obvious pleasure in it— and still more in keeping, folded within its breast pocket, his release papers, which proved that he had been twice honorably discharged: once in 1918, after being wounded at Belleau Wood, then again in January 1920, after serving sixteen months with the American Expeditionary Forces in Siberia—under some of the worst conditions the U.S. Army had ever seen. From time to time he would take the papers from his pocket, and smooth the crease between his fingers, almost absently, before placing them carefully back inside. The suit had been inherited, of course, from the Salvation Army—he had never otherwise owned a suit in his life—but the papers were his own.

—

IN THE KELLY HOUSE, IN THOSE DAYS, IT WAS A RARE EVENING THAT did not end with the Judge and his son nearly coming to blows—and always over the subject of the bonus, and the Bonus Army. The Judge was of the opinion, which he often expressed, that there was something deeply skewed at the very heart of the affair—indeed, Waters's assertion of the "all-American" intentions of his men was certain evidence that this was the case. In contrast to what Waters seemed to assume, *patriotism*, the Judge said, was not a thing that could be bought or sold. No, indeed. Patriotism which is *bought*, he said one evening—just as the cook, Germaine, was bringing in the hot dishes and they were all sitting down to their meal—cannot, properly, be considered *patriotism at all*. Do you know who said that?

He was speaking, as usual, pointedly to his son. But Alden kept his head down, and continued only to work away at a piece of meat on his plate, which stubbornly refused to detach itself from the bone.

I am speaking to you, son, said the Judge.

In answer, Alden's knife scraped noisily across his plate. He stabbed the loosened meat with his fork and chewed slowly for a while, before nodding in his father's general direction.

Yes, I hear you, he said.

The meat—unswallowed—was visible in his mouth as he spoke.

Alden, his mother warned, that's repugnant.

The thirtieth President of the United States, the Judge said. The greatest leader this country has ever seen and—I have strong reason to suspect—*will* ever see. Yes—he continued—I am starting to get the distinct impression that you and your friends may be right, after all; that this great country of ours really will go the way of Rome, and somewhat sooner than expected. *Eight years ago*, Calvin Coolidge himself spoke those words. *Patriotism*, he said, is not something to be bought or sold— or, worse, he might have added, to be *bartered* with. But even he gave in, said the Judge; made certain compromises back in '24, which we are surely paying for now. Everything at a price! Certain *compromises*—the Judge repeated—which threaten the very principles this country was founded upon; the soundness of which the Kelly family itself is living testimony! Had the Kellys not—the Judge asked, taking increasing pleasure now at the sound of his own voice—*raised themselves up* (as it was the clear right of all men in this country to do) from nothing at all? Had they not managed to build for themselves a life, the proportions of which only a generation before—from their tiny half acre on the Dingle coast—they never could have dreamed?

A half acre, yes! Upon which, for a thousand years or more, they had toiled without hope of progress or change. When the crops failed—the Judge said—they'd simply starved. Were pushed off the land.

That was 1847, the Judge said. (Though they had, all of them, heard the story—word for word—more than a dozen times.) The "Gregory clause" had just been put into effect. They had no choice but to sell! To move to a farm near Castlemaine, and work for other men. But before long, even that was gone. Their small cottage destroyed—literally *lifted from under them*. With a rope tied to each corner of the house, the Judge said, and the help of a single oxen team, the "crowbar brigades" could accomplish in minutes what otherwise might have taken ten men and a whole afternoon.

After that, there was nothing to do but wander the streets and *beg* for a living—there being no longer any chance to earn one. They began to build their coffins with little trapdoors, so that they might easily reuse them. Imagine! The Judge shook his head. Three times the Kellys placed their dead inside coffins like these, and pulled the latch.

Then (here the Judge's voice rose as it always did at this point in the story) *then* came the rebellion of 1848 in which your Great-Grandfather, Michael (a nod, briefly, at Sutton and Alden both) was always proud to take part; he and his eldest brother, John. There being nothing more they could do for either themselves or their families in Castlemaine, they made their way to Tipperary. Joined O'Brien and his gang. They stood next to O'Brien himself, the Judge said (the same O'Brien who was soon to become—though nobody could have known it then—the most feared sheriff in the state of Montana; he cleared the plains of the Indians almost single-handedly, they say), their guns pointed at the farmhouse of a certain Mrs. Margaret McCormick, where the police (the scoundrels) had locked themselves, along with her five surviving children, inside.

Later John would be shot through the heart by a stray bullet, and your great-grandfather would just barely escape with his life. In any case (and here the Judge sighed happily), the battle was lost. Michael, he didn't know what to grieve for most—the loss of the battle, or his brother, John. Still, he was proud he had tried. But now there was nothing to do but leave the country that had thrice spurned him—once when it took his land, a second time when it took his brother, and a third and final time when it took his pride.

Through all of that—the Judge said (his voice trembling now, as he stared around the table at his own family, each of whom, for their own private reasons, stared down instead at the table or their plate, or past him, toward the darkened window, refusing to return his gaze)—he himself, his wife, and three of his children, my father among them—the youngest, barely two years old—had *managed to survive.*

They made their way first to New York. And from there—a more difficult journey still—on to the Indiana plains. *Why?* (The Judge was looking directly at Alden now. In his voice, for a brief moment, a note of genuine appeal.) *What was there for them, there?* (He slammed a fist on the table, to emphasize the words.) *Nothing but dirt!* But they turned that dirt into a *life for themselves*. By the labor of their own hands, they profited by it! That was the reason men came to this country—and *thrived*. They knew the meaning of words, then, when they spoke them—and the worth of the money they earned. They knew, then, that patriotism—*patriotism* (the Judge said, having found himself with some satisfaction back at his starting point)—was *not* a thing that could be bought, but something, instead, that grew in a man's heart in accordance with the value he himself invested in the land he profited by.

ALDEN HAD REMAINED CURIOUSLY calm while his father spoke, but now two bright spots appeared on his cheeks.

How dare you, he said quietly—when, after only a moment's triumphant pause, the Judge at last began to tackle his food, which for some time had been growing cold on his plate. How dare you talk about "fairness," Alden said. I don't believe that, for all your talk—about the meaning of words, and your pride in the fact that once—*once*, the Kellys, too, *worked* for a living—that you yourself have the slightest idea—

But he did not have time to finish. Slamming both fists onto the table now, and knocking his plate back so that a newspaper, which had been concealed beneath, fell to the floor, the Judge had already risen. Alden continued to speak—his voice trembling with fear now, as well as indignation: what that word means, he managed. The Judge towered above them all, his face dark and swollen with rage. Again, he hit the table with his fist. The silverware bounced. A water tumbler poured its contents across the tablecloth, leaving a dark, temporary stain.

You—the Judge said. Glaring across the table toward his son. But then something strange occurred. He became, suddenly, unsteady on his feet, and where his face had darkened with rage it was now blanched of color as a vague panic fluttered across it. After one uncertain moment, in which it was unclear to anyone—least of all, it seemed, to the Judge himself—what had happened, or was about to happen next, he sat down again, looking stunned. His wife's eyes had remained riveted on him from the moment of his first shout. They did not look panicked or alarmed, only frightened in the way that they always looked frightened when something unexpected happened. The same expression had crossed her face, for example, only moments before, when she had exclaimed in unrestrained horror at the sight of Alden's semi-masticated food.

No one spoke. The Judge's breath, though raspy and audible, soon regulated itself, and it seemed that the crisis—if one had indeed occurred—had passed. Sutton glanced briefly at Alden, then away.

That, the Judge said bitterly. Right there, is the problem. You think if you give a thing a different name it changes that thing. You call them lazy, dishonest, you call them misjudged and underrepresented. At the end of the day it amounts to the same thing. Ten thousand lazy, dishonest, misjudged, and underrepresented men threatening to overthrow the very principles upon which this country has been founded. Oh, sure, you can put a different shine on things for a while. But you know how quickly it's going to wear off? You know how long you're going to look good with that shine on you?

But I wonder—the Judge cleared his throat. I'm serious now, he said. It's a question that's been plaguing me. Do any of your friends down there in the swamps really understand what it is they're after? It's kept me up nights. Do they, I wonder—the Judge said—even know what it is they're asking? A bonus, my boy, is just another "name" we gave to the most basic sort of life insurance policy back in '24! Payable at death— or 1945—whichever for these poor lads comes first. Do they understand that, I wonder? All of those boys are worth more dead than alive! Insurance, see. It's a thing, like anything, you buy into. Something you *earn*. A calculated investment in chance—a commodity like any other. *Bonus*. If you're looking to define your terms, you might want to start with that one. And here's a hint, which you might pass on to your friends. Pressing for the payout now means the amount of money due is only a *small proportion* of the money *that would be* paid out in 1945. That's how it works! The very principle of economics!

The Judge began to chuckle. Alden, who had remained silent all that time, betrayed himself only by two small red squares, which had once again inflamed themselves on his cheeks.

..

SUTTON COULD NO LONGER clearly remember when what had once been mere playacting became something more. There had, at one time, been only what seemed to her the same endless battle waged in the back room, where they had played, before their mother established herself more permanently there. Sutton was, for the most part, assured an integral part in the world Alden created for them, because she was always willing (so aware was she at all times of how ultimately expendable she was—it was, in the end, always *Alden's* world) to take the less glamorous roles. She was endlessly taken for prisoner, locked behind a complicated network of their mother's chair cushions, or publicly executed—her head dangling over the edge of a tipped chair. But she was never troubled on these occasions because she would, of necessity, be revived almost instantly—in order to serve as a messenger or, on rare occasions, an officer or even a general in the tireless operations of Alden's imagination. It was so gradual, when it happened—that the imaginative battles gave way to real ones—that, at first, Sutton hardly noticed the transition at all. Hardly realized that the pamphlets Alden had begun to bring home (which he first read to her out loud, then left out around the house, in order—when they were not first prudently removed by their mother or Germaine—to be discovered by the Judge), or the copies of *The Militant* (which he had, on occasion, with the same glint in his eye with which he had launched all his previous campaigns, pressed into her hands) belonged to the *real* world. When she did realize it, it struck her as a great loss, not only to herself personally, but also to the world that she and he had once inhabited—so happily—together. By contrast, what little she knew of the "real" world seemed rather limited in scope and possibility.

Still—like any child of a certain age—she had no choice in the end but to follow him there.

AND SO, THE FOLLOWING Sunday, she went again with Alden down to the camps, which she found quite transformed even from the week before.

It was not just her imagination, Alden told her. The camp had certainly spread. New shelters lined the makeshift streets (each named for a different state of the Union), constructed from scrap metal and whatever else could be salvaged from the mountain of refuse that rose—the highest point in the vicinity—from the Anacostia Flats. As more and more men flooded in, the mountain diminished, and the city grew. Boxes, rusted frames and bedsprings, old barrels, sinks, fence stakes, scraps of lumber, bits of wrecked cars—all were hauled away and transformed into the homes and headquarters of the Bonus Army. There was a veteran from Ohio, for example, Alden told her, who lived inside an oil drum, and twin brothers from Tennessee who shared a piano box—ACADEMY OF MUSIC still stamped in big letters on its side. A grizzled veteran from Delaware—who, it was rumored, had been a Confederate messenger in the Civil War—slept in a burial vault mounted on a rusted trestle.

At the intersection of Washington and Oregon their progress, already slow, was stalled completely. A fight seemed to have broken out, and around it a large crowd gathered. Alarmed, Sutton willed Alden to retreat, but he pressed on, instead, and Sutton had no choice but to follow. Soon, however—to her great relief—it became clear that the fight was contained within a makeshift ring; that the immovable crowd was merely jostling for position from which point they might observe the undersized contenders: two small boys, around the ages of nine or ten.

When finally they'd managed to pass—pressing their way along the crowd's outermost edge—their route continued to be so meandering, and their progress so slow, that after a while Sutton began to suspect they had lost their way. Alden, however, continued to push steadily on, and she did not detect in him the least apprehension; not even, indeed, when they turned a corner and death itself loomed up to meet them!

It was true: there, at the corner of Idaho and Maine, an open coffin stood upright before them, blocking their way. Inside was a dead man dressed in a crumpled black suit. Though the mood of the crowd was more lively than Sutton knew to be proper for funerals, this did not immediately surprise her. Perhaps they were Catholics, she reasoned. But just as she did, the dead man sneezed loudly, and the crowd erupted in shouts of laughter. It was only a stunt, Alden explained. Now—too late—Sutton was able to see this quite clearly. Above the "dead man" a signboard even advertised the fact in plain letters: the man was in the process of being "buried alive." All the while, another man passed a hat, declaring that, in contrast to the "dead man," it was now time to "rise up!" Were the good men, he shouted, who had risked their lives for their country over in France now going to simply "turn over and die," let the government "bury them"? Occasionally the "dead man" would raise a stiff arm from the grave. Hear, hear! he would shout. Or else: I should not have died in vain! Still otherwise, for humorous effect, he would simply sneeze or yawn— his body convulsing vigorously before once again reassuming the rigid posture of death.

Not long after they left the "dead man" behind, they turned a final corner and arrived at their destination. So unprepared by this point was Sutton to arrive anywhere at all that she did not recognize the tent they had visited the week prior until they were upon it, until she herself nearly stumbled over the boy, Douglas, who—perched on a crate outside the tent—was whittling away at a stick of dry wood.

She'd surprised him, too. Now he jumped up and grinned—first at Sutton and Alden, and then at the pot Alden carried, which contained the remains of their afternoon meal.

AFTER THEY'D EATEN, JOHN and Arthur lit pipes of tobacco, which filled the tent with smoke, and soon all the men, Alden along with them, began to talk among themselves, just as they had the week before.

After a while, Aida tossed Sutton a look and grinned.

Douglas, she said, why don't you take Sutton outside? Then, nodding toward two empty buckets by the tent door, she added: Water to collect.

Douglas stood up, nodding, his hair falling in front of his eyes.

Uncertain at first, Sutton stood up, too, then followed Douglas to the door.

THE WATER HOSE WAS connected to a fire hydrant about a hundred yards away. They had to wait half an hour or more in a line that stretched approximately the same length. A large man with whiskers, who—dressed in ordinary civilian clothes, none too neat or clean—wore six military medals strung in a row on his breast pocket, oversaw the operation with a genuine air of authority, making certain everyone waited their turn.

Sutton was not permitted to carry either pail on the homeward journey. Douglas took them both, one in each hand, so that his muscles strained and blue veins stood out on his forearms. He walked stiffly, each step checked by the counterweight of a heavy pail. When they arrived back at the tent, Douglas deposited both where they had found them, just inside the tent door, but did not himself go inside. He sat down on the same overturned crate he'd been perched on when they'd first arrived, picked up the stick he'd been whittling, and examined it silently for a while.

Sutton did not know if she should leave him—go inside, with the rest—or remain.

Before she could decide, Douglas looked up. He squinted at her past the glare of the afternoon sun. I'll show you something, he said.

All right.

They walked together through the crowded streets to where the shacks gave way at the edge of the camp. Here they encountered only a scattered pup tent or two, and a few chained dogs docilely finishing off some scraps of a meal. Then they left even these behind. Finally, there was only an empty stretch of grass, and then more grass—giving way only at that farthest point, after which nothing (least of all their own fields of vision) could stretch farther, to a stand of trees. Here Douglas drew up short and turned back—nodding in the direction they had come. Below them, the camp spread in patches of reds and grays. Here and there they could make out an American flag, tugging impatiently at its strings, or a wisp of smoke, rising vertically over the landscape—like the thin tail a cloud makes when you know it is going to rain. They stood, looking out over the camps together like that for some time, observing the patchwork pattern the streets made, which had been invisible to them below.

It struck her, then—funny how she hadn't thought of it before. How the world they overlooked was, in that moment—as perhaps in any other—just as foreign to Douglas as it was to her. How he was no more than a child, really. He could be no more than—what? Twelve. Thirteen at the most. She felt a sudden tenderness toward him at the thought of it.

Do you miss it very much? she asked—surprising them both. Where you come from, I mean, she added. Almost by way of apology now.

Douglas pushed the hair from his eyes, and squinted into the distance as though looking for the answer there. Then he dropped his gaze, shrugged, and said nothing.

Well, Sutton said quickly—trying to in some way reestablish the boundary she now felt certain she had crossed. It . . . can't last forever, can it?

But even as she said it, she felt the words snag at something otherwise indiscernible in her mind. She did not want, she realized then, for any promise to be finally met—any solution finally found. For things to return—on account of it—to the way they had been before the Bonus Army had come. Before she had marched with Alden through the twisted streets of the camps, seen men raised from the dead, cradled the child of an Indian in her arms . . .

Anyway, said Douglas abruptly, interrupting her train of thought, we won't be goin' back.

Sutton looked up sharply.

What? she said. Why's that?

Again Douglas shrugged and dropped his gaze.

Once we get our bonus, he said, my dad and me. We're gonna buy us some land—in Virginia, maybe. Or Tennessee. After that, we'll send for Momma. Isn't one of us goin' back to Kansas now.

There was no hint in the words, or in the way that Douglas spoke them, as to whether what he'd told her made him happy or sad. Because of this, Sutton did not know how to respond; whether she herself should seem pleased or dismayed by the news. Before she had time to consider the matter any further, however—or say anything at all—Douglas had turned. For the first time, he looked at her directly.

If I tell you something, he said—his voice low and urgent now—will you promise— But here he paused, glancing quickly away. Will you promise, he began again (his voice softer and steadier now) not to tell; I mean (again, he looked at her; his blue eyes flashed) not another living soul?

Sutton nodded. Then, because he was not looking at her, and said nothing: Of course, she said.

It's . . . the Indian. John, Douglas said. He's—he's *murdered* a man. I saw it. We all did.

Color had begun to creep into his cheeks and now he shook his head, so that his hair fell like a shroud, and it was difficult to read his features.

Sutton could feel the beat of her own heart in her throat.

When? she said. Where?

Slowly, then, pausing often in order either to correct or further obscure the details, Douglas related what he could of the incident he now recalled. It had been the first evening he and Chet and his father, who had traveled together all the way from Beloit, Kansas, had ever laid eyes on the man. They'd been Washington-bound; had just stopped off in East St. Louis for something to drink and a meal. He had hardly noticed it at first, Douglas said; had no idea how the fight had begun. But he did see (they all did, he said) how it ended. The dead man's body carried away, in the arms of six men.

And John?

Gone. Fled first of anyone. Then the police came; we all fled. It wasn't 'til the next day we fell in with him—John. And Aida. By pure accident, see.

And had they been followed?

No, Douglas said. He supposed they had not. As far as he could tell, the Indian was in no danger now. And it had never been mentioned—

not once, so far as he knew—between them. What had happened that night. Everyone else, he supposed—his own father, even—had forgotten it had even occurred.

Somehow, though (Douglas said), he himself could not get the thing out of his mind.

SHE CONFRONTED ALDEN THAT evening.

John's a Red, she said. That's how come you go down to see him all the time.

She did not know how she knew this—and, in truth, was not absolutely sure that it was so, until the expression on Alden's face confirmed it.

Douglas, she told him. And Arthur. Chet, probably. They don't know he's Red—I'm sure of it. And I'd hate to think (her voice trembled with a sudden conviction she hadn't known, until that moment, she felt) that—she continued—in not knowing, they should be placed in any danger.

By now Alden had collected himself. What gave you this idea? he asked. What did you hear?

I don't need—Sutton snapped—to be told what I can just as well see for myself.

In any case, Alden said, they're better not to know.

Alden, Sutton said. *He's killed a man.* Douglas saw him—they all did. With their own eyes.

Douglas said that?

Silence.

Alden shook his head. You keep whatever you heard to yourself, he said. It may not be true, of course—but if it is . . . He paused. He must have had his reasons.

Reasons? Sutton asked. What reasons?

But Alden had already turned away.

—

WITH SCHOOL OUT, SUTTON WENT DOWN TO THE CAMPS WHENEVER SHE COULD— even without Alden's company now. And nearly always when she went, she walked with Douglas out to the far end of the camp where they could see it spread below them in its patchwork of reds and grays. She pressed him when she could: Had he noticed anything about the Indian's behavior that might be considered in any way . . . unusual? But Douglas was reluctant to speak of the Indian again. And, despite her fears, there was no sign that either Alden or the Indian, rarely seen together, were involved in anything beyond what had been officially sanctioned by Waters—or that their sympathies (never once, at least in her hearing, voiced out loud) threatened either Douglas, Arthur and Chet in particular—or, more broadly, the "all-American" intentions of the Bonus Army as a whole. Perhaps—Sutton considered—even Douglas's story about the Indian had been nothing more than—not a lie, exactly, but somehow a *stretching* of the truth. Some way of expressing his own abstract fears (young as he was, and so far away from home) through some concrete, easily transmittable form.

BY THAT TIME—THE BEGINNING of June—twenty thousand veterans had arrived in Washington, or were on their way. Railroad workers added empty boxcars to trains in order to accommodate the steady stream of men who continued to arrive from every corner of the country, often with whole families in tow. Despite—or because of—persistent rumors of Communist infiltration into the camps, the city's residents opened their homes, and donated to the cause what little they could: food, clothing, even money when there was any to be had, and (the one thing of which, in those days, everyone seemed to have plenty) time. Volunteers flooded into Camp Marks to help distribute the food supplied by private donors like Mrs. Evalyn Walsh McLean. The Salvation Army set up a huge green tent, replete with a small lending library, and a letter-writing station where veterans were encouraged to write home or to the government. (The addresses of several congressmen, including Judge Kelly, were posted along the inside tent walls, along with the recommendation that each man might: "Write, and tell your story!")

And always, there was music. Brass bands, and the "official" Bonus

Expeditionary Force orchestra played regularly, gathering massive crowds. But there was always an ad hoc band playing somewhere—on whatever instruments had been carried from home, or otherwise fashioned from the junk heap that continued to rise from the flats—though now at a diminishing angle. There was always somebody singing and stomping along to "My Bonus Lies Over the Ocean" or "God's Tomorrow Will Be Brighter than Today."

But the exuberant optimism that abounded in the camps during those first weeks couldn't—and didn't—last. Despite the support they received, as the population grew it became increasingly difficult to keep everyone fed. Soon it was hunger more than anything else that the veterans felt—and shared with one another.

Accordingly, on the ninth of June, the police officer S. J. Marks, whom, like Glassford, everyone knew to be sympathetic to the veterans' cause (it was for him, indeed, the camp had been named), personally invited the men to return to wherever it was they had come from.

We've got trucks, Marks had roared—indicating the one in which he stood, and the others that, just then, were drawing up behind.

He waited several long seconds, but there was no reply. The veterans stared ahead, then, nervously, at one another. Finally, it was Marks himself who broke the silence. He cleared his throat and tipped his hat to the crowd.

I suspected as much, he shouted. And I don't blame you! I hope you stay and get your bonus!

ON ANOTHER AFTERNOON NOT long after that, a priest named Father James flew in from Pittsburgh. Sutton and Alden had just arrived with the remnants of their previous night's meal, and whatever else they could reasonably take from underneath the nose of Germaine, who—it was clear—was well past the beginning stages of noticing something. Unable to push their way through the crowd that had gathered, they never managed even a single glimpse of Father James—but they heard his message clearly. Everyone did.

Stick it out, boys! he yelled, his voice booming through a megaphone. Don't let them back you down!

Thousands of veterans were still on their way, he told them: their numbers would only grow. By the time the whole thing was over, the preacher promised them, the Bonus Army was sure to stand one million strong.

If they won't give you this little bonus, he roared, offered you because your wartime pay was less than common labor—well, then, turn them out of office! If they turn you away . . . go home and organize against them! Send men who want to look after *the people*, he shouted—not the five hundred millionaires who currently control our national wealth!

Around them, veterans screamed and cheered.

Will you promise me this? shouted Father James.

Everyone, including Alden, roared back in the affirmative.

Will you, Father James shouted—raising his voice, and his arms in their military dress skyward, and pumping a fist into the empty air—as God is each and every one of our witness, will you make this solemn promise to me today?

BUT THAT SAME DAY also brought a storm of leaflets distributed by presidential hopeful Norman Thomas. When finally Sutton and Alden managed to reach Chet and Arthur's camp, they heard about that. He was encouraging the veterans to abandon the fight, Arthur informed them crossly; to direct their efforts instead toward permanent government relief. "We address you not only as veterans of the World War but also as veterans of that larger and unending war against poverty," the leaflets read. Chet, Arthur, and Douglas had spent the better part of the day collecting as many pamphlets as they could in order to burn them.

After all the progress we've made, Chet said, shaking his head.

John, who had just joined them and as yet had not said a word, coughed, then peered quizzically at Chet.

Progress? he said.

In his arms, Felicity slept peacefully. She was wearing a pretty white dress with blue stitching, which she had inherited from Mrs. Evalyn Walsh McLean.

What, I wonder, is that?

Chet snapped his head in the Indian's direction and swore softly.

We've got one hundred thousand men, he said. We could have a million. This thing is getting bigger, not smaller—that's progress, in my books. When it comes down to it, politics is just numbers, after all—and we got 'em.

Politics, John said calmly, is more than just numbers. Or at least—he paused—there's more than one way of adding them up. If we start counting, for example, how much money they have up there versus us down here, then what happens? And what about guns? Have you calculated ammunitions?

Again, Chet swore under his breath, but said nothing.

ON THE WEEKENDS THE tourists arrived carrying cameras and picnic baskets filled with food to be shared with the veterans. There was also an influx of journalists—each more eager than the last to report the "truth" about the camps and the Bonus Army. Sutton clipped the articles that were subsequently published, along with a corresponding rash of conflicting editorials and letters—organizing them together in an old school notebook she had allocated for the purpose. Sometimes she underlined her favorite quotations, such as the comment in *Survey* magazine by Gardner Jackson, who wrote that the veterans could be observed to practice "the first large-scale attempt to mimic Mahatma Gandhi's passive resistance." Alden had laughed out loud at that. Imagine saying that to Waters! he'd said. He'd have you thrown out for a Red! Or Roy Wilkins's report for *Crisis* magazine, which described his surprise upon finding, in the camps, "black toes and white toes sticking out side by side from a ramshackle town of pup tents, packing crates, and tar-paper shacks." In the Bonus Army, he wrote, unlike the one within which they had fought the war, "black men and white men lined up equally, and perspired in sick bays side by side."

But not all Washingtonians were weekend picnickers or reporters for *Crisis* magazine, and soon, no matter where you stood, or from which direction you looked at the thing, there could be no doubt any longer that (despite how many times Waters insisted on the "all-American" integrity of his army, or how many times cast-off suits were washed by his men) key factions of the BEF were now controlled by the Communists—who would (if no progress was made through more "legitimate" lines) soon control more. But still, even when pressed, Alden denied any involvement with the Red element. He was careful, however—Sutton noted—never to go as far as to disown their approach. Even when the problem spread to the city and ordinary citizens began to complain of being accosted by Reds on the street. Stopped as they exited grocery stores, and asked for donations—then berated if they insisted on taking any more than half of their own purchases home.

Mary Kelly herself had been accosted in this fashion one afternoon, arriving home some time later, stricken and pale. The Judge, ordinarily dismissive of his wife's "nervous" complaints, was enraged by the incident.

Now they're attacking decent women in the streets, he shouted that evening—at no one in particular, because Alden had not yet arrived. He paced the room with a heavy tread, his feet on the bare floorboards sounding louder and louder, as if building momentum toward some unknown end.

When Alden did finally arrive, his father greeted him with a roar.

Decent women in the street! he repeated. What will it be next?

At her husband's request, Mary recounted her story once more so that Alden could hear. Perhaps, the third time through, she was even beginning to enjoy it a little.

Well, said Alden, when the account was complete. Are you all right?

Yes! the Judge shouted, before Mary herself could reply. She's all *right!*

In that moment, it became clear—to Mary, as equally as to the rest— that the real issue had never been, for the Judge, Mary at all. Sutton saw this knowledge cross her mother's face: the brief moment in which she had seemed, once again, to have captured the Judge's attention had just as quickly been stolen away, or had never existed at all. Her shoulders crumpled and she was wracked, suddenly, with violent sobs. No one went toward her to comfort her, so finally Sutton went herself, placing a hand tentatively on her mother's shoulder.

Well, if she's *all right*, Alden was saying over the noise, then—

All right! the Judge shouted. Are you going to wait until women are beaten to death on the streets before this amounts to a problem for you? Is this the country we live in? Where if a woman can make it home without being accosted by vagrants and Communists then everything is *"all right"*?

But the Judge, as he continually reminded his son, did not seriously doubt that the matter would be fully resolved before long—and in the government's favor. Training, he said, had been under way at Fort Myer for more than a month.

Yes, indeed, he informed his family one evening with some satisfaction, the government would very soon be prepared (should anyone be foolhardy enough to press them on the issue) for all-out war.

The next day Alden repeated what his father had said to Arthur and John. Arthur swore through his teeth, then quietly shook his head.

We went to France to bury the war, he said, not bring it home.

The Indian, however—observed Sutton—remained curiously silent.

NOT LONG AFTER, the whole camp was roused in the middle of the night. Waters had recently returned—cured of a mysterious ailment—and his first order of business was to rid his troops of all Communist influence. After that, he promised to lead an attack on the Communist organizer John T. Pace himself, who—in Waters's absence—had established his own camp nearby.

The enemy has infiltrated! Waters shouted at his troops in order to rouse them from their beds. He's among us!

When, having stumbled from their tents, his men had assembled before him, Waters ordered them to take with them what weapons they could find: bricks, iron bars, scraps of metal from their makeshift homes—then he led the attack.

By the end of the night hundreds of alleged Communists had been "evicted" from Camp Marks—evictions so violent in nature that, finally (adding a strange twist to the affair), government troops had to be called, in order to defend Pace's men. By the time they arrived, however, Waters had already caught and tried at least half a dozen men—sentencing them, by his own authority, to fifteen lashes across the back.

When Sutton heard all of this, she wondered aloud to Alden what would happen if his own allegiances—and those of the Indian—should be discovered. Two men, merely *rumored* to be Communists, she reminded him, had recently turned up drowned on the banks of the river, just outside the camp—victims of Waters and his men.

Don't worry about me, Alden had said sharply. Then, by way of apology: Anyway, sooner or later it'll dawn on all of them that we're on the same side.

THEN, SUDDENLY, THIS SEEMED to be true. On the fifteenth of June, the Bonus Bill swept through the house, and two days later nearly one thousand veterans—Pace's as well as Waters's men—assembled on the Hill to await the Senate's final ruling. Everyone (Sutton included—with only a tinge of regret in her heart) felt certain that the "Bonus Army affair" would very soon be at its end, having resolved itself happily—despite her father's dire predictions—in the veterans' favor.

Instead, the Senate returned with a decisive no.

A palpable shock rippled through the crowd; the police stepped forward. After only a moment's hesitation, Waters did, too. The Senate vote, he declared, was only a temporary setback. The BEF could, and would—he promised, his voice ringing in anger—stick it out. They would not back down until the bonus had been paid in full, and to every last deserving man.

With that, the veterans turned, and—very slowly—began to make their way back to the camps.

IT WAS NOT UNTIL much later that it occurred to Sutton to wonder how those *inside*—her own father—must have felt during those hours before the verdict was read. How even the bravest among them must have felt

their throats go dry at the sound of the men assembled on the hill outside. How they must have felt their hearts quicken in their chests—as
they ducked through evacuation tunnels in order to avoid what they
could only anticipate would, very soon, be an angry crowd.

They might, perhaps, have mustered some courage by imagining
themselves, briefly, in the tradition of the Founding Fathers, who had
similarly fled when, in June 1783—one hundred and fifty years ago
almost to the day—Revolutionary soldiers had poked their bayonets
through the windows of the Philadelphia capitol, demanding instant
payment for their own services to the new country, which had at that
time not yet even cooled into a solid shape in their minds.

It would have been then, perhaps, some comfort to remind themselves of their proximity to history in this way—of the way that things
repeated themselves, if in ever-widening circles. Some comfort to
remind themselves that the *sole reason* the Capitol had been built in the
very spot from which they now fled was to avoid *precisely* the sort of
unruly, antidemocratic behavior that had once threatened the Founding Fathers and now threatened them. It was, they would have assured
themselves then, *their duty* to protect both themselves and the principles they had been entrusted to uphold! (That Congress had eventually
given in to the demands, and that the last beneficiary of the Revolutionary War had received his final payment as late as 1911—well, that
was beside the point. It had been a different war, a different time, and
if a "bonus" payout now was not downright impossible, as it surely
seemed to be, it was at the very least—they would have reminded
themselves then—inadvisable to make decisions in the present moment
based on the grounds of the past.) To be connected to history by a singular narrative line, thrust through the ever-widening circles of history, was one thing—but the trajectory had, always, to be forward!
Now, of all times (they would have thought encouragingly to themselves, as they retreated underground), was not a time to look back!

EVEN MORE DIFFICULT TO imagine was how it actually came to pass,
that—a month later—the United States government, led by General

Douglas MacArthur, stormed the Pennsylvania Avenue and Anacostia camps, smoking out ten thousand men, women, and children—including at least several veterans of the 42nd "Rainbow" Division, which he himself had led into battle at Verdun and through the Marne. In the weeks leading up to the riots, it had been increasingly difficult for Sutton to get any sense of the situation at all. Not only had she been forbidden to go down to the flats—she hardly saw Alden anymore. He began to leave earlier each day, and return later; when their paths *did* cross, and she pressed him to tell her what was on his mind (it was hardly like him to keep his cards like that—she told him—held so closely to his chest) he reacted violently. He had no idea what she was suggesting, he said. Indeed, he *wished* he could say he had some knowledge of what Pace had planned—but he did not. At any rate, he hoped it would be better than what *Waters* had up his sleeve. Which was (he said), as anyone could observe, *nothing at all*. Marching around down there—making a fool of himself, and everyone else. *Anything*, Alden insisted, before turning away, would be better than that.

DESPITE HIS PROMISES, WATERS'S first political move following Congress's negative ruling had, in fact, been to officially resign. But the words had hardly been uttered when he had a sudden change of heart. He would, he announced, continue to lead the Bonus Army—but only on the condition of absolute power.

I'm going to be hard-boiled now, he told his men after they'd sanctioned his pronouncement with a rousing cheer. If any man refuses to carry out my orders, he will be dragged out of Washington by the military police. To hell with civil law and General Glassford, I'm going to have my orders carried out!

He ordered military drills, beginning that very afternoon, and the formation of a force of five hundred "shock troops" à la Mussolini's gang. The Italian leader, who had done so much for the veterans of his own country, had for some time served as Waters's chief inspiration. Now he even went so far as to rename his men the Khaki Shirts—a move that went over especially well with the Italian element.

Waters led his Khaki Shirts—Douglas, Chet, and Arthur among them—in their first big march on the Hill on the second of July. That same afternoon, Sutton went down to the camps for what—though she could not have known it then—would be the last time. When she arrived, she found Aida alone with the child. The men had been gone nearly three days straight, she was told. They returned only late in the evening—exhausted by the long hours they spent performing drills on the flats beneath the hard glare of the sun.

And John? Sutton asked. He goes with them?

She was not surprised to learn he did not.

Oh, no, Aida said, and shrugged. He doesn't go in much for Waters and that lot.

Sutton held on to Felicity for a time while the child slept. An hour passed, then two. She was about to give up (she would soon be missed, she knew, at home—where it was becoming increasingly difficult to explain her long absences), when Arthur ducked through the door of the tent. Chet, then Douglas, followed. They greeted her kindly, but—as Aida had said—they seemed exhausted, and sad. Even the plate of food Sutton had managed to beg from Germaine that morning did not seem to revive their spirits—though they thanked her sincerely for it, and began—hungrily, if rather mechanically—to eat.

There was not much; it did not take long.

The march, Arthur said, after they had finished and the plate had been wiped clean, had proved a disappointment—to say the very least. It was a long weekend holiday (a detail Waters had somehow over-looked); by the time they'd arrived at the Capitol, everyone had already gone home. Well, they'd stayed four hours anyway. Waters shouting the whole time about the change of tide the new President would bring.

Arthur raised his hands, then let them fall. I don't know what to believe anymore, he said. I don't.

Then the child began to cry, and Sutton was reminded of how late it had become. She handed the child back to Aida, gathered the empty dish, and—expressing her regret that it had not been more—took her leave as quickly as she could.

..

IT WOULD BE MANY years before she came to learn with any sort of accuracy what took place between that moment—as she bade them all, Chet and Arthur, Douglas, Aida, and the child, a hasty goodbye; then turned, in order to make her way for the last time through the rutted streets back home—and when, three weeks later, "all hell broke loose," just as her father had promised it would. Or how it was that Alden had managed, in that brief interim, to find himself in possession of a powerful explosive, at (depending upon how you looked at it) precisely the right, or precisely the wrong, place and time; or that Arthur had found himself, the afternoon following, wearing another man's ill-fated hat.

Many years before she would learn, for example, of how—on the morning of the twenty-eighth of July—Waters read aloud the eviction notice he'd received, which ordered the immediate evacuation of the Bonus Army. The Penn Ave. as well as the Anacostia camps would need to be cleared, read Waters—his voice shaking with rage—by no later than ten o'clock that morning.

Or of how—at exactly ten o'clock—Glassford and six members of the United States Treasury arrived at the armory building off Pennsylvania Avenue, which now housed Pace's men. The building—along with an adjacent concrete block once owned by the Ford automobile company—had been slated for demolition since early spring, in order to make room for the new Federal Triangle. That morning, however, as the first cranes and wrecking balls came into view (looming up suddenly in the distance, from behind the approaching Treasury men), it still belonged to the Bonus Army.

This armory is not for sale! shouted a veteran posted out front, when Glassford and the first of the Treasury men drew near enough to hear. It's the headquarters of sixteen hundred men of the Sixth Regiment of the BEF! All of whom have been honorably discharged, and eighty-five percent of whom have served in France!

Aside from this—single—show of resistance, however, there was little dissent as Glassford and the Treasury agents pushed past, then entered the building; or as they returned, only a few minutes later, with the first startled veterans, their wives, and a few children. Once more, then, Glassford and the agents turned and plunged inside—this time making their way up a rickety flight of stairs, left exposed due to the building's demolished western wall. And once more, it was not long before they were on their way down again—a stream of veterans following steadily behind.

The eviction carried on like this more or less without incident. By one forty-five that afternoon, the building had been cleared. Only the police were left—sweating in their summer uniforms and pacing the grounds. The veterans and their families, who had just been fed a spartan lunch (personally provided by Glassford), lounged at a distance of about hundred yards—and if it were not for the desolate backdrop and the stricken, half-starved appearance of most of the crowd, it would have looked more like a Sunday picnic than an unruly evacuation scene. Even the mass of onlookers who had gathered to witness the drama unfold were beginning to move off.

But then a shout went up in front of the old Ford building, and several of the police officers who had been guarding the empty armory rushed over to the Ford building instead. The disturbance continued—the noise echoing into the yard below. Then two shots were fired, followed by a moment—so brief that afterward it was impossible to be certain if it had even occurred—of deep silence. Then the noise and confusion resumed. Glassford yelled, Stop that shooting! But it was too late. One of the officers, who had been hit with his own nightstick just before he'd fired, now stood facing the crowd—turning in bewildered circles. Even at the sound of Glassford's command he did not lower his gun.

William Hushka, age thirty-five—a Lithuanian immigrant and veteran from Chicago, who had sold his butcher shop to join the U.S. Army in 1917—and Eric Carlson—thirty-eight years old, from Oakland, California, who had survived the most brutal of the trench war fighting in France—were dead.

Within minutes, ambulances had arrived and the bodies of the dead men, along with the injured police officers, were carried away.

..

MEANWHILE, GENERAL MACARTHUR HAD called up Dwight D. Eisenhower and, despite Eisenhower's protestations that suppressing a potential riot was "beneath the dignity" of any Army chief of staff—or even, by implication, a low-ranking aide—had begun briefing him on the full-scale combat operation he was about to put into effect. An hour later, Glassford arrived at the Ellipse on his motorcycle to find MacArthur in full dress uniform. When he asked what the plan was regarding military presence on the Hill, MacArthur replied without hesitation. We are here to break the back of the BEF, he said. We'll move down Pennsylvania Avenue first, sweep through the billets there, then clean out the other two camps. The operation will be continuous. It will all be done tonight.

Glassford requested a ten-minute delay, which he was granted. He raced to the Penn Ave. camp to spread the word among the veterans still billeted there. Then he ordered the message carried to the other camps, urging the immediate evacuation of at least the women and children. He then cleared Pennsylvania Avenue, where a sort of ceremonial order had fallen over the crowd who had gathered there, waiting for the troops.

IT WAS A LONG WAIT. The troops were still being sailed upriver from Fort Washington. More were arriving from Fort Myer—having left, for the first time in its history, the Tomb of the Unknown Soldier alone and unguarded. Finally, the first of them came into sight—accompanied by a half dozen flatbed trucks and tanks, which, as Judge Kelly had warned, had been transferred to Fort Myer in early June, should the occasion for their use arise.

At four-thirty p.m., armed with tear-gas grenades, and the instructions from MacArthur to use "such force as necessary" to accomplish the task, the troops, with sabers drawn, their feet clicking like wrought iron on the hard pavement, approached Camp Glassford. Many of the veterans and bystanders along the route cheered, thinking the procession merely a demonstration of strength—but the mood soon changed when, after arriving at the Ford building, the first troops stopped abruptly and fixed their bayonets at a crowd of veterans, just then lining up for mess call.

The last time I saw bayonets I was going through Marne, came the shout of one veteran.

A whistle rose through the crowd. A few men laughed.

You got three minutes! yelled an officer. Three minutes, I warn you!

And then what? a veteran called.

Then it's the Marne all over again, another replied.

A stone soared through the crowd. At first it looked like a bird. Then the riot began. The infantrymen donned gas masks and approached the billets, tossing tear gas grenades behind them as they went. The recently evacuated buildings were set on fire, and before long the entire city seemed engulfed in gas and flame. An officer moving between his ranks said, Be careful, men, don't burn any flags. But everything was burned. The scraps of wood and other materials that had been used as shelters for those billeted outside the government houses—everything.

The veterans retreated. There was nothing else to do. A few stood their ground and were grazed in warning by the sabers of approaching soldiers. One man, blood streaming from his ear and holding aloft a tattered flag, screamed, Hit me! Hit me, you yellow bastards! I took it then and I can take it now!

And somewhere—amid it all—Arthur and Douglas were moving, Alden with them. Somewhere, Chet. Somewhere, John and Aida. This more than anything was difficult for Sutton, later, to imagine. The child pressed tightly against Aida's breast to protect it from the choking gas. The child, breathing in terrified gasps, forcing her head against her mother's hand—unable to tell the difference any longer between the protection, which the hand delivered, and the smothering air.

What thoughts would have flickered through the mind of the tall Indian as he pressed himself, along with his young wife and child, to the outer limits of the crowd? Only to find that everyone else was pressing in the same direction. Only to find that there was, therefore, no outside or inside any longer to press toward, and that likewise it was impossible to discern between the shouts of the veterans and the shouts of the soldiers; between his own thoughts and the noise of the street—or even, indeed, between the future and the past. So that the stories of his ancestors (which had been passed down from generation to generation, and which now, as ever—so profoundly had they been etched there as to become nearly a physical trait—trembled in his brain) mixed indistinguishably with his own deeply personal and most ardent desires. How they had once been driven by cattle prod, from the fertile Mississippi River Delta over seven hundred miles, through fire and flood and driving hail, into the dusty center of the beleaguered continent where nothing grew, and how they would, at last, be relieved of that history, became one, a single element, which the Indian moved through then; his arms stretched out as far as he could extend them, as though moving—or attempting to move—through the impassable space of a uninterpretable dream.

Finally, though, there would have been—there would have had to have been—some sudden, dramatic shift in pressure. By whatever outside force: some change, some slight shift, and then—no more resistance. The crowd, unexpectedly released from whatever it was that had kept them knotted, both pressed upon and pressing against one another, suddenly free to move in any direction they chose.

Without pausing to consider any other option, the Indian, his wife and child—absorbed by the singular determination of the crowd—would have turned, then, as one, and headed back toward the camp. There was something irresistible about it. That final blaze on the horizon: so big it lit up the whole sky.

II.

Douglas

ON THE MARCH. JUNCTION CITY, TOPEKA, KANSAS CITY,
EARLY MAY, 1932—WITH A BRIEF DETOUR TO BELLEAU
WOOD, FRANCE, 1918, AND SILVER PEAK, NEVADA, 1930—
SIBERIA, 1918–1920.

L ater, what Douglas remembered best was not really his father at
all, but the shape of his father, from behind: head bent and leaning into the wind—the entire empty state of Kansas opening off around
him, from every side. Douglas's own lungs, as he ran, would be filled
nearly to bursting, his brain hot with thinking how much, how badly, he
wanted to catch him this time. But each time, equally, he would not.
Each time, when his father halted, he would find himself still several
paces behind. He would pull up short and stand there while his father
caught his breath. Sometimes his father would even have to drop to the
ground; sort of arch his back up—his head thrown at an angle so that his
two missing teeth showed, and the thick tendons in his neck stood out
like hard wire. It was a wonder Douglas never could catch him, the way
his father choked and sputtered like that at the end. His own breath came

back so easily. It was like, after it was over, he hadn't even tried—while his father's heavy breathing and slow recovery attested clearly to the fact that he'd expended nearly everything he had. That was, of course, the difference: the exact distance by which Douglas always lagged, and each time, because of it, he swore that next time he'd try harder. He'd throw himself into the race like there wasn't going to be anything he would need his heart or his lungs or his legs for ever again after—but next time would always turn out the same. His father spluttering and half dead with exhaustion and him just standing there—as though he had hardly even moved, but just followed with his eyes.

When his father had caught his breath again, it was always the same. *Well, I ain't beat yet*, he would say. More to himself than to Douglas. Then he'd pick himself up and the two of them would walk together back to the wagon, which seemed, suddenly, from that distance, small and insignificant, like it could never hold anything—even if they filled it up and emptied it again a thousand times.

Then his father would start to laugh.

Ha, ha! he'd shout. If the Duke could see us now!

It was in those moments, when his father laughed like that and invoked the Duke by name, that Douglas got his first, brief inkling that the Duke did not preside over time itself—deciding at any moment what was and was not to be done with it. Everyone was always talking about it like that. It was always "the Duke's time and money," and how much of it went into, or came out of, any given thing. Never once as a boy, that he could later recall, did he hear of time falling under anyone else's jurisdiction.

But just before they returned—before the wagon once again established itself in correct proportion to the field and their approach—Douglas's father would pause again, suspending the moment just that one beat longer, before he bent again to his task, and Douglas followed. Before their minds, in unison, began revolving slowly, once more, around the same narrow groove that countless rotations had already worn: wondering to themselves, for example, what was cooking up at the house, though it never turned out to be more than one of two or three things, about how much longer it was until quitting time, and how many more rocks they would pick until then, Douglas's father would stretch his hand out, in the direction they'd come, and say, By God, would you look at that, boy? And then he'd turn to Douglas, and Douglas would turn in the direction his father pointed, and strain his eyes as far as he could see. Because, even though he was never mistaken by his father's tone to imagine there really was some particular thing to see out there, he always looked anyway, as if there might be one time, and was always, therefore, equally surprised when he saw, again, only an empty Kansas sky. Hardly ever even a cloud, as he later recalled it—and the field below, so flat and big and empty that at a certain point it was impossible to tell where the field ended and the sky began. There was nothing, nothing, not even a bird that would stay still long enough for him to fix with his gaze. And it would not be until many years later that he would finally realize that what had stirred in his father, in those moments—what had impelled him to pause, to turn back, to strain against that emptiness for something he could, if briefly, share with his son—was not any *thing* at all. That there existed in the very act of looking, or rather in its brief— and almost wholly imaginary—arrest, some resistance to the slow constriction of the heart brought about generally by the passage of time, which had, almost certainly (though this, too, Douglas had no knowledge of then), already narrowed the passageways leading toward and away from it to such a degree that it was for that reason and that reason alone that he both ran harder, and gasped longer, after running a certain distance across the Duke's—unmeasurable—field.

It makes him sad to think of it now, so many years later. Of the way that his father, and his mother, too, no doubt—with her surprised eyes and her mouth always set in a thin line, making it seem as though she were forever attempting to cure herself of the hiccups by holding her breath—must have also felt that slow constriction over the years from some equivalent point in their own childhoods, when they, too, must have felt the same way he did, while chasing after his father, whom he never once could catch. He can't help but wonder, when he thinks of it, if there might be another, different sort of world, or a way of living in it, where the heart would not constrict. Where the skyline would always seem as it did in childhood: irrelevant, nearly abstract. But then he always gets stuck wondering about it, because it is only in retrospect, after all, that he is able to recognize—in the way he wanted to, so badly, then—the sort of beauty in the landscape his father had pointed to when he stretched his hand toward it, and, with that gesture, conjured it into being at all.

So then it was quitting time. They'd walk, the two of them, to wash themselves in the cold water, which, after a few strong thrusts, the handle screaming, gushed from the pump's long snout. It felt good, the way that water poured over Douglas's head and down the back of his neck, wetting his shirt. His father would take his handkerchief and find a clean corner of it to scrub behind Douglas's ears, and before he tucked the rag away, he'd show Douglas the dirt that he'd gathered. Then they'd turn together toward the house, and as they approached, a black shape would appear from beneath the eaves to take the form of a crow—a big bird with a damaged wing his father had tamed, and whom he called Faustina, though never in front of Douglas's mother. (After an Italian girl with a wooden leg, he'd said, whom he had known, briefly, during the war.)

Each evening when they returned from the field she would appear from beneath the eaves, at first dark and indistinct, to become a bird and sit on Douglas's father's shoulder and poke her beak into the thinning hair on top of his head, and his father would sing a few lines of "Roses of Picardy." It was the only song Douglas ever knew him to sing, but he sang it well—his voice vibrating deep in his chest on the lower notes. Then, when they reached the porch, he would lift the bird from his shoulder and place her down lightly on the porch rail before ducking into the kitchen ahead of Douglas, where his mother would have already laid out the meal. She kept it waiting each evening, either on the stove or in the oven, 'til the loud squeal of the pump across the yard warned of their arrival. It was at that point that (though Douglas himself never witnessed the moment) she would bring it out and then disappear into the kitchen again, so that it would always be there, waiting for them, when they arrived—the steam still rising—as though no one had had a hand in its making.

IN THE EVENINGS, DOUGLAS's father drank. It was always a mystery to him—like in church—how it happened. How the liquid diminished in the bottle, and how something arose slowly, inside—or alongside—his father as it did so. Something other than himself, and yet himself all the same. Something he always associated, for some reason, and at some level, with the Holy Ghost. His mother would sit in the corner, with the basket of clothes she perpetually mended, as though it were impossible to fix anything. As the night wore on, and Douglas's father spoke louder and louder, she stitched faster. Pausing only, once in a while, after no particular interval, to say his name, sharply. *Douglas*, she'd say. Sometimes just that. She knew that he knew what it meant. Other times, she would say it more to his father than to him. Douglas, *it's time*. But his father would not hear and, because he did not, there never was anything for Douglas to do, or anywhere for him to go when she said it, because he slept right there on the hard cot by the stove, upon which his father would at that moment be sitting—his eyes bleary and glazed with the presence, already, within him, of the Holy Ghost.

So he would not move at all, except to give a slight nod in his mother's direction, acknowledging to her that he knew she had spoken. He would not look at her directly. He would only turn his head slightly. Aside from that, he would remain very still, a book open before him, though by that time in the evening he never could understand what he read there. He would just stare down at the book and let his mind go kind of numb so sometimes it seemed that the Holy Ghost was mysteriously unsettling the very forms of the letters on the page. That they were rising up before him with his father's voice as he told the story once more— a story both Douglas and his mother knew by heart and could have recited themselves—of the terrible night he'd spent in Belleau Wood; half buried beneath the body of another man.

RIGHT FROM THE FIRST moment he'd woken he'd felt it, his father said. Something heavy and strange. He just . . . . knew, somehow (though the feeling had hardly returned to his body, and he could not yet see). Then he tasted blood on his lips, and was certain. It brought him back to life, he said: the taste of another man's blood. Its very strangeness on his lips revived him; stirred his own blood, once again, in his veins.

And do you know, Douglas's father would inquire of his mother and of himself then, how they came to recognize me as alive among all those dead men? But instead of waiting for a reply, or answering, he began to sing. The only song he ever sang: *And the roses will die with the summertime* . . . The words would rumble just as they did when he arrived with Douglas, home from the fields. Only this time there was the Holy Ghost in them. *And our roads may be far apart* . . . His mother's needle would be going at such a pace that by now there was no time at all between the stitches in which to discover there would be no time to finish anything. There was just the needle going in and out and the thread extending— not attached or attaching to anything at all—but just drilling and drilling itself through a single hole. *But there's one rose that dies not in Picardy!*

Go to bed now, Douglas. It's past time.

Douglas would nod again, his eyes pointed straight ahead as if trained on the page, and the voice of his father would swim up from the blur of words there, which he could no longer make out, so that it would not be his father but the Holy Ghost that spoke. Then, in another moment, standing above him, his father would hold out his hand and say, Give it here a moment—meaning the book. He would not be angry, just—suddenly—sad. And so Douglas would hand over the book and another change would come over his father's face as he looked at it. When he handed it back he would say, simply: I read this, too. Or else it would be: Didn't. Never had the chance. He would place the book back into his son's hands, which he had not withdrawn, and tell him he was a good boy to study hard, and that he would grow up to do great things if he kept at it, and used the brain God gave him for more than counting rocks, or glasses of whiskey at the bar.

But then, just as suddenly as it came, he would abandon the sad, far-away note that had crept into his voice. After all, he'd shout: it's not like this is Amer-r-r-rica! Here, we all have to *work* for a living! Which was something he had once heard said by a Frenchman in Paris, who rolled his *r*'s in a way his father could imitate. Then Douglas's mother, her needle driving itself into the solitariness of its singular, fathomless hole, would say (so quickly it might easily have been between a still-uncured case of hiccups that she spoke), Arthur, really, that's enough now. The *boy*, and his father would look up, surprised.

Enough? As though he didn't recognize the word. He'd repeat it again, quietly to himself. Enough. Then louder. Enough! Oh, is it? My dear! Is it? he'd ask. My *putteet shair-ee*? He would look abstracted and thoughtful, as though the question as to whether it was or was not "enough" were a mathematical problem to which some absolute and unwavering answer might still be found. His face would take on an expression of genuine concern—as when he had lifted the book from Douglas's hands and discovered the title to be something he either had or had not read. But in another moment he would begin to laugh, at first softly to himself. It would start almost like a tickle at the back of his throat, but then it would get bigger and bigger until he nearly choked on it.

Marry him for his pension! he would roar out, finally—between belts of laughter. Who's the sorriest of us now!

He was—it seemed—genuinely delighted by the words, and from time to time would scoop Douglas or on rare occasions even his mother up, so that her mending went flying (abandoned, permanently unfinished) to the floor, and steered one or the other of them around the little room in a sort of tuneless waltz, which kept time with his repeated exclamation: His pension! Yes! That will do! Until he collapsed, exhausted, and his mother was able, her small hand under his broad shoulder, to steer him to the adjacent room (really only a closet, at the back of the house), where they slept. She would give Douglas a single, final glance over her shoulder before she disappeared. In fact, she did not really look at him—just as he had not, all evening, looked at her. There was never any point, that is, in which his mother's eyes made contact with his own. She only tossed her head in his direction—but he understood. That he was to do as he had been told some hours before: make his own way to bed, and pray heartily to God for forgiveness for whatever sins he or his father had committed that had brought the Holy Ghost once more—as though, indeed, he were one of them—into that house.

—

THAT LAST SPRING WAS AN UNUSUALLY WET ONE, SO IT WAS NOT UNTIL the second week of May that all the corn had been planted. At the end of the week his father was paid, and when he was he went into town and came back with a lot of new things, which he laid out on the kitchen table. Everything was perfectly quiet. There were no cicadas outside, and no ghost inside, holy or unholy. As he laid down each object he had bought he pronounced its name—and each, together, the object and the word, made a heavy sound against that quiet.

Douglas's mother was not in her usual place by the stove. Her usual pile of mending was there, where she would otherwise have been, and Douglas felt the exact emptiness of the space she did not fill. His heart beat faster as if to fill it but it did not fill it. He was alone with his father as his father named things and placed them on the table: Rope. Ten feet. A silver canteen and a box of chewing tobacco. All of this and more were placed into the Army-issue rucksack on which his father's surname: SINCLAIR—also, of course, Douglas's own—was stitched in uneven red letters.

It was late. Douglas's father said: Time to turn in, son.

He wished his mother would return, but she did not. Even after he had, at his father's request, crawled into his bed by the stove for what would be the last time, he tried to stay awake. He tried to wait for her. It felt important that he should hear her familiar step on the porch before he slept. But he did not. He drifted to sleep despite himself, and woke only to his father shaking him softly on the shoulder. And so, the sun not yet fully risen, they went on their way that morning without taking leave of his mother—who, asleep now in the adjacent room (his father said), it was best not to wake.

AFTER A WHILE—SOME MILE and a half—they came to the crossroads. Chet was waiting for them there. Douglas saw him from a distance, sitting by the side of the road. When he saw them coming, he got up with a grin. He was so tall and thin it looked like if he turned around sideways he might disappear. But he didn't turn, and came forward and shook Douglas's father's hand. Then he shook Douglas's hand, like he was grown-up, too, and then they all kept walking. His father and Chet talked a lot between themselves. Once, his father turned and said, Isn't that right, boy? But Douglas didn't know what it was that had been said, let alone whether whatever it was was right or wrong, so he didn't reply. His father gave him a shake and said, What's the matter with you? Look alive, now, son! So he tried to look alive, but it was difficult what with also having to try to keep up with their pace, and think about all the things he was busy thinking about just then. But then he heard his mother's name and paid attention.

She was gone all afternoon and half of the night, his father said— longer than he'd expected. But sure enough she'd come back with the ticket. Kept—he said—like a pledge at her father's house, since his return from the war.

How's that? Chet asked. And so his father explained how it was that, fresh from the service—with nothing to show for himself but his name— he had promised every penny of his bonus to his wife. Just as soon as it came through.

And it didn't seem too shabby a thing! his father said. A pension— ha! More than most could offer then. And now? Well. Somethin' better than gold. I gave that ticket to her daddy on the day we was married, so's he could see I was good for it; that I meant my word. And by God, I did—I *do*. Still—it was all I could do to convince her, now. It's a fair lot to risk—she said—losing a job, when most folks don't have none. And what with leaving her all alone (I was dead set, I told her, on taking the boy) . . .

Here Douglas's father paused. With the back of his hand, he wiped the sweat that had begun to collect on his brow. Well, that was a small price to pay—he continued—when you thought of it. Of what they had coming to them, if they just dared stand up and ask. I won that bonus fighting—Douglas's father said. Blast me if I'm not going to win it again by doing the same. And sure enough—he continued, after they had traveled a few more paces together in silence—she'll thank me, once we get what it is we've been owed. We'll quit this place—that's one thing sure; start us up someplace new. Get us a plot of land somewheres. Virginia, maybe. Tennessee. Send back for Lou once everything's paid. That's right, Douglas's father said; I can swear it to you now, Chet, as God is my witness. Neither I nor my boy will be coming back this way, to work for the Duke or any other man.

Though Douglas's heart had, a moment before, thrilled at the sound of his father's voice—at the thought of the plot of land, in Virginia, or Tennessee, which would soon be their own—another feeling, more difficult to place, mixed in now as his father spread his arm in a wide arc behind them and Douglas traced the path that it made with his eyes. A dull pain—too deep to trace to its particular source—as he thought now, in whatever dim way he could, of the time and distance they would have to cover before everything was "paid," and they could send for his mother.

His mother, who—at that very moment (Douglas's heart lurched at the thought of it)—was first waking. Was realizing again (if, over the course of the night, she'd forgotten) that she had—as his father had promised—been left quite alone.

Both Douglas's father and Chet were quiet now. Only their feet, marching roughly in step—though Chet's legs were so much longer—made any sound. Douglas's father had placed his right hand over his breast pocket—where, inside, his bonus ticket lay—and Douglas looked at his father's hand, and the breast pocket beneath it, then down at the road, at his father's feet. After a while, without noticing at first, he began to count his father's steps beside him. One. Two. Three. Four. Why his father's instead of his own? Five. Six. Seven . . . It kept his mind occupied, and at the same time reassured him of the progress they made. If he looked out, instead, too far down the road, it seemed they were hardly moving at all, and so never would get any nearer to anything, or farther away.

—

IT WAS THE MIDDLE OF THE AFTERNOON BY THE TIME THEY REACHED Junction City. By evening, they had boarded a train heading east, toward Topeka and Kansas City. They shared a car, and the last of Douglas's mother's bread, with two men also bound for Washington. In exchange for the bread, one of the men, a broad-shouldered man named Jim, opened up a can of beans, from which they took turns eating from a single spoon. After each bite, the men licked the spoon so clean it shone, even in the dimming light. Then, just as they finished the can, and the bread was gone, the train ground to a halt, though they hadn't arrived anywhere. They stayed put like that for nearly an hour. Douglas wondered if they would ever move again, or if they would stay put like that, and have to walk all the way to Topeka, or farther than that, in the morning. His shoes were already nearly worn out with walking, and they had only been gone a single day. There was even a hole in the toe of one of them, and the other was split along the inside seam so that it was no trouble at all for dirt and sand to get in and he had to shake his foot every third or fourth step in an effort to get it out again. But it never did come out, once it was in. Not until they stopped and he cleaned the inside of the shoe with a corner of his pocket handkerchief. Only then, for a short time, when they first began walking again, was there no sand in his shoe. Then there was again. And the more sand that piled in there, the more would come, or so it seemed. And no shaking or hopping would get it out, but still Douglas shook and hopped until they sat down again, and his father said, What's wrong, boy? Are you going to dance like that all the way to Washington? And when he showed his father the hole in his shoe, his father told him not to worry. He was going to get him some brand-new shoes in Kansas City when they arrived there, he said, and in the meantime they would patch the ones he had up good and solid. He took out a thick wool sock and told Douglas to put it on and then he said, Now see if that ain't better, see if any of that dirt can come in now; for a while it could not, but his foot sweated and got sore, and the wool scratched at the places on his foot that had already been rubbed raw.

It had been a relief because of that when they first climbed onto the train to take his shoes and socks off and prop his feet up on his rucksack, next to his father's feet, which had also been put out to air. He laid his head on the rolled-up blanket he'd carried, because it was too hot to roll it out. His father was propped up by his own rolled-up blanket and, the way he lay, his Adam's apple stood up straight like the point of a knife in his throat. He let out a low whistle. If this ain't living, he said. Chet laughed, and Jim nodded, but his companion, a short brown-skinned man, who looked to be a Mexican, said, And what if it ain't?

Don't mind him, Jim said. He's still sore over losing three dollars to an Indian.

Well, now, what did he do that for? Douglas's father asked.

Jim shrugged his big shoulders and the Mexican swore under his breath. He's lucky he didn't lose more, Jim said. Them Injuns get mean when they want something. They're liable just to take it right out from under you most times, give 'em half a chance. Whole world's getting like that, more or less. Real savage-like.

Yes, that's so, Jim continued. No one pays any mind to the next man now. Take tonight, for example, when we passed 'round those beans and yer missus's bread,'til there wasn't any one of us got more nor less than the other. If everyone did like we did—shared things out, civilized-like—I figure there wouldn't be no need of getting robbed by Indians. Nor stealing from them neither.

Well, that sure is a pretty thought, Douglas's father said. Don't you like that, Chet? I sure am liking to imagine ol' Duke spooning me out just as much bread and molasses as he sits down to each night. Chet laughed, then his father did, too. Jim stayed quiet; his feelings were hurt.

But see, now, that's dreaming, Douglas's father said after he and Chet were done laughing. Things just ain't like that, nor will they be, and if you start believing they are, or wishing too hard on it, you're liable to get a whole lot more'n three dollars stole.

Just then the train gave a lurch and began to roll slowly. The moon followed. Douglas's father settled back again, his head propped on his bedroll. Yessir, he said. We're on our way now. Then everyone was quiet for a time, just appreciating the steady racket of the wheels on the tracks as the train picked up speed.

Yessir, Douglas's father said, as though speaking to no one now. If you don't go ahead and take what's yours, sooner or later you'll be left with nothing at all. Might as well, he said—and now he gestured toward the open cargo doors, where outside the moon trailed heavily over-head—be nothing more'n—a—a wild animal, out there. All alone, scrambling t' just—

But he didn't have a chance to finish his thought.

What's that? Jim said. What did you say? He was leaning forward now, his eyes dark suddenly, and mean. Say it again, he said.

What again? Douglas's father said.

Jim's eyes flashed. *You* know, he said. Who you calling a—

Well—hold on, Douglas's father said. Hold on. Nobody's called nobody nothing yet, so far as I can tell.

Well, Jim said—his voice was uneasy. It shore sounded like some-body did.

Awww . . . come on, now, Chet said, raising himself on an elbow to look at the two men. We're all right.

Yeah, Douglas's father agreed—after a moment in which it seemed he might say more. We're all right. We're *civilized*, ain't we?

Uncertain whether he was being made fun of or not, Jim didn't say anything for a while, but then he and Douglas's father went back to talking, pleasantly enough, and from time to time Chet's voice joined in—but never the deep growl of the man who had got himself robbed by an Indian. Jim didn't talk like anyone Douglas had ever known before, and he tried to imagine what it would be like to be from a place—like California—where he had never been. To not even know a place like Junction City, if you didn't want to, and didn't happen to pass through it one day. It was strange to think about. About how many people there were all over the world who had never been to or even heard much of anything about Junction City. Who didn't know what it was like, or even think to imagine what it was like—to be there, where he was just now: somewhere in between Junction City and Topeka and on his way to Kansas City, then beyond. All the way to Hoover's door, Douglas's father had said—in order to claim what, by rights, was already theirs.

Did that make them—Douglas wondered—civilized? Was it that? *Knowing* what was yours by right? Having a paper to prove it? Rather than just . . . taking things, like a wild animal or an Indian?

He figured that was probably right. Though just at that moment he thought it might be nice, after all, to be an animal instead—a mountain lion or a grizzly. To never be afraid of anything at all, except maybe fire; to never feel lonely because there was no open space in your heart for anything at all, let alone loneliness, to get in. The heart of a mountain lion, he thought, would be as solid as that. Their brains, too—quick and hard. All the different parts fit together inside like the cars on a train; thoughts like light streaming in through a semi-open door.

As he drifted to sleep, Douglas heard his father's voice rise and fall alongside Jim's—until at last there was nothing to tell them apart, the familiar and the strange—and he hardly noticed when even the familiar dropped away, and only Jim's voice remained.

By God, said the voice, *I was there.* Saw it *with my own eyes.* When General Pershing knelt to kiss the sword Napoleon himself had carried all through the Battle of Marengo. Then Stanton—he knelt, too. Said: Here we are. And we *were.* Staying in those crummy barracks outside town. Getting eaten alive by the descendants of lice who'd once eaten Napoleon's men. I considered it a privilege. Especially for those of us, like myself, who, before we shipped, had never even fired a gun. Well, if we didn't whip them anyway. There was something in us—in all of us. Some instinct for survival—for freedom above all—which did us proud. And it was that, mark me, more than any general or any gun, that won us the war. But now—the voice paused. The train measured four long beats. Nobody remembers any of that now.

Douglas's father and Chet had been asleep for some time, and now Douglas suspected that the Mexican was sleeping, too. Everyone in the whole world was sleeping—except Douglas and Jim. But then, he could not even be certain of that; perhaps he himself was not fully awake, and Jim neither. Perhaps he had already, as he had for some time suspected, ceased to be able to properly discern where Jim's reminiscences of the Great War left off and his own dreams began, and before long, despite his best efforts, there was little use in attempting to make any distinction at all; the two combined, and were one. And that was how, a few moments later, Douglas arrived, along with his father and Chet, the Duke, the Mexican, and Jim, at Hoover's doorstep, to be greeted by a crowd of French soldiers, who shouted and cheered and stamped their feet, and sang "Roses of Picardy" in rich tenor voices, which sounded just like his father's had always sounded, after returning at the end of the day from the field, back home.

—

WHEN HIS FATHER ROUSED HIM IN THE EARLY MORNING, IT MUST HAVE been from a very deep sleep. For some time he did not know where he was. The sun had already risen, but it seemed to be coming from the wrong direction. There was no time to dwell on the problem, however. His father had already rolled up his blanket and was now pulling on his boots.

Come on, now, son, he said. Before the ticket collectors come.

Douglas knew what that meant. He woke up all the way, and sure enough, then, knew where he was. He gathered his blanket and reached for his shoes. His feet were swollen, though, and so sore that he had trouble, only managing to get the left shoe on before he was forced to hop from the train.

There was a heavy fog, and the dew was very wet on the grass as if it had rained, but still Douglas could see where the sun had begun to burn its way through the heavy cloud cover, lighting the far edges of the land-scape. All that blankness, interrupted only by the rubble of the train yard. Metal spikes and rusted barrels littered the grounds everywhere Douglas looked. Half of a disassembled train car—in which, as Douglas approached, it soon became apparent one or more persons had taken up residence—rose at an oblique angle. A line of laundry had been slung in a homely fashion from its tipped-up end to an adjacent post. It was dif-ficult to imagine how anyone could have slept in it any other way than standing up. A dog tied to a post outside looked up at Douglas as he passed, and then away. He looked lonely and bored, like he hadn't seen anyone who mattered to him in a long time.

So this—Douglas thought—is Kansas City? This, too, was difficult to imagine. It seemed that instead of getting nearer to anything, they had, in fact, only gotten much farther away. That, indeed, they had arrived at the very ends of the earth, and in another moment, if they took a few steps in any of the directions that now lay open to them, they would find the earth itself preparing to give way, dropping off at the same star-tling angle with which the abandoned train car dropped from its axle to the bare ground below. But Douglas did not have long to contemplate this possibility, or its consequences. His father was moving quickly—once more, Douglas had to double-step to keep up. And the earth did not give way. It remained so solid beneath them that he winced as his dam-aged feet hit it with every step.

Finally, they came to a road with a long row of low houses strung along it. Douglas's heart lifted at the sight. An illegible sign swung limply on the door of one of them, which Jim now entered. The Mex-ican—then Chet and his father—followed. Douglas, the last to enter, closed the door behind him so that the sign banged against it, star-tling him.

Inside, a low light burned, only partially illuminating the back wall and leaving the rest of the place as full of shadows as the early morning had been. By that time, though at most only half an hour had passed, the sun had managed to burn its way through nearly all of the fog and had risen perpendicular to the low clouds. Next to that sudden, persuasive brightness, they were revealed to be no more than thin phantoms. Soon the inside of the tavern began to appear in just this way. Objects emerged against the dark background that had, until then, absorbed them. There were six stools at the bar. And a heavyset barman—studying them curiously from beneath a low brow.

Both Douglas's father and Chet chose one of the stools at the bar, then Jim sat next to Chet and the Mexican next to Jim. Douglas did not sit, but only stood in the space between the seat where his father sat and the next, until his father turned and indicated that he should sit down, too. Soon they all had a plate of potatoes in front of them, and then whiskey appeared, and every man hollered and raised his glass above his head before he drank, and then the barman laid down another, and said it was on the house.

Don't take much to guess where you're headed, he said. I hope you get your bonus.

Glasses were raised once more and drained, and Douglas ate solemnly all the while and felt the warmth and the weight of the food settle slowly within him. But before long his father turned and said, Now we'll have to be looking into a decent pair of shoes for the boy. His stomach felt cold again all of a sudden when he heard that, though he didn't know why. His father had turned back to the barman and now he consulted him about the various establishments in town and what the likelihood of their being open for business was, and the barman shook his head and said that there wasn't any likelihood at all, it being a Sunday, and then his father said he would see what he could do. It being the Lord's day, he said, after all, maybe something will work out all right. He got up, but told Douglas to stay where he was, and Douglas nodded, grateful to be allowed to stay in the bar. Then his father went out, and Chet with him, and that left just Douglas with Jim and the Mexican. The barman placed a tall glass of white milk in front of Douglas. At first he didn't know if he was intended to take it—or, if he was intended to take it, if he was intended to pay. He didn't have any money. On account of this, Douglas just looked at the milk where it had been placed before him, until finally the barman laughed and said,

Don't just gape at it, son! And then he was sure he was intended to drink it and he wouldn't be expected to pay, and so he did, and it was very white and cold.

It seemed a long time to wait before his father and Chet returned. But then they did and Chet slammed down a note on the table, and his father said to Douglas, Come on, now, we've got some distance to cover yet. The barman raised one heavy brow like whatever it was that Chet had put before him was a great deal more or a great deal less than what he'd expected. Chet stood still, his feet spread and his head back, so that his Adam's apple cocked itself like a gun in his throat, and with how tall he was, despite his thinness, he cut an impressive figure. Jim and the Mexican stared dimly from their corner of the bar. It was hard to make out their expressions. Jim started to speak, but before he could get a word out, Douglas's father cut him off, saying, We'll be seeing you boys. Then he was out the door, following Chet, and neither one looked behind to see that Douglas had followed, but he did. And so, once again, they were out on the street, with the sun high in the sky now, and only a few scattered clouds—so thin it appeared that a man might, with a single breath, have blown them away.

IT WAS THEIR LUCK THAT, by the time they arrived back at the rail yard, a freight train was already loaded, ready to depart. They scrambled into the first empty car they found, and only then did they turn and look behind them. There was nothing there to see but spools of rusted wire, discarded engine parts, and, of course, the abandoned train car, propped at its incongruous angle, still pointing to the sky.

Chet let out a long breath, as though it were the first time he'd breathed all day, then he stretched himself out to his full height in the far corner of the car. Douglas's father remained sitting upright. He didn't say anything—or even seem to breathe. In one hand, he clutched his rucksack so firmly Douglas noticed his knuckles were white. It was not until the train had picked up speed, until the wind began to blow in through the half-open door—joining them like a fourth, especially lonesome, traveler—that Douglas's father finally relaxed his grip and laid his bag down beside him. But even with the wind and the speed of the train, and his father's evident, correspondent relief, Douglas continued to clutch his own bag as tightly as his father had clutched his, without knowing why. And when his father dug from his bag two brand-new leather boots and extended them proudly toward Douglas, Douglas took them hesitatingly slow. He pinched them together, the way his father had done, and held them out, away from his body, like they were an animal he'd killed.

Well? Douglas's father said, after the boots had dangled in this way between them for some time. Douglas said nothing. Finally, though, very slowly, he lowered the boots to the floor and began to ease them onto his throbbing feet. First one, and then the other. Where the leather touched his raw right heel on its way down the shaft of the boot, he winced in pain, but as the boots were two or three full sizes too big for him, once inside he had plenty of room for his feet, even with how swollen they were, and sore. He tied up the stiff laces of the boots, which had never once yet been tied, and then he leaned back to admire them, and his father and Chet peered around to get a good look at them, too.

Damn if those ain't a pair of boots, Chet said. Then he whistled— one long, low note—and when finally all his breath had been pressed out through his teeth and he had no more left, he inhaled deeply and began to laugh. Then Douglas's father joined in. The two men laughed and laughed as though their sides would split and there never had been, or would be, anything funnier to them in all the world.

BY THE TIME THEY arrived in St. Louis they were hungry again. They found a place near the station that served food. When they were asked to pay up front, Douglas's father was almost too happy to comply. He counted out his coins slowly, taking physical pleasure in the task. Shortly after that, the food arrived. There were plates of cold meats and potatoes. There were corn fritters and fried onions. All of it vanished as quickly as it appeared, and still their hunger did not subside. So they ordered more, and ate that, too. The place had begun to fill up by then.

It was getting toward dusk. After a while, two men—who must have been twins, they were both so tall, with identical round faces and round red beards—came and sat down at their table in the corner of the darkening room.

Washington? the man nearest Chet asked. I've half a mind to go myself.

The other man snorted through his nose. And half a mind not to, he said.

It went on like that for most of the evening. Whenever one of the men said one thing, the other said the opposite. Everyone was drinking now, including Douglas's father and Chet, but no one could keep pace with the twins. The more they drank, the more urgent the opinions of each man became, and the more and more opposed. Soon a crowd began to gather, and everyone was shouting either their unconditional support in favor of the veterans and the Bonus Bill, or their uncompromising disapproval. No one seemed to fall in between. Douglas was literally caught in the middle, with one twin on his left and the other on his right, so it was some time before he noticed the growing commotion at the center of the room. Soon, though, the crowd fell away and the cause could be plainly seen: two men, one just scrambling to his feet, the other still reeling from the recent impact of a blow. Douglas's father stood up on his bench to get a better look, then the twin men stood up on either side of Douglas, so that Douglas had to stand up, too, in order to see anything. He saw the downed man stagger, then watched as they both began to pace like caged animals, moving first one way and then the other, their heavy fists poised. The downed man was faultier on his feet than the man who had dealt the first blow. He looked like he'd sooner duck and cover than make an advance, and when he did it was with a strange sort of flailing motion, like a wounded bird. To make matters worse, each time his arms descended—uselessly—to his sides, the poised arm of the steady man would shoot out as though it had been mechanically sprung, and it could not be stilled again until it had exhausted all possibilities of movement and direction. Again and again the steady man's arm shot out—each time with a force that seemed wholly new.

When his opponent fell again he made no attempt to rise, but still the blows continued to fall until, at last, the crowd—which had been lulled into a hushed silence by the steady man's insistent advance—suddenly roused itself.

Get that man off him! they shouted. Get him up, get him off!

A group of four or five men descended upon the combatant then, but even their combined strength could not hold him at first. Indeed, rather than diminishing the fist, and the power it still contained, their five sets of hands only served to draw attention to it, so that even when at last it was stilled, it was that fist that still held every man's attention in the room. More even than the man himself, whom only now it had become possible to take in as a whole. He was—Douglas realized, in apprehension and awe—a full-blooded Indian. The biggest Indian—or, for that matter, man of any breed or variety—he had ever seen. By the time Douglas realized this, however, the Indian had already shaken off the hands that held him—as though he might easily have done so all along—and made his way alone to the door.

NO ONE FOLLOWED. The door slammed shut and the crowd rushed to fill the empty space in the middle of the room, obscuring the injured man from view. A general confusion erupted. Everyone shouted and pushed against one another, barking out questions and orders. The twin men had leapt from their seats and were now pressing toward the center of the room. Once in a while Douglas caught a glimpse of one or the other of them. Clear out! Clear OUT! came the call. But Chet and Douglas's father remained where they were. They didn't move, and no one else did, either. Then, when the body of the downed man was raised and carried aloft, like a prizefighter, from the room, a hush descended over the crowd. He looked, as he was carried away, anything but a champion. His head slung heavily to the side like the neck of a bird that had been broken. His shirt and face were drenched in blood.

Now everyone emptied out into the street, following the downed man.

Murder! someone yelled. The word rippled through the crowd, and with it, something new and terrible trembled on every man's tongue.

Even Douglas—who could not bring himself to speak the word aloud—felt it. Stirring in his heart as though it had always lain there.

But then another word was pronounced, disrupting the progress of the first.

Po-lice!

Instantly the crowd broke, splitting into countless, conflicting directions. Douglas ran too. As if by instinct. Not looking up to see in what direction his father or Chet had gone. It was only, therefore, by what seemed a great coincidence that, after some moments had passed, he looked up and saw them both, only a little ahead.

They ran together then, for something close to a mile—turning from the paved road onto an uneven gravel track, and then again, down a sloped grass path and into a large and open field. Only then, panting for breath, and careful, for some reason, not to look one another in the eye, did they stop.

They were alone. Douglas looked back toward the road, but he could not really even see it now. Perhaps they had left it behind them much longer ago than he'd thought.

Then he felt something—almost like the sensation that had stirred in his heart just moments before when the word—*murder*—had hesitated, unspoken, on his tongue. Only different this time. A terrific, electric sensation, which shot down the length of each of his arms and—without making contact with anything there—coursed through them again before settling in upon, and scorching, his heart. He was—he realized only now—too late—empty-handed. His bag, with his father's name embroidered in red letters on its side, had been left behind—wedged beneath a table in the corner of a bar in which a man had been murdered, and which they themselves had recently fled.

—

LYING BETWEEN THE FEET OF HIS FATHER AND CHET THAT NIGHT, wrapped in the thick sweaters they had dug from their own packs to cover him, Douglas felt heavy and warm. Still, he was very far from sleep. That was all right, though—he didn't wish to sleep. He concentrated on the known shapes of his father and Chet beside him, so that he would not. He was just barely able to make them out—two dark outlines against that further darkness beyond.

Only a few minutes must have passed, though it felt like much longer, before one of the shapes sat bolt upright, then lit a cigarette.

It was Chet.

Goddamn, he said. It's dark as hell in these woods.

It did not occur to Douglas until that moment that Chet might also be afraid.

A short time later Douglas's father sat up, too.

Dark as hell, he agreed. But not the darkest wood I've seen—not even close. And then, as on so many occasions before, he began to speak of the darkness of Belleau Wood. But there was something different in his voice this time. The Holy Ghost, if he was present at all, was as still and unseen behind it as the darkness itself.

The woods—Douglas's father began—were choked with such a darkness that night it was impossible to tell where one thing ended and the other began. There was the darkness of the wood itself, of course, but there was something else, too. Some other darkness, which had no adversary, so that you might just as soon pause to rest slumped against the stump of a man's leg as against the stump of a tree. It was something . . . other, he said. Something at last—finally—removed from the earth, and therefore from men. So that it didn't even have anything to do, any longer, with war—it was just . . . darkness. A wasteland of downed trees, their leaves gone—as if they had never existed at all. Even the earth, blasted by shell craters and shallow, hastily dug trenches, had begun to give way. Suddenly, and without warning: a leg would be plunged knee-deep into a dugout, or a bloated corpse, or a simple absence of ground. And all around—everywhere—as if someone had taken the known world and shaken it upside down, there were helmets and guns strewn on the ground. Blankets, half buried in mud. Boots, Mauser rifles, Springfields. Letters, unopened; fragments of letters. Unexploded grenades.

No—it wasn't war, Douglas's father said. It was something else. In each moment, newly defined. In each moment, abandoning every possible definition. It wasn't, that is, any *thing*. It was only . . . a crushed nose, a gouged-out eye. You might even find yourself confronted by a corpse, and think it was your own grave you had stumbled into. It would not be, then, without some pleasure that you might observe your own body—that you might marvel, from that distance, at the neatness of your wounds. At how even the most violent ruptures of the flesh and especially the bone revealed beneath them a finite, observable system— like the busted-up insides of a clock or a car. Even without understanding the particular function of any one individual part, or being able to imagine that it had ever been, or would be again, a working, functional whole—there was, you found, a limit to the mystery that each part, in itself, contained. You could confront yourself like that out there, Douglas's father said. In all of your simplicity. Naked of mystery. You could stare, like that, into the face of your own death, and find in it something so familiar and strange, and with a pull so deep, it was a wonder it was possible to look away from it again. That you could, in fact, be startled from it so easily—by something as simple and inconsequent as a shell, fired at close range.

And just like that, Douglas's father said, we were startled from it at last. On the twenty-fifth of June, the darkness broke. We stormed down the hill like madmen from the grave: there was nothing to stop us. It was less a question, then, of victory, and more . . . just . . . the absence, for the first time, of any resistance at all. Enemy or otherwise.

Then anger overtook us. A deep fury, which we had not known we could contain but that seemed now to be the only thing we ever had contained, or would ever be likely to. It was according to this anger that we were driven, then. What a sight it must have been. As though we were the dead themselves, raised from the earth and, lit by the fire of hell, come swarming down the hill in a final charge. *This* was war. It was a relief to feel it finally. I'd been fighting in those woods a week and this was the first time I'd felt it. War, yes. That was the hellfire burning inside us. My first taste of it. A wholesome power that burned with an incinerating power that laid, or promised to lay, everything it touched to waste. And all along I had thought that the waste itself was war. That it was the human detritus in which we had wandered for days. The horror of that, the madness. I was wrong. I understood it then. War was not waste. It was the furthest thing from that. Its power was not in its destruction—but in its promise of something. And so I knew then what I know now: that there is nothing equal to that promise, once it gets born inside you. Once it burns its way in, licking at all the empty spaces there, inside. All the stories of my ancestors came back to me then. The Great Plains wars and the men—my grandfathers—who killed other men with their bare hands. Of how they carried in their pockets the scalps of the men they had killed, and from time to time, for simple love, would reach into those depths and rub that taut skin between their fingers. For love, yes, of the man himself—the negative shape of whom he held in his hand. His fingers would be aquiver with it, and he would be filled again, at that moment, with the same sensation: that promise—its burning ember alive in him still. For the first time, as I stormed down the hill at Belleau Wood, I understood what I had done, whom I had killed, and for what reasons. I could feel it in my flesh. It took the shape of a man—my own body. It was, perhaps, for this that rage burned within me as brightly as it did as I flew down that hill. It was, perhaps, for this that I screamed along with the rest, and at so ungodly a pitch that to this day the thought of it still rattles my bones.

It seemed, during all the time that Douglas's father spoke, as though Douglas himself hardly breathed. But now that his father was silent, his breath—evident again in his throat—seemed surprisingly loud, as did the disparate noises of the wood: the chirruping of crickets in the distance, as well as the more proximate sound of the leaves overhead as they were stirred on their branches by a distant wind. Chet's cigarette had long ago been extinguished, but he had not moved. Douglas could still make out the known shape of his shadow, propped up on one elbow, against the surrounding darkness.

Ten minutes or more went by like that before Chet finally cleared his throat.

I guess we'd, all of us, better get some sleep, he said.

Then that denser blackness that was his upright shadow dissolved, leaving only blackness in its wake.

AS USUAL, THE MORNING came much sooner than expected. The leaves overhead—once so impenetrable—were in fact no match for the sun, which, from its earliest hour, shone through.

Douglas woke to it, then his father and Chet did, too, staring blearily at one another. The terror the woods had inspired in them just hours before seemed, suddenly, very far away.

They exited the woods and easily crossed the field to where the road waited for them, at a distance of only fifty paces. The streets, littered with the refuse of a quick retreat, were empty, and even the establishment they'd fled—when, far more quickly than Douglas imagined to be possible, they once again arrived there—appeared unassuming and innocent, as though it had no idea what had transpired.

Douglas followed behind Chet, who followed behind his father; one after another, they pushed through the swinging door, which hung loose on its hinge. A single gentleman, his hat pushed over his eyes, was sleeping in a far corner, but their entrance did not disturb him. Douglas hovered by the door as his father moved toward the table where they had sat the night before. But it all seemed now so long ago . . . or perhaps it had not even happened at all. The twin men, the Indian—even, or especially, the murdered man, who had been lifted and carried like a discarded object on the backs of six men! All of it seemed as distant to Douglas now as if it had been a dream. But then, as if in testament to the reality—if not of what had been dreamed, then of the dreaming—Douglas's father reached his hands under the table in the corner of the bar and pulled from beneath it the missing bag, upon which, sure enough, his father's name—which was also his own—was still written in red, uneven letters.

—

THE BAG WAS HEAVIER THAN HE REMEMBERED IT, BUT NOW DOUGLAS WAS grateful for the weight as they made their way back to the station. No one in the town had yet stirred—all the houses were still shut tight—but at the station the day had already begun. A crowd of veterans were busy breaking down their makeshift camp. Nearby, an old man sat alone, stirring hot coals in the overturned lid of a barrel. When Douglas's father wondered aloud if there would be empty cars enough to take them all, the old man laughed. Hadn't they heard? The railway men had been attaching extra cars on all the eastbound trains, he said. More than fifty thousand men were now on their way to Washington—expected to arrive before this time next week. How else were they going to get there?

AS PROMISED, AN EMPTY car was easy to find. They climbed in, Douglas's father and Chet repeating, incredulously, what the old man had said. Fifty thousand men? And even the railway men now on their side? It was not until they had sunk into place against the train wall, their bags deposited beside them—not until, that is, they had given up all possibility of a hasty retreat—that two shadows suddenly flickered and emerged against the facing wall—one of them much larger than the first. Indeed—larger than life. They turned, and—as their eyes adjusted to the dim light—their worst fears were slowly confirmed.

It was the Indian.

And so they continued east. Now in the company of the Indian, John, his pale wife, Aida, and their small, moon-faced daughter, whom they called Felicity. The two of them, the Indian and his wife, were about as unlikely a pair as you were liable to meet, and slowly, over the days and then the weeks that followed, Douglas learned the extraordinary story of how they had first met, and come to know each other.

—

FOR JUST ABOUT AS LONG AS AIDA COULD REMEMBER, SHE SAID, HER father had been working a claim out in Silver Peak, Nevada. Then, one day—when even the old man hardly expected it anymore—he struck gold. He went into town and came back with four hired men, the Indian among them. They'd agreed to work on credit, but one week turned to two and then a month went by and still the cracked earth yielded nothing more than the single rock the old man had already found. One by one the hired men left—taking with them, when they did, whatever was not staked to the ground. A pot, a shovel, a deck of cards, a spoon. One night, even a framed photograph of Aida's mother—dead by then for many years—was stolen from its place beneath the old man's bed.

It was just to show: nothing was free.

Only the Indian stayed. For by that time, for some alchemical reason that would perhaps now forever go unexplained, John loved Aida, and Aida loved John. When the old man discovered it, however, something changed inside him, too. It was a change so deep that at first there was no outward sign of it—but still, John felt it, and was afraid.

And sure enough, soon after, while the Indian slept (one eye always open now), the old man crept with a knife (the one possession he had managed to protect, and so the one thing he had left to him now in the world) to the spot where the Indian lay. But the Indian had heard the old man approach, and now he saw the blade, and the mad look in the old man's eye, glinting above him with the same cold glare. He recognized that glare; knew, in an instant, that it had nothing to do with him, or with Aida, or even with the old man himself anymore.

A great battle ensued. Even with the Indian's strength, which was the strength of ten men, the old man had on his side that purest, coldest flickering light, which glinted inside him like the blade of a knife. It was not, the Indian felt very certainly then, against the hope or fear of a man, or even of an animal, that he struggled, but of some more remote ancestor—a plant, or a stone. It seemed that nothing would end it, until—finally—Aida herself leapt silently from the shadows with the Indian's knife and felled her father with a single blow. It was not certain if he had been instantly killed, or if some life remained in him still, but in either case, the old man's body was still and, soon after, the Indian was able to shake himself free.

Taking nothing—not a pot, nor a rope, neither the Indian's nor the old man's knife—they ran. The Indian barefoot, Aida dressed only in her father's coat (pungent even as they plunged through the darkness with his smell). The Indian streamed with blood from a gash in his chest that he would not notice for several hours. The wound left a trail through the woods behind them—but there was no one to follow. When finally they rested, the girl made a bandage with a piece of cloth she tore from the inside lining of her father's coat. Then they ran on, and no one followed. And yet—they were not alone, for the girl was already carrying with them their child.

In the end; something always begets and is begotten by something. To prove the point, the Indian would sometimes raise his shirt and show the mark his wife's father had etched in the middle of his chest. It was a great mystery how, in the chaos of the altercation, which both man and wife described, it had been done; how, with what looked like great patience and care, an almost perfect circle had been drawn on the Indian's skin.

Months later—just weeks before the child would be born—the two would meet by chance one of the hired men who had left the prospector's claim nearly a full year before. He had taken with him the old man's pocket watch when he left, and it was in fact on account of this watch, which he wore like an amulet around his neck, that he'd been recognized. Otherwise, he would have looked like any other man. Nothing was said of the watch, however, or of the past at all. Instead, the thief imparted what he knew of the old man now.

It happened, he said, a month or so back, that the old man had stumbled into town with a rock the size of a fist in his hand.

You'll never believe it, he said. But sure enough. It was gold. Lord knows what he'd been through to find it. Looked like he'd been raised from the dead. One eye gone, leg busted, dragging—hardly any use at all. An ear on crooked. But in he came, and laid that rock down and stared hard with his one good eye as it was appraised of its worth.

And there was no mistake. He was a rich man. Because there was more where that had come from—much more. The rock he had brought was only what he could carry away with his two hands. It was like something had changed under that earth, the thief said. Remember? Turning up nothing but granite and dust? It was like something was lit underneath it to change all of that. Now, everything the old man touches turns into gold.

So—Chet said, leaning in. You went back?

The Indian shook his head. No, he said. Then the child gave a shout, and the jug, which had been going around, got passed, and one after another every one of them, including Douglas, took a swig from whatever was inside. A peace descended over them then, and—side by side, around the low-burning coals of a nearly extinguished fire—they drifted off into a deep sleep—undisturbed by even the most remote and insubstantial flickering of dreams.

Most evenings it was like that. A bottle or two of whiskey or moonshine was acquired, and they shared it freely among the passengers if they were traveling by boxcar, or among those nearby if they were camped in a rail yard, waiting on a train. Stories were told. Sometimes a crowd would gather. There were always more men. Navy men, Army men, Air Force men, Marines. There were privates first class, there were lance corporals, lieutenants—even officers sometimes. It was funny, Douglas's father said once, everyone is equal on the road. Officers just as much as enlisted men were in need of a hot meal, a friendly face, and an empty car. That's what it came down to, in the end, those three things, and perhaps in that order. And every man equal on the road, and in the eyes of God.

Why, I wonder, he would ask on other occasions, is it only over the railway lines that God keeps his watchful eye? Why is it only there he distributes the bread evenly—that each man takes care to lick his spoon as a courtesy for the next? Take that same man, his father would say. Give him a plot of land, or a few dollars in his pocket—and watch—see if that all doesn't, soon enough, fall away.

But it was not always like that. Sometimes God watched the railway line no closer than he watched over the rest of the world. Twice they were robbed. Once, a knife was pointed, unsteadily, at Aida and the child. Without a word, Douglas's father handed over two dollars in coins and John handed him two more and a jug of whiskey and Chet gave him the other half of a loaf of bread they had shared. Douglas looked at Aida, and tried to detect some trace of fear in her face. He thought if he detected any they were lost, but—though she held the child so tightly it was a wonder the child didn't wail—he saw in her face no trace of alarm, and sure enough, after the outlaw had collected what had been offered from the three men in turn, he cleared his throat, lowered the knife, and ran.

There was always the sense, though, after that, that they might not be so lucky again. And always, there was the threat not of what *might* happen, but what already had. When they heard rumors of police on the line, their hearts beat more rapidly in their chests. When they saw an officer in the distance, they steered their course—without acknowledging they had done so—quickly, in the opposite direction. Never once, however, did they speak their fears out loud, or mention—directly, at least—that night they had first seen the Indian. It happened, though, that one evening, Chet—forgetting how close the story brushed the Indian's own—recalled the night Douglas's father had recounted to them the story of Belleau Wood. It had served to strangely comfort them, Chet said. Because—strange to say—it is not always a tale of comfort that comforts a man. After being scared half to death—

Here he faltered, and an uncomfortable silence ensued. Chet looked at the Indian, then at Douglas's father—then back at the Indian. At last, it was Douglas's father who spoke. Who picked up his story where he had left off before, so that soon the Indian and the more recent past were just as forgotten as they had been on that other fateful night—camped outside of East St. Louis, where something less than an hour before the Indian, John—whom they all now knew well—had murdered a man. Though the memory of that night still haunted him (and would for a long time yet to come) it felt, somehow, remote and strange to Douglas as he recalled it now—as if it, too, had happened under the cover of Belleau Wood. Or whatever other darkness falls over things that happened a long, long time ago.

—

AFTER BELLEAU WOOD—DOUGLAS'S FATHER SAID—AND EVERYTHING else he'd seen, he didn't feel too much like going home. He'd been discharged in June, on account of a wound to his side, but had healed quickly and, as soon as he could, had joined again. So that was how, only a few short months later, he found himself a newly minted member of the 27th Infantry Regiment, and on his way to western Siberia.

Helluva time that was. It would be months before their provisions arrived. They starved, half froze. Thank goodness for Russian women, Douglas's father said. For a time, along with the dirty business of staying alive, they'd proved so distracting the regiment had hardly noticed the *real* problem. There was no enemy in Siberia. And no missions. In short: no war. Life was not, in fact, so dissimilar then from now. They lived on the railroad line, guarding of it whatever section they could. It really didn't matter what you held—or who you had to bargain with to keep it. The Japs, the Jews—the Czechs, even. Just so long as you could hang on to that line, you had something.

The boredom—Douglas's father continued—that was the worst. Men were driven mad by it. It ate away at them. Gnawed at the edges of things, until there weren't any anymore. When an attack was ordered, it was a relief to be sent out in columns, away from the railway line. A relief to have something—anything—to break up the monotony of their days, and allow them to realize, again, that there was something to discover out there. So it was always in that state—of exhausted, bewildered relief (the kind a blood cell might feel in discovering itself suddenly connected to the heart), combined with a mounting anger (also, perhaps, of a blood cell, at nonetheless being kept so far from the source)—that the American soldiers destroyed the villages they found. And with a simi-

larly vexed pleasure that they discharged their weapons, lit houses on
fire, lined up "suspects" who fled (every man, woman, and child who
fled from their homes was automatically suspect—what reason did a
Russian peasant *not* inspired by Bolshevik ideals have to live?), and
watched them drop: a sudden jolt to the chest plunging that region more
rapidly to the ground.

There was an order to it, which the soldiers quickly learned. So that
after a while even the brief respite the raids had once provided ceased.
They became one more formal procedure. Even the results, once tallied,
always seemed to add up the same. American casualties (very few of
these; the civilians were almost always surprised, and mostly unarmed).
Bolshevik (a rough estimate). Prisoners—and of them those suspected
to have Bolshevik ties (the dead were automatically Bolshevik). Along
with this information, the estimated location of the village—or rather,
where it had once stood—was recorded, and after that they returned to
their segment of the railway line.

Yes, there was a system to it. They were not like Admiral Kolchak's
or the Japanese soldiers, who roamed the countryside like animals. Killing, raping, burning, looting, without any sort of method or record or
intent. For those soldiers there was no mission at all, certainly no war—
they followed instead only an odd sort of patternless migration, fueled
by a boredom, emptier and more terrifying still.

For the most part the Americans lived on friendly terms with the
Russians themselves. They loved the women best, of course—and the
women loved them. For those who did not go mad there arose even,
after a while, a bemused acceptance of the absolute aimlessness of
their situation there—then even a desire to preserve it. To maintain,
for as long as possible, the perilous imbalance of their ledger books; to
keep their enemies on strings (which could, when necessary, be easily
disconnected). Otherwise, they liked to boast that they had no real
adversaries, and held no grudges. That even the Bolsheviks were "not
too bad" if you got to know them. Perhaps because of the easygoing
manner they generally adopted toward them, they were sometimes
even rumored to be Bolsheviks themselves—a rumor they perpetu-

ated through the stories they would sometimes tell as regards to their own missing men. No one ever died in that wilderness, it was said. They merely defected—then roamed the countryside with the Bolsheviks, like wild dogs with wolves. And maybe it was true, because sometimes even the one genuinely verifiable number provided in the ledger books—the number of deployed Americans—did not add up at the end of the day. They would be less a man, who could be officially recorded neither as living nor dead; his body—overlooked somehow in the accounts—left to the final, unforgiving judgment of the desert instead. By reinventing these missing men as Bolshevik soldiers, the Americans gave them up—but only to the other side. They imagined each of them as heroes, gaining instant stature and glory—a sort of Bolshevik Kolchak, if there could be such a thing. Twelve or thirteen women, one of each race and hue, in his tent at night; his lapels slung with the borrowed medals of Japanese, Czech, even American soldiers . . .

As much as the fantasy further abstracted the already abstract enemy lines, it also served to give some sort of structure to the great void into which the Americans lost their men—a void that threatened them also, and from every side. To imagine death not as the great emptiness they feared, but as a foreign army with an express and certain purpose at final odds with their own. It was easier to imagine it that way than any other, because no matter how they resisted it, no matter how many times they rubbed their crosses or recited their Hail Marys into the desert, the emptiness of the landscape just ate up the words. If there was a heaven—if there was an afterward to anything at all—it was easier to imagine that it was as a Bolshevik soldier.

And it was not all talk, either. There was actual proof in some cases that defections did, at times, occur. Douglas's father himself had known of a certain case where a young American soldier—only seventeen, he'd admitted, when he'd signed—had come over with the sole intent of joining the revolution. A little Jewish kid. Scrawny, but tough, too, and with so many brains it made you wonder why he wanted to have them blown away—splattered in every direction across the Siberian landscape. But he did, and there wasn't anything anyone could do or say to stop him. When he talked, it was *you* who doubted, instead. Maybe the kid was right. There were moments when even Douglas's father found himself very close to *actual belief* when the kid spoke about the possibility—the *real* possibility, the kid said—of *justice*, and *liberty for all*: poor and humble, red-skinned, black-skinned, Semitic or white; women as well as men. Moments when he wanted to follow him—that scrawny little kid from New Jersey—out into the desert, so beautiful did what the kid say seem to him then.

It was, at any rate, a comfort later—after the kid disappeared one night—to imagine him out there, with that direction still. Even after all the talking he'd done, it had seemed sudden when it happened. An accident. As though the kid had been sucked up like a Hail Mary into the oblivious blankness of the landscape. But he had not. Douglas's father knew for a fact this time, and it did—it gave him some comfort to know it. To imagine the kid carrying out his plan just in the way that he had said he would. It had been, after all, a very simple plan, and barring any unforeseen circumstances—illness, capture, or death (circumstances which, it had to be admitted, the kid was just as susceptible to on this side as the next)—there was no reason to believe that he was not out there still. That his plan was not indeed being carried out, perhaps even now, all these years later, when the Americans and even the Japs have retreated and Kolchak, even, and all his women—of every race and hue—and his cache of stolen wealth and treasure has dissolved, without leaving of itself even a trace, into the seams of the earth.

Now, Douglas's father said, when what had once been unimaginable (this present moment) has indeed come to pass, and we sit for some equally unimaginable reason on another segment of another railway line, it may be that a kid from New Jersey is the indispensable commander of a division of the Red Army. That, as we speak, he is on his way to delivering to all of us the justice he once promised he would bring. And though we might not recognize it as such when it comes, it will, you can be sure, be the final justice—having been conceived of, and wrought, like the earth itself, within an emptiness greater than any of us can imagine (even those of us who have witnessed it with our own eyes). Because, you see, if something—anything at all—is ever delivered, Douglas's father said, from that great void, it will indeed be a justice that can at last not be registered in any book, and before which (we will have no other choice) we will have to prostrate ourselves, as before God. Yes, Douglas's father said, we will have no other choice but to lay our souls down at our feet—just as Abraham once laid down his son.

So—he said, leaning back on one elbow, and extending his free hand above him toward the blanketing sky—you can thank whatever you have to thank on this green earth that the day will never come. That no matter how many times you pray, no matter how many Jews from New Jersey, or Negroes or white men from heaven or hell, are plunged into the frozen desert of Siberia, or anywhere else, that final justice *will not come.*

You can keep your children, Douglas's father said. No one will ask for them. If they do—you can be sure it is the Devil who does. No, there is no justice that will now, or finally ever, prevail over that darkness. I know, because I have seen it. And so I can tell you: It is nothing but darkness.

—

IT WAS THE RUSSIAN GENERAL SEMENOFF WHO CONTROLLED ALMOST the entire area around Mita, near where Douglas's father and the rest of his unit were stationed. A legend long before any American arrived, Semenoff once claimed that he couldn't rest easy at night unless he had killed at least one person that day. He did not—Douglas's father assured them—suffer too many sleepless nights. From his roving base, constituted by three armored trains—the *Terrible*, the *Merciless*, and the *Destroyer*—Semenoff and his men cast a wide net of fear in every direction. It was, fittingly, the *Merciless* in which thirty of the most beautiful women in all of Siberia were kept in constant, rotating supply—never a single woman more or less. Even the most flesh-starved mind did not entertain too many thoughts of what went on inside that particular train. It was enough to have heard the rumors of Semenoff's raids in which he wrenched the gold from old men's teeth and flayed alive any who dared protest—to scream, to cough, or in any other way remind the general that he was, before he was killed, indeed, *alive*. For that offense, he would be punished rightly. Have his life, rather than snipped at the thread, slowly drained from him until there was nothing left but the thread itself, twanging sharply against bone—making the most unlistenable music for all who had the misfortune to hear. These rumors were enough to turn even the most foolhardy soldier's heart cold with dread. And just so, when Douglas's father found himself, along with the rest of his Army platoon, steadily approaching the *Destroyer* one night, his own heart was laden with such a crippling dread that, to this day, it drowned—very nearly—even the memory itself.

WE WOULD NEVER HAVE done it, he said. We would never have dreamed of disturbing the Devil like that, in his lair; would, instead, have let him continue to rape and pillage the earth for the rest of time—if he had not struck first. We were woken abruptly; it was the strangest thing, there was hardly any sound. Just, suddenly, dirt and sand, which—ripped loose from the earth—rained down upon us as we slept. Because of it, Douglas's father said, I was not sure at first in which direction to turn. It even occurred to me that I had not yet fully awoken. That I was somehow still locked inside that alternate gravity of dreams. But as I watched and waited, I realized that even if that were the case there was no freeing myself from that hold. I waited. It was all I—any of us—could do. We waited, and we prayed that the sting of sand, which was the earth itself—ground by the force of opposing pressures over an unmeasured, unimagined interval of time into a fine dust—would not kill us before the cold new composite forms of bullets and shells.

We survived. We did not lose one man—even to the Bolsheviks. And three nights hence, we drove ourselves like bullets into the belly of the *Destroyer*, seeking our revenge. And by the grace of God—we had it. We captured the *Destroyer* at the expense of only two of our men—one dead, one "missing." But I knew nothing of that until later. And, until I awakened alone in perfect darkness, I could not have guessed that, this time, the "missing" man was me.

IN THE PARTICULAR DARKNESS in which I woke, there was nothing—not even sensation at first, certainly no object, or gradation of light—against which I might measure myself. This, I thought, surely, is death. The moment I thought it I felt a great sense of relief, and then a deep gratitude—for whatever God had granted that I might take with me into death my own thoughts, or whatever it was that marked me as somehow separate from the rest of the world. It had been a thing I had much doubted, while living—even as a child. It was only something dreamed up, I thought, by men who could not bear the thought of dissolving into the simple mystery of things. Who had finally made of that mystery something so foreign to themselves they could almost look it in the eye. Confront it—like an enemy. Forgetting, of course, in doing so, that it is—that mystery—the very material from which they themselves, and all the guns and swords and shields that they fashion against it, have been drawn.

But still, in that moment, first waking in total darkness, what a relief it was—to be waking up inside that dream! To have not yet been required to dissolve into those unremembered, unknowable spaces—from wherever it was, that is, I had come. But quickly, that relief turned to cold panic in my heart, because all at once I knew I wasn't dead, but very much alive. I could not feel my body—still could not test it against any presence of light or of matter—but I knew, suddenly, that it was there; that I had not, and could not, escape it.

After a very long time, which would have been impossible to measure, I managed to raise one hand. It felt like it weighed one thousand pounds. But I raised it, and felt with it for something to grasp. Something against which I might, at last, measure myself and thereby reenter the world of the living—within which I was still uncertain if I was fully contained. Above me, my hand hit dirt. Then more. I stretched it out as far as I could, first to the left, and then to the right. On either side, I hit dirt again. Only then did I realize. I was not, after all, and just as I had first assumed, lodged fully within the world of the living—but I was indeed "contained." More fully then than I ever had been, or am ever likely to be again.

I had been buried alive.

I DO NOT KNOW how long I lay there; how many days and nights, or if perhaps it was only a matter of mere minutes or hours. There was no measure of anything except my own bare life against that darkness. But at a certain, unmeasured point I became aware of footsteps overhead and was overtaken by a new sensation, which even now I find difficult to name. Perhaps it was hope—but if it was, it was a hope so pure, so unattached to anything that might have taken the shape of a real or imaginable thing in which to hope, that I could not identify it. And then so quickly did it dissolve itself to dread—when, in the next moment, a door above me was raised and a blinding light entered my grave—that it would have been hardly possible, with any assurance, to distinguish it from that subsequent emotion. In fact, the light with which I had been so unexpectedly assaulted was only the dim light of an underground cell, but its contact with the absolute darkness to which I had by then grown accustomed nearly blinded me—and, indeed, blinds me still. So that even now, as I speak to you, a dark shape hovers above you, where that same light once imprinted itself in the negative—in the precise shape of the hope, mixed irreconcilably with fear, that I felt as the door to my grave was lifted and the living world streamed, unexpectedly, in.

AFTER THAT THERE WAS a different sort of time. A time I could mark in the usual way, by the relation of light to object, object to light. I could measure it according to the regular intervals at which the door to my grave was opened—perhaps a space of six hours. Perhaps longer. But it doesn't matter. In any case, I began to be able to keep time, to think backward as well as forward again. To brace myself at the sound of approaching footsteps, against the blaze that would soon rend the darkness, by shutting my eyes tightly against its incumbent glare. It was as though there was only one long moment that suspended itself between the all-consuming darkness and the all-consuming light. As though that silence, that blackness—which nothing, not even the functions of my own body (my heart, which continued, presumably, to beat, or my breath, which continued to traverse the distance between my lungs and my throat, or my kidneys and bowels, which continued to empty themselves, though there was increasingly less for them to expel) could interrupt—was the slow tick that preceded, however many hours later, the tock of the approaching footsteps and their accompanying blaze of light. At which point I would be hauled from my grave and strapped—my hands first, then my legs—to a straight-backed chair. The world would spin and then hover like a shadow above me. It never did take on any definitive shape, so that when I think back on that time now there is no image for me there to recall. And even the voices that echoed, that shouted at me in syllables I could not comprehend—even the pain with which my body greeted the lashes of the object with which I was beaten (making meaning, finally, of my throbbing head and limbs)—seems to fade into the indistinct shades of my memory, leaving only the faintest, lingering trail.

LOOKING BACK, YES—DOUGLAS'S FATHER continued—those days or weeks (I am not sure how much time went by like that) appear to me as though peering backwards down a dim corridor; not from the present into the past, but from the past forward. Because it is those days at the beginning—when the pain, and the glare of the light and the insensate syllables that rained down upon me, indistinguishable sometimes from the lashes of a whip or a chain—that remain most vividly in my memory. As the days progressed—as I myself edged slowly closer toward my eventual release—things become much more murky, more difficult to recall. So that it is at the murkiest and furthest possible reach down the dim corridor of my mind as I peer ahead, into the future, that it happened I *was* released. This time onto quite a different sort of blankness.

I cannot therefore tell you exactly how it came to pass. That, as the door opened one day to the glare—which, as all things must, had receded over time to a shadow of its former brightness, against which I hardly squinted anymore—I reached up and felt my hand connect with a throat. That I felt my hand close on that throat. That I felt beneath my hand what for all I knew was my own flesh collapse under my own weight; felt its resistance give way beneath the pressure of that hand, while the hand itself, exhilarated by its own strength, held fast—until there was no resistance at all. It was not until then that I realized the hand was my own, and I lowered the dull weight of another man's body very slowly—almost with tenderness—so that at last it came to rest.

It was not until that moment—coming alive beneath the body of a man I had killed—that I began to reason with a certain faculty of mind that I had for some time forgotten. In short, I became human again. I began to think, to dream. I noticed things. I noticed that the light, for example, was dimmer than it had been at other times. That no one stirred. That, though it was surely strange, no one hauled the body from my own, in order to expose me—his murderer—below. No, it was only my own breath that stirred. Everything else was plunged into the darkness and stillness of death.

Slowly, then, I began to ease myself from beneath the body of the dead man. We moved together, a sad, slow sort of dance—in which, neither being able nor fully willing yet to disrupt the connection between us, I slowly shifted my weight and at long last succeeded not in separating myself finally, but at least in switching positions. So that now— except for my broken leg, which was still partially pinned beneath the dead man (though I would not realize it until later)—I lay on top of him, rather than he on top of me.

Now my heart—and the blood in my brain—was beating quicker and then again quicker, and the quicker it beat, the more I desired for it to continue beating. In a sudden burst, I managed to extract my leg from beneath the weight of the dead man and in the same moment realized it had been pinned. Only then—having severed that last bond between us—did I manage to raise myself from my shallow grave and make for the open door. Though it seems to me now that that first moment—that first free moment above the earth—lasted an age, I believe that I moved, in fact, quite quickly, despite my broken limb. That I surveyed the cell and, finding it bare and the door ajar, a key dangling in its hold, made my way toward it without hesitation. That indeed I paused only once to reach—for some reason—for the key in the door, and that having torn it from its hold I plunged with it into a night that was itself plunged, nearly, into the same breathless stillness as the grave I had so recently left behind.

Dragging my useless leg, I headed in a singular direction—so singular, in a landscape replete with possibilities of directions I might equally have tried, that it was, on the contrary, no direction at all. I didn't pause—to survey the land, to test the wind, to reason with whatever faculties I had begun to regain—I only plunged ahead, with a great shuddering panic of joy in my heart, which beat now only with the joy of its own beating, and with each beat there stirred again in me the impossible human faith with which all human hearts beat: that it would continue to beat. And it was by that faith, which had nothing to do with gods, or even with men, that I managed to make my way from the small camp, barely glancing back as I went.

Almost at once I became aware of time in quite a different way than I had from within the cell. Of the way that it existed, deeply, within the earth—distinct and yet inseparable from the predictable comings and goings of the sun. It was according to these comings and goings (in order, that is, to survive first the brutality of the heat in midafternoon, then the crippling cold with which the landscape was seized by darkness) that I relearned time. That I regained, that is, or more particularly, a sense of *continuum*—of the manner in which time was not constituted merely by the tick, tock of two moments as they swung, alternately, back and forth, but proceeded according to a more encompassing rhythm of which that alternation was only the most minute part. Without this sense—just as without water or food—I would surely have perished. But water and food were, of course, necessary, too, and both of which I was lucky enough to stumble upon on the third day of my travels when I came upon a recently abandoned village—torn through (I could not tell) days, maybe even hours before, and perhaps by Semenoff himself.

The sight of that village as I approached it was to me like the sight of the kingdom of heaven—if, that is, there were such a kingdom, and I a man of faith. Being a man, instead, of an empty stomach, parched throat, and broken bones, it was equal or better to me than any glimpse of paradise. There was still water in the flasks that hung on the scorched and crumbling walls of the houses I entered—and I drank. There was flour and even a little dried meat to be found inside a leaning cupboard, whose door, fused shut by fire, I managed to pry open with the end of a spoon. I then mixed the flour with the water from a flask into a paste and placed it on my tongue. It is impossible to describe the sensation that spread through me in that moment. It was as if every cell of my body unfurled at once. I did not move for half a minute or more, or even swallow, but only sat and felt within me the thrill of contact between the food and my tongue. I felt it rush right out to the ends of my fingers—felt it reach every last follicle of hair on my body. Only then did I swallow.

FOR FOUR DAYS I lived in that village alone, except for the rats and the unburied corpses of the dead—before I realized I was *not* alone. On the fifth day, toward evening, as I prepared my usual meal—stirring into my ration of flour six drops of the precious water from the flask (it gave me, I remember, such pleasure to count them, and even greater pleasure, after I had counted out six precisely, to allow one more—a mistake, a single, unaccounted-for drop, a pure gift!)—I caught sight out of the corner of my eye of an odd shape, darting quickly between the burned-out beams, fallen crossways, along the path. I turned and squinted into the oncoming darkness. At first I thought my eyes had simply tricked me. Perhaps it had been only a mirage I had seen—resulting from hunger, or the shifting light. Or perhaps, and just as likely, it was a passing ghost, finally rising from one of the bodies I had not had the strength to bury—whose stench and shame I lived among, as if it were my own. I was not then, as I am not now, unsusceptible to the idea that spirits linger sometimes, semi-embodied on the earth, and that it is even possible on occasion to encounter them. Whether in real and physical form, I don't know, but at least, certainly, in the dream images—which do not ever just come from nowhere—of the mind. But at the same time as I accepted this possibility (as well as the inarguable fact that I was very hungry and very tired, and that my eyes were apt to make mistakes in the descending darkness), I did not believe that either explanation was true. I believed very strongly, and I could not be swayed from this belief, that I had indeed seen—moving between the beams that had been strung across the path—the shape of a man. I left my spoon and the flour and the water I had yet to allow myself the pleasure of releasing, drop by drop, from the flask, and made my way to the adjacent house. My leg had healed slightly, though it was stiff still, as if frozen beneath the knee, so I could not move quickly. Still, I moved quickly enough to catch a second glimpse of the moving figure as it disappeared behind a fallen tree. It was no wonder I had managed to track him—I saw now that he was a very old man, that he moved half doubled over, painstakingly slow. My impression that he had been a ghost had no doubt been influenced by the fact that he was dressed entirely in white.

It is difficult for me now to say with what sort of caution I myself moved then, in the direction of the fallen tree behind which the old man had disappeared. What was I afraid of? What was left for me to lose in that ruined village over which, until just moments before, I had thought I'd had sole dominion? In truth, I had not thought past the last flask of water the already nearly empty cupboard contained. I had not thought past the immediate salvation that had presented itself to me in the form of a ruined village; of white flour, a severely limited supply of water, and a side of dried meat, which I had not yet had the stomach to touch. What would I do when the water was gone? When I had stirred the last of it—

forgoing the final surplus drop—and there was nothing at all? Over what would I maintain dominion then except precisely that nothing? What, therefore, could I claim dominion over now? And thus with what caution did I move, except with the caution of a doomed man toward his own death—finally away from dominion over anything at all?

But when I reached the collapsed tree—fallen crossways over the charred entryway to the adjacent house—and peered beyond it, it was not death that I saw, but only an old man. Bent nearly double—perched on a fallen beam just beyond the barrier the fallen tree imposed. He did not see me at first, but instead stared straight ahead—toward what, I didn't know. Nor, indeed, given the blankness of his gaze, if he saw anything at all. I waited for a moment, my ears perked like a dog's, listening for any indication that I was in the company of any more strangers whose presence I had just as equally failed to anticipate. But no, there was just the familiar sound of the empty air through the broken limbs of the tree and collapsed beams of the houses—which, exposed at various angles to the approaching wind, created a series of obstacles it overcame in a single breath. After some time passed like this, and I was certain the man was indeed alone and indeed a man, I approached, extending my open hand in an expression of—I knew not what. But then, as I continued my approach, as I continued to extend my empty hand at that particular angle toward the old man, suddenly—I knew. *Peace*, said my hand—and I knew in that moment, for the first time, the true meaning of that word, and also why it proves so difficult to say among living men. I had, and expected, nothing. And immediately as the old man turned, sensing my approach, he knew and accepted that. We were two men, with nothing to give, and nothing that could be taken away, and so we sat down next to one another, side by side, and were at peace.

FOR SIX MORE DAYS and nights we remained like that, the old man and I. I wetted his flour with my water, and he wetted mine with his own. Together we now had six full flasks of water. I carried mine, along with my pot of flour and the side of meat, still untasted, to the old man's home, which was still standing and looked, perhaps, much the same as it always had—except that the roof had been burned, exposing the little house's single room to the open air. We placed our provisions together by the cookstove, which appeared as though it might also have functioned as it always had—except, of course, that its chimney had been made irrelevant by the gaping sky that it, and the rest of the house, now opened upon. Our joint provisions, gathered together there, gave the impression almost of plenty, and for several days—until my growing thirst and hunger interrupted the impression—I would find myself glancing over to the stove where the flasks remained, arranged together in a solemn row, simply to admire them there.

THOUGH WE COULD NOT properly speak to one another, I understood before long that on the night of the raid, the old man had lain in the bed in which he still slept; that he had heard a noise, which had made him shake with fear. That he had turned to where another—a wife? a child? It was difficult to be certain—lay. That he had been surprised to see that they were not there, where he had expected them to be. That he had begun to call out. That for a long time he called and called, and no one came. That the noise became louder. That he smelled the smoke of the village as it burned. That he fell to his knees and prayed. That he prayed to God for the return of the woman or the child. For the flames to retreat. For the village to be saved. That, afterward, he lay down on the floor and covered his face with the cloth of his robe. That he crawled under the bed, wedged between the mattress and the floor, and closed his eyes. That he waited—perhaps for death. But that, after some time passed, he opened his eyes again and found he was alive. That he went to the door, which now gaped open, though the branches of a fallen tree obscured the street from view. That he had pushed his way through the branches and, because he was nearly blind and did not need to shield his eyes from what he knew lay before him, covered his heart. There were no words for what the old man had felt then, and those that he had up until that point used—words that, though I understood him well enough, had fallen uselessly on my ears—dropped away, and there were no words at all but only his hand, lifted from his heart, and extended—open and waiting—in the same way I had held my own when first I approached him.

All this I learned from the old man, but I was at a loss to tell him, or to have him comprehend, my own story, and after only one or two failed attempts I no longer tried. There was no vocabulary, not even of gesture or sound, by which I could convey to him the great distance I had traveled, or for what reason I had come.

BUT ON THE THIRD DAY of our residency together a curious thing, which seemed close to miraculous at that time, occurred: we discovered, the old man and I, that we had between us a shared language, after all—however cursory and incomplete. It happened in this way: The old man, his toothless gums still gleaming with the paste of flour and water that we had, toward evening, shared, uttered three simple words: *Oui, c'est bon*, in appreciation of his meal. He spoke them quietly; he had not expected me to hear, let alone to understand. But the words resonated within me. They traveled the ill-used channels of my memory, and my own nearly forgotten childhood came flooding back. Though I was still a young man, the memories that returned to me then had not been stirred for many years. So far removed did I feel from them then, it might easily have been someone else's childhood I recalled. Someone else's language—which perhaps I had only read in a book, or heard recounted over a fire, in the same way I am recounting this story to you now. (Someday—who knows?—these words I am using may resurface within you in a similar way—as a dimly recalled version of your own life.) That was, in any case, how the memory of my mother—last seen by me at the age of six—and her language—last heard by me at that same age—came back to me. And so it was, that for the remaining four days we lived in the single room of his house—surrounded by an emptiness that could be neither gestured toward nor named—the old man and I spoke French together. It was a language the old man had learned as a child, dreaming he would one day visit the great cities of the world where he knew it to be spoken. A language that, perhaps at the same age the old man had undertaken to learn it, I had already begun to forget. It was my mother who had taught to me what little I knew—for she was a Frenchwoman, from Upper Canada. My father, a trapper and a gambler, had met her while traveling through that region in the early part of the century, and by the time I was six years old she had disappeared again—back to that mysterious part of the world from which she had come. The language she had spoken to me in those, my earliest years, had—I thought—also been lost, wrenched from me in the exact manner my mother had been. I could not, therefore, recall her language, when finally I did, without a certain amount of reflexive pain. It was as if each word I recalled, as the old man spoke, were pulled from an actual location in my heart where it had remained, without my knowing it, even after all those years.

We did not speak in full sentences, the old man and I. Or try to convey our meaning, as we had before, with gestures and the accompanying words of our own languages. In part, this was because we did not have enough words between us in our shared language to really communicate anything—but mostly it was because that was not what we desired. For neither of us was there any longer a need, therefore an impulse, to attach the language we shared to any meaning at all. Instead, we took pleasure in listening to the sounds the words made when we spoke them—knowing they were sounds that connected us, at least by a tenuous thread, to one another, and therefore to the world. It was enough to know that when the old man pointed to the wall and spoke the word for it that I also not only saw the wall, and knew it was a wall, but also had within me a wall of my own—an almost forgotten wall, but a wall nonetheless, which corresponded perfectly to the sound of the word the old man spoke. Back and forth we went, naming the things that we saw, and that remained to be named in the half-demolished house. This went on until, on the sixth day of our shared residency, the old man uttered an unrecognized word and pointed to the empty space beside his bed where some days earlier he had indicated an absent wife or child. I did not understand the word at first,

and it took some time for me to realize that it was not a word at all—
but a proper name. This interruption of the simple rules of our game
destroyed, at once and entirely, the initial joy we had taken in our
shared language. It became, in that moment, a language like any
other—which spoke of things that could neither be pointed to nor
held in hand. To this day I cannot bear to hear a word of French spoken, and we did not speak it, the old man and I, again, to one
another—not even to name the flour, or the water, or the spoon, with
which we were nightly fed. And very shortly after that, indeed, we
did not speak to or see one another again, nor sit in the perfect peace
we had—after having for a second time given up language—regained.
Because, on the seventh day, there arrived on the limit of our horizon
a band of soldiers, moving swiftly in our direction.

AT FIRST IT WAS impossible to tell from what army, or for what cause,
they came. Perhaps it was their own. There were plenty of those,
too—self-governing bands of soldiers, fashioned after the mode of
the great Admiral Kolchak or General Semenoff. Those who could
see no reason for the spoils of war to be directed into the hands of only
two or three men—or why, if it did occur that way (as it was always
wont to do), they themselves should not be among the chosen. It was
rumored that some of the American "deserters" had joined wandering bands such as these, and it was impossible for me, I realized, as I
watched the approaching soldiers waver at the limit of the empty
landscape, not to get the idea of these fearful wandering tribes of
deserters and outlaws mixed up in my mind with the idea of the dead.

Once the soldiers had advanced far enough that it became clear
there was no other possible course for them to take except directly to
our door, the old man and I returned to the half-demolished house.
Obeying the old man's hurried gestures, I followed him to the bed,
which on one other occasion had saved him. Cautiously, he slid his
slight frame between the sinking mattress and the dirt of the floor,
and, when he was settled there, turned and directed me to follow.
Though I was smaller in frame than I am now, there was no way I

could have fit myself beneath that narrow bed. I shook my head and indicated my breadth and height, exaggerating it by at least three times my actual size. Indeed, I felt that overlarge as I looked around for another location in which to hide. I felt each moment as it passed thicken like an object in my throat. Everything was open and gaping, blasted or shot through or collapsed or in some other way exposed to the air and every approaching eye or blade or gun that might arrive in the hand of any man, living or dead. I knelt again to the floor and peered in at the old man. He lay perfectly still, his thin chin pointed straight ahead, but I saw that his lips moved in what I took to be a half-whispered prayer. I listened carefully, and found that if I stilled my heart and pressed my ear as far into the emptiness that stretched between us as I could, I could hear the sound his words made against that emptiness. I could hear, that is, not the sound itself, which rang in my head without meaning, but instead the space of encounter between the words and the air. Between his utterance of those words and the air's receipt of them, which was as dumb and uncomprehending as my own. And at that moment, though I had not prayed for many years, it occurred to me to hunt in the depths of my memory for a prayer of my own. I located one or two words, but when I said them out loud they sounded embarrassingly hollow and insincere—especially next to the reverent, though unintelligible, murmur that continued to emanate from the old man. For a moment, comforted by that sound, I thought I might just stay beside him like that, until the end came—whether at the hands of marauding bandit soldiers or the hands of time. I would stay, pressed as nearly as I could into the emptiness of the old man's voice as it made its negative impression on my heart and my ear. But then I realized that, if I stayed, I gave away not only myself but also the old man, and that brought me to my senses again. But as I made to go, the old man—sensing my retreat—interrupted his prayer with a muffled shout, and once more I turned and pressed my face into that dimness and saw his face was now turned toward mine. He reached his hand toward me as I knelt again by the bed. It was more like an empty claw of a bird than the hand of a man—a crippled claw, which had grasped nothing for a very long time. I took that claw in my own hand, and saw then that there were tears in the old man's eyes. In the dimness they stood motionless, like a thick cataract, but somehow it was not sadness but a sort of joy that I sensed in him then. I could not explain it at that time, nor fully now, so counter to the fear and the trepidation in my own heart did that joy run. We are always so quick, aren't we, to translate what we see—the pure material of the world—into our own image. We refuse to let it rest, even for the brief moment in which it is given to us to do so, as it first arrives. To feel it, that is, even for that brief time, for what it is, or might have been, before converting it through the machinery of our hearts and minds—which can be such dark and merciless implements sometimes—to what we already know. And just so, I took the old man's joy and I turned it into sadness and fear inside my own heart. Though there was something of that joy that lingered in it still—something I am only now beginning to crack into and understand. But it is a slow thing, and I do not think that I have understood yet, or will for a long time, what it was on that day that I was given. Not until, perhaps, I myself am an old man—if God or whatever powers-that-be grant me that—and I have wedged myself into the very last space available for me on the good earth to hide.

I LEFT THE OLD MAN'S house and skittered between the fallen walls and archways, avoiding as best I could the bodies of the villagers, which had begun by then to decompose—their bones bared in places. Indeed, it occurred to me, as I fled aimlessly through the ruined streets, that the inner structure of the entire town and all of its inhabitants, save one, were as utterly exposed, or in the process of exposing themselves, as I was in that moment.

I was still thinking this, and skittering beam to fallen beam like a frightened squirrel, when I heard rather than saw the soldiers approach. Perhaps I had never heard any sound so sweet; I remember I actually sank to my knees, overcome with sudden gratitude and relief. It was not that the words I heard then held any meaning for me. In fact, just the opposite. I did not recognize the language the approaching soldiers spoke at all; I knew only that it wasn't Japanese, or Russian, and—because it certainly wasn't English—that meant there was only one other language, so far as I knew, it could be. The soldiers were Czech. And the Czechs were—or so it was rumored, and indeed proved for me that day—everyone's friends. In the end, I did not hide at all, but instead gave a sort of a shout. Immediately the voices ceased, then—after a brief pause—returned, now hushed and confused. I realized only then that I had made a mistake. In my excitement it had not occurred to me that the approaching men would not also have known immediately that I intended no harm; that I, too, was a friend. I hadn't thought—so empty, and so grateful and so willing my heart—that there could be detected anything in my voice save the most defenseless, benevolent note. The soldiers continued to approach—but cautiously now. Silently, my hands raised above my head, I waited for them to appear.

When the first soldier came in sight he paused, his weapon raised. He spoke—a single phrase—once more in that gloriously unidentifiable tongue. Then four or five men appeared behind him, their weapons also raised. They stood facing me like that for some time, saying nothing now—not even among themselves—just regarding me in bleak surprise. What a sight I must have been! Only half clothed, my chest bared and still dark with bruises where I had been beaten not long before, my hair grown matted and long. Then there was the pure desperation of my posture: my hands raised above my head, and the wild note with which I had announced my presence—a sound which still must have lingered in the air.

I tried to steady my voice as best I could before I spoke again. American, I said, lowering one of my arms and pointing to my chest. American, I said again. Slowly, the Czechs lowered their guns. The word having achieved, in this way, a welcome result, I repeated it again and again. It was as if it were the only word I knew. American. American, I said. As if *that* were the prayer I had tried to utter beside the old man only minutes before. A prayer that had sounded so empty then, as if it had not existed at all.

..

AND INDEED, WHEN I directed the soldiers to the old man's hut not long after, having managed, with the help of one among them who could understand and even speak a little English, to indicate that I was not alone—when I pressed my face again into the darkness under the sagging bed and called out to the old man—I received no reply. My words echoed against a profound stillness. And when we hauled the old man out from beneath the bed, it appeared as though he had already been dead a long time. The Czechs looked at me and then at the old man—confused. Just a moment ago—I said. I left him, but just for a moment. The English-speaking soldier now appeared even more confused than the rest. This man, he said, finally, has been dead for a week. I could not deny that this appeared to be so. But I also knew that when it came to the interior matters at the heart of all questions of life and death, things never were, or would remain for long, exactly how they appeared. It was, however, useless to press the issue. There was nothing to be done about it now. The space and time by which I was separated from the old man was now so profound, and so unbreachable, that it did not matter in human terms if it was measured in decades or hours. Also, the confusion with which the soldiers had initially regarded me had turned quickly to concern. It is difficult to trust a man who does not understand the difference between the living and the dead. I closed the old man's eyes, which had until then continued to peer glassily into the distance—as if still hoping to recover something from that void—and turned my attention as best I could to the living. I asked for only one thing—that we bury the old man, with our own hands. Still puzzled, the Czechs agreed to my request. Two of them departed, returning several minutes later with a broken shovel and a hoe. It was funny to think that those implements, as well as who knew what else, had been lying exposed in the dust all that time: ready to hand. We carried the old man a little distance from the town, to its western-facing edge. I could have carried him myself, and indeed it would have been easier, less awkward to do so, even with how weak I had become. Despite my battered chest and painful, stiffened leg, it would have been nothing to lift the old man on my shoulder and carry him out to the western limit of the demolished town. His weight on my shoulder would have had no more meaning than a perched bird. But even with how eager the Czechs were to depart, we all somehow seemed to agree that it would have been indecorous to carry the old man simply slung over a shoulder, and so we proceeded through the village, stepping over the awkwardly thrust beams and bones that interrupted our course, with the old man's body stretched between us.

A shallow hole was dug. It did not look sufficient in depth to cover anything at all, let alone a man, but when the old man's body was laid within it we found that it was deep enough. We covered his body with the extracted dirt, and the Czechs bowed their heads and one of them spoke a few words that—appropriately, I thought, for the occasion— I did not understand. But when the soldiers began to move off in a group, back toward the village from where we would shortly depart, I turned back and traced a single word in the dirt over the old man's grave: PAIX. A word that we both, to greater and lesser extents, now understood. That, indeed, for a brief time we had shared. Then I turned and followed the Czechs and we made our way back to the railway line, which I would find was not at all far from the little village. There, the Czechs had been established for many months. They had known the village well—though not, until very recently, of its devastation. They had come to investigate only after their young spy—a hired boy of twelve or thirteen—had failed to arrive at the appointed hour.

EVEN IN THE SHORT time the Czech soldiers had been away, their camp had shifted slightly—a little farther south of the line, and for a moment, before spotting the relocated camp in the distance, we turned in circles in the spot where it had once stood. I sensed in the soldiers only the vaguest surprise that of what they had expected to find there was now only the most impermanent trace. Later, we were informed that the move, which had indeed been slight, had occurred the evening prior after a particularly unwelcome "delivery" from General Kalmykoff. It was the habit of this general to throw the corpses of horses or Yakut ponies into Czech or American camps from his trains as he sped through. When one particularly fetid corpse had interrupted the Czechs' evening meal, they had disbanded their little camp and relocated to a safer distance.

Kalmykoff was another legend in Siberia at that time. Unlike Semenoff or even Kolchak, who had positioned themselves outside of the law, Kalmykoff had brazenly positioned himself above it. He had already tried and hanged two members of the Swedish Red Cross, for one example. But despite this, American money and troops poured in to support him. Like it or not, we were on the same side. We sat in camps on the railway lines Kalmykoff blazed through, and were sent in columns to the villages to rout out and kill whatever he had not already destroyed. And we did this. We even began to enjoy it. Death got under our fingernails. It tingled, clinging to the ends of the hairs on our forearms and the insides of our noses. Anything to break up that dull expanse of time, which otherwise threatened to destroy us. Yes, there existed among us a boredom so great that it was a heavy exertion just to bear it. Some of us were lost on account of it—beyond any mere swapping of allegiances. One man going mad, another torn to threads in front of our eyes. Still another's life leaking out of his mouth in such a slow vermilion red that it was impossible to imagine it had existed inside him all of that time. Inside a man you either liked or disliked, it didn't matter. I remember one particular case, a man named Rabinovitch, who had cried into his soup for no apparent reason on several occasions, but who, when approached—when offered the slightest brotherly commiseration—would rear up, his eyes flanked suddenly on either side of his head and his hard fists prancing in front of him like the hooves of a horse. There was not, in the gesture, any seeming object—just a desperate disavowal and distrust of human contact of any kind. You might think, from his name, that he was a Jew, but he said he wasn't. He hated Jews, he said. As well as Negroes and Italians. It was his fear, see. I noticed it, and he noticed

I noticed, so he hated me, too. I would stand near him sometimes just to feel the air change between us. Just to feel the way his breath would suddenly stiffen in his throat. Outwardly, nothing or nobody otherwise scared him. He would go hurling himself headlong into a fight as if he were as hell-bent on destroying himself as he was on destroying the enemy. He bragged a lot, too. About how many Bolsheviks he'd killed, and how many had been the result of hand-to-hand. And no one told him, as many of us no doubt thought quietly to ourselves: Anyone could kill one Bolshevik or a hundred on the ground. They were kids, nearly all of them. Less properly outfitted for combat than even we ourselves had been our first winter when we arrived and our munitions, along with our winter gear, did not. It was only because it took so much energy not to freeze or starve to death that winter that we didn't die of boredom. But that was the way it was for the Bolsheviks all the time. It's a miracle they survived at all, let alone drove out everyone else. But that's just it. They knew how to survive. They had something over on every single one of us in that respect. Jap, American, and even Kolchak soldier. It was not only death that had gotten under their fingernails and into the hairs inside their noses, and lungs. The country itself had infected them. The sand and the grit and the cold had got under their skin. It made them part desert, part air—which was, after all, all that country was. That was why they were so supreme when it came to fighting out there. It was where they—very literally—came from, and would return. You would be reminded of this fact often—of how ultimately foreign and dispensable you were to them—and to that landscape. Especially when a shell whistled nearby and then exploded in a way that made you pause as if out of respect for the shape of your own death, which had just a moment before been brilliantly illuminated beside you.

They dropped gorgeous shells. Shells which hung suspended in the air for whole minutes sometimes, lighting up everything below and making you want to stop and look up and just wonder at it all for a while. Just as stars will sometimes take you unawares so that you begin to ask yourself—not with your head or with your tongue, both of which have long ago given up such impossible questions, but with some part of your heart that never will—what is a star? What is this rock, suspended for some minutes, beneath them? And what am I—suspended, most briefly, there? Those are the questions, anyway, that would spring into my own heart some nights when we stood outside and saw the Bolsheviks, in their true element, alive and raining down on us from the air.

But then, I have not finished telling you about Rabinovitch, and how, for all his talk, he got blown apart just like anyone else might have by a Bolshevik shell. About how when I ran to him I found the upper half of his body at a distance of several yards from his lower half, and his eyes wild in that way, like the way they'd looked when he got fighting mad—as if he had eyes, yes, like a fish or a horse, on either side of his head. I can't say why, but as I knelt beside him, I remember I felt more remorse for his passing than I ever had before, for any man. When I saw his life, in vermilion red—I never saw a life so bright as his—bleed out from between his teeth, I felt a terrific and unassailable sense of sorrow and loss. Maybe it was those eyes—the way they bulged, like gills, on the side of his head—or the way that I detested him. His commonness, and petty cruelty—the sort that did not take on the guise of war, but was always somehow, instead, personal and small, utterly his own. Whatever it was, it opened within me, as I knelt beside his diminishing body, his life escaping in vermilion red between his teeth, a profound pity, which I will never forget. It made me weep—real tears streaming down my face—as all around me the beautiful Bolshevik shells streamed like the supreme mysteries of heaven and hell to the earth.

I told myself then that it was not Rabinovitch I mourned. I could not make sense of that. It was the old man, I thought—for whom I had never properly grieved. It had been all that I could do, after all, to follow the Czechs back to the railway line, and not long after that I was returned to my own camp—another surprisingly short distance, among all those distances—where my company, battered but intact, had remained. Almost immediately things settled back into the old pattern, as if I had never been away. As if I had never been buried alive, or had light scoured into my eyes, or fed an old man like a bird from a spoon, or uttered clumsy prayers into the darkness that had separated me from him—a space that was at once infinitely vast, and yet at the same time, somehow, too small—beneath his sagging bed.

As I have said—the company had lost only two soldiers in the capture of the *Destroyer*, and my unexpected arrival brought that number down to just a single one. As I recounted what bits and pieces of my story I could (they surfaced tentatively, at first, were hardly narratable—I struggled especially with sorting my impressions into some semblance of chronological time), my return was proclaimed a miracle, and it revived in all of us the belief or hope, or whatever it was, that the men we had lost to that great, empty, unconquerable terrain—to that unwinnable, indeed, unfightable war—were not really lost, but had only been absorbed into other as yet unrecounted, or unrecountable, stories. That they would someday return to us, just as I had done, and make sense of their absence in some—however unbelievable—way. Or, if they did not, it was only because the story had become, finally, too complex—too ultimately removed from our own realities. It was impossible to know how deeply this belief, if that is what it was, penetrated—or if it was only something (an object, like a doorstop) that we wedged into the small opening that revealed itself sometimes as the absence of any sort of belief at all.

Whatever the case, there persisted in the atmosphere of the camp a rare sense of triumph in the capture of the *Destroyer*. A sense that had been only partially dampened by the train having been promptly returned to its owner. Kolchak's Washington supporters had, without too much trouble, succeeded in persuading the government that there was nothing for it but to give Semenoff back his train. You see, the idea was that whatever Kolchak's men—including General Semenoff—were doing, the Bolsheviks were doing (or would be doing, given the chance) much worse. The official report was that they were the greasiest type of Russian Jew we were all too familiar with in America. That many of them, having spent time in the Red-hot zones of either New York or Chicago, had returned to their native country, having absorbed every one of the worst phases of American civilization, and without the least knowledge or racial understanding of what was meant by the word so dear to, and so inseparable from, what it meant to be an American: *liberty*. It was my experience, to the contrary, that the Bolsheviks—being the only ones who seemed to have any idea at all of what it was they were fighting for—were the most honest of all of us over there.

But still, I was troubled by something, which I can't help but puzzle over to this day, and that is that, as I later learned, the date of the *Destroyer*'s return corresponded exactly with the estimated date of my own escape. It is only natural that the emptiness of the camp from which I'd fled, and the ease with which I was able to make my way, should strike me in this light as less the miraculous stroke of luck I originally believed it to be. It is possible that the location at which I had been held had been only a temporary camp inhabited by Semenoff's men during the brief time the *Destroyer* had been occupied by American troops (my own company). That it had, upon the train's subsequent return, been abandoned—the diplomacy of the Americans having been rewarded perhaps, if not directly with my official release, at least with a loss of interest in my affairs. If this was the case, who was it, that night, who had visited me in my grave, and with whom I had gratefully traded places? Was he indeed an enemy? A lingering marauder, only semi-connected to the Semenoff gang? Or had he instead arrived to grant me my release—the "diplomatic" proceedings of my capture and subsequent interrogations being now unnecessary? But why in the middle of the night? Why alone? Why had the semi-unconscious workings of my body achieved an end that, were it not for a chance sequence of events over which I had no control, would seem utterly impossible?

It is, as it always is, easiest to imagine him as an enemy. But something in me resists this, and—perhaps as a result of the pact that we sealed together that night—makes me think of him, instead, as a friend. But everyone knows there is no firm line that separates the two. Even the most powerful generals and secretaries of war know that. They especially. That is, after all, what every war is. An attempt to draw that impossible line—to separate out one half of the story from the other. But it can't ever be done. Not with any sort of efficiency, or finality, or purpose in the end. And even the most hardened and battle-weary general will, in his final days, be forced to retreat from physical struggle into the quiet corners of his mind where he will continue to hunt among the shadows for the very same enemy he had been searching for outwardly all those years, and—needless to say—without any more luck. And so it is for me—that I reconstruct, again and again, in the quietest and most ill-lit corners of my mind, the man who released me from my grave that night, and who, for his trouble, was himself laid to rest. To help ease my conscience somewhat, I remind myself that the "release" my visitor may or may not have granted me that night would have, most certainly, been according to his own terms, not mine—but when indeed will it ever be otherwise granted? Darkness is darkness. Emptiness opens only onto further emptiness. I know this now not from any sixth sense, but from my own skin, which brushed up against it, from my own lungs, which emptied themselves into, then breathed it in, in turn. A perfect, impenetrable darkness. Those are indeed the only terms upon which any one of us may one day finally be "released," and short of that there is always and must remain just the vain attempt at procuring from that darkness some identifiable shape—something to fight against. The promise, still, of eventual victory. When there is no longer any enemy to conjure from that emptiness, you will know that there is nothing to fight for any longer. You will have dissolved into it so finally, then, that there will be no shape to it at all. And you yourself—you will find—will have already been dead, like a star, for a thousand years.

—

EVERYONE WAS SILENT FOR SOME TIME THEN, AFTER DOUGLAS'S FATHER had finished speaking. The Indian nodded slowly, and then Douglas did, too. Chet, who seemed to have been sleeping, raised his head from where it had rested on the back of a tree and stared around, as if bewildered by a world in which Douglas's father's steady voice did not hum. The baby cried softly and Aida rocked her, and Douglas hoped that she would begin to sing in the strange and tuneless way she did sometimes, which put their minds and hearts at ease, but she did not. She only rocked the child silently, and the child continued to cry. After a while, though, even without the comfort of her mother's voice, the child's cries dissolved into sighs, and Douglas's father said: It's another long day tomorrow; I believe I'll turn in. He put his hand on Douglas's shoulder as he said it, and something about his touch surprised the boy. It was not a protective gesture, and it was certainly not an embrace—it was just a moment of contact across distance—but it made him feel, somehow, and for the first time, as though he were an equal, and served to close the distance introduced between them by his father's tale. To return them to themselves, and to the regular passage of time, as it continued to proceed at an undisturbed pace from the point where they had left it. A point that—untroubled by their departure from its course, or indeed by their existence at all—absorbed them easily, as though they had never diverged, or thought to diverge, from its singular, uninterruptable flow.

Douglas and his father rose then, together, like men, and moved away from the fire to where their blankets had already been rolled out side by side. They fell into them gratefully, and soon Douglas heard his father's breath achieve the level pace of untroubled dreaming. He himself lay awake, however—his eyes wide, braced against the darkness, waiting until John and Aida had also lain down quietly, the child between them exhausted now. Until Chet, who sat out a long time after John and Aida and the child had retired—stirring the coals as if they actually required his tending—finally stood up and undid his fly and pissed into what was left of the fire—his back arched so that his head and neck, with its great Adam's apple, were thrust defiantly forward into the night. Until, having rebuttoned his fly, he traversed in a few cautious strides the distance between the fire and where his own blanket had been rolled out below Douglas's father's and his own. From his position, Douglas could not see but only sense the way Chet's arms extended themselves in front of him in order to measure his pace and—though the night was as usual empty and blank and there were no obstacles in his path—protect himself against anything that might interrupt his course. Finally, he lay down and, after clearing his throat several times, in preparation for the hum of heavy breath that would soon begin to whistle through his nose in a sopranoed snore, he, too, fell fast asleep.

But even then—when the night had truly come to an end, and even the stars seemed to dim in acceptance of the total dominion of darkness—Douglas did not sleep. For the first time, perhaps in his whole life, he felt utterly alone. He let the feeling settle. He measured it—its distance from himself, and from his father and Chet—who remained, no nearer or farther away than they ever had been—then from John and Aida and the child. What was it against which he had been drawn that night, so different from all the nights that had passed before? What space had taken shape before him, suddenly, as a result of that encounter, and what was he in relation to it, and to that unmeasurable space beyond? He experimented—attempting to enter in and out of that shape, so newly introduced, at will. In, out, in, out, in, out, he went—until he began to forget which space he had always known, and wonder if there was perhaps no real difference at all—that he had known both all along. In which case the resulting shift in pressure between the two zones through which he imagined himself to move was not a shift in pressure between an actual interior space finally separate from the rest of the world and a space prior to that definition, but instead only a way of shifting the mode and quality of his perceptions—so they might seem at any point either to emanate from some central source within him, or to disperse themselves in horizontal waves, across a world both of, and not of, his own making.

—

MONTHS LATER, IN LONG STRIDES, IT WOULD BE CHET ALONE WHO would make his way back to Douglas's mother's door. He would stand awkwardly there, refusing to enter, a letter from Douglas's father extended toward her in one hand. He would not exactly cry—he had never done so before, his whole life—but the tears were understood between them. They existed in the thickness of his throat and an inability to look the woman in the eye. He would say: I'm sorry, Lou—which was Douglas's mother's name, or what everyone called her, save Douglas. Finally, Douglas's mother would take the note from Chet's hand. She would read it several times through before she understood what it said, because her eyes could not train themselves on the words in the correct order, but—as our eyes and hearts are always wont to do—kept skipping ahead, instead, to the end. She would read, in Douglas's father's scrawled hand:

Chet will have told you that things have not gone off as expected or planned, but he will also assure you, as I will assure you myself, that I am an innocent man, as I hope you will know in your heart. I promise to get clear of this mess before too long. Until then, you needn't worry about either me, or the boy. The boy's safe, and has found employment—best he stay put for now. Tell your father I'm sorry, but that I'll make it up to all of you soon. Don't think I won't.

Your Arthur

When, after a long while, she had finally succeeded in reading it through, Douglas's mother would hand the letter back to Chet, confused, as if she had only by accident taken something from him that did not belong to her.

Well, thank you, Chet. For coming all this way, she would say. And not another word would be passed between them, nor any mention of the events that had come to pass in all that long time, between the early morning her husband and only son had risen before dawn and made their way, while she slept, out to the same road down which Chet had just come, in order to begin their journey, and the day that only Chet returned, to bring her the last news of her husband she would ever receive. Because even when Douglas did manage to write he never men-

tioned his father. Having no more news of him himself, there was nothing to say, and so he spoke, instead, as his father had always done, about
the bonus, and the progress that they'd made (a deal was always "just
around the corner" whenever Douglas wrote). And then about the house
and land in Virginia, or Tennessee, that would soon be theirs—just as
soon (Douglas—as his father—always said) as that deal came through.

He repeated all of this, nearly word for word, each time he wrote
until, one day, a letter was returned to him unread, and he learned that
his mother had passed on.

But that was many years later. Many years after Chet had bowed his
head and, feeling it disrespectful somehow to turn, backed slowly away
from the door, afterward to make his way along the crooked path that
led to the crossroads, where he would then turn toward the house of the
Duke and, after a mighty apology, begin once more to pick from the
earth—just as he and Douglas, and Douglas's father, had done before
any of them had ever dreamed of the Bonus Army, or indeed of anything
at all beyond the limit of that seemingly endless Kansas sky—the stones
that each year were churned from it in an endless rotation of soil, and the
combined forces of the earth's heavy gravity and the nebulous, always
invisible and unpredictable forces of the climate and the air.

III.

Alden

UNDERGROUND. WASHINGTON, D.C., 1932–1934—WITH A
BRIEF DETOUR TO THE DON RIVER VALLEY, 1932.

Alden had been waiting so many weeks for precisely this moment
that at first he hardly understood when the Indian, John, simply
handed him the object. Weeks in which he had been forbidden to speak
to John directly; to inquire after what, if anything, was delaying the plan
(whatever it was) from finally being put into effect. After a while, he had
even begun to suspect that the whole thing—his part of it anyway—had
been some sort of a mistake. A joke, even. That Biggs (who had introduced him to the Indian at the beginning of May) had simply made it all
up; created the story from nothing—just, as usual, to make him look the
fool. Maybe the Indian didn't even have anything to do with the party—
he certainly kept quiet about it, if he did. Maybe he'd never done underground work in San Francisco, Wichita, or Carson City; was not, as
Biggs had claimed, an expert on explosives—having worked with dynamite since the age of ten, in the gold and silver mines of southern Nevada.

But here it was. The Indian's nod, and the object, by now carefully stowed in the inside pocket of the large leather satchel he always carried (recently emptied of the last remains of his family's midday meal) in anticipation of precisely this moment—now very much at hand.

It was, he considered only later, due to his tremendous excitement over the fact that the moment, against all expectation, *had in fact arrived*, that he announced his departure at all. He might easily have simply slipped away, just as he had done on so many occasions before.

But he did not.

And because he did not, but instead announced both his intention to depart and the direction he planned to depart in, Arthur had looked up and said, I'll come with you. Me and the boy. And turning to Douglas, then: Come on, boy, he'd said, smoothing the lapels of his threadbare suit. Let's go see what's happening down on the Mall.

ALDEN HAD BEEN INTRODUCED to the Indian by a mutual acquaintance, Fred Biggs, whom he'd met three years before. Though Biggs was several years older (they'd overlapped in high school by only a single year), he had so far managed to maintain both the physique and countenance of a rather luckless adolescence. As unassuming and indifferent as Biggs outwardly appeared, however—wearing clothes, like his features, one size too big for him, a terrifically bored look, and a hat pulled down so low it was nearly impossible to look him in the eye—he had been active with the more militant branch of the CPUSA since sometime well before Alden knew him. It was rumored that his demeanor—coupled with his young age—made him a perfect candidate for some of the party's most dangerous jobs. Because of this, Biggs had (before Alden had even managed to make his acquaintance) been elevated, unquestioningly, to the rank of local hero in his mind.

Alden's own association with Biggs—even once he was finally able to meet him and make his own allegiances and ambitions known—had proved disappointing. After a while he began to suspect it was not just Biggs anymore: that, for some reason, he was being deliberately spurned by the party. How, he wondered, had *Biggs* managed to rise so quickly and easily in the party's esteem? So consistently aloof did he appear, it seemed impossible to Alden that he might have been able to impress upon anyone the integrity of his intentions—especially at so young an age. But perhaps, he considered, he was looking at the thing the wrong way around. Perhaps it was precisely Biggs's aloofness that had so ingratiated him with the party. It made a certain sense. Wasn't it, after all, easier to trust—and come to rely upon—*dispassion* than its opposite (as vulnerable as passions were, to every shift and change)?

Settling on the idea, Alden began to cultivate for himself as indifferent a persona as he was able. He wore a hat a size too big—which he cocked, à la Biggs, over his left eye—and did his best to restrain his natural outspokenness (speaking instead with a sort of improvised drawl). It was a feat he could only manage when devoting to it his absolute, undivided attention. Inevitably, his mind would drift—an issue would be raised that would rile him—and, in a moment, his cool and deliberate manner would be altogether forgotten. The overall effect of his efforts was that he began to come off as even more hot-tempered and erratic than he had on any previous occasion. This unreliability—coupled with the inescapable fact of his lineage—certainly did not help to ingratiate him any further with Biggs, or the rest of the party; and so he remained—at least until May 1932—just as much an outsider as he'd been before.

It had been Biggs, then, who approached *him* with a proposition that changed all that.

That very morning—Biggs said; it was the tenth of May, 1932—an important party member had arrived in Washington, whom Alden would, very shortly, have the privilege to know. He would be staying out on the flats with some of Waters's men. After they were acquainted, it was there that Alden should go to see him every day—arriving and departing (this was important, Biggs said, twisting the unlit cigar he perpetually chewed between his back teeth, and without in any way altering his tone) no later, on any given day, than three o'clock. If his new acquaintance did or said nothing, if he did not seek Alden out, or even speak to him directly, Alden was simply to return the next day, before the agreed-upon time. Rest assured, Biggs said, one day—a date and time no one (least of all, Alden) could know in advance—his new acquaintance would transfer into his care a small explosive, which (Biggs could not help but betray, here, a note of respect) he had fashioned himself. The object was not at all dangerous unless tripped—but even so, Biggs said, Alden should take sufficient care. It would be easy enough to conceal, as it was only (here Biggs made a careless gesture, indicating an object no larger than a small box of cigars) of roughly such a size. Once he had done so, his job was simply to transport the object to the Capitol. To make his way, as quickly as he could, and without, of course, drawing to himself any undue attention, in the direction of his father's offices there.

Alden's heart, which had—all the time that Biggs had spoken—been hammering loudly in his chest, now began to beat even louder. His mind raced. He had certainly made it clear to Biggs that he was willing—that he was absolutely willing—but did Biggs actually expect—?

He was not (Biggs was saying) to go *so far* as to his father's office, but was to locate, instead, the small antechamber *adjacent* to the office. Did he know the one?

There was a small table there, Biggs said, wedged between two large stuffed chairs. It was here that Alden was to deposit the object. Another party member—already well established *inside*—would take all the necessary steps from there. (He needn't wonder *whom*, Biggs added quickly; Alden himself would have no dealings with the man.) Once he'd delivered the object, nothing more would be expected; Alden should simply leave the building as quickly and quietly as he'd come.

Alden's heart had, by this time, quieted in his chest. His thoughts, too, regained their more regular pace. So he would not be expected—But still— Biggs could hardly think—

He cleared his throat. What— he began. That is, may I ask. Again, he cleared his throat. It seems only right, he burst out, finally, that if I am to *carry this object* I should, at least, know to what purpose and direction it's bound!

For the first time, now, since the conversation had begun, Biggs removed his cigar and—for a long, contemplative moment—examined its pulverized end.

You must understand, he replied at last. The importance of— utmost—secrecy in this matter. In order, of course, to protect the party—but also those, like yourself, who have already, at any level, gotten themselves (he peered at Alden from beneath his hat's low brim) *involved*.

Alden looked away. Biggs shrugged. Then continued, leaning ever so slightly in Alden's direction; his voice soft, little more than a whisper. If you trust, he said, as I do, that the party has both your, and this country's, best interests at heart—and that therefore everything you do to serve the party serves this ultimate end—

He drew back suddenly. Coughed. Then returned his cigar between his teeth.

That—he concluded—should be enough.

—

IT TOOK SEVERAL MINUTES, ONCE ALDEN WAS ON HIS WAY—FOLLOW- ing Arthur in the direction of the Mall—before he could relax again, and begin to appreciate, in the way that he'd hoped that he would, the weight of the object he carried: its great, explosive potential at his side. The problem was easily overcome, of course. He would simply announce to both Arthur and Douglas that he was needed back home, make as if to depart, and then (when he was quite sure he was unseen) double back toward the Mall. With this decided, he allowed his mind to drift, more pleasantly, in other directions. He saw himself at some indeterminate point in the future explaining to an admiring crowd his own (admittedly small, he would modestly protest) part in bringing the whole thing off. But, enough of that, he chastised himself—as he often did when his imagination ran away with him. If he imagined something like that, in exactly the way he wished it might occur, well—it was quite obvious that it would not. If, however, he managed to leave his projections of the future—his hopes and ambitions, his greatest desires—to the best of his ability *unthought*, there remained a greater degree of chance that the arrangement of events as they actually came to pass would take the shape and particularities of those as yet unarticulated desires. It worked the other way as well. If something terrible crossed his mind (as just at that moment, walking beside Douglas and Arthur, it did: How could, he wondered, the explosive power he had recently been charged with possibly be contained within the precise and limited dimensions of the device he carried? How could any who regarded him not instantly recognize what he himself recognized so well? It was the *future itself* he bore upon his person now, exposing it—and himself—at every moment to the inherent risk that it be wrested from him—and before it was time!) another thought would occur to him, and that was that, since the latter thought had been thought at all, it would not now, *could* not (by some law of reason, the details of which he could not be aware) come to pass. The complicating fact that he had *also* thought this second thought—that the first could not come to pass—did not trouble him overmuch; at least he was guaranteed that it should not.

So distracted by these thoughts was he that Alden hardly noticed when the crowd around him, which had until then been largely moving with them, thickened; then began—so slowly that at first it seemed accidental—to move in the opposite direction. To push back upon itself, pressure building, until there was just: a sudden swell of bodies. Moving as one, and according to a will and direction all its own.

Alden moved with it. There was no time to consider why, or in what direction; to wonder what was happening, or how it had begun. There was no way of measuring distances, in either space or time, and because of it—of those moments, as he was pushed along; through and under; as the crowd surged around him like a wave—he remembered hardly anything at all.

Nothing, that is, until the hit. Until a sound like hard gravel being ground underfoot caused him to turn; to realize that the sound had been a brick, just then connecting squarely with the skull of Douglas Sinclair.

In response, Douglas had lurched forward, uttered a startled cry, which, even above the noise of the crowd, Arthur (already several paces farther on) heard.

He turned. Saw his son's forehead glistening with blood, and—a look crossed his face. Then his fist went soaring through the air, and (as though it had known in advance, even before the brick had been thrown, where it would land) connected with the jaw of a soldier from the 12th Infantry Regiment, just then advancing with the rest of MacArthur's men.

There was nothing then—no memory at all—until he found himself sitting beside Douglas and Arthur on the hard, ridged police van floor, Douglas's forehead gushing with blood. Arthur with his hand pressed to the scalp of his son, his voice a low, repetitive moan, which seemed, even as the words were spoken—*My boy*, he said; *my boy, my boy*—already lost.

There was: Being ordered to stand. Being searched. The bag he still carried slung over his shoulder wrenched from him. Opened. There was his own horror as the hand of an officer lifted the small box entrusted to him less than an hour before; himself being shoved, brutally, from behind, so that in another moment he was sent sprawling to the floor, choking for some reason, the air emptied from his lungs.

There was a sudden flood of relief. Not only at the return of breath to his lungs, but at having been relieved of the object—in whatever way. It hardly mattered to him now. He sat, choking and spluttering, even weeping a little with the pure relief he felt at having whatever it was that had been begun—whatever it was that he had, in a capacity he could not name, found himself part—was now, however ingloriously, at an end.

There was the dark underground cell; his back pressed to the wall, in order to cool the bruise that was quickly forming there. There was: The door being opened. Once again, being ordered to stand. There was Arthur, ordered forward. Arthur hesitating. Unwilling, or unable, to remove his hand from the forehead of his son, though the bleeding had stopped now. Had dried in a thick crust (more black than red) in the boy's hair.

There was: Arthur, again, ordered forward. Arthur, complying this time. Then two men, talking in low voices; seeming to agree. A tattered hat placed, for some reason, on Arthur's head. Arthur's hand flying up—defensively—in order to remove it. Two men holding it fast.

IT WAS NOT UNTIL much later—a week or so after his return—that Alden came to know anything more about the hat Arthur had worn that afternoon, or any of the other circumstances surrounding his release. When, once more, the cell door clanged and he was informed that he alone was free to go, he simply rose and—nodding once, grimly, in Douglas's, then Arthur's direction—followed the officer to the open door. It is possible that—having accepted, without question, the exceptional quality of his fate—he did not think of it again. That he did not pause, even for a moment, to consider under what exceptional circumstances he might have been allowed (without once being questioned regarding either the origin or direction of the lethal object wrested from him the day before) to be so simply returned to his parents' home—bruised and embarrassed, but otherwise unscathed.

He was sullen and, especially at first, did his best to avoid all but the most necessary contact—even with Sutton. He felt personally affronted whenever she, or his parents, or even Germaine, interrupted his painful musings on what had, or had not, so recently occurred. But this did not happen often, as they, too, were wary and left him, for the most part, alone. And as the days passed, and the dark bruise on his back began slowly to heal, he found it became easier for his mind to drift away from the past. Before long—though from time to time the riots, the Indian, Arthur and Douglas, Biggs in the distance, would swim again into view—it became nearly reflexive for Alden to push them, whenever they surfaced, quite altogether from his mind. What was done was done, he counseled himself; it was hardly worthwhile to dwell on the thing. And besides: it was absurd, and even somewhat vain, to suppose (with the way things had gone in the end) that any action on *his* part might have

had even the slightest effect on the event as a whole. In fact, it was probably for the best he had been intercepted when he was, the object confiscated, and no greater harm done. At times he even indulged in a certain
feeling of smug superiority. If he had only been entrusted, he thought to
himself, weeks, days, even hours before, the whole thing might have
gone off differently. From the safety of the present, it was easy to imagine himself in the past far braver and more willing than he really had
been, or was. Despite this—and whatever he might be able, quite reasonably, to say in his defense—he did not fool himself into thinking that
either Biggs or the Indian would be quick to ask for his help again. Perhaps there was some relief in that, too. It would be best for all involved,
he decided emphatically, to avoid them—and anyone else connected
with the party—for some time.

—

IN THE EVENINGS, HE WAS PRESSED INTO HIS MOTHER'S SERVICE IN
the assembly of a large, seemingly unsolvable jigsaw puzzle, which she
had spread out on a low table in her private room at the back of the
house. Very slowly, as the days and then the weeks began to pass, an
English country garden gradually emerged into view. A white trellis,
laden with red and yellow flowers. Shutters, a cobbled path, the fine
spray of a weeping willow at the bottom-left-hand edge of the frame.
Though Alden had protested at first (Sutton, without hesitation, had
flatly refused), he was, in truth, grateful for his mother's silent company
come evening. For the mild frustration, a sort of rigorous boredom, that
overcame him in those quiet evening hours when confronted by the scattered pieces of that unsolvable puzzle, and its small satisfactions, as—
piece by piece—they brought it closer to its end.

   One evening, however, his mother broke the silence he had come to
rely upon—to take almost for granted—since his return to his parents'
house. Not even his father had yet spoken to him directly about what had
occurred (or failed to) and, in sharp contrast to the atmosphere that had
reigned in the house before the riots, the only sounds to be heard during

mealtimes now were of Germaine's heavy tread as she delivered the plates from the kitchen, and the persistent clatter of cutlery on glass. He could only assume—so silent had his father so far remained on the subject—that his mother and Sutton knew nothing (or very near nothing) of what had happened at all.

You know, his mother said to him, however—quietly, one evening, and in so casual a tone that at first he suspected she might simply complete the sentence with "I've been hunting for this piece for over an hour"—it's Sutton you have to thank.

What? Alden said. So surprised was he by his mother's words that it was really as if, at first, he hadn't heard. Then, having made sense of the words, but not yet even beginning to guess at their meaning, he added, incredulous: *For what?*

His mother was regarding him carefully now. Alden could not remember a time when she had looked at him like that. Not since, perhaps, his earliest childhood. As if she could . . . *see* him. And not just him as he was in that moment, but—all the way down. As if she *knew* him, better than he knew, or was ever likely to know, himself. He shifted uncomfortably under her gaze, and realized with a hot flash of shame how unreasonable it was of him to suppose that there was anything at all his mother did not know.

It was she who saved you, his mother said. It is probable that—without her help—even your father wouldn't have been able to; the sort of (only now did she drop her gaze) trouble you were in. Only now did her hands become suddenly restless, smoothing, nervously, the fabric of her pleated skirt, before returning to the table in order to hunt out the missing pieces still scattered there.

Alden, confused, sat opposite, shaking his head. What? he said again.

So his mother, in a steady voice, which surprised him—neither gentle nor severe—as though she were recounting to him a subject that had now, to either one of them, only the most immaterial connection—explained to him everything she could about what had passed between Sutton and the Judge on the morning following the riots. About the hat—and the man who would be wearing it, and about how (as the Judge told Sutton then, and Alden must surely—his mother urged him—know himself) what at first might appear to be a stretching of the truth at times corresponded more accurately to the truth than the truth itself . . .

Alden's mind spun.

The hat, the hat.

He remembered it all too clearly. How Arthur had locked arms with the tall officer, attempting to remove what had not—what never had—belonged to him.

How could Sutton—he thought—*knowing?* She must—he considered—have *recognized, known*—and not merely *because she was told,* been able, simply—

But then the rest of the story began to settle in his mind.

Who, then—he considered, finally—would have been left to take the charge? A cold chill—of recognition; at last, of understanding—ran the length of Alden's spine. He got up unsteadily. His right leg had fallen asleep beneath him, he found, and now the feeling returned painfully.

I just thought you should know, his mother said, looking up at him. Uncertain—apologetic now. I just thought— she said. But he did not wait to hear what she thought. And he never would know, because the subject was never broached between them again.

AFTER THAT, JUST AS before the riots, Alden began to spend as little time at his parents' house as he could. He left early in the morning, shortly after rising, and did not return until after dark. Now, though, because he had nowhere else to go—it was to Jack Nancy's house that he went.

—

JACK NANCY, THE YOUNGER—ONETIME ALEXANDRIA COUNTY FOOT-ball star—had been laid up all that summer, 1932, with a strain to his lower back. Alden spent most of August laid up alongside Jack—at Jack's mother's place in Kalorama. They stayed inside, in Jack's big upstairs room, ringing the bell and ordering more tea and food. The maid, a Negro, by coincidence also named Nancy, lumbered, frowning, all month long, up and down the stairs. The more old Nancy frowned, the more young Nancy rang that bell. Alden laughed.

You got it coming, Li'l Nancy, he'd say.

But he never did. The lines of old Black Nancy's frown only deepened throughout the afternoon, finally becoming so dark and set, her eyes so fixed in her head, and her movements so increasingly rigid as she set down each tray, that by three o'clock in the afternoon it seemed that instead of, like everyone else, being made out of flesh and blood, she had been carved out of stone. They whittled away at her all afternoon. The trays arrived, growing so heavy as the day wore on that soon the glasses were rattling and the tea was sloshing around in each glass, spilling out sometimes over the rim as it was set down abruptly before them, and left to puddle on the tray. As if to compensate for Black Nancy's increased sourness, young Nancy stirred more sugar in his tea, and with every teaspoon became more lighthearted, so that by midafternoon his misery would be quite forgotten. The pain of his lower back would slowly dissipate, and soon he would be raised on an elbow, regaling Alden with fantastic accounts of his past and future glories. He was like his old man in that way—Nancy the Elder. He liked to hear himself speak. He was an old money man, the elder Nancy—who had somehow got himself tangled up in politics. Now he was a senator. Funny the way life goes, he'd say, as though he had had no hand in the business. Everyone, including Judge Kelly, had always liked the elder Nancy, especially from a little distance. Once you were in the same room together and got him talking, though, it was nearly impossible to get him to stop. Everything reminded him of something else, and when you finally managed to escape, it was through a gap in the story that in no way resembled the one through which you came.

It's like his tongue isn't hinged on right, the Judge said. It flaps.

Nancy the Younger was just the same, only he had less to be reminded of and so less to recollect. With him, it was always the fifty-six-yard field goal with which he'd managed to secure the championship win for Eastern High as a freshman back in '29, or the time he'd caught his sister in the hall closet with his father's secretary—who, when Li'l Nany had discovered them, had covered his face with his hands, neglecting his more private parts. Never once did he talk about the one thing Alden was genuinely curious about: the occasion when, at the age of five or six, Li'l Nancy (who apparently had a knack for stumbling upon his family members at their most compromised) had discovered his grandfather, Old Mister Nancy, dangling from a ceiling hook at the old Kalorama place. That was shortly before they had moved to the Hill and their fathers, then they themselves, had become friends. And when it came to it, if it was a friend you wanted, you couldn't get much better than Li'l Nancy. Alden knew that. Especially that summer. He would talk your ear off, that was sure, and never about the thing you wanted him to, but still you'd never be bored, listening. Even when you'd heard the same story a thousand times. There was something about him that held your attention that way— and even Black Nancy, though she pounded up those stairs with a fatally heavy tread in the waning hours of each day, was so crazy about him that when he died, ten years later—late September 1942— his plane spiraling into the waters of the North Atlantic, she cried for six days straight. Then, on the seventh day, Mrs. Nancy suffered a stroke, leaving the left side of her face completely paralyzed and destroying her ability to eat or speak. This brought Black Nancy up short. She said, If it ain't the one thing, it's sho' enough the othah— and there wasn't any use in crying about it. This was all recorded in a letter Sutton wrote to Alden shortly thereafter, so that was how he came to know about it.

That was the same year, incidentally—1942—their own father, Judge Kelly, died. Mary Kelly, who had for some time by then resided at St. Elizabeth's Hospital, just outside the city, and who rarely involved herself, even by way of the most cursory response, in the more ordinary happenings of the world, including those most ordinary happenings of all, life and death, and who barely batted an eye when her own husband's death was announced, had shaken her head when she heard.

Black Nancy, she said, was the only good thing that ever happened to that family.

But that was all still sometime in the future.

MRS. NANCY HAD BEEN an inveterate "cave dweller," as the old money types of the Kalorama District were known, who couldn't "hack it" (her own words) in town. When Jack had been twelve, she had divorced the elder Nancy and moved back to Kalorama for good, taking Jack and Black Nancy with her. (Alden had heard her say it himself: "I couldn't hack it," she'd said—her sensitive nose pink at the edges and quivering slightly—as if her marriage had been nothing more complicated or binding than a challenging round of golf.)

So it was in the company of three of the Nancys: Mrs. Nancy, Li'l Nancy, and old Black Nancy, that Alden spent that last, unsufferably hot month of the summer of 1932. Stuffing himself on Black Nancy's sweet tea and sandwiches.

I'm going to be a big fat man, just like my father, Jack would say miserably, just before noon. But by four o'clock he would be raised on an elbow again. I am, after all, within my rights, he would inform Alden smugly, to be a fat man if I so choose and desire. But you—he said—pointing a thick finger at his friend, or swiping away the half-finished plate of sandwiches as Alden reached for another—you have no excuse. Who—he said, his mouth, at the corners, already beginning to break into a wide grin—ever heard of a fat *Commie?*

Before even finishing the sentence he would already have busted out laughing, muffling the final word. The force of the laughter, however, would always serve to remind him of the crippling pain caused by the dislocated disc in his lower spine.

Goddammit, he would yell. Goddamn you, you are killing me.

DURING THE DAY—LAID UP in Kalorama with Jack Nancy—Alden's mind would be blank and calm. But when he returned home at night, he would often find himself, against his will and better judgment, once again running over the course of events in his mind, and wondering in what way, or at what point, he might have recognized within them some sort of pattern; some way, that is, of recognizing—and thereby affecting—what was (though he could not have known it then) already to come. But he could detect no pattern; no, nothing beyond the brute facts of what had occurred: the sudden—material—onslaught of bricks and metal from the approaching cavalry; then the manner in which one of them (as though there had existed for it all along no other course) connected with the skull of Douglas Sinclair.

In none of it—no blow given or received, nor the manner in which, shortly afterward (though he could hardly recall it) their hands had been bound behind their backs, and he, along with Douglas, still bleeding, and Arthur, had been led away—could he find one single immaterial thing that he might have seized upon in order redirect the course of things. Still, he continued to trouble over it, his thoughts repeating themselves; turning over the same, stubborn groove. By what method, he wondered, might he train them toward some different end? (It was, as he had reflected on countless occasions, hardly worthwhile to dwell on the past.) If there existed any way of affecting the future, it would have to be—he reasoned—not, as he had so far supposed, in the discovery of some auxiliary route based upon and beginning from the moment at hand but in altering the direction of the route along which one had already come. Where he had previously envisioned, that is, a complete break with the past, it was obvious no break could possibly be! The future, he realized, quite unmistakably now, would always arrive in some recognizable form. He recalled, for example, the look in the eyes of the Bonus Army in the moment they had turned—as if a single man—to face the approaching cavalry, who had just then begun toward them at a charge. There had been fear— yes. And anger. Both of which Alden understood. But there had been something else, too, which at the time he'd found difficult to place. It occurred to him now what it had been: a look of absolute recognition. The look of a man who stares at his own face in the mirror, say, and— though he does not always like what he sees—registers, through the simple fact of his gaze, an exact equivalence. A complicity with image and form, which at once cancels out both true judgment and every course of action that has not already been tried.

And so it was, and had always been, Alden thought—throughout history. Where no man or woman had any other manner of looking at the world, except to stare back at the past. No wonder they found themselves so hopelessly trapped there! Yes, he thought, it was that . . . simple acknowledgment—of there being no actual distance to traverse between the future and the past—that had filled him suddenly, in the moment of the cavalry charge, with a horror more devastating than the rush of smoke and dust, or the volley of guns, or even his own intentions (the probable effect, that is, of the small block of wood he then carried on his person; an object that, though it appeared innocent enough and measured less than six inches in diameter, soon promised—by means of a small vial of sulfuric acid, a blasting cap, and a stick of dynamite lodged within its hollowed core—to achieve for itself a very different meaning).

Yes, it was quite clear to him now: where he had previously envisioned the future as arriving with the same force he then carried (that pure, unalloyed potential), having no correspondence with either the present or the past . . . it could never arrive that way; quite possibly, it could never arrive at all! The future, he saw now, would always arrive a moment too late, in what would (by the time it arrived) already be the past. It was therefore not the future that needed to be anticipated and arranged, but the proper recognition of it when it came. What was necessary (Alden thought to himself now, with some satisfaction—having arrived, finally, at a loophole in the trap that had otherwise been made of his mind) was some method of inspiring within the hearts of men not an *idea*, but some substantial form according to which they might, in a moment of sublime recognition when it came, actually *become* the future, rather than, as usual, pitting themselves against it as though it were the most rudimentary foe. But he was at a loss to understand how this might be done: how any *thing* might resist—when transferred either in time or in space—becoming, at least in part, an *idea* again. And even his own thoughts—in direct proportion to his efforts to contain them—continued to erupt in the most impulsive manner, as though disconnected from any progression, let alone any tangible *form*, so that it was a very difficult process to train them toward anything that might be considered of any substance at all. Proof of this was that, though he might spend an entire sleepless night attempting to work through the problem, first one way and then another, the next day not even the slightest trace of his efforts would remain.

There was never anything to do in the morning but to eat the breakfast provided for him, and depart, as soon as he was able, to Jack Nancy's, where—sweet tea in hand—he would be regaled by Jack with whatever details he had been able to glean about preseason training, or his sister's varied exploits with men. This latter topic, in particular, was one that held for Jack considerable interest because of the fact that he had so far had none of his own. This was a regret that was, of course, never spoken out loud, but was always implicit—and quite possibly taken to his grave. It is quite possible that Jack Nancy plummeted to his death in the North Atlantic—his scrotum pinched with cold and the pressure of terror and wind—a virgin. But that would occur many years later, and the future was never a subject that interested Jack. Neither of course was the past, and thus he never was able to satisfy Alden's own niggling and morbid curiosity as to the nature and dimensions of the death he'd been witness to as a boy. The smell of it, say, or its other lingering aftereffects. Did it scald itself, for example, onto your eyes, so that even when you looked away, and possibly for a long time after, it left a tiny white light dancing at the outer field of your vision as after staring too long at a naked electric bulb? And as it was well known that to die by one's own hand was a very different matter from dying by natural cause, he wondered further if there was not, perhaps, some instant knowledge that the body, remaindered by such a death, imparted to the onlooker—a knowledge that, if briefly, illuminated the origin of the death itself, which had arisen, somehow, deformed and monstrous within the soul?

After all of Black Nancy's sandwiches had been devoured and they had begun to hear the telltale signs of evening falling in the form of the clinking of ice in Mrs. Nancy's glass downstairs, and her heavy sighs, which became even heavier as the sun descended behind the trees and spread its shadows like soft blankets on the ground, Alden would glide home, his brain a bright red ball glowing in his head, and it would only be as he neared the gate to his own house and saw the light in his father's window and felt, before he saw, the pale echo of the light in his mother's back hall and the contrasting pressure of Sutton's bulb pulsing with a betrayal and resentment he could neither admit to nor understand, that he would be filled suddenly with the sweeping, nearly unbearable sensation of the relativeness of his own small glow, which would suddenly both dim and flare: an erratic, searing pain.

WHO KNOWS HOW MUCH time would have passed in this way if the future had not suddenly arrived, then, in the last days of August, looking—as it nearly always does—so very much like the past? It was the Indian, John, who appeared one day, just after Mrs. Nancy's lengthening sighs had alerted Alden to the fact that he would shortly be due home, pacing the length of Mrs. Nancy's Kalorama drive. The Indian had, over the course of the weeks that had passed, become pale and thin, so that indeed he appeared to Alden almost like a ghost of himself as he approached in the waning light. Having no experience with the matter, Alden failed to recognize what he might well have years later: that what he mistook in the Indian as the effects of inadequate food and sleepless nights, was actually the result of a slow-burning dread that had gradually begun to overtake him. Alden was, at that time, still very young; he could not foretell the future. He could, just barely, see ten feet ahead of himself—what with how quickly the darkness had come, and the great distances that always existed between lampposts in the more fashionable neighborhoods.

When finally Alden reached him, the Indian turned stiffly, as though suddenly unused to his overlong limbs, and, without extending a hand or a single word in greeting, began to walk slowly in the same direction.

The two walked together then, without speaking, their pace checked by darkness.

Why don't they light these goddamn neighborhoods? the Indian said.

Alden realized only then that he had been walking as stiffly as the Indian. At the sound of his familiar voice, however, Alden relaxed; his knees bent. Pretty soon there were lights in the distance. They walked faster toward them as though drawn on by the light. The hill hurried them, as though pressing from behind—ushering them out of the darkness of Kalorama, and into the future. He wanted very badly to arrive there.

Finally, after twenty minutes or more, the Indian stopped abruptly on a well-lit street, under a low awning. Alden waited for him to speak, but he only continued to regard him silently. It was impossible to tell what he was thinking.

Come on, the Indian said finally. Let's go inside.

Then, turning, he knocked twice on a heavy door adjacent to where they now stood. Shortly afterward, when the door opened inward, he ducked inside, without motioning for Alden to follow. But Alden did follow. He entered the house after the Indian, and shut the door behind him.

Perched on a large stuffed chair at the far end of the entry, a thin man in spectacles—very serious-looking, in what was perhaps a rather premature middle age—had evidently been waiting. Whoever it was who had opened the door was nowhere to be seen. It had evidently not been the man in the chair—unless, that is, he had raced back across the room very quickly, in just the short time it had taken Alden and the Indian to enter the room. This did not seem very likely—though he did appear poised in such a way (balanced as precariously as the book held open on his knee, or the spectacles at the end of his nose) that it was not out of the question he had either recently arranged himself in that position or was preparing at any moment to spring.

Now, abruptly, he closed the book on his knee and looked up, toward where the Indian—Alden behind him—hovered just inside the door.

Ah, he said, addressing Alden as a professor might an especially promising new pupil. A pleasure. He extended his hand, but did not get up or move toward him, so that Alden was forced to do so himself. He did so; allowing his hand to be taken up firmly in the professor's own. He had not expected so firm a grasp, however, and returned the pressure only after the professor had released his own—in doing so, extending the handshake a beat too long.

It has been brought to my attention, the professor said, after returning Alden's hand, that you are quite (here he paused, allowing him to put extra, though delicate, emphasis on the word that followed) *dedicated* to our cause. Would you consider that to be the case?

Alden could not help but shift, uncomfortably, from one foot to the next, but he nodded.

The professor nodded as well, then leaned back in his chair, his fingers clasped tightly around the book on his knee. Automatically, Alden searched its spine for a title, but found it was covered in a protective leather case.

I would, the professor said—gazing off somewhere beyond Alden, into the distance—accept your word on this matter more readily if something else, of late, had not *also* been brought to my attention. Now he let his gaze drift back toward Alden, who concentrated on meeting it. Were you not charged, the professor said, adjusting his position so that once again he sat forward as though ready to spring, with the possession of some very . . . *sensitive* materials some weeks past? *Sensitive materials* (he pronounced each word as if they themselves might explode on his tongue) which never *did* arrive at their destination and, in failing to do so, directly resulted in the obstruction of a major element of our operation?

I was, Alden said, charged with . . . sensitive materials. Yes.

Which did not reach their destination.

Yes. Sir. You see, I—*they*—were intercepted.

His voice broke a little on the final word.

I was, Alden said—clearing his throat before beginning again— taken . . . But he could not finish the sentence. I put myself, you see—he began a third time—at great personal risk, sir—I hope you understand.

The professor eyed him from behind the reflective lenses of his spectacles, as though peering at him from a great distance.

I have heard, he said slowly, after a weighty pause—still gazing at Alden intensely—one other thing of the affair, which I will tell you, and then we'll be done with it—put the whole thing behind us, so to speak. I have heard . . . that your personal *risk*, as you say, in this affair was significantly *reduced* due to some very *worthwhile* connections. Again, the professor paused. Would you say that this was true?

It is, of course, he continued after a moment or two, when it became clear that Alden had no reply to offer him, a great *disappointment* to us that the materials in your charge were intercepted—the interruption of this operation came indeed at great cost. But what is *most* important, as always, with the sort of work that we do, is that we are able to *learn* from our mistakes. That we are even able, from the new configuration of events and circumstances within which we find ourselves, to recognize some new *advantage*. Now—he said—leaning forward still more, and redirecting his gaze so that for the first time he appeared to be looking at Alden directly, I see before me a young man with every mark of one day becoming . . . a great *leader* within our party. Is this a thought that has occurred to you?

Again, Alden made no reply. His mouth felt remarkably dry.

The professor raised his hand and, as though she had come from nowhere, a thin woman dressed in a long dark gown, as from a previous century, and carrying a tray with four tall glasses, entered the room.

Why don't we have a toast? the professor proposed, rising. He then turned to the thin woman, indicating to each of them that they should take a glass. After they had done so, he took the last for himself.

To the future! the professor said, lifting his glass in the air—a gesture the others copied—then drinking the contents in a single swallow. Alden attempted the same but could only manage a little. He measured the quantities of alcohol still left in the Indian's and the tall woman's glass. Neither one of them had drunk as quickly or as heartily as the professor.

During all this time the tall woman appeared not to have noticed that anyone else was in the room. She stood with them nonetheless, silently, towering a full head above the professor and nearly as much over Alden, so that his gaze fell level with the point at which the prominent bones of her chest conjoined, exposing a most vulnerable V shape between them, from which he found it increasingly difficult to look away. So mesmerized had he become that it was some time before he noticed that the professor had begun speaking again, this time in a foreign language he could not understand. After another moment or two, he at last recognized—from a few scattered words familiar to him—the language as Russian. Now the tall woman turned to the Indian, and spoke to him in the same language, and—to Alden's immense surprise—the Indian replied. An Indian speaking Russian! He did not have long to ponder the strangeness of the scene, however, because very soon the professor, in a startled voice—as though he had for a moment forgotten Alden entirely—interrupted the Indian, saying, Please forgive us, and the conversation continued in English. But because Alden had already missed so much by that point, what passed between them was no more understandable to him than it had been before, and he turned his attention instead to his glass so that it might more quickly empty itself and he might have some excuse to depart.

IT WAS SOME HOURS later that Alden stumbled, alongside the Indian, into the street. The solid lines of the buildings they passed, and the hard, perpendicular angle of the street, were a disorienting contrast to his own muddled head. Beside him, the Indian seemed even larger and more solid than usual, and when, once, in faltering slightly, Alden reached out to steady himself against him, he felt an almost physical shock at the touch.

Before long, the Indian pulled up short just as he had in front of the house of the professor a few hours before. The houses in front of which they now stood were of a very different sort: long and swaybacked, they huddled together, seeming almost as temporary and haphazard as the shelters at Camp Marks.

All right? the Indian said.

Alden nodded yes.

The Indian returned the nod, then he ducked through a low entry-way, motioning for Alden to follow. Once inside, they were enclosed in almost perfect darkness. Alden followed the Indian hesitantly down a short flight of stairs, his hand on the rough wall beside him, so that he wouldn't stumble. At the bottom of the stairs, he could see that the small cellar they had just entered had been converted into sparely furnished living quarters with a bed in one corner of the room and a table at the center. A small lamp on a high window ledge cast a limited glow.

What—? Alden began—but the Indian put a finger to his lips, and pointed toward a third figure in the corner, at that moment just rising to greet them. It was Aida. Though Alden's eyes had not yet fully adjusted to the light, he recognized the contour of her shape immediately as she approached. What a relief it was to see her!

Alden, she said. She, too seemed relieved; she approached quickly, then drew up short suddenly, just before she reached him.

Alden nodded, swallowing hard for some reason—though for some time his throat had been dry. He placed his hand on the back of the child, whom she held in her arms. He would have liked to extend his hand farther; to have placed it lightly, instead, on Aida's cheek, which looked in the dim light even more drawn and thin than he recalled. He would have liked to have filled that space, whatever it was; to have brushed away whatever shadow had fallen there if it was only, as he hoped, a trick of the light.

Come. Sit down.

She indicated the corner of the low bed, and the Indian went to the window to remove the lantern still flickering there. Soon all three of them, along with the sleeping child, were seated together on the bed. The lamp cast only a small circle of light from the point on the floor where the Indian had set it; beyond that it was ringed with what seemed an even more complete darkness.

He'll sleep here, the Indian said, to Alden as much as to Aida. He isn't fit—

Alden tried to protest, but even as he did he felt a heaviness in his mind and on his tongue and the words that he did manage, if indeed he managed them, only reinforced what had been said. Aida nodded, and began to make up a bed on the floor.

And did you——? she began, looking up shyly from her work. The Indian shook his head.

We'll speak about it later, he said. Then, to Alden: Sleep. You are tired, and unwell.

I am well, he said.

I have just to look at you to see that you are not.

Perhaps not, he said. Perhaps I haven't been well for a very long time. But still——the professor is right. I have not suffered, I have——failed——

But here the Indian rose abruptly from the bed.

I would advise you to sleep, he said. Then, over his shoulder, gruffly, and not to utter that word again in this house.

Alden nodded gravely. He understood.

I will not, he said. The dim lamplight, and the solemn beauty of Aida, as well as the vast quantities of alcohol that had gone to his head reverberated within him, making him feel sentimental and sad. He continued, therefore, to quietly admonish himself. No, he said. It is true. I have not suffered. I have not yet even *begun*——

But he did not have time to finish his thought. He found himself suddenly breathless and choking, his body pressed flat against the wall. It was several seconds before he understood what had happened——or recognized the Indian, John, his large head nodding in front of his own, as the force that held him there.

What did I tell you? the Indian said, his white teeth flashing.

Alden's mind reeled. Certainly, he thought to himself, he must know the answer to this. But just as a word "at the tip" of one's tongue retreats further and further from reach the more eagerly it is hunted, so the information he so desperately required seemed to retreat further away from him——disappearing finally into the deepened shadows of the room.

What did I say? the Indian said again, but his voice was so close and his face so obscured by darkness that the voice did not seem to be coming from him at all. It seemed instead to be only—a voice, and Alden began to wonder if it was not according to the force of a man, but the force of the voice itself that, in another moment his body was slammed again against the hard wall, causing a sharp pain to shoot through his shoulders and down the length of his spine.

I said, the voice replied—because Alden was very far from responding now—not to speak that word again in this house. Do you understand?

The pressure suddenly released from his throat, Alden slid from the wall—slumping against the Indian's shoulder. He heard another voice then, which at first he took to be only the sound of his own throat as it gasped, in confusion, for air. But then he realized it was the sound of Aida, crying. He strained to lift his head from the Indian's shoulder and saw that she had knelt behind her husband on the bed. That she still clutched the baby, who had not woken, white tears glinting on her cheeks.

Do you understand? the Indian asked again. But now his voice had changed; had become soft with regret.

Alden, Aida sobbed. Do you hear him? He is saying he is sorry. Speak, she begged of him. Speak.

He was able to respond only with a low groan, but even this proved such a relief to the girl that she began to sob again, this time out of gratitude, saying, Thank you, O my Lord, for your everlasting kindness.

Slowly, as the oxygen once more entered his blood, Alden began to search back through his memory and, little by little, like a man retracing his steps in badly drifted snow, to recall what had transpired. His mistake, he realized finally, had been in assuming that the word most terrible to the Indian's ear had been the same word most terrible to his own. As if in confirmation of this, he could hear the Indian remark, almost under his breath, but with a vehemence that rendered the words, nonetheless, even in Alden's state, distinct and clear: There has been enough suffering.

In that moment, as Alden realized more fully the extent of the mistake he had made, he felt powerfully—almost unbearably—sad. There existed, he realized then, in every word the possibility of just such a mistake. And, as he sat there on the bed, the blood just beginning to return to his brain and to his heart, it occurred to him that the likelihood of his ever being able to speak aloud any word that would communicate within it the meaning he intended and desired was very slight. The realization swept over him all at once, indistinguishable from a wave of overpowering fatigue.

Very soon after that, he fell asleep where he lay—waking again only after the first fingers of light had pried their way beneath the makeshift curtain of the room's single window, which opened onto the street.

AIDA WAS ALREADY AWAKE. She paced the floor slowly, as the child, Felicity, cooed—her small voice dissolving the moment it was uttered into the warmth of Aida's hushed replies. The comforting sound, as well as a dull pain in his throat where it had been bruised, distracted him temporarily, but soon—as, gradually, he made sense of his surroundings and recollected the events of the night before—a powerful shame swept over him.

Just as it did, the Indian's step was heard on the stairs and, a moment later, he appeared before them. To Alden's great relief, however, the Indian merely grinned in Alden's direction—then inquired teasingly (as if what had transpired between them had little to do with either of them, and was of little consequence) after his health. Attempting to match the Indian's tone, Alden assured him he was well. But as he rose from the bed in order to prove that this was so, he found that the throbbing of his head increased, and that his feet under him proved unsteady. Slowly, he made his way to where the Indian and Aida, along with the child—who had begun to call out in a shrill repeated cry—were already seated at the table. By the time he reached them, the child had grown quiet, and too late Alden realized this was because Aida had raised the child to her breast. As eyes will on anything uncommon to them, Alden's lingered longer than was necessary on the child's head—pressed there, against its mother's breast—before, remembering himself, he averted them sharply, his cheeks burning.

If the Indian sensed Alden's discomfort, he did not let on. He had already begun to speak in a deep and measured voice, as though recounting an old story, which he knew by heart. And yet it was not an old story. It was, instead, the recent events of the twenty-eighth of July that the Indian recounted then—beginning from the moment he had last seen Alden; just before he had departed, along with Douglas and Arthur, in the direction of the National Mall.

He made no mention, in front of Aida, of the "sensitive materials" he himself had, a moment before, transferred into Alden's care, but instead began his account immediately after the three of them—Alden, Douglas, and Arthur—had taken their leave.

It was very soon after that (the Indian said, his eyes darkening), that the trouble broke. He and Aida herded—suddenly—like animals from their tents. Then a noise like a shot—or a whip being cracked. And after that . . . it was as if all the pressure that had built up in that stinking swamp over the long months broke at once, and now there was nothing to do but be swept along with the force of the tide that moved to fill the breach that had been torn. To pour out—a great mass—moving not because they had direction but because they did not.

And so it was that in my one hand, the Indian said, I held Aida, and in the other the girl, and we fled through the streets and it was as if we were one body moving, pressing toward the opening at the end of the row, where there was no opening now. We moved like sleepers, he said, in frustratingly slow motion, only half aware of the fact that we were not making any progress toward our goal, if indeed we had been able to determine one.

Then, just as we reached the end of Delaware Row, Aida screamed. And so I *heard* it before I felt it myself: a searing pain. It seemed as though it was the pain itself that blinded me, independent of any cause, because there did not appear to be one. But then I felt it, and the child—felt her go stiff in my arms. I worried that I had held her too tight and squeezed the life from her, but I could see nothing and I was scared that if I loosened my grip she might slip from my grasp and that then I might never be able to find her, so I continued to hold her tightly, but now I was frightened by my own strength and the pressure of my arm against her body, which I could not gauge. I tried to speak, to say something in warning or comfort to Aida or the child, but when I opened my mouth I only choked on the air, and I felt as if it would kill me before I managed to bite from it a single word.

AIDA AND ALDEN, AND even the child, were still; they had hardly breathed while the Indian spoke. But now he was silent, and Alden realized that both he and Aida had redirected their attention to him. That the Indian had asked him a question.

Douglas. Arthur.

He shook his head. Both Aida and the Indian continued to regard him silently, still waiting for his reply.

You see, the Indian said, when still Alden said nothing, it seems that Arthur's been detained—for a reason yet to become clear. There was some—he continued—altercation with the police, the boy said. But beyond that he knew nothing. Now the Indian looked up at Alden sharply.

Chet's looked into it, he continued, but has not been able to get very far. The charges, you see, are not exactly . . . proportionate . . . to the boy's account of what transpired. Again the Indian paused. He seemed— he began again—to be under the impression that you were also there— at the time of the arrest. I thought perhaps—still he regarded Alden, his eyes seeming to see deeper and deeper with every word—you might be able to help us understand the situation, and that perhaps if we knew more, we might—

Alden shook his head. No, he said. His voice harsh, and feeling particularly painful now in his throat. Again the Indian's gaze dropped swiftly away.

There was some confusion, Alden said. I believe . . . a policeman was hurt. But I did not see what happened—and I know nothing of what happened to either Douglas or Arthur after I was released.

This was not altogether a lie.

And the negotiations—the Indian was saying—for your own release. Was there anything in their nature that might shed any light on the charges that Arthur is faced with now?

Alden was beginning to feel ill. He was certain the Indian could see it; could detect—but what, exactly?

He shook his head. The Indian was silent for a time.

Finally, it was Aida who spoke—raising her head from where she had buried it in the child's dark hair.

Well, she said, I suppose in that we are no closer we are no further away.

After that there was nothing but silence between them.

—

LESS THAN TWO WEEKS LATER—IN A MOVE THE PROFESSOR CONSID-ered inspired (and which, incidentally, he had thought up himself), Alden had a job at the *Washington Post*. Judge Kelly (just as the professor had anticipated) was relieved, in light of current circumstances, by Alden's sudden expression of interest in anything at all; he had therefore been more than happy to approach Mr. Gradon Stanley—editor in chief—with whom he happened to be personal friends. Alden had flunked out of two of the four core subjects in his final high school year, and flatly refused to attend college in the fall—but despite this, as a favor to his old friend the Judge (who was not at all a bad man to have on your side), Mr. Stanley welcomed Alden with a firm handshake, and with that—he was a newspaperman. He was given a desk in the corner of the room by the door, which—swinging open and shut all day—caused a constant draft and rustled the pages in both the incoming and outgoing files.

This was merely a preliminary measure, the professor assured Alden. As such, his main job was . . . to do nothing. To behave as any entry-level copy editor might. To be ambitious—but not overly. To do his work—neither poorly, nor too well. He was expressly forbidden to involve himself in party affairs, or express his opinion to anyone regarding the party—or politics in general. All of this—to be neutral and inconspicuous in every way—should have been easy, but for some reason—he couldn't help it—he was nervous as a cat. He would shuffle the papers from the piles in front of him until he wasn't sure any longer which ones were coming and which ones were going, and whenever anybody passed by, giving him an unsuspecting wink or a wave, he would begin to perspire, his heart slamming violently against the inside of his chest.

Once or twice a week, just as he exited the office at five o'clock, he would be met by the Indian, and the two of them would stroll through the Mall.

It is only a matter of time, the Indian would reassure Alden on these occasions. Patience—and time.

And the professor. He feels this way, too? Alden would ask—though he knew what the answer would be.

The big Indian would nod solemnly, and, aware of Alden's real purpose, add in sympathy: What we need to establish is trust, first of all. You must understand, of course, the importance of that.

But they did not always speak this way. As the weeks and then the months passed, they conversed with increasing ease. More and more, the Indian began to share with Alden from his seemingly inexhaustible stores of knowledge. He had, for instance, an incredible head for languages (he spoke Choctaw, Russian, and a spattering of French), politics (he kept up on all sides and knew the capitals and leaders of countries Alden had never heard of), and poetry (he was a passionate reader, with a particular memory for Shakespeare). He would often pause, hold up his hand—as if receiving a signal from a distant planet—and recite for his young companion a stanza or two from *Macbeth* or *Richard III*. His voice would change as he did so, quivering with a slight lisp, and favoring his *r*'s in a way that was incomprehensible to Alden until, later, he heard the radio recordings of these productions, and therefore firsthand the accents of the British actors whose lilt the Indian imitated with precision—a way of speaking that was altogether alien to anything he had ever heard. At any rate, a far cry from the accents of those one or two Brits to whom he had so far been introduced—by his father, of course—who, when invited into his father's study, had extended their clammy hands and said a how-do-you-do in a way that sounded as though they were holding marbles in their mouths (a cure, he had once heard, for stuttering), so that he forever afterward associated the British with that unfortunate speech impediment—something that went hand in hand, so to speak, with manual perspiration.

If it were done when 'tis done, then 'twere well / It were done quickly, the Indian would say, his hand aloft and his voice hovering above the *r*'s, so that it seemed for a moment the words themselves were suspended above them—even causing Alden, on a few occasions, to glance up, as though he actually expected something to descend.

If th' assassination / Could trammel up the consequence, and catch / With his surcease success; that but this blow / Might be the be-all and the end-all here, / But here, upon this bank and shoal of time, / We'd jump the life to come.

And then they would. The words would descend upon them, all at once. They had been sent off as all words are, one by one, as though not even intended for one another, and then, at some point in the middle distance as he and the Indian continued to walk along, unsuspecting, they would align and fall together, with a great blow. They would knock themselves against their teeth and into their hearts so that it was always with the solemnity of beaten men, who know that they are beaten—who give in, at last, to final blows—that they walked on after the Indian had finished speaking. The night would seem, then, unnaturally quiet and there was nothing to say until, when they were almost at their customary stopping place at the far end of the Mall—from which point Alden would make a left and continue on toward his father's house, and the Indian would continue straight ahead, toward where Aida and the child would be waiting for him—toward the one lamp that Alden knew for a fact would be lit for him there—the Indian would turn and speak again, for a final time. In mid-autumn, the Mall was still filled with pedestrians; though it would be getting late, carriages and automobiles would still be barking and rattling their way along the adjacent streets, and from time to time they would hear a shout or the high, long laugh of a girl, but still they would be plunged together in a silence that was in itself complete, uninterrupted by these or any other sounds. It was this silence more than anything else they shared, and which, as the months progressed and the weather became cold and the Mall was plunged into actual silence, and even the ducks had flown, became even more profound, so that not even the ruffle of the feathers on the backs of the birds as they shuddered the water from their backs (that sudden, almost interior flutter, like blood rushing in the vein) disturbed it.

But, always, just before they parted, the Indian would raise his hand as though speaking an oath and leave Alden with some final, parting words. Something different every time, but always—equally—it would ring out as though he had spoken it a thousand times. As it did on what would be the final occasion that the two of them parted, when the Indian lifted his hand and recited these words:

But in these cases, / We still have judgment here, that we but teach / Bloody instructions, which, being taught, return / To plague the inventor.

Then continued. In the direction he had already, and for some time, been bound.

BUT THAT WAS STILL several months away. In the meantime, Alden continued to shuffle pages back and forth between the incoming and outgoing piles on his desk, and after a while his nervousness dissipated so that he no longer got them confused, or jumped like a cat, or tapped at his cigarette until its bright end glowed as sharp and fine as a knife. Indeed, after only a few weeks he no longer needed to pretend that he was neutral in every way—he became so. His life began to stretch out before him, as behind, in the same regulated and more or less comfortable way that it does for any salaried man. Even the small discomforts of the day—the early rising, the treacherous commute, the excessive boredom of the late morning and early afternoon, during which time itself (sagging between the taut ends of the day) seemed to enter into an entirely different measure all its own—began to hold for him a certain pleasure, which could be owed, in all probability, simply to the fact of their being so recognizable. He knew that he could absolutely count on each day to occur nearly exactly as it had the day before, and the day prior to that, and so on. But after only a brief respite, in which he recognized and appreciated that this was so, he suddenly became restless again, and resumed his anxious tapping.

Perhaps the natural nervousness of his constitution demanded something upon which to fix itself—something to lend context to the persistent disquiet of both his body and mind. Because he now had nothing of the sort, he began to invent circumstances of his own; in a word, he became paranoid. So much so that he began to walk several blocks in the opposite direction before turning and doubling back in the way that he actually intended to go—even when he was going somewhere, as he nearly always was, as simple and innocuous as the corner grocery, or to the Nancy house in Kalorama, where he still visited—though less frequently. Li'l Nancy was up and walking around by then, going to practices but sitting out games, and growing a little fatter and a little more restless himself. More and more Alden began to see the way that his friend was just exactly like his old man, after all, and that was how it happened. If you didn't use up all the energy you had inside you when you were young—it hardly seemed to matter in what direction—it just sort of turned sour inside you, as it was doing just then inside of Li'l Nancy. So that when you think about it, and if it hadn't have killed him, it was almost a shame that the war didn't come sooner for him. But anyway, as the fall wore on, Alden saw less and less of Li'l Nancy and finally he didn't see him at all—or anyone outside of the fellows in the office, and from time to time the members of his family, when such sightings were in no other way possible to avoid. His only real pleasure was his once- or twice-weekly stroll around the Mall with the Indian. Sometimes he wouldn't even listen to what the Indian said. He would hear only the rhythm of his voice, the energy and insistence of it; let it enter his veins, and as it did, make silent prayers to himself that he would not allow his own energies to be

mis- or falsely directed—to be burned up or used up or allowed to
fester, at least for long, in some stinking office somewhere.

FINALLY, WHEN HE COULD bear it no longer, he confronted the professor. He was certain that by now he had "paid his dues," and therefore
demanded he be immediately reassigned to some more active duty. He
thought of Biggs, whom he had not seen since well before the riots.
He—Alden was sure—had never been put through such a lengthy or
exacting trial.

I can understand your feelings, the professor replied, rubbing his
chin. It is, of course, natural that a young man like yourself would
feel that his . . . talents and energies . . . were being wasted in an occupation that has none of the direct and obvious recompenses that he
might, or that any of us indeed, might wish. I, also, you see—the
professor continued—am sometimes of the mind-set that there might
be a more direct and . . . expedient . . . method of achieving our ends,
but there are those who, for reasons it is neither necessary nor indeed
even advisable for me to be privy to, see it differently. I am, after
all—like you—only taking orders.

THE NEXT DAY, ALDEN met the Indian as usual, and told him what the
professor had said. After hearing him out, the Indian had nodded grimly
and agreed.

Patience, he said, was the most difficult but also the most necessary
thing. As for the hunter, he said. The early shot always misses its mark.
You have to wait what feels always one beat too long.

That day, as on every other, the Indian had appeared, as if by accident, alongside Alden as he made his way from the office at the end of
the day toward the Mall. Sometimes he managed to get nearly halfway
up the street and even around the corner before the Indian appeared,
and sometimes he did not appear at all, but at least once or twice a
week at first, and then more frequently as the weeks progressed, he
did. Alden was never even sure from what direction he came, when he
did, or what he did when he did not come, or during the rest of his day.

Often he would wonder about it, the mysterious alchemy of the Indian's profession, but he could never bring himself to ask directly—the materials with which the Indian worked too "sensitive," perhaps, even for words. Oftener still, he would find his mind wandering back to what Sutton had said that day, sometime before the riots. How her head had bent toward his, her features taut with concern: *Alden. He's killed a man.*

His own response—*He must have had his reasons*—would quiver within him in reply. But it was not a statement; it was a question.

Finally, one he steeled himself to ask.

When he had done so, the Indian was silent for a while. Then, without slowing or in any way altering his pace, he pointed off into the distance.

Do you see that? he asked Alden.

Alden was not even entirely sure if it was something in the near or the far distance toward which he was being asked to direct his gaze.

No, he said. What?

The Indian dropped his hand, but continued to gaze steadily ahead. Into the far distance—Alden was sure of at least that much now. Toward some place, just beyond the line of the horizon, made indistinct by a heavy bank of cloud.

There are many things—the Indian said, after a moment or two had passed, again in silence—one cannot see. It is only a fool who imagines it's because they're not there.

But to answer Alden's question, he continued. The man at the bar that night had once—he said—been a friend. But then (here the Indian paused, in order to more carefully choose his words)—he'd had (the "*friend*," that is, not the Indian) a sudden change of heart. Had turned against the Union, even helped break up the Harlan strike in May of '31. Had fought against his own men, the Indian said. And for what? Nothing more—he supposed—than the promise of a steady check.

A man's got to choose, the Indian continued sadly. There's never going to be for him any more than one side.

Something about the way he said these final words—Alden could later not put his finger on it—frightened him. Caused him, whenever he thought back on it, a quick, involuntary shudder; his heart, for some reason, turned cold with dread.

Then, toward the end of November—the twenty-second of that month, to be exact; it was easy to remember the date only because of what followed after—the economist Raymond Robins, a well-known party member who had mysteriously disappeared nearly two months before, suddenly reemerged; discovered in a North Carolina boarding-house under an assumed name. One moment he had been on his way to Washington where he had an appointment with the President, and the next— All he could later recall was a sudden darkness, descending.

Two months later an emissary from Washington unpacked a series of photographs and documents from his briefcase and passed them over the counter to a bemused Mr. Rogers, from Whittier, North Carolina, who had agreed to meet with him briefly over lunch. Mr. Rogers shuffled disinterestedly through the photographs, then returned them to his companion, who continued to stare at him over the tops of his frosted glasses, blinking almost compulsively—a habit that undermined his otherwise (though he was a man of rather diminutive proportions) commanding presence and authoritative glare.

Know the man?

Why—no, Mr. Rogers had said apologetically. I am afraid I have wasted your time.

Later it was reported that as he spoke, he *glanced nervously* left, then right, as though *subconsciously*—

No? asked the deputy, blinking twice. Once again, he pushed the photographs toward Mr. Rogers. Nothing at all—he said—*familiar* about the fellow? This fellow—here. In the photograph. Nothing *at all*?

Here the deputy paused again, smoothing his mustache, which looked as though it had been brushed sharply against the grain. He looked hard at Mr. Rogers, who was now *beginning to sweat*—his face growing red with a confusion that was, even to himself, becoming *more and more difficult to explain*.

No! Mr. Rogers said again. His hands flew to his face—*a dead give-*

away, as any observer of human beings in compromising situations well knows. With one hand he adjusted his eyeglasses, and with the other he relieved a phantom scratch beneath his left ear.

No, I can with some confidence declare— he said. But here his voice faltered and he failed to complete the sentence.

Mr. Robins, the deputy said. Mr. Robins, Mr. Robins. Blink, blink. Raymond, he said. Come, now. It's all right. Everything will be all right now, Mr. Robins. Come home.

So that was how, in the second-to-last week of November 1932, Raymond Robins was returned to New York and the care of his wife, where—after only a brief stay at a well-appointed sanatorium outside the city—he regained his senses fairly quickly and was reestablished in his usual role in politics and society.

ON THE AFTERNOON THAT Raymond Robins returned from the dead, the Indian and Alden walked together and mulled the story over, turning it this way and then that. Perhaps, they considered, the real R. Robins had not returned at all—still holed up in some other out-of-the-way town somewhere, or else, having become more of a pain in Hoover's backside than everyone already supposed (he had, over the past months, become increasingly vocal about his disappointment in the government's continued refusal to recognize the Soviet Union), he had been hauled off somewhere to be otherwise disposed.

It is of some interest to note, on account of what happened next, that the Indian had a curious look on his face as the case was discussed. That, after a while, he became thoughtful and said that it did not seem to him to be, as it had seemed at first glance, a story of resurrection— but of death; he just wasn't sure whose. It could be Robins's, he reasoned. Perhaps a doppelgänger had been unearthed somewhere to replace him. That Mr. Rogers had been a real, honest-to-goodness businessman quietly going about his own life in Whittier, North Carolina, only to be surprised one day by the image of R. Robins, to whom he did bear an uncanny resemblance but of whom he—not a political fellow—had never until that moment even heard, let alone known.

That Mr. Rogers's hand had thus fluttered to his face not in *feigned* but in *genuine* confusion, whose dartings, left to right, of the eye had not revealed any *subconscious* doubts or fears, any panic at having been finally *routed out, exposed* . . . That, instead, everything was quite on the surface. That he was merely attempting to *make sense of*, and simultaneously searching desperately for *some way out of*, the bizarre predicament within which he had found himself. Perhaps, the "sanatorium" toward which "R. Robins" was at this moment, thanks to the loving direction of his wife, bound was really only a metaphor—the Indian suggested—for a state-of-the-art reeducation center that would include various different levels of "motivations" for the new "R. Robins" to comply with the constructed story of who he was and why, and what he would do next—which was, of course, the most interesting part of the story. No matter if the current R. Robins was "real" or not, it was certainly interesting to ponder what was *at stake* now in his *being* R. Robins in a way that no one, no doubt even R. Robins himself, had ever thought to ponder before, and it was just as they were beginning to ponder this that the Indian set off on a story of his own, after mentioning in passing that he did not believe that any one of us had any real or final right to the body that was his own.

When you think about it, he said, we all live our lives out in borrowed bodies, do we not? And as Alden nodded, considering this in the philosophical light he believed it had been thrown, the Indian added that it *did* happen, quite literally sometimes—as it had, for example, in the case of Arthur Sinclair, whose body had been borrowed from a prison guard in the Siberian wilderness back in 1919. Arthur had told him about it himself, the Indian said. About how he had walked for three days on borrowed feet, too tired to guess the connection they had to another man, before he woke up one morning and they were his own.

Alden must have looked incredulous. Even at the best of times to speak of Arthur, of whom nothing more had been heard since the afternoon following the riots, made him uncomfortable—and now here was this absurd story, which the Indian recounted with a straight face, as though it were something he should actually *believe*.

Yes, the Indian said, nodding. It was true. He had not even had a chance to look the man whom he had borrowed those feet from in the eye—on account of being surrounded by such a powerful darkness. A darkness, perhaps—the Indian added, after a moment of reflection—not so very unlike the darkness R. Robins had known before he, too, was "raised up" into the body of another man.

Their pace had slowed—it had become as ponderous as the Indian's tone. Alden waited for him to explain; for him to establish, somehow, what he had just said safely within the bounds of . . . a joke, or a metaphor for something, if that's what it was.

When he did not, Alden hesitated.

Do you—? he began. But then again he paused. It was all too ridiculous even to warrant further inquiry. Still, something compelled him to ask. Believe that? he finished finally.

When the Indian did not reply, he added, Arthur's story—what you just said.

The Indian's step faltered. He glanced briefly toward his companion, and as he did so, Alden's eyes slid, unconsciously, away. Something in the gaze disturbed him. He wondered what sort of information this subtle shift in his own gaze might have revealed, if there had been anyone present interested in its being so revealed—but then he saw very clearly that there had not. The look that he had, just a moment before, found too penetrating to bear, and from which he had averted his eyes, had not even been directed at him. He saw now that the Indian was in fact looking straight past him, toward some invisible point on the horizon—as if he were not even present at all.

Still, the sensation of that gaze—which had not even been directed at him—was one that he could always recall later, whenever he thought of the Indian—or of Arthur. And so vividly that he would almost feel it again—touching every hair on his head, and sending itself in ripples down his spine.

Shortly after that, they parted. As they had done on so many occasions before. Alden's path veering to the left and the Indian's continuing straight ahead, in the direction he'd been bound.

..

THE INDIAN MUST HAVE traversed the distance between the point at which their paths had finally diverged and the basement flat he shared with Aida and the child in record time. Alden was unfamiliar with the pace of the Indian, naturally, when he was not accompanying him, but there is no doubt that he walked at a rather quick step because, as Alden later calculated it, it took the Indian no more than forty-seven minutes after they had parted, at half-past five, to return home and get himself blown into so many unrecoverable parts.

The next day, the front page of the *Post*, as well as every other newspaper in the city, reported that the explosion occurred at exactly 6:17 p.m. That it had ripped through the building in which the Indian was found, reducing it—and two neighboring houses—to rubble, and killing not only the Indian, but two Polish sisters, and a stray dog that had reportedly been seen pacing the streets all day. The wife and child of the Indian (who'd had, the newspaper confirmed, known Communist ties) had avoided the blast; the wife was, at that moment, being held for further questioning.

Alden tried hard to appreciate the fact that—at least—as the newspaper indicated, Aida and the child had survived, but—perhaps because this fact was weighted equally against the fact of the Indian's death, and the deaths of a stray dog and two Polish sisters—he could not seem even to register the news. The details included in the account seemed, he reflected to himself, to create not a story at all, but only the effects of a distant constellation—each point equally suspended by and disconnected from the last. In this way, the Indian, John, existed in equally direct and abstract relation to the explosive materials that were later detected on the premises, and the time of day, 6:17 p.m., when these materials had apparently erupted—so that as Alden read over the article several times it became unclear to him if it was the materials or the time of day that had killed him. But there was one point in this constellation of facts as they assembled themselves before him on the page that stood out. He soon realized it was because it was not a fact at all. So closely did it resemble the rest of the points of the story according to which he had so far oriented himself, however, that he read the article through several times before he noticed it. The recovered materials did not seem, the article reported, to either "indicate or merit" the explosion that had, at 6:17 p.m. at the corner of Heckman and First, subsequently resulted, the known details of which the article then went on to explicitly state. The question—upon which, Alden realized, all the disparate points in the story were hung—was: What missing element had caused an explosion nearly three times the velocity of that indicated as a possibility by the materials retrieved at the scene of the crime?

He must have read the article through three hundred times, until the words on the page danced in front of him, and recombined in increasingly meaningless sequence and, finally, the article held no meaning at all. All day people came and went, banging through the door, causing the ever-increasing pile of loose pages in his in-box to scatter uselessly across his desk. When this happened he would merely collect the pages and return them to the in-box, before retraining his attention to the front-page news, where, once again, he combed the words for content that it would not and could not possibly reveal. How badly he wanted to give that flimsy paper a shake and have the facts settle somehow differently on the page! But no matter how many times he read the piece, or shook the paper between his fists, or turned dully around in the small office only to sit again at his desk in order to confront the page once more, the facts stubbornly remained, perfectly detached from one another, and yet refusing to be in any other way arranged.

THERE WAS NOTHING TO do at the end of the day but go home. He started out of the doors as usual, and turned toward the Mall. He could not help but slow his pace as he approached, waiting for—with every moment, expecting—the Indian to arrive. Though he told himself he would not come; though he contained within him the hard knowledge (precisely the size and shape of the letters that had assembled themselves that morning on the *Post*'s front page) that he would not, there was something in him, larger and more substantial, that told him that he would. It settled in his chest, very solid and real, and he walked all the way home with that very real thing inside him that told him that the Indian's footsteps would, at any moment, intersect with his own.

A whole week went by like that. Alden walked to work and numbly attended to his tasks. By the end of the next day he had regained the usual equilibrium between the incoming and outgoing files on the corner of his desk, and after a while he even began to take some pleasure in the methodical rhythm of the tasks—the same tasks that had, just days before, driven him nearly mad with restless boredom. He wondered, as he gazed around the office at the people around him who were bent to their own respective tasks—accomplishing them methodically and with the same vague pleasure that had previously bewildered him, but with which he now accomplished his own—whether they had not also experienced some terrible shock as disruptive to the system as the Indian's death had been to his, and whether the diligence with which they bent to their tasks, despite—or rather because of—their tedium was only the effect of that lingering trauma. Perhaps, he thought further, it was in this manner that one detached oneself from a constellation of facts from which one was finally excluded. It was, after all, he saw then, in the same detached manner with which he now moved through his days that his mother, and even his father (in a blunter and more ruthless way), moved through theirs—as if intent on protecting that one single thing at the center of themselves that remained real and unbroken. He had not known, until that point, what it was to suffer a great loss, or even a loss at all—so he did not realize at first that what he at that moment identified as "real" and "whole" inside him was not that way at all. That he was, as he would realize only much later, merely suffering from the common effects of a broken heart.

—

EACH DAY, AS HE LEFT THE OFFICE, SLOWING HIS PACE AS HE APPROACHED the Mall, he expected the Indian to appear, and each day the Indian did not, until finally Alden did not expect him anymore. And just as he ceased to expect the Indian—or much of anything at all any longer—

the professor appeared. He did not intercept Alden's steps as the Indian would have, but stood waiting for him in an oversized coat at the corner of Fourteenth Street and Pennsylvania Avenue, his eyeglasses frosted with the steam his breath made against the cold air.

Hello, he said, as Alden approached.

Hello, Alden replied.

He did not extend his hand toward Alden as he had done when they had first met, and Alden did not extend his own. Instead, just as Alden came level with him, he simply turned on his heel and fell in step beside him and they continued on together, in the direction of the Mall. They had walked almost to Fifteenth Street before the professor spoke again.

You'll be pleased—he said—then paused. He looked at Alden, a smile playing at the corner of his lips. They want you for one of the party's *special institutions*. (He added singular emphasis to these final words.)

Alden looked at him blankly.

Underground work, the professor said.

They continued in silence.

I thought it best, the professor began again, clearing his throat and hunching his shoulders as if against the wind, though it was blowing at their backs, to wait a while before speaking to you. Before . . . making any decisions.

Quickly, but pointedly now, he glanced in Alden's direction. So quickly, indeed, that Alden failed to catch his eye.

AND SO WINTER PASSED and spring began. Toward the end of April, and owing, in the end, more directly to the professor's connections than his own, Alden left his position at the *Post* and was given a job at the State Department. At first his responsibilities and the pattern of his days seemed hardly to change at all, but still Alden felt pleased by the professor's obviously increased confidence in him, and he began to see much more of him than he previously had. On one occasion—perhaps three months had gone by, perhaps more—the professor had even said to Alden, with a teasing glint in his eye, You know, I am almost feeling that we can begin to trust you. However—he had continued hurriedly—you still have much to learn. *Humility*, he'd said—laying heavy emphasis on the word—perhaps, most of all. Before his downfall a man's heart is always proud.

IT WAS AROUND THIS TIME, shortly after Alden left the *Post* and took up his job at the State Department, that he first met Joe Hodge. Joe was only a few years older than himself, but had already completed two years at Columbia Business School, read everything that Marx, Lenin, and Louis B. Boudin had ever written, been sent overseas on "underground" work, and was now rising steadily through the ranks of the State Department. Joe was solid—a man on whom anyone could depend. He was even built that way, with the thick neck, broad shoulders, and big bland eyes of an ox. Even the way he spoke was so steady and sure that by the time he had said anything you were already convinced not only that you'd heard it before, but that you'd probably said it yourself. It was this that made him such a good spy. In fact, though, by the time Alden met Joe (and despite how solid he still appeared from the outside, right up until the end), he had already been badly rattled.

Alden's own position at the State Department had been arranged, once again, through a mutual acquaintance of both his father and the professor—Barney Coates. Coates was a longtime party member, but in the fashion of Joe he was the last person you would suspect to have any belief or opinion that differed from your own—it didn't matter what those beliefs or opinions might be. From time to time, Coates might have been accused of being a tad "sentimental"—which was what, back in 1933, they were still calling anyone who leaned a little left—but like Hodge, he was "solid," and there wasn't even a whiff of suspicion surrounding him or his various "sentimental" endeavors and affairs until just before the war, when nearly everyone else had been shaken from the tree.

So it was Coates who got Alden the job. At the suggestion of the professor, he'd approached Alden's father personally about an opening that Alden (he'd said) might be just the man to fill. They needed someone quick and smart, Coates told the Judge—but without too much experience. They generally preferred it that way, he'd said. To train their men themselves. Not have them come in with *bad habits* already thoroughly ingrained. He was sure the Judge would understand. And didn't he also agree—Coates wondered—that (even with how young Alden still was) it was about time to seriously think of the way he would make his way in the world? And that there were a lot more avenues that a man might travel down, were he so inclined, within the government, than along "newspaper row"?

Judge Kelly had, of course, heartily agreed. But mentioned, as it was only fair to do, that there *had* been a time in the fairly recent past when he himself had questioned his son's sense of . . . proportion in certain matters. Alden had, however—he was quick to add—certainly learned a lesson or two since then, and—he added even more quickly—he certainly appreciated Coates's offer; opportunities like that, as they both knew for a fact, didn't come knocking every single day.

Coates had nodded solemnly—then assured the Judge that the job he proposed (one with some "real direction and responsibility") was just the thing for someone Alden's age, with a questionable sense of proportion. At that, the Judge offered Coates his hand—gone, uncharacteristically, limp with gratitude.

IT WASN'T UNTIL HIS third week at the office that Alden first met Joe. He came into the office with that swivel of his head, first left, then right, that Alden would come to recognize. It was not as if he were looking for anything over his shoulder—just as though he were straightening out a kink in his stiff neck.

Then he pulled up a chair and sat down squarely in front of Alden, hanging his hat on his knee.

Joe had grown up in New York, on the Lower East Side, and had been involved with the party since the age of fourteen. At first he had gone to all the meetings and rallies; had even helped organize the last great Young Pioneers Christmas celebration in Madison Square Garden in 1930. He had decorated the revolutionary Christmas tree himself, and stood ringside during the boxing match that had been organized between "science" and "religion." Heywood Broun, that eternal champion of the underdog, had acted as the referee; no wonder, then, that "religion" won in the seventh round by KO before "God" himself walked in—dressed in a business suit and followed by a coterie of priests and rabbis (fifteen-year-old boys and girls dressed in oversized bathrobes) to present the award. It had been, Joe recalled, a terrific party.

But then, just a few months later, as Joe was finishing up his second year at Columbia, he was asked to go underground. At first he was flattered—but pretty soon he understood what sort of sacrifices "underground" work required of him. He quit school. That was fine by him, he said. But then they asked him to quit the party (the great Christmas celebration of 1930 was his last hurrah) and move to Midtown. He hardly saw his friends any more and spent his time shuffling between the docks, in order to greet Soviet spies (who came off the boats without speaking a word of English), and their apartments (which, in contrast to his own modest digs, were aggravatingly well appointed). It had driven him crazy, he told Alden, after they'd established their odd friendship—in which, over drinks after work each evening, Joe would mutter away over his whiskey, becoming increasingly distracted as he spoke.

At first—on account of the intense aggravation and loneliness of underground work, and the time he had spent in the Don River Valley and the Upper Caucasus—it had been a relief for Hodge when he got the State Department job. But by the time Alden met him, only six months on, he was getting nervous as hell again.

What are you worried about, Joe? Alden would say. They'd suspect the President before they'd suspect you.

It was true. Even if you counted Joe's Young Pioneer days, he was the least sentimental person you were ever liable to meet. Still, when the subject turned, as it often did with Joe, to the Don River Valley—the five weeks he had spent there in the spring of '32, just prior to landing his job with the State—his voice would begin to tremble, then break.

You know what I'd like? he'd say—and as he spoke, his thick hand would shake so much it rattled the ice in his glass. I'd like the President himself to go over there. See if that wouldn't inspire him a little. Make sure he did everything he could to keep that sort of thing from happening *here*.

But look, Alden would say, that's just what he's trying to do.

It was the spring of 1933, Roosevelt's first hundred days. Even the most sentimental among them believed, at least, that the worst was over.

Just because it's not written down in a book somewhere, Alden said on one occasion in an effort to cheer Joe up, doesn't mean we can't recognize a good thing when it comes. Hell, you might miss the revolution, he said, if you've got your nose buried, looking for it in the pages of a book!

At that, Joe had nodded seriously over his drink, but his pale eyes strayed. He glanced quickly to his left.

Yes, I would agree with you there, he said, but he seemed distracted now, as though he no longer remembered what it was he was agreeing with, or what had been said. Then in no time at all they would be back at the Don River.

If he could just see those kids, he'd say. Staring up at us like that. If he could just see it like I did. Hear—like I did—what *hunger* sounds like. Hear a man, turning on his own children; saying, *Why don't you kids just go ahead and die*—

But that last word would get so stuck in poor Joe Hodge's throat, he'd have to stop to clear it. Then he'd glance around, like there was that crick in his neck, before beginning again.

The "New Deal," he'd scoff, sensing Alden ready to cut in—that's politics for you, not revolution.

But *that's*—Alden would burst out, exasperated, and referring to the story to which Joe repeatedly returned—*the past!* At this, Joe would nod solemnly; say that, in principle, he agreed, then glance first left, then right once more—as though he were actually looking for it to catch up with him.

AT THAT TIME, IT was still commonly believed that the famine in Russia, of which there were still only scattered reports, was a mere invention

—a propagandist's ploy of the most conservative type. But the Utopian vision of Stalin's Russia, in which Joe, too, had once fervently believed, and been so eager to see with his own eyes, could not now be scoured from them. As hard as he tried, he could not rid himself of it. It had a stranglehold on him so tight that, he admitted—after a few drinks had loosened up his throat enough so he could speak of it—he often found it difficult to breathe.

It comes over me, he told Alden one evening, all of a sudden, like that. Like someone's got their hands on my throat. I see them. I see those kids in front of me—just like I saw them then, and I get this sick feeling inside.

They don't look human, see! Just . . . looking at them—I can hardly bear it. Even then, I just wanted to—to get the hell out. But then I thought about that. About how despicable that was. To look straight into the face of something like that, and think only of myself. About *getting away*. Getting *out*. Out of that filthy little hole . . . with those filthy kids staring up at me. As if—as if I could *do* something!

There were the rumors, too, Joe said. That those, you know, who had managed to survive had done so only by eating the flesh of their own kin. Can you even imagine—? Joe said. No. Thank God. You can't. But I can, he said. Do you know what it's like to live like that? (Staring straight ahead, past Alden now.) All those images, mixing about in your head the way they do in dreams, so you can't even tell any longer what's real and what's not?

At dinner with my wife, say— Joe said. Hovering over a bite of food. The color might drain suddenly from it; I won't be able to move my fork an inch closer to my face. The entire meal will start to stink. And then even the color of my wife's face—my beautiful wife—will begin to drain. I'll start to hate her. And—and all of it. It all just starts to— *disgust* me, see. The way she—my wife—just continues to sit there and eat—as though ravenously—digging at her food. She starts to look like a jackal, sitting there—ripping the tiny carcass of a duck or a quail on her plate. Picking at the little bones. Once in a while taking one from her mouth and laying it at the side of the plate—her bright white teeth, the only thing suddenly with any color, flashing.

I start to wonder to myself if she would eat me—if it came to it. I start to feel afraid. I can feel the cold fingers of fear, like little nails scraping against the inside of my throat. And because I think I might start to scream, I have to get up and go out back, and pace up and down a little just to cool myself off. I try to think about other things. I do simple arithmetic just to calm myself down. To convince myself that there are still simple equations in the world—the existence beyond me of something larger, more enduring, than the images that shift and change so constantly before my eyes.

But I can still feel it. Even as I calm myself, and make my way back to the table. To my wife, my comfortable rooms. Even as my wife looks up and says, Is everything all right? And I say, Yes. *Yes.* I can still feel it in the back of my throat as I speak. It doesn't ever go away. It lingers, and each time it comes over me it stays a little longer, so I fear that one day it won't go away at all. That one night I will not be able to return; that I'll leave my wife to line up her little bones at the edge of her dish alone; to clatter her knife and her fork on an eternally emptying plate and wonder what's keeping me; why I don't return . . .

ONLY THEN WOULD JOE look up. A little puzzled—to see Alden, still there, staring back at him—as if he had, indeed, only just then awakened from a long and complicated dream. He would shake his head, even smile a little. A sort of shyness, Alden thought—embarrassment, even.

But it was not that. Like every solidly built American man, Joe was not easily embarrassed. It was simply not in his constitution. It was only later, when Alden thought back on that smile (it was really just the hint of one, his thin lips curled up only very slightly at the corners), that he recognized the look Joe Hodge gave him in those moments for what it really was.

It was pity. Pity that Joe extended toward him then. Not the sort of self-satisfaction that is so often mistaken for pity, but the genuine kind. A pure gift—an offering. And so the shyness that Alden had detected a moment before, from the great, impassable Joe Hodge, who, at the age of only twenty-seven and at the peak of his career as a Soviet spy, might have been in full daylight mistaken for the thirty-first President of the United States, was due to the fact that in those brief moments he was completely unprotected, unguarded, and in so being, recognized in Alden what Alden did not: his ignorance. Which, in a pure moment of generosity, Joe took as his own. So for those few moments as Joe looked across at Alden, they were ignorant together—though Alden did not know it then. Joe felt then, for both of them, what it would take Alden many more years to understand. That they did not, either of them, deserve their fates—whatever they were going to be.

And then it was over, the look was gone. Joe would get up, pay both of their bills, and then, with another little shake of his head, walk out into the night—for a very brief moment a carefree man—leaving Alden to mull over, and make what sense he could of the stumbling confessions that had tumbled from Joe's mouth, like a man in a dream.

IT WAS NOT ALWAYS like that, though. In a different mood, Joe would talk cogently about the time he'd spent in New York working underground. Brag, almost, about how different things had been back then.

That had been real spy work, he said. Now everything was just politics—too easy. Before, all communications between Moscow and New York depended on microfilm and invisible ink. Codes had to be smuggled in. By Germans, for example, working on the Hamburg-American line—slid beneath the glass of Woolworth's pocket mirrors, or the backs of dental plates. Even once they had safely arrived, it was no easy process to decode them. They'd be triple-typed and in need of a bath of potassium permanganate before, at last, the red-brown ink of the Russian text suddenly appeared between the lines. How easy the Soviet spy had it now! Joe said. If he had even a few of his wits about him. How simple it was for him! To make "a clean sweep of just about anything he wanted, and, to boot, a whole lot he didn't."

He'd become agitated just thinking about it. Even angry. Which was odd, when you considered the situation. How he, too, would have found himself suddenly in a very bad position (as soon enough he did) if it turned out not to be quite so simple anymore.

The problem, Joe complained, was not too *little* information—but too *much*. There were too many factions and divisions, he said—and all of them working at cross-purposes. But there was one thing they all had in common, Joe said. They were all glutted with opportunists—those whose "investigative" efforts so far had only served to make them greedy and soft. They just enjoyed it all a little too much. Shopping at Woolworth's, eating American food—even making American babies (whose citizenship served as a security device for them, just in case the revolution failed). And their "spy" work? Joe said. It consisted of nothing more rigorous than the research of a graduate student! In Russia, American spies had trouble getting their hands on a phone book! In America—everything was open and for the taking. At first they couldn't even believe their luck. They bought up patents by the truckload, Joe said. Ordered technical manuals for aircrafts and explosives. Bought endless amounts of sample powders directly from the explosive manufacturers—who sent them out indiscriminately, eager for business. It was with sheer amazement that the newcomers settled into their new lives. America. Where everything, including spy work, came easy!

He recalled, for example, Vladimir Burtinsky—whose orientation was one of his first underground tasks—gloating over his drink (of which he was overly fond, and which would soon prove his undoing) that the country was in fact *built* for spies. (Less than a year later Burtinsky was killed as he exited a bar. He had been last seen flashing a roll of bills recently won at a game of craps—in sheer delight at the incredible role of chance in his affairs! Shortly after, he was mugged, and left to die in the street.)

It was discovered only later that Burtinsky had, some time before, been taken in by a con man: code-named Crumb. For a price, Crumb supplied Burtinsky with false transcripts of recorded conversations between foreign ambassadors, the authenticity of which Burtinsky did not doubt, and the sensational quality and content of which he was particularly proud. For months—until just shortly before his death, when at last he became suspicious—Burtinsky passed these false documents on to Moscow. Finally, though, he had no choice but to cable Moscow, admitting his error: "We now must assume that there is no Vernon," he wrote, referring to a previous wire. "That he and others were fictitious creations by Crumb, which served his own purposes and sizably increased his remuneration."

It is an open question, if Burtinsky had not met his own end in the way that he did due to the pleasure he took in his newfound freedom to increase or decrease his own remuneration at will (he had, apparently, spent the majority of his money and time in America gambling and drinking—often appearing at party meetings either still drunk from the night before or fighting such a terrible case of alcohol-induced vertigo that it was necessary for him to lie down prostrate on the floor during meetings, insisting from time to time, with his eyes closed, "I'm still listening"), whether or not he might have met the same fate as so many other spies who, after some similar gaffe, toward which so many of the spies who made their way into the country were prone, would be recalled to the Soviet Union only in order to swiftly disappear.

There was a growing awareness of what this meant around that time—due mostly to people like Joe Hodge who had returned from assignments in Russia as rattled and pale as he, and recounted, in the stunned monotonous rhythm of sleepwalkers or the criminally insane, what they had seen. Many returning spies, they reported, were simply being shot. This was, if uncomfortable, at least relatively easy to imagine. More difficult were the accounts of the gulags, and not least because it was nearly impossible to get anyone to talk with any sort of certainty about what they'd witnessed there if they'd been. They would rub their eyes and shake their heads as if they no longer trusted themselves or their memories—which seemed to them now more like nightmares than anything they'd actually *seen*.

BY 1934, AMERICANS, TOO, began to be "recalled" to Moscow—only then to disappear. Most of these disappearances were so cloaked in mystery, or obscured by conflicting information if any could indeed be gathered, that they were hardly worth speculating about—and, at first, the majority of American party members remained largely unconcerned. If you weren't careful, or didn't play by party rules, it was little wonder— they told themselves, and one another—there were some "accidents" along the way.

Alden, like nearly everyone else at that time with connections to the party, thought of these incidents in more or less the same way they had thought of Burtinsky's penchant for gambling. If one was foolhardy enough to play with chance, sooner or later one was bound to lose. It was the most basic American principle, which they continued to take on faith: people, for the most part, asked for, and therefore deserved, what they got.

But right after the creation of the first New Deal projects, there was a rash of prominent party defectors and, as more and more of them began to speak out, an increased sense that—when it came to Moscow—not much was ever left to chance. One of these defectors was Elizabeth Gregory, an acquaintance of Joe's from his Pioneer days.

Alden was introduced to Elizabeth one night shortly before she disappeared. She had been visiting the capital "on business," and, for company, had taken along her disarmingly beautiful cousin, Bits—whose one intelligence (Elizabeth said on her behalf) was that she kept well out of political affairs.

As far as Joe and Alden could later recall, Bits herself never uttered a single word of her own the entire night. She wore her blond hair in tight curls like a china doll, and once Alden caught a glimpse of her teeth—each one small and pointed like a fox's, in perfect rows—when she cut the evening short with an exaggerated yawn. Except for that one—final—occasion, though, she kept her mouth shut tightly in a painted line.

Elizabeth was the opposite of Bits in every way. She was a big, soft-looking brunette. The sort of girl who made you want to just go up to her and squeeze. Not attractive, exactly, but not unattractive, either. She had big lips, which she painted sloppily with bright red lipstick, and her mouth hung, just a little, so you almost didn't notice, to the side. Joe said that was on account of some early childhood paralysis, but if you didn't know that you would just assume that she had developed the habit of talking out of the side of her mouth.

And she talked. Nearly incessantly. But it was the sort of talk—just like Alden's old friend Jack Nancy's—that you hardly noticed. It was more like listening to yourself think. One thing just slid, naturally, into the next. That was why it was such a surprise when Bits suddenly opened her mouth and cut the evening short—flashing those perfect little teeth. Everyone got up in a hurry after that and went home—made shy, suddenly, even after the six or seven drinks they'd tossed down and the relative obscurity of the darkened corner of the bar in which they had taken cover. The ordinary boundaries (which had seemed, for a very short while, gloriously, to have been expunged) had been, in that moment, suddenly, disastrously, reimposed.

But before that happened, they had felt—all of them—the way that one only can when one is young and has drunk a little too much in the company of strangers. And years later, Alden had to admit (though he was not then, and never had been, a religious man) that there existed in him a hope—an expectation, even—that at the end, regardless of when and how it came, he would be granted at least some semblance of the feeling that coursed through his veins that night, as he drank steadily with Joe Hodge and Elizabeth and little foxlike Bits, when they were all still, more or less, who they said they were and believed themselves to be, and no one had yet fled, or gone thoroughly underground, or fallen ten stories to their death, or otherwise disappeared. When, to the contrary, they were all very much alive, and even Joe, with his heavy head and his stiff shoulders, seemed to be part of an unstoppable buzz inside Alden's brain, and everything was lit from the inside by a single *glow*.

Maybe he was in love with Elizabeth, or Bits, or even with Joe himself that night—it was that sort of a glow. Even though all night Elizabeth talked only of her work with the Agricultural Adjustment Administration, of its—her eyes had flashed—*absolute corruption*, and though she even intimated at times that she feared, if not that she *foresaw*, in its entirety, *what was to come*, as she flashed her dark eyes again, and her slightly off-kilter smile hardened at the edges—an expression that Alden would read only later, against the grain of time, as a kind of desperate *plea*—he felt it. For the first time, he was in love. But was it not, perhaps, after all, with that possibility itself, that he was in love? The possibility that it was already too late for anything—even, or especially, love? Did he not feel a distinct thrill, that night, of their proximity to everything going, as it very soon afterward did, so terribly wrong?

But still, there was no way of knowing then, despite how that *not knowing* might have thrilled them, what would become of Elizabeth—or of themselves. It was that very night, you see, that Elizabeth made up her mind to quit the party. She announced her decision definitively— just before the fox's yawn interrupted their little party and they were scattered shyly again, out into the street.

ONLY THREE MONTHS LATER, Elizabeth Gregory disappeared. Suddenly, and without any explanation. No trace of her was ever found. And, although at one point, early in the war, it was suggested that several dozen American "former employees of the Soviet Union" were being held in Russian prison camps, by then there was a real war, and Russia was an ally, and the rumor died out after having made only the slightest ripple.

Joe was the one to tell Alden—one afternoon after work. He drank more, and more rapidly than usual, as he spoke, but it was as if each drink, rather than making him drunk, made him more and more sober, until he seemed to become absolutely frozen and Alden had to steer him from the room like that. He very nearly had to lift Joe's legs for him in order to get him into a cab, and then try not to worry about what would happen on the other end—if he would recognize his own house when he got there, and be able to make it inside. Or if instead he might, over the course of the short ride, solidify into a final, unmoving effigy of himself, and this final loss. A loss that was, indeed, perhaps the last blow for Joe, because it was by then only a few short months before he, too, would disappear, leaving only slightly more of a trace.

Alden knew he should have gone with Joe that night, but he couldn't bring himself to do it. He couldn't bring himself to look at him one moment longer, in fact, and packed him off more perfunctorily than he should have, or than the situation warranted. He turned quickly, before the cab had even rolled out of sight, anticipating the relief he would feel once he was released from his company—which had become, in the past weeks, even before Elizabeth's disappearance, increasingly oppressive. But, instead, he was greeted only by a familiar emptiness, then a sudden sweeping sensation of his own loss. One that stretched into the furthest and most unreachable corners of his heart, which until that moment he hadn't known had existed at all.

LATER, ALDEN WOULD RECALL the way Elizabeth had, in support of her sensational announcement, listed off the things that had, she said, *pushed her over the top.*

One, she said, counting the point out on one hand, was the famine—which, "as Hodge here can attest," had been anything but a fantasy. Two: the lengths the party had now gone in order to recruit new members. Dressing up like Ku Klux Klan members, for one example, she said. Had they heard that one? In order to scare up the black vote. Three: the absolute lack of concern for the security of party members doing underground work. She herself had already seen half a dozen friends disappear "underground" forever (Alden could not help but feel a chill run down his spine at this—had this already happened to him? he wondered. How would he know it if and when he himself, finally, "disappeared"?). And then, of course, there was the issue of those "invited" to Russia, for training or to sort out a delicate "misunderstanding." The list went on.

In fact, Alden didn't realize until long after that night—until he had folded Joe's stiff limbs into the cab and it had driven away—that, despite the chill that had inadvertently run down his spine at Elizabeth's words, he had failed to properly listen. In part this was because of the disarming beauty of Bits, who had been seated across from him, and in part it was because of the (not unrelated) growing warmth that had all that time been spreading through him. It was nice to have company. To be buoyed by the flirtatious vitality of Elizabeth's steady stream of conversation—

an interruption to the monotony of his days—and he remembered thinking that he would need to find more women to spend time with after that.
That they really did provide the necessary release from the strain of the
working day. That without women, one might become—like Joe
(though even he had a wife)—on the whole, really quite dull. By the
time all of Elizabeth's fingers had been counted out flat, Alden found
that he had missed more than half.

Sooner or later, Elizabeth had said then, everyone who once supported the party (and here her eyes flashed at Joe, causing Alden to wonder suddenly if there was anything, or had been anything before, of a
romantic nature between them, if such a thing was possible) would be
grossly disappointed.

But Alden was himself not terribly troubled by the warning. And as she
continued to speak, he was still hardly listening, instead thinking primar-
ily now of the possibility that Joe had indeed had *relations* with Elizabeth,
and if so, what kind. Wondering if Elizabeth was as freethinking in her
sexual practices and policies as she was in other areas, and if perhaps
tonight was not a night that would end triumphantly for them all.

THINKING ABOUT THIS MONTHS later as, after disposing of Joe, he
walked home alone, made him feel about ready to burst with longing. It
was a strange, inside-out feeling—almost as though he had burst already,
and so wanted now only to be able to put everything back together again.
He hadn't felt that way since he'd read the news about the Indian on the
front page of the *Washington Post*. Everything in little pieces inside
him—even his blood coursing through his veins suddenly in pieces, like
little bits of glass, so that as he walked he actually began to itch all over
in this crazy way. He had to stop in the middle of the street, even, in
order to scratch at his skin, and the way that his fingernails felt on his
arms—their absolute impotence on the surface of his skin, as they failed
utterly to disrupt whatever it was that was at that moment coursing
through his veins—was so enraging to him that he simply sat down on
the road and cried.

He hoped, as he cried, that he did so mostly for poor Elizabeth Gregory, who had so recently disappeared, but it was more probable—and he recognized it, as he continued to weep—that he did so for Joe, and for himself. And perhaps a little for the Indian—though he had been dead by then nearly two years. Or (but here he began to tremble) for Arthur. Whose name he could hardly bear to pronounce inside his mind.

It was almost as if even the rough idea of the man he had betrayed—in so vast a way, and so irredeemably, that he could not even understand exactly how, or in what form—touched too close to . . . whatever it was . . . that knot at the core of himself, which he could not undo. On account of it, whenever his mind drifted even close to Arthur, or Douglas, or the events of the twenty-eighth of July, 1932, he flinched in almost physical pain. He thought of what the Indian had said (it was, he realized only then, very nearly the *last thing he'd said*), about Arthur—how he had lived out at least a part of his life in the body of another man, and he wondered if perhaps such a thing, without his noticing it, had happened to him. That somehow it was Arthur's life and not his own that—having inadvertently stumbled into it somehow—he was obliged to carry on with now. It would explain the physical pain he felt, increasingly perhaps, at the memory of him—when he could not, by his usual means, keep it at bay—as well as why Arthur himself, so far as he knew, had all but disappeared—

Perhaps that was just it, he thought. What had happened to Elizabeth. To anyone that just . . . "disappeared." They found themselves living out their lives in other people's bodies: too exhausted by the effort of it to guess at how they had arrived there, or why.

WHAT LITTLE JOE KNEW of Elizabeth's actual "disappearance" he had told Alden that night. Just as she had promised, she had—shortly after they had met in Washington—*quit the party*, as well as her related (unmentioned, but no doubt intricate) involvements with its more sensitive inner workings. And just as she herself had anticipated, an invitation to Moscow had followed promptly—an invitation she had the audacity to refuse. It was directly after that she disappeared. Bits reported that she simply didn't return from work one day. After quitting her job at the

AAA she had got a job as a secretary at a small law firm, Johnson and Mallory, in the Bronx—thanks to the assistance of her uncle, Bob Mallory (Bits's father), one of the partners there. Bits herself worked in the office, but had taken the day off sick. Elizabeth had left in the morning for work at the usual time, but was reported to have left the office at the end of the day half an hour after she ordinarily did—five-thirty in the afternoon. She had appeared, by all accounts, "her usual self" throughout the day, but, after she took her hat from the hook in the office's small antechamber, poked her head around the corner to the inner office, shared by three Johnson and Mallory employees, including Bob Mallory himself, said good night, and offered a general wish that the weather would turn soon and relieve them all of the unseasonal humidity (it was only mid-April), she was never seen again.

ALDEN REMEMBERED VERY LITTLE of the rest of that spring. He went to work. He returned. He rarely talked to Joe anymore. Sometimes he saw him in the coffee room at work, and when he did they would both nod solemnly and then one or the other of them would duck his head back into his sandwich or mug of coffee or give a little jump and turn on a heel in an unexpected way as if he suddenly remembered he had forgotten something in another room. To see big Joe Hodge jump was unusual, but it became less and less so as April gave way to May and then to June and the humid air settled in, as if it had no thought any longer, nor ever would, of any other place to go. Then, sometime in the middle of June, Joe suddenly became very still and quiet again, almost like he had the night Alden had sent him off by himself in a cab. Alden thought that this was probably on account of the weather. Imagine that. The man was about to jump to his death from a tenth-floor window, and Alden attributed the strange calm that had settled over him to the oppressive heat.

But by the time Alden learned of it, he had his own worries, and so the details of Joe's death, accompanied by whispered speculation as to whether or not he was a spy, on whom and what he had or might have been spying if he was, and the sequence of events that led to his untimely end, Alden barely heard.

Just two weeks before, he had been approached by Ted Wainwright, Coates's boss. It had been brought to his attention, Wainwright said, that there were certain *arms* of the party that stretched into the very *highest* government positions, and the thoughts of the repercussions of such an extended *influence* were making it difficult for him, and most conscientious right-thinking Americans, to sleep at night. Was Alden so afflicted?

Alden swallowed, and nodded yes.

It was not a lie. He had not been sleeping properly since Elizabeth Gregory had disappeared, and that was going on two months. Without the company of Joe after work he went on solitary walks, which extended longer and longer into the evenings. The light didn't fade until about nine o'clock that time of year, and it would be dark by the time he got in. He would then enter the silent house and go into the kitchen, where he would help himself to whatever he could find. Sometimes there would be a plate left out for him, other times not—there never did seem to be a pattern to it he could rely on. He would wash down the cold meal with a glass of milk, and count the interval between the humming of the refrigerator and the moment it shuddered loudly and was still. Sometimes—and for this, too, there was no regular pattern, at least not one he could easily discern—his mother would call his name out in her high, brittle voice. More often than not this occurred in the moments just after the shuddering motor of the refrigerator had dropped him momentarily into deepest silence.

Is that you? she would call, and each time, without fail, no matter how much or even at times how eagerly (so desperately lonely was he in those days) he waited for it, it would make him jump to hear it when it came. His heart would quicken and he would have to pause in order to regain his composure before he responded—a note of annoyance, on account of being surprised, always therefore pronounced on his tongue.

Yes, it's me, he would say. Who else?

Sutton would already be tucked upstairs, where she now spent most of her time. His father, equally, kept to his end of the house; more and more they heard from him only the steady *swish swish* of the old riding whip as it beat time against the empty air.

Despite how much Alden anticipated it, even longed for it, each time his mother's voice actually arrived—when he was reminded, with the sudden introduction of her voice, that he was not alone; that she was waiting for him behind her semi-shut door, and, now that his identity had been confirmed, expected him to enter; to duck his head down to hers, be kissed by her pale mouth, and sit beside her afterward for a while, her hand from time to time reaching out to touch his own—he would feel a deep resentment begin to stir in him. He no longer wished to be in any company, least of all his mother's. He did not wish to seek out the correspondence any longer between the voice that had disturbed the brief calm of his after-dinner quiet, as he had swallowed the last of the milk from his glass in the dark kitchen and the refrigerator had shuddered to its brief repose, and the lips that had raised it. Though when the voice did not come he would always await it with anticipation (which was, he told himself, not truly desire but only the usual degree of anxiety produced when there is any degree of uncertainty about what the immediate future will bring), once it came, he could with conviction regret it bitterly, and it was a relief to do so—because it had come.

After he left his mother, planting a final kiss on her thin hair, saying, Good night, Mother, I must leave early again tomorrow, she would often delay him, one excruciating moment longer—reaching up to catch at the sleeve or the lapel of his coat.

You are less and less yourself these days, Alden, she would say.

Given this, or a similar excuse for genuine annoyance, he would bat her hand away.

Good *night*, Mother, he would say, and climb the stairs to his bedroom, making a note of the pale glow from beneath his father's office door. The perfect symmetry of the light that leaked from beneath it to lie in a triangle there at the foot of the hall never altered in dimension, day after day. It existed there just as surely as the silence of the house existed—aside from the occasional throat clearings of the refrigerator, or the other small sounds, so ordinary and rhythmic in nature as to not even be heard. (What else, he would wonder sometimes when by some chance occurrence his attention was drawn to them, did he fail to hear?)

Sutton's room, her door shut tight, would confront him at the top of the stairs. Often, he would linger just outside it for a while, pacing back and forth in as natural a pattern as he could, so that the loose board by the rail would make its characteristic squeak—according to which anyone within hearing range was always alerted to any traffic in the hall. But the door always remained firmly shut, and after a time he would locate his own room, and at the center of it, his bed, and would fall into it with such intense exhaustion that he could almost *see* sleep as it approached him in a wave.

But then, just at the peak, when he was certain there was no escape—that in another moment it would be upon him—he would be wide awake again, and there was nothing to do but lie there in the darkness—sometimes all night—only falling into a fitful sleep in the early hours of the morning. But this early-morning sleep, with its repetitive dreams of ordinary waking tasks (of the alarm's buzz, of greeting his father as he descended the stairs), would be so tedious it never seemed to provide him any rest at all. So real did it all seem that if it were not for the fact that he could nearly always count on a single skewed detail—a missing tooth in the mirror, an egg that refused to boil, a stranger's face looking back at him where his father's should have been—he would never have known that he was dreaming and quite possibly never have awoken.

So HE COULD ANSWER the question posed to him two weeks before Joe Hodge's death in all honesty. He was certainly one of those who was losing sleep. It did not take much, after that, for Ted Wainwright to persuade him to report everything he knew: of the professor, of the Indian, of Elizabeth Gregory, and of Joe Hodge himself.

Two weeks later Joe was dead, and Alden was making arrangements to leave the country, with the help of a letter from Wainwright and his father's connections to the embassy in France. By the middle of August 1934, he had already reached Paris, having purchased a second-class ticket bound for Liverpool—then traveling overland to Dover and, by ancient steamboat, to Calais.

IV.

(INTERLUDE)

THE CANDIDATE OF MANY PARTIES.

A Phrenological Examination to Ascertain What His Political Principles Are.

18724—Holes Torn Out by Huge Shells, Where Our Boys
Fought in Belleau Woods, France.

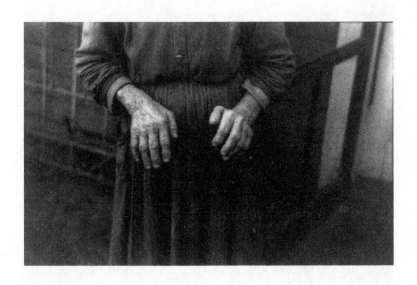

No. 8. Original Drawing.

Mr. Birchall and Miss Relph.

No. 8. Reproduction.

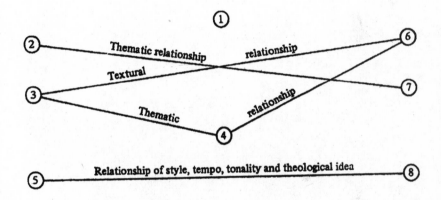

TABLE I   Frequencies of One Million Digits

BLOCK NO.	0	1	2	3	4	5	6	7	8	9	X²
1	4923	5013	4916	4951	5109	4993	5055	5080	4986	4974	7.556
2	4870	4956	5080	5097	5066	5034	4902	4974	5012	5009	10.132
3	5065	5014	5034	5057	4902	5061	4942	4946	4960	5019	6.078
4	5009	5053	4966	4891	5031	4895	5037	5062	5170	4886	15.004
5	5033	4982	5180	5074	4892	4992	5011	5005	4959	4872	13.846
6	4976	4993	4932	5039	4965	5034	4943	4932	5116	5070	7.076
7	5011	5152	4990	5047	4974	5107	4869	4925	5023	4902	14.116
8	5003	5092	5163	4936	5020	5069	4914	4943	4914	4946	13.051
9	4860	4899	5138	4959	5089	5047	5030	5039	5002	4937	13.410
10	4998	4957	4964	5124	4909	4995	5053	4946	4995	5059	7.212
11	4948	5048	5041	5077	5051	5004	5024	4886	4917	5004	7.142
12	4958	4993	5064	4987	5041	4984	4991	4987	5113	4882	6.992
13	4968	4961	5029	5038	5022	5023	5010	4988	4936	5025	2.162
14	5110	4923	5025	4975	5095	5051	5035	4962	4942	4882	10.172
15	5094	4962	4945	4891	5014	5002	5038	5023	5179	4852	16.261
16	4957	5035	5051	5021	5036	4927	5022	4988	4910	5053	4.856
17	5088	4989	5042	4948	4999	5028	5037	4893	5004	4972	5.347
18	4970	5034	4996	5008	5049	5016	4954	4989	4970	5014	1.625
19	4998	4981	4984	5107	4874	4980	5057	5020	4978	5021	6.584
20	4963	5013	5101	5084	4956	4972	5018	4971	5021	4901	6.584
TOTAL	99802	100050	100641	100311	100094	100214	99942	99559	100107	99280	13.316

V.

Douglas

THE BONUS TRAIL. ANNANDALE, VIRGINIA; JOHNSTOWN,
PENNSYLVANIA; HARRISBURG, PENNSYLVANIA; WASHINGTON,
D.C., AUGUST–DECEMBER, 1932—ALBANY, NEW YORK;
WASHINGTON, D.C.; STAFFORD, VIRGINIA, 1933—VARIOUS
LOCATIONS ALONG THE EASTERN SEABOARD AND THROUGH-
OUT THE MIDDLE WEST, 1933–1934—WASHINGTON, D.C.;
WINDLEY KEY, FLORIDA, 1934–1935

Each day Douglas rode into the city with Chet to look for his father, hitching a ride with one of the farm trucks that drove in from Annandale every morning and returned every afternoon. Douglas would sit up on top, and more often than not Chet would tuck his long legs into the cab and sit talking to the man who drove. Sometimes there were two men in the cab, and then they would sit three abreast. When there were three in the truck, Chet would ride up top with Douglas. Douglas liked it best, though, when Chet rode in the truck and he rode on top, so that he was all alone up there for nearly an hour, which was the time that it took them to get into the city. In that time,

sitting up there alone, with the wind rushing by him, Douglas's mind
would be blank and clear, as in the days, which now seemed so long
ago, when he had worked beside his father and it had seemed that nothing had ever or would ever change, and the hours stretched as long and
unbroken as the Kansas sky. When the only interruption he could have
imagined was the look that would come over his father's face sometimes just before he'd take off running, Douglas after him. His heart
pounding in his chest—bursting with the twin desires he could not
separate in his mind: on the one hand, to overtake his father, and on
the other for him to remain, as he always did remain. Just ahead. His
strong back tilted at an angle to the flat field, the sweat on his neck
gleaming—wetting his shirt in the *V*-pattern that birds make when
they fly, all together, in a known direction.

Having until very recently known only the repetitive, instinctive
rhythms of the seasons and of parental love—the latter interrupted only,
also as if instinctively, by his father's habitual bursts of anger toward his
mother and himself, and his mother's fiercely reactive affection, which
she used against them both—it was strange to discover that there were
countless other patterns, possibilities, and limitations to things, and that
the endlessness that had so far defined his concept of the world in fact
opened off onto something even more endless, which he was incapable of
conceiving at all.

THEN THE TRUCK WOULD lurch to a halt and Chet would say, All right,
boy, and Douglas would jump down, and feel the heavy thud of his feet
hitting solid ground.

They learned nothing of what had happened to his father and did not
speak of it—or any other thing. When they returned in the evening,
they would sit together in silence, staring up at the sky, and there would
be only the clattering sounds of pots and pans, the intermittent shouts of
men from the surrounding camps, and, once in a while, the high-pitched
yip of a dog.

It was into the space of that silence, or near silence—just as the
increasing weightiness of the night sky pressed its vastness and its mys-

teries upon them, and its utter incomprehensibleness began to take—for each of them—the form of sleep that Chet told Douglas one night that he'd heard of a farm that was hiring. Just south of where they presently were, he said—and that he did believe Douglas stood a fair chance of landing a job.

Douglas was wide awake again, then, in a hurry. He propped himself up on one elbow and looked at Chet, who was sitting up, too—his hands on his knees, staring off in the dark.

You could start tomorrow, Chet said. I believe it's what your daddy would have wanted. Rather than hauling into town every day, risking trouble on his account—and half starved, too.

He looked at Douglas. The cut on the boy's forehead, received on the day of the riots, had healed, leaving a purple scar—just visible beneath his low fringe.

What do you say? Chet said.

But there was nothing to say.

THE NEXT MORNING DOUGLAS woke early. He stood up, and stomped his feet to get warm. It had been a stifling hot summer and even the night before, as he had finally drifted off to sleep, he could still taste the sourness of humid air. But sometime during the night it had turned cold.

Chet was still sleeping and the whole rest of the world must have been, too, because there weren't many sounds—only the call of a bird here and there. Douglas rolled up his blanket and sat down on it, and as he sat there—waiting for Chet to wake—it seemed very certain to him that everything that had happened or was going to happen had already happened: that there was nothing unreal, or unrealized, in the world. That everything, instead, was material—existent before him.

The first tentative, almost plaintive notes of the birds he had heard when first waking had grown by that time into a terrific swell of noise, but it had grown gradually—so gradually that he had not attended to the transition, and so could not account for it now. He closed his eyes and tried to hear each sound as it had first occurred, when each was still itself alone, independent of any other, and after a while it seemed to him that he could hear the way each note wove its way among the others. But then he was not sure whether it was the notes themselves he heard, or whether each, in intersecting with the other notes in the air, had already changed, and he could not help perceiving them that way.

He was wondering this, his eyes closed, when Chet woke—his voice (as he cleared his throat, swore out loud, then got up to shake his arms and legs just as Douglas had done, to get warm) interrupting and thus changing all the other notes around him once and for all. By the time Douglas finally opened his eyes, Chet was standing in front of him, looking at him. Then Chet turned, picked up his blanket and bag, and said, Let's get a move on, then.

So Douglas stood up and everything was as it had been and would be. The ground solid: stretching empty and cold in four directions. And the birds just noise overhead.

THEY WALKED FOR ABOUT a mile 'til they reached the junction where, on previous days, they had flagged down a ride into the city. This time they waited and let four or five trucks go by without waving or thumbing a ride. Then the same truck, a great big flatbed, that had picked them up the morning before pulled up. The driver was the same. A thin man, who kept glancing around him, as though he didn't want to get caught looking at anything.

This is the man can find you work, Chet told Douglas. The man leaned from his truck, gave them a nod, then let his eyes dance around for a while, asking them how did they do, and if the sudden cold hadn't taken them by surprise.

Without waiting for a reply, he ducked his head down to light up a cigarette, which turned out to be packed so loose that its flame leapt up and would have singed his long eyelashes if he hadn't just in time waved it like a match, so that at last it settled itself into a fierce and single glow.

All right, Douglas said. To Chet, who was standing with his hands out as if he had been asking a question.

Douglas shrugged his shoulders and shifted his bag—his father's name on its side, ablaze in red letters—from one shoulder to the next. He had a hard time looking at Chet, and Chet at him. Neither was looking at the other and there was nothing to say, but Douglas said anyway, I hope it won't be a very long while, and Chet let his hands fall down abruptly as if what the boy had said were the answer he was looking for.

No, no, son, it won't, he said. You can count on that. I know where to find you, so your daddy will, too. He cleared the phlegm out from where it had collected; as he did so, his Adam's apple reared in his throat. Then he reached out his arm again, and held Douglas by the shoulder, this time hard enough that Douglas could feel the pressure of it through his coat. Then Chet dropped his hand and said, Well, good luck to you— and Douglas turned and opened the door opposite the thin man, who had by then nearly breathed in the entirety of his cigarette, it burned so fast, and the door creaked on its hinges and made the most god-awful noise as Douglas got in beside him, clutching his bag tightly to his chest. Then the thin man flicked the still-burning end of his cigarette out the window on his side and gave a short wave to Chet, who stood, still shivering a little, by the side of the road, though the sun had come up by then—and they drove.

WHEN THEY GOT WITHIN a mile of the place, they could see that a crowd had gathered outside a locked gate.

The thin man drove up and tailed a group of men walking at the far end of the crowd.

What's this? he said. Though it was clear as day.

Hullo, said the man nearest to the truck as it idled beside him. Lemme guess, he said. You all lookin' for work?

Well, yes, sir, said the thin man. This boy here. I promised his daddy I'd find him some work, and that's what I am plannin' to do.

Well, let us know where it is when you find it, said another man without turning his head.

Yes, send us a postcard, said another.

But nobody laughed, and the thin man swore under his breath.

We've been crossed, looks like, he said to Douglas. Then he stopped the truck by the side of the road, got out, and kicked it. Douglas waited a moment and then he got out, too. He didn't know what to do or where to go or if the thin man would expect him to go along with him or not, or how he was going to wait for Chet or his father for very long at all if there wasn't any work.

The thin man appeared to be waiting for him, so he double-stepped to catch up and they wandered up the road, catching up with the stragglers they had spoken to a moment before.

Where you all headed, then? the thin man asked, and the near man swept his arm ahead of him, indicating a general direction.

Some of us is going on to Johnstown later today. They say the mayor there will put every man to work who comes.

Johnstown, eh? said the thin man.

There was no reply.

Well, yesterday I heard the same about this place, the thin man persisted. I bet you did, too.

Yesterday it was probably true, one man returned. But today ain't yesterday and they ain't hirin'.

We got here 'round six o'clock, the near man offered. Looked about like it does now.

Well, you figure there'll still be work left in Johnstown when you get there? the thin man asked.

Nothin's sure, the near man said.

It'll be yesterday again already by the time we get there, said the far man. But the way I figure it, it might as well be yesterday as today or tomorrow.

The thin man hesitated. His eyes danced as he walked, as though it were his eyes rather than his feet that were trying to keep pace. He glanced toward Douglas quickly, then away.

You figure you could take the kid? he asked.

They had slowed their pace just outside the gates where the crowd gathered. The mood was dark but subdued—as though everyone had come just in order to be turned away, and no one had expected any different.

The near man said, What? Because he hadn't listened or hadn't heard.

I said, you figure you could take the boy? the thin man said, nodding his head in Douglas's direction. I promised his daddy I'd get him some work, but I ain't headed as far as Johnstown. If you took him along with you there, I figure he could get work just as right as anyone. He's young, and I ain't known him long but I could almost swear he's a good worker and wouldn't trouble you none.

He turned to Douglas. That right? he asked. You a good worker, son?

Douglas nodded his head, but the near man was already shaking his.

I ain't got nothing like a guarantee, he said. Still, if the boy wants to come along, I ain't gonna stop him.

The thin man nodded his head gravely, his eyes still dancing. The near man stretched his hand out to the thin man, who hesitated before taking it briefly in his own.

Much obliged, said the thin man.

I told you, the near man said. I ain't offerin' anything.

Much obliged, the thin man said again, not hearing. Then he turned to Douglas.

I'll let your daddy know, he said. I'm headed back that way tonight. I figure it's the best I can do for you and him both and that he can find you there just as well as anyplace. You can be sure, he said, when I see your daddy—

He's not my daddy, Douglas said.

When I see him—the thin man said again—I'll tell him where you'll be.

Douglas stood there shaking his head, but he couldn't reply now because if he opened his mouth he would cry. So he kept his mouth shut. But when the thin man looked at him square again he was still shaking his head.

Well, I don't know what else yer gonna do, the thin man said, and he shook his head, too. For a while they stood there like that, side by side, both of them shaking their heads.

There ain't no work anywheres else.

The thin man took off his cap then and rubbed the top of his head, which was bald and glistening. Douglas still did not risk a word as, finally—returning his cap to his polished head—the thin man touched Douglas on the shoulder, then turned.

—

CECIL CADON AND THE REST OF THE CADON CLAN TOOK CARE OF HIM pretty well after that, almost as if he were one of their own—though it was three days before anyone remembered to ask for his name. He was always just "son" or "the kid" until, on the third day, Cecil pointed to the name written in red letters on the side of Douglas's bag and asked if it was his. No, Douglas said. It was his father's name.

Only when Cecil looked at him funny did he remember to add that—of course—that also made it his own.

The Cadons were from Texas. Cecil was eldest. He'd been a rodeo clown but one day he busted his knee getting thrown and he wasn't any good clowning anymore. Next there was Mick, and Mick's son, Curly. Curly was a half-wit, and never said a word. His hair wasn't curly but straight and hung on his forehead limp and slick, and when one day Douglas asked about that, Mick wound his finger in a tight circle around his left ear and stared at him.

You never noticed the kid's brains is curly? he said.

Oh, Douglas said. All right. I noticed.

Finally, there was Smoke, who was youngest, aside from Curly. He was almost as silent as Curly was, but not so stupid, and after a while Douglas got to notice that it was Smoke and not Cecil who decided the way things went, even though that was not how it appeared. It was Mick and Cecil who did the talking. Smoke just sat there and nodded his head. But whenever he did say something, even just a single word sometimes, or head off in one direction or the other without announcing where or why, well, the rest of them would always follow. So after a while Douglas got to see the sense to his name, too. Whatever direction Smoke headed—that was the way they went.

THEY ARRIVED IN JOHNSTOWN on a boxcar that was full nearly to overflowing—and every one of them, like the Cadons, Bonus Army men. Each time the car pulled into the station it seemed more boarded the train.

Ho' up, they'd say. Move on over, soldiers, you got room for one more.

More often than not there was a bottle of something to pass around, but there never was anything to eat among them. It got to bother Douglas; he couldn't put his finger on it. How it was these soldiers could lay their hands on whiskey like it was water, but couldn't ever find a loaf of bread to eat. But the reason was simple enough, and he realized it after a while. Liquor didn't always have to be liquor, but bread always had to be bread. And it always cost something.

From time to time a fight would break out when the jug had been passed around a reasonable number of times, but it was always quelled pretty quick, and usually it was Cecil who did it. He'd yell out, *Yeeeehaaauup*, and everyone would turn, surprised, and stop whatever they were doing or whatever it was they were fighting about. You boys jus' gonna make the road stretch out longer than ever if you keep on involvin' yerselves like that in dis-agree-ment, he'd say.

Sometimes it wasn't a fight at all—just a sideways glance or a discussion that rankled the clown, and he would let out his yell and everyone would ho' up. But as the ride wore on, some of them began to get sore about it, and say, What's it to you, Tex, can't a man open his mouth around here without hearin' you yip?

This ain't no dis-agree-ment, one man said, mocking Cecil's Texas drawl. He had just been called out by Cecil for suggesting that Waters (who had disappeared again) could only be bothered to look out for his men when it suited him. Is there any one of you, the man asked, looking around, hard, at the collection of soldiers slumped against one another, and against the rattling wall of the train car, in dis-agree-ment with that?

No one said a word, and Cecil didn't, either. Only the *clickety-clack* of the train could be heard—every man's face trained on Cecil.

After a while, Cecil just shrugged. So long's there ain't no trouble, he mumbled, pulling his hat over his eyes.

For a while, peace did reign in the cramped boxcar. Douglas closed his own eyes for a time, then opened them again and looked around and saw that nearly all of the men had their eyes shut tight, too. They were slumped against the walls of the car in such a way that their shoulders bounced and rattled and even their heads banged sometimes against the metal of the car with a steady beat, but even that didn't wake them. At times their faces were briefly illuminated in the moonlight, which came in, in fits and starts, through the gaping door as the train trundled into open country and then plunged (disappearing once again into darkness) through a tunnel of trees. The night was so clear and the sky seemed so open and vast that it was a wonder to Douglas that God could not see straight down from above and see all the faces of those men lit up as clearly as he could in that light—which he himself had thought to throw on them. Most of the time it seemed to Douglas there was good reason why God did not take notice of every-thing that was going on all the time. Even though it is said he can keep his eye on every living thing and keep dominion everywhere, Douglas was more often of the mind to forgive him when, from time to time, things got overlooked, because human beings—they made it very difficult, the way they were always so foolish and mixed up and confused and never knew themselves if they were coming or going and would do one thing and say another or the other way around. It would be no wonder that in looking down from any sort of distance, a being might become confused as to the general direction and intent of actions down here on the ground and there-fore would have a terribly hard time knowing which way to direct a man or what would be the most obvious thing to say or do to lend a hand. And then there was the weather, too, and the terrible distance that seemed always to exist between the earth and the sky, and so most times it seemed to Douglas no wonder that certain things went unnoticed or ignored.

But on a night like that one, there seemed no excuse in the world; no reason that God could not look straight down from wherever he was and see, just as clear as Douglas himself could, how dead tired those men were, and how hungry and desperate and poor, and find some way to comfort them. See how all alone in the world Douglas was, and his father—wherever he was at that moment—was, too, and do something about that. See how poor Curly's brains had got all twisted up in his head and unwind them for him, and just generally take stock of the situation down here. In those moments there seemed to be not much mystery at all, and everything seemed very wide open and plain to see, and as Douglas looked at all those men's faces in the moonlight, empty of whatever resentments or expectations they generally had, he thought that each and every man was deserving and that there wasn't any sense of bringing any man into the world if he wasn't going to be in some way provided for and looked after, or at the very least checked in on from time to time.

Then, just as the sun was starting to come up, creeping its way through the low branches of the trees, there arose a new quality to the stillness, and with the sudden introduction of form (the trees just beginning to sharpen their edges against the sky) and the introduction of sound (that first sharp call of a bird, still hidden among the branches, which would seem not to lessen but to heighten the silence, to bring it personal and near) that stillness would deepen and deepen 'til you could hardly stand it anymore. Even the steady tread of the wheels on the tracks below seemed to become present in a way that it had not been all night. That steady rhythm, the sound of their own passing, seemed to become a part of the quiet. It seemed to sing out—to answer the lonesome cries of the birds, who were just being discovered in the trees—and everything was, for a moment, utterly changed and changeless. Just as—Douglas thought—it always had been, and always would be, as far as he could tell, with the dawning of every new day.

ON THAT PARTICULAR DAY, however—the last before they would arrive in Johnstown—the train ground to a halt just as the sun had begun to rise. The abrupt alteration in momentum roused everyone from their sleep. It occurred to Douglas in that moment, as he watched the men stir and wake, that a man could and would become accustomed to every discomfort just so long as it was regular. If, like the steady rhythm of a train, which had pounded the men's heads against the walls of the car as they drove, it continued to pound. So, it was not (he considered) nor could it ever be, discomfort or suffering that roused a man, or made him seek change in the world.

Well—what was it, then?

No one said anything for five minutes or more—everyone still expecting the train to move again; for it to establish the rhythm and regularity according to which they might drift off, once more, into much-needed sleep. You could almost feel it—the way the men willed it to begin; willed themselves to be lulled back to sleep—for the train not to have arrived yet at its destination. For it—perhaps—never to arrive there. It was easier, after all, to exist between points of arrival and departure as the train made its way, with no seeming direction at all, precisely because there was only one direction to go in—the one that had already been laid out ahead. In every man's heart, therefore, as in Douglas's own, there was the same secret dread of the next port of call.

After something more than five minutes had passed, one of the men finally spoke, interrupting the silence. With that, the delay became real, and very soon after that it became interminable. There was a general stirring of bodies, uncomfortable now, and a rumbling of voices as sleep lifted itself, and was soon so quickly and cleanly forgotten that (though just moments before they would not have parted from it for anything in the world) no man desired it, and they were all once more firmly established within the waking world.

The birds began to call with greater insistence as though truly hopeful now that they might communicate something, and everything seemed to take on a shape of its own.

Another minute passed and the men became even more restless.

Do you see anything? someone asked, leaning from the car. It was as though he were asking himself, because no one else had such a wide view.

Swinging back into the car of the train, he shook his head in reply. Nope, he said. Can't see a damned thing.

If I was you I'd get out now and walk the rest of the way, someone else said. But he himself made no move to go.

It was another ten minutes or more before they heard the railway police coming down the line. They could hear them banging their sticks against the cars from a distance of a quarter mile, the metal ringing like an empty bell. Now everyone moved at once. Mick, who had still been seated as though sleeping, his hat pulled low over his eyes, leapt up quickest of all and pulled Curly up by the collar, too. Curly made a loud low sound like a startled deer. He had nothing to gather because he had not unrolled anything from his pack, which his father now fixed to his back. Soon everyone was pouring out of the boxcar and making for the woods, but there were so many men that many of them, including Douglas and the Cadons, who were nearer the back of the car, did not have time to exit the train before the guard arrived. He shouted at them to disembark, but the way he spoke—even with his voice raised like that—it came out sounding more like a question than a demand. Douglas's heart stopped beating so hard in his chest. It almost made him laugh out loud to hear that voice now. They all piled out one after the other as they were told, but now no one was in a hurry, and once they exited the car they all just stood around lazily, as though they were paying customers waiting for a missed connection.

It wasn't until they were all out of the car that someone piped up: Well, hold on, wait a minute now, how come? Why can't we ride in on this train same as ever? Let it get us where we're going same as it's going to get you and itself there?

We've got our orders, the voice said, adjusting itself to a lower—steadier—note. There isn't to be anyone riding in this car when it pulls into Johnstown. Johnstown's full, and they can't use any more travelers—coming from any direction. Personally, I don't care where you fellers are headed, I just know it can't be by train. There's strict orders about that.

He continued up the line, then, and Douglas watched with interest as he went. An ordinary man, his stick ringing on the emptying cars that still stretched out ahead. Once, he looked back over his shoulder—not enough to see them, really, just enough that they registered the glance, and its direction. In a different voice, still—as though neither the one (low and steady) nor the other (troubled and high) he had so far used belonged to him at all—he said quickly: Sorry about that, men.

In response, Cecil hooted like an owl. The rest of the men stood sullen and quiet. Then, when the policeman had rung his way up the line some six or seven cars farther, they began clambering back on board.

Ten minutes later they were on their way to Johnstown again.

THE BEF CAMP WAS set up in an abandoned amusement park just outside of town. It was not hard to find, but when they got near they saw a police checkpoint set up in the middle of the road, which made Mick stop dead in his tracks. Smoke, however, continued straight ahead and soon the rest of them followed, and they just walked right through—the police had their hands full already with a dozen other veterans, both coming and going.

It was clear at a glance that any job or promise of a job in Johnstown had evaporated long ago—but since they had come so far and had nowhere else in particular to go, the Cadons, and Douglas along with them, set up camp, too. The old rides—though they had long since rusted shut—made as good a foundation as any for makeshift homes; some men even claimed the empty swinging chairs of Ferris wheels for their beds, fashioning ladders out of scrap metal to enable them to clamber into them at night. In many ways, life in Camp McCloskey, as the settlement came to be known (in honor of the town's mayor, who had first issued the veterans an invitation to his town), was not so very different than it had been in Camp Marks.

McCloskey had not foreseen the number of veterans who would take him up on his offer, and in response to the flood of men who did—who continued to pour in, even long after Douglas and the Cadons arrived—he organized a special committee that solicited money and food from local and national corporations, in an effort to at least keep everyone fed. But it was impossible to keep up with the demand, and soon McCloskey urged those veterans who, like the Cadons, had arrived long after the last jobs in Johnstown had been filled, to move on.

Most, however—having nowhere else to go, and no way to get there, even if they had—stayed.

A profound hopelessness settled over the camp. The days slid by, one dissolving into the next. Even Waters was now encouraging his men, from Washington (where he was searching out a permanent headquarters for the BEF) to "go home." Just until December, he promised, when Congress reconvened. But December sounded as remote to many of the veterans, by then, as 1945.

For them, Johnstown began to feel like the end of the line.

—

AROUND THAT TIME, A GOVERNMENT INSPECTOR CAME TO THE CAMP. He was a big man who walked a dog, and the dog and he held a curious resemblance to one another. They hadn't been in the camp long before everyone knew them as "the cousins"; the word spread through the camp quickly: The cousins are coming. The man carried a thick book under his arm and consulted it from time to time, but nobody knew for what purpose, and some suggested that it wasn't to any purpose at all. That it was just a big empty book the man carried. Just something to poke his nose in from time to time and make the men nervous as hell.

You reckon they got us all figgered in there, or what? asked Mick.

Sure, they got you figgered, Cecil said. Had you figgered in '17, they sure as hell got you figgered now.

They can figger this, said Mick, and gestured in the cousins' direction.

Oh, hold on, now, brother, said Cecil, but not in his usual tone.

BY THE TIME THE cousins arrived at the Cadons' camp everyone had their honorable discharge and their bonus ticket laid out and smoothed flat before them. Douglas had his father's out in front of him. He had carried it with him ever since, after the riots in July, he'd been released and his father had not. His father had pressed it into his hands at that time and told him to look after it and after himself. If the bonus came through and he wasn't around to do it himself, he told Douglas to take that ticket, cash it in for what it was worth, and send for his mother. Then, just like they'd planned (his father had said) the two of them should buy that little plot of land for themselves—in Virginia, or Tennessee—and not worry after him one bit. He would find them wherever they were (Douglas's father had said)—and just as quick as he was able.

Douglas had kept the ticket in his front shirt pocket ever since, and though he never did take it out to look at it, it gave him pleasure just to know it was there. It gave him even more pleasure to unfold it and smooth it out now, and read again what was promised there. It made it seem real again—which it hadn't in a long time. Like they weren't just—like the Oliver brothers—swinging their fists at the empty air.

THEY WERE JUST KIDS—the Olivers—nine or ten years old, but they used to box together, regular, back at Camp Marks. Somehow (though neither one of them, as far as Douglas could recall, had ever won a match) they always managed to draw a crowd.

It was their father, Mr. Oliver, who organized the fights. A tall man, with a melted ear. Douglas remembered him in particular. He had always found his attention drifting, for some reason—when he was supposed to have been watching the fight—toward that central swirl of melted skin on the side of Mr. Oliver's head. It used to glisten under the glare of the sun; still hot-looking.

His boys—Jonas and Ike, they were called—were pretty evenly matched, though Jonas was older and had a good four inches on Ike. Ike, though, despite being shorter, was solid, and probably the stronger of the two. Also, he had a broad grin and knew how to use it. Jonas was more solemn, but there was something fierce about him, too—a little desperate—which made you want to watch him. Made you want him to win.

The crowd got so thick sometimes that you couldn't even see the fight. It had to be shouted down to you—relayed along the crowd—so that it often arrived conflicted and confused. He's up. No. He's down, he's down. It was sometimes unclear how much of the information eventually received in the more remote corners of the crowd reflected the actual progress of the fight, and how much the progress of its communication. But then it didn't matter, because each fight always ended up the same way, in a draw. Mr. Oliver would suddenly be there in the ring, gripping in his right hand the fist of solemn Jonas, and in his left the fist of grinning Ike. It got to be that you could pretty much count on it. Douglas could not remember a single time when a fight had ended any other way. But people bet on one or the other boy all the same, and instead of serving to decrease interest in the fights, the crowd around them only continued to grow, and every time, just like the last, Mr. Oliver would stand in the middle at the end of the fight and hold up the fists of each son and say, "Draw."

The crowd would just go wild. Not because they wanted it to have ended that way but because more than anything they didn't. So each time that man stood up there and announced that it had ended that way it fed their desire that it should not have ended that way. Douglas remembered how his father and he had shouted first for one boy and then for the other—his father changing his mind halfway through the fight when the mood hit him, because he never wagered, and Douglas following his cue—and how, when it ended and the two boys' hands were raised in a draw, his father would whistle a long, low note and turn to grin at Douglas and say, Well, what do you make of that, boy? I thought that time, Ol' Jonas, he really had a chance. And then they would move off, and the crowd would disperse around them, and Douglas would nod his head as if he, too, had been surprised.

So the cousins made their way, finally, over to the Cadons' camp and inspected their papers, both man and dog with small, dark eyes, short noses, and drooping chins jutted out in identical fashion.

Shaking his, the man opened up his big black book and made a note; then he shook his chin some more. Douglas could see Cecil sort of inch his way over to see if he couldn't get a look at that book, but before he got close the cousin snapped it shut, then looked at Douglas and said, You don't look hardly old enough to be *born* in '17, son—let alone to have carried a gun—and Douglas said, That's right, I ain't. These are my daddy's papers—I'm just holding on to them for him.

Where's your daddy then? the cousin said. If he ain't here.

Douglas shrugged. He didn't want to say. But the cousin glared at him and finally he said, He got locked up a few weeks back.

The cousin grinned.

Wasn't his fault, Douglas said.

Oh, sure, the cousin said. I know what that means. His eyes got darker. Red, eh? He left his mouth open just a little after he said it, so that his bottom teeth showed. They were small and spread apart evenly, so that they looked loose.

Douglas shook his head and Mick and Cecil and even Curly shook theirs. Only Smoke continued to stare hard at the cousins in an impassive way as though nothing had been said. As if the cousins themselves, like everything else, were just a puff of smoke on the breeze that would soon drift by.

No, sir, Douglas said. He sure isn't. None of us is. We're Waters's men.

The cousin snorted. The dog started sniffing the ground but the man soon yanked his nose up in the air and the two of them trained their gaze on Douglas again, then on each of the Cadons, before, at last, they turned to go.

I could write you up, the big man said over his shoulder as he turned. I won't this time. But you remember that. And the rest of you, too, he warned. I know the tricks that get played. I bet half of you ain't ever laid eyes on France; just takes one look, I can see how it is.

Then he and the dog lumbered on to the next camp.

Cecil looked at Douglas. That ain't right, he said. I'm telling you, son, it ain't right. But you best remember what the man said. If I was you, I wouldn't show that ticket—not to no one, no more.

Douglas nodded. Slowly, he began to fold up his father's ticket again.

Don't look so sick about it, Cecil said. It's just—time's all. What it takes. He pressed a hand to Douglas's shoulder. It's going to work out all right, he said. In the end.

Mick let a long breath escape as though he had held it for ten minutes or more. Time, he said. Sure. It ain't likely we're gonna lay our hands on that any more than on anything else, he said. Then he held up his discharge papers and his bonus ticket, pinching them together at the corner so that they fluttered in the breeze and everyone in the little group could see for themselves just how thin they were, and how well, on account of it, the wind blew through them, as if they weighed nothing at all. For a moment Douglas thought Mick was going to let go and have them blow away and be gone, and the rest of them thought maybe he would, too. Maybe even Mick himself believed he would. But then Curly gave a sort of moan. It was just something he did sometimes, so it wasn't connected—not in any particular way—to his father's bonus, or how the wind blew or did not. He would just make a sound like that, all of a sudden, for no perceivable reason at all—high and long like a strangled bird, or something more like the low growl of a stuck badger, sometimes, or a cornered deer. He'd lift up his head so his bare throat was exposed, and you could almost see the noise as it traveled up it. It always gave Douglas the creeps to see it when he did, even though he knew the boy wasn't right in the head and you couldn't blame him for it. But in that moment, the exact moment when Curly made his sound, a sort of fierceness came over Mick's face, and it occurred to Douglas that it was not a thing that a person—not even someone's own father—got used to; the boy being different like that. For a moment or two more Mick let those papers flap in the breeze, but he didn't let them go in the way that everyone—briefly—expected he might, and after a while he folded them up and put them back in his pocket just like the rest of them had done.

It was strange, though. It would have made them sick to see Mick tear that ticket up or to have it float away, but somehow it made them even sicker not to. Everyone, even Curly, detested Mick a little as he tucked his papers carefully away. They hated him and themselves for the thing—whatever it was—that stopped him from doing what, for a moment, he had wanted so badly to do.

When it was done, Smoke leaned back a little. Even he was relieved. He looked straight at Mick, and then at Douglas, and Cecil, and all of them, even Curly (each for their own private reasons, which they could not have said out loud), bowed their heads, and were ashamed.

—

SHORTLY AFTER THAT, McCLOSKEY HIMSELF SHOWED UP AT THE CAMP. He was an ex-prizefighter with a cauliflower ear who spoke out of the side of his mouth.

God sent you here and I'm sending you away, he told them.

A few scattered hisses and boos spread through the crowd.

Hey! McCloskey shouted. I'm asking you. I'm telling you nice. That's more than Hoover ever did for you!

But no one was in the mood to make distinctions. The noise grew louder.

All right, then you bums can walk! McCloskey roared. I'll see you get a damned good start! I won't call in any troopers to massacre you, he shouted at them. I'll put hell on you myself!

CECIL AND MICK, WITH Smoke observing from under the broad brim of his hat, made the arrangements for the Cadons' departure. There wasn't much to arrange: there was nowhere to go, and no way to get there. But for them, like most of the rest of the men, it didn't much matter. One place, after all, was as good as the next.

For Douglas, though—it was different. And now, as he listened to the Cadons assemble their haphazard plan, and considered the arbitrariness of his own progress and direction, he felt a by-now-familiar panic begin to rise. In vain, he attempted to comfort himself (as he had often been able before) by recalling his father's final words. It didn't matter (his father had said) where he ended up, or how long it took him to get there; his father would find him. Him, and his mother, too. Just as quick as he was able.

But this presumed, Douglas reflected painfully to himself now, he might actually *arrive* somewhere. They were words that were true only, that is, if and when the bonus came through and he didn't—on account of it—have cause to travel anymore, in any direction. If, to the contrary, he allowed himself, as he had so far done, to be blown, first this way, then that, in whatever direction, it seemed unlikely—if not downright impossible—that he might, by chance one day, be blown once more across his father's path.

WHEN THEIR PLAN HAD been settled, Cecil and Mick retired. Resting their packs against a miniature railroad tie, they themselves rested against their packs. From time to time, Cecil made a smacking noise as he sucked at his teeth, a habit of his that seemed to comfort him. Other than that, there was only the rumbling sound of voices in the distance, interrupted from time to time by the clanking of tin cups or the creaking of machinery as people settled into their makeshift homes for a final time, or scraped from the profitless bottom of an empty bowl. Peace descended over the camp, but not, despite his best efforts, over Douglas's heart. With every attempt to calm his nerves, they only quickened; his thoughts raced more wildly; his blood pounded more and more insistently in his veins.

When he could bear it no longer, and everyone but himself and Cecil (who continued, from time to time, to gently smack at his teeth) seemed to have long ago drifted to sleep, he approached the older man.

I—I can't go, he hissed. Leaning in, so that he spoke almost directly into Cecil's ear.

As was his custom, Cecil had pulled his hat down low. Now he adjusted it so that he peered out at the boy with one eye. When he saw Douglas staring back, his own eyes wide and frightened, he again adjusted his hat so that now it sat squarely on his head and he could easily regard the boy.

Ah— he began, shaking his head.

And then Douglas knew. He knew, and Cecil knew. That he— Douglas—*would* go. That he would depart, along with Cecil and the rest of the Cadons come morning. That he was as helpless as Curly was to the insistent chance with which he had and would continue to be blown farther and farther from the course that his father or himself had intended or desired.

Ah— Cecil said again, and again he shook his head slowly. But surely your daddy won't think to look for you here, where no man is or will be? Imagine (he said) staying—all alone. Ducking the blows of the mayor as he swings at you from his merry-go-round. If, instead, you come on along with us, and the rest of the army; return to Washington in the fall . . . why, it's there (the older man promised, pulling his hat down again, low over his eyes) that your daddy'll find you.

—

THE TRAINS WERE DANGEROUS NOW—ESPECIALLY TRAVELING EAST. They were often stopped; arrests were made. For a while men were happy enough to turn themselves in at the stations, just to wind up in jail for the night and get a hot meal—but soon enough the jails were full, and nobody gloated anymore over the food, or anything else they might acquire over the course of a night there.

They stuck to the roads instead. Got what rides they could; climbed on the backs of wagons, or stood on the edge of a truck if the load was full, for a couple of miles. More often than not, though, they walked. Douglas was grateful for the boots his father had procured for him what now seemed so long ago. They were still comfortable and firm, and despite the fact that he was always hungry, he had grown at least an inch over the course of the summer, and his feet were not as loose inside them as they had been before. The other men were not so lucky. Once, Mick even offered to buy Douglas's boots for the promise of his share of bread for a week, but Douglas turned him down flat and after that kept his boots on all the time, even while he slept—though Mick, along with the rest of the Cadon clan, was trust-worthy and kind.

··

TOWARD THE END OF August they arrived at Harrisburg—a junction where the road met the Susquehanna River and split, going one way, south toward Baltimore, or the other, toward Bethlehem. A hundred or more veterans, who had arrived some days ahead of Douglas and the Cadons, had already set up camp in an unused factory yard and posted a guard at the "gate"—two busted tractor tires—to control the flow, and quality, of the BEF men who came and went. They had not touched their papers (which they still kept, as always, folded in the breast pockets of their shirts) since they had been inspected some weeks before by the cousins. It was a pleasure to take them out, now, among friends.

Cecil swore to the guard, on behalf of them all, that they were not Reds; that they neither subscribed to nor supported those or any other sabotaging measures that might be used against the Bonus Army; and then they all swore allegiance to Waters, and their ultimate loyalty to the army itself. After that, they were ushered through the "gates" and—their spirits high—began to set up camp next to a former sergeant major, Dudley Sterns, who had led his men in the Big Push at Chateau-Thierry in 1918, and described to them in some detail, as they tightened the pegs on their tarp, those last hours before they "went over the top," when something began to shift within the men in his charge, and in himself. Something so deep, Sterns said, it is often mistaken as having very little to do with men. And it's true, the sergeant major said—his big chest thrust forward in his quality overcoat, which he wore even on that warm September night—it is indeed a thing apart, the thing that a man feels, as he lets go of his last pretensions to a singular life; as he gives himself—his own life—back to the source, and becomes, in the moment he does so, a man among men; which is to say, *more than a man*; which is to say, a great surge, instead, of *energy and power*—

It was from the sergeant major, too—later that evening—that they first heard the news that the officer, Shinault, who had shot and killed two men on the day of the July riots, had himself been shot and killed. A week before—mid-August, Sterns said—he had entered a house on Front Street SW in Washington. He had been shot twice: once in the stomach, once in the head. He'd died instantly. On this much there was very little argument. The rest of the details, however, as they soon learned, significantly varied—depending on whom you spoke to, and when. Most agreed, however, that Shinault had ended up at the house as a result of a domestic dispute between a colored man and his wife. It was the colored man, they said (a certain Willie Bullock, member of the BEF) who had shot Shinault—departing, afterward, through the front door, then swiftly disappearing without a trace. Others, though, maintained it was the *wife* who had done it—and a scattered few supposed it was a third party, yet to be accounted for; that the whole thing had been only later blamed on the colored man due to his (rather loose) affiliations with the army, with obvious intent to undermine the BEF.

Two days later the police had two black men in custody—both named Willie Bullock. Neither, however, turned out to be the right man.

—

DOUGLAS STAYED ON WITH THE CADONS AT HARRISBURG FOR TWO weeks before they continued on together—following the river south until they reached the railway line. It being too risky to ride, they followed the track on foot. Though the going was slow, they had plenty of company, and the closer they came to the city, and fell into step alongside more and more Bonus men, the more Douglas felt certain that—just as Cecil had promised—he would soon be reunited with his father there.

But when they arrived in mid-November, there was no sign of either Chet or his father. Together, Cecil and Douglas traveled the length of the city, inquiring at every Bonus camp they found—but no one ever had any news to share. And as the days passed and still they came no closer to learning anything of his father at all, Douglas began to find his mind occupied less and less with thoughts of finding him. Instead— more often that not; for a reason he could not entirely explain—it was toward Sutton his thoughts began to turn. Wasn't he (he thought), after all, just as likely to run into her on those streets as he was his father—or anyone else? The more he thought of it, the more likely it seemed, and the more likely it seemed, the more he thought of it. The more he remembered (and so acutely that, when the memory came—always as though from nowhere—he had to stop in his tracks, nearly, in order to catch his breath) the way she had spoken to him that first afternoon they'd walked together to the edge of the camp. Her voice soft—almost shy.

Do you miss it very much?

Something about the way she had said it; the way she had looked at him then.

But it was foolish to think of such things. And anyway (he reminded himself) it was Alden, not Sutton, who might be of some help to him now. Alden—who had been there. Who knew for a fact that his father was (except for a single, wayward blow) an innocent man; that somewhere along the line a terrible mistake had been made—which, once perceived, might easily be corrected.

This was, at any rate, what he believed most of the time. Other times—a creeping doubt entered his mind. What if the Indian had finally been caught? If his father's association with him had been discovered? What if his own bag, found that night at the scene of the crime—his father's name stitched in red letters on its side—had been used as evidence against him? He shuddered with shame at the thought of it. But why, then—he considered—if this was the case, would he himself, or Chet, or any of the others not also be detained? And how could a man be held for long, or indeed any time at all, for a crime he had merely witnessed—in which he himself had no part? (This, though, would always send his thoughts directly to the boots on his feet—the mystery of their acquisition ablaze, suddenly, like a hot flame inside him. What if the barman back in Kansas City—? If Jim—?)

But no. He stopped himself. This couldn't all—he reasoned—be about a single pair of boots. Inevitably, then, the thought would briefly flash into his mind: so, what if his father really *was* a Red—as the cousins had suggested? But *no*. It was impossible. He did his best to push the thought—and any other—from his mind. His father was *innocent*. A thing to which Alden—like himself, and anyone who knew him—could easily attest.

But he found as little trace of Alden as he found of Sutton or of his father on the streets of Washington that fall. And when, in early December, he and Cecil approached the courthouse, having at last exhausted every corner of the city—along with the memories of all the veterans, shopkeepers, layabouts, and even schoolchildren who crossed their path—they had even less luck there. No record existed—Douglas was told—of his father or himself having ever been detained there at all.

After that, they stopped looking. But still . . . All through the rest of that fall, and into the winter, Douglas continued to expect his father, and (until they left Washington; he couldn't help it) *Sutton*, to arrive. It could be at any moment, he told himself, over and over again. He—or she—might, suddenly, just . . . *be there*. Arriving, unannounced; in the same way that all things, and every moment (even as they are anticipated) always come.

—

DECEMBER PASSED SLOWLY, AND MORE OR LESS WITHOUT EVENT. JUST after Christmas—his every effort having met with overwhelming defeat—Waters shifted his attention to the spring. Then he moved his troops north, near Albany; Douglas and the Cadons followed.

The Bonus Army could only grow! he promised them. After a winter of training, it would rival any of the world's armies in size and skill—and when it came to sheer determination, it would surpass them all! There would be no *way*, come spring, for Congress to refuse them: by June 1933, Waters vowed, the Bonus Army would march again down Pennsylvania Avenue, one million strong.

BUT DESPITE THESE PROMISES, a cold apathy crept into the Albany camp. Even Cecil became quiet as the winter wore on. He no longer hooted like an owl, interrupting the fights of other men to start one of his own. He grew thin. First just like the rest of them—like a man who has had too little to eat for too long—but then it was different from that. By February, when it came time to divide what little they had managed to procure for a meal at the end of the day, he politely refused his portion. More for you men, he'd say. Then, when they continued to look at him, their food suddenly unswallowable in their throats: I'll come round.

But he did not, and, in the middle of February, he died—sitting upright against a tree at the edge of the camp. It was Curly who found him. He stood out at the edge of the lot one day and howled like a dog—from pure instinct, everyone supposed. Because, like a dog, he failed to understand the great distance that had been introduced between himself and the dead man, and kept tugging at Cecil by the hand as if he could wake him. But one thing he did know as well as everyone else: something was terribly wrong that could not be set right. Poor Curly could not be comforted and continued to moan all night long, and it helped the rest some to have their sorrow spoken out loud like that, in the wild and impenitent tongue of a half-wit. It made it easier to say nothing themselves, and they buried Cecil like that, almost silently, and never said among them any but the most necessary words.

—

BY THE BEGINNING OF MAY, EVERY NEWS REPORT IN THE COUNTRY was already announcing that (just as Waters had promised them) ten thousand veterans were, once again, on their way to Washington. Maybe more.

Even when this did not prove true—when it became clear that the Bonus Army had in fact, over the winter, dramatically dwindled in size; that they did not, nor would not now, stand ten thousand, let alone one million strong, the newspapers, Waters, and even the government itself continued—out of either fear or desire—to say that they would.

In a way, then, it continued to be true. In the way that any promise is true. There were always more troops coming—hovering just beyond, and therefore blurring the edges of what was, within each moment, certain and known. So that, in Douglas's mind, ever afterward—even when the Bonus Bill had been passed for many years and every dime of it spent and forgotten, and all of it had been turned under the wheels of time so finally as to seem as though it had never occurred at all—the Bonus Army was still approaching. Barely visible—an indistinct glow on the horizon: that point at which (as just beyond the last known curve in the road) everything drops away, finally, into darkness; becomes the limit of all things knowable and known.

It was from this direction that Douglas's father, all that winter, also arrived. Transformed: a winged thing in Douglas's heart. Indeed, over the course of that winter, for Douglas and the rest, the entire Bonus Army was transformed in this way, to become something more than it was. Hardly—or, at any rate, purely—real anymore, it took root in the most fragile and remote corners of their minds. After a while, it hardly seemed to have to do with them anymore at all. It was as though (thought Douglas, as he climbed aboard a Washington-bound train one early May morning with—except for Cecil—the rest of the Cadons; as the train lurched and continued unconsciously along its known route, ignorant of the weight he and the rest of the men—their expectations, both personal and shared—added to its load) he had dreamed it all up. That he had dreamed the promise itself: the emptiness upon which it was based—and upon which, consequently, they rode. Yes, everything was still to come, he thought. There was nothing certain at all, and the future—at that moment—was just as distant as it had been or would be at any other. He felt that quite certainly, as he climbed aboard. Felt—as the air began to stir against the conflicting forward motion of the train and then to howl through the open door—how the promise—the desire at its root, which was desperate and primordial; as instinctive as a fish or a bird, which steers itself by some internal compass ever northward in the spring, or southward in the fall—and the emptiness were one; how they could not be separated, and that their union was in fact *the only union*. The very substance—or lack thereof—upon which all dreams, waking or not, are founded, and therefore the single source of all things certain and uncertain in this world: past, present, and yet to come.

—

THERE WERE ALREADY NINE MEN IN THE CAR BY THE TIME THE FOUR of them—Mick, Smoke, Douglas, and Curly—clambered aboard. That made, as one old man pointed out to them then, the unlucky number, thirteen. He had one blind eye, the lid swollen shut, and his good eye blinked and blazed as they came on board. It almost seemed to glow in the dark as he counted them. Then it flashed: One of you all's got to go.

Aw, said another man. He had his hat pulled down low, to cover his eyes. There's fourteen, he said. You just can't see the one hid behind your busted eye.

This made some of the men laugh. Then another man cut in, saying how it was he knew for a fact that the number thirteen was lucky to some, and that luck and most things like it were all in the way that you looked at the thing. This was discussed for some time until the blind man, his one eye still blazing, raised himself to his feet and began to shout.

This train is going to start moving, he said, and if one or more of you is not off it I am going to have to throw you off myself.

Finally, a man who looked too old to have fought in France—perhaps he was a veteran of the Civil War, or of the War of Independence, or of the Indian Wars; perhaps he was a thousand years old, and had seen every battle the country had ever fought from the time the first man encountered its shores, and stood dumbstruck and wondering—mumbled, Well, hell, that's all right, I can understand how you feel, and exited the train.

That made everyone shut up fast, and no one said anything for a while. Douglas didn't know for sure, but he thought it likely that every one of them, including the blind man, was thinking the same thing he was then. Wishing suddenly, like he was, that it had been him to say,

Well, hell, and find another car to board somewhere, and all the way up the line he kept a lookout for the man who had given up his place; who had reminded him, he realized (too late, only after he was gone) of his father—if his father had grown, in less than a single year, into an old man. And also of Cecil. At least the way Cecil had looked in that last month when all of a sudden the flesh fell off his bones and he was hardly recognizable anymore. He got scared thinking about that. About the way that the old man had looked like his father in some ways and like Cecil in others: about how he had recognized him right away, but only realized it too late. So that it was certain (so surely had he recognized him when at last he did) that the images in your mind don't just disappear, but stay with you, always—no matter how much it seems that you come to forget. Also, it got him thinking about the way his father would have changed in all the time that had passed since he had last seen him, which seemed now like such a long time. Not quite so much as he might, briefly, have imagined—but changed nonetheless. Just as he, Douglas, had also changed—because he felt very certain he had.

It worried him to think of it; of how, should he ever see his father again, there would be some things recognizable about him, and some things that would not be—but that he would never be so unrecognizable to Douglas, nor he—Douglas—so unrecognizable to his father, that they'd fail to know each other. He would never be able to simply turn away, even if that was what he wanted. No, he would never be able to pretend he didn't see his father, if his father appeared; to pretend there was another man he was looking for instead—a man who hadn't changed at all. No, his father would be recognizable to him in an instant—but that instant, as with the old man on the train, might come too late. He might just as easily be the thirteenth man on some train car some night as any other man—which Douglas might realize only after he was gone. He might allow him to disembark. Might not cry out after him, or offer to accompany him into the night, or say, You're all right in here, let me be the thirteenth man, and substitute himself, until it was too late. It seemed (Douglas thought then, sadly, to himself) that time moved at such a pace—always at odds with the mind—that you might never come to recognize anything for what it was, or at least not at the precise moment in time when it was, indeed, that thing.

—

ROOSEVELT WAS NOT A BONUS MAN, AND NEVER HAD BEEN. DESPITE this, Waters was confident the bill would pass that spring. And, indeed, things looked very good for the army at first. Arriving veterans were directed to camps set up just outside the city, where—at the government's expense—they were provided with a roof over their heads, an army-issue cot, and three square meals a day.

Even those who, from the start, opposed the "safe distance" the camps proposed between themselves and the Hill did not complain as they drifted to sleep in their beds at night, or lined up for a meal. Douglas regretted the distance for a different reason. It was hardly likely, he reasoned—so far away from the city—that his path might cross with Sutton's now. But it wasn't otherwise all that bad a deal. And besides, as many of the men happily maintained, if the President was willing to feed and house the army, he would surely be willing, sooner or later, to give in to their other demands. A scattered few, however, believed that just the opposite was true. The onetime bandit—Arizona—whom Douglas met around that time was one of those.

You never get anything free, the bandit would say, and he should've known. He was wanted in three states—and it wasn't (he told them) for standing in line. If the BEF veterans were willing to stand in line now, they all might just as well give up and go home, he said. He himself might just as well go back to Arizona (which was the closest thing to home he had, and how he got his name) and get himself hanged. But still, as he said all this, he didn't get out of line, and neither did the rest of them, and very slowly it inched forward, and the closer he got, the more Douglas could feel the emptiness in his belly. It got hotter and hotter, until he thought he was going to burn up from the inside, and when he got to the front and held out his cup and it got filled up, he thought he might bust before he got a chance to sit down and eat, and it wasn't until he had taken a bite or two that he remembered enough to be embarrassed at how hungrily he ate. He slowed down a bit then, or tried to; tried to pretend that each bite was going to be the last, but it didn't change the fact—whether he ate fast or slow—that after only a few bites more all the food was gone, and the bandit—he seemed to read his mind—said, We've been fooled again. You can see that now, can't ye?

But later that same day they were visited by the President's wife, who led them in singing "There's a Long, Long, Trail a-Winding," and sure enough nearly all of them, the bandit included, sang along. It made the bandit sick to think of it later—to recall how all those men had waggled their heads and said, Why, yes, ma'am, when the President's wife had asked if they were all just as happy as could be—and Douglas always wondered if that was because the bandit had waggled his head right along with them: Douglas had seen it with his own eyes. If it was because he suspected that, on account of it, he really wasn't any different from the rest.

Much later, just to irritate him, Douglas would whistle that same tune under his breath, and it would without fail cause the bandit to curse and that for some reason always gave Douglas some satisfaction. And there never was any consequence to it, his riling the bandit like that, because a moment later, as it always was with the bandit, the whole thing would be forgotten. You see, the bandit, he would fire off at the least provocation, but the next moment it was like nothing had ever even happened at all. One time, when Douglas mentioned this, the bandit got to thinking seriously on it and told Douglas that he hadn't always been like that but he figured that he had been at least since Verdun. That after that, whenever his blood rose to a certain temperature, it stopped up the circuits of his brain and there'd be a short fuse and he'd go a bit blank, and that was why he did try his best to keep calm, and, the way he said it, it was obvious he thought he had made a success of it. And why not? He couldn't ever recollect any different, and Douglas didn't tell him.

—

IT WAS NOT JUST FOOD THAT WAS ON OFFER THAT SPRING—THERE were jobs, too. At first they went just to the young, unmarried men, but after a while these restrictions were waived and anyone could apply. And plenty did—despite the unflattering rumors that began to circulate soon enough about the conditions in the field.

How's that for equality? a white man shouted one afternoon in the government camp, raising his fist in the air. Now everyone's a slave!

All the black men and the white men cheered together.

To hell with reforestation! someone else shouted.

Everyone cheered again.

Still, though, every job on offer that summer was soon filled. Even Smoke finally signed up and went his own way—leaving Mick and Curly behind.

Curly, see, he couldn't do any work like that, where you needed any wits.

Douglas stayed, too, on the advice of the bandit, who said that surely something better was just about to come along.

When it did, Douglas, too, left Mick and Curly behind. And he never did find out any more about either one of them—or about how Smoke got along up there in the big woods. He felt bad to leave them because he knew that was the way it would go. Sure enough—it did.

THEY TRAVELED SOUTH, THEN, he and the bandit, and, before too long—just as the bandit had promised—they'd got themselves jobs at a tobacco farm just outside Stafford, Virginia. It was not the best sort of work, the bandit said—but it sure as hell beat working for the government. They would be up before sunrise every morning and out in the fields. That was, as Douglas soon learned, the best—really the only halfway decent—time of day. In the heat of a long afternoon when he would feel about ready to drop dead he was so tired and sore, and the sun on him felt like it had burned its way all the way through, so that it wasn't just burning his skin anymore, but his brain and his heart, he would think back to the way the day had begun, and it would seem to him so good that he wished he could, if nothing else, return to those moments after first waking. When they were just rolling out from underneath the blankets and splashing cool water on their faces from the bucket that hung on a post in the yard. To those brief moments when he'd been waiting in line behind the next man, with sleep still lingering, clouding his brain. Just waiting; anticipating the cool water and then actually feeling it, as it splashed over his face.

It would feel as if that moment were right inside him, when he thought of it; that the water had got in through his ear to his brain. In the middle of the day, he would remember the way that his head had felt then, cool and alive. But then the next morning when he was actually standing in line, waiting for the hit of the cold water, for the blood to rush to his brain and for everything to feel like that—fresh and sharp and alive inside him—he would not feel that way at all. More often than not he would feel (save for the desperate, unbearable heat) just like he'd felt when he'd stood in the field and thought longingly of the coolness of the water—even as he lingered behind another man and anticipated its blow.

HE SPENT THE DAY crouched behind Jo-Jo Hadley—a big man, nearing sixty, whose skin had turned red as a beet and hardened that way, giving him an odd sort of sheen. He had been working those fields longer than he could remember and, because of it, made up for Douglas's slowness in the field before Douglas caught on. He took some pride in that. In showing Douglas the way it was done.

Like this, see, he'd say, expertly spudding the plant he'd taken from Douglas's fumbling hands. When Douglas got quicker he would grunt his approval and beam up at him, saying, You got it now, son, there's nothing to it, and when he did get the hang of it, it got to be that he could do it—

take the plants from Hadley as they churned toward him, with the passion and endurance of a threshing machine—without thinking of it at all.

Soon everything began to blur together, so that he could no longer tell the difference between the cool mornings and the heat of the day, or between any single step in the process of planting, which had by then become one long, interminable task. Because of this, he could never be sure—then or later—how long it was before he woke one morning with a tingling numbness in his hands. Perhaps only a little more than a week had gone by, but perhaps more time had passed.

At first he thought he had only somehow slept on his hands funny, cutting off the circulation to them temporarily—but no matter how hard he shook them out or wriggled his fingers the numbness remained. He was slower than usual that morning, but Hadley didn't say anything. Finally, around midday when they were all gathered to swallow their few mouthfuls of bread alongside of the shaded pathway that ran through the two largest fields, Douglas said, Damn if my hands ain't numb, like I slept on them funny, and Hadley and one or two of the other men, including the bandit and a midget—whom everyone called El Niño, because even though he was small he was still a force to be reckoned with—laughed.

That's nicotine, son, Hadley said. First it gets into your hands and then it gets into your brain, 'til you can't hardly think straight anymore.

One by one the men showed Douglas their hands and he saw that all of them were cracked and swollen, and he wondered how he had never noticed it before, and then he looked at his own hands and he saw that they were red and swollen, too, and he saw very briefly in a flash the way they were the same hands as everyone else's hands.

You got to be careful, nobody ever tell you? the midget said. You got to keep your fingers clean, else they're liable to fall off.

Douglas must have looked pale as death, sitting there with his bread half chewed, his throat too dry suddenly to swallow—just looking back and forth from his hands to theirs. The men laughed again and then someone changed the subject and they forgot about Douglas, and he was left to try to swallow his food, and though finally he did, he could feel it all afternoon. A tight knot in the middle of his throat, like Chet's big Adam's apple must have felt in his.

But then, when they were walking back together through the row at the end of the day, Hadley ahead of him, Hadley turned and said, You don't worry about what they say, son, y'hear? The feeling will come back in yer hands, sure enough. Next week; I promise. Soon's we get paid.

But they didn't get paid next week, and the feeling did not return to Douglas's hands. The morning they were supposed to be paid the field manager said that it would be the week after next, if then. Could be, he said, not 'til the end of the season. And it did no use to grumble, he said, because everyone was in the same boat—himself and the farmer as well.

A week more passed—then two. And though still no one was paid and Douglas's hands became with each passing day increasingly numb, the days began, at last, to take on recognizable form, and just as they did Douglas began to see that they would end. The season wouldn't, he could see now, last forever—and soon enough the men began to speak of the next. Some would head farther south, they said, where the planting went on longer. Some would head west. A man could pick fruits and vegetables there. Though the pay was not so good, at least a man's hands did not go numb, or his brain twisted.

Being able to distinguish between days and see that the season would end meant that Douglas, too, trained his mind around that time toward the future: he began to expect his father again. When there had existed for him just one long moment that he could not measure, he had hardly thought of his father, nor expected anything at all—but now, and against all logic, every moment became one in which his father might arrive. Nearly a hundred times every day he would look up and expect to see his father swinging down the shaded road, Chet alongside him—shielding his eyes with his hand. The way Douglas imagined it, his father was always looking. Sometimes the image of it was so clear in his mind that for a moment when he himself looked up to scan the skyline he would actually *see* his father there, looking back, and for a very brief moment their eyes would meet. But—at that precise moment of contact—his father would disappear, and Douglas would realize that it had once again been only his imagination that had summoned his father briefly into being; that he had not yet arrived, and would not. But despite the fact that he told himself this each time, his father not yet having arrived did not close, but rather opened the possibility that he *would*. And so until the final moment when they were paid out and everyone moved on, he still looked for his father, and still expected, every time he did—even if he looked up a hundred times in a day—that his father would be there, looking back. It got so bad he had to force himself to wait; to count to five hundred, say, before he looked again, or run through the lyrics of "Roses of Picardy," which his father used to sing, six times in his mind. Sometimes he could do it, and sometimes not. He would always be disappointed when he disobeyed his own rules, as he often did, and looked up too soon, and punished himself by picking an even higher number to count to, or an even longer song.

—

BUT THEN AT LAST THEY HAD BEEN PAID, AND THERE WAS NO WORK OR anything else one morning but the heavy stink of liquor lingering in the air. Douglas woke up before anyone else had risen; he sat up suddenly, bolt upright. He only later realized it was on account of the alcohol he'd drunk the night before, because every time he indulged afterward the same thing happened. He would be wide awake suddenly, like he had never been more sober or more awake or alive in his life, and when it happened he couldn't do anything else but get out of bed and jangle his feet around, try to shake out whatever demons had lodged themselves overnight in his legs or his soul.

And so on that particular morning he woke up very early, while everyone else was still sleeping, and walked outside. It was very quiet; not even the birds spoke. There was a heavy blanket of gray mist that had crept up over the hill and covered the tobacco fields—the last plant spudded just hours before—and it occurred to him for the first time that the world was beautiful. It was a terrible, sick feeling, he felt then, as he realized it. He felt it shoot all the way through his body—from the tip of his head, which was bare and open to the chill of the morning air, to the ends of his fingers, which tingled with a by-now-familiar sensation, which was almost no sensation at all. A sensation, or lack thereof, which (though Hadley had promised him it would) had not gone away now that he'd been paid, and in fact never would. He would still feel it even many years later—all during and even long after the war. Not as sharply or as vividly as he did then, but still—an echo of it. A memory of numbness that, through the confusions of time, he later connected not with the pain of the work, but with the beauty of that landscape, which had just then revealed itself to him.

He stood out there that morning with that chill in his heart as equally as in his head and his hands, and he prayed that he might sense in that terrible beauty some sign, something that might indicate to him the path that he should follow. He looked up into the sky, which was just begin-ning to lighten, into that thick blanket of mist just beginning to disperse itself into the coming day, and he prayed. He prayed out loud—to God or whatever force was out there that might instruct him best.

He did not know why he formulated his question in words that he actually spoke out loud, and perhaps that was his most grievous mistake, for the words came out sounding dull, nearly meaningless in the open air. And no answer came. Perhaps if he had not spoken, but had found some language equivalent to whatever was just at that moment beginning to stir in his heart, then he might have been answered in kind. The risk was, of course, that the reply would come back as mysterious and as incompre-hensible to him as the feeling that currently resided within him; that there would have been nothing to understand. No simple word, no sign. So he spoke his request in simple words, but still there was no recognizable reply, and the longer he stood there in the empty field, the emptier and more alone both he and it became; so much so that, finally, when he turned his attention inward—the world having offered him no guidance at all—he seemed to himself as scoured and hollow as a reed or a shell.

Finally, when the sun had burned away what was left of the mist and the first sounds of the men breaking camp interrupted what had until then been perfect stillness (disrupted only by the occasional call of a bird and, once, the rattle of an old truck on the road, its motor popping in tired, slow retreat), Douglas turned back to the camp. And later that morning, because he had arrived at nothing else, he found himself—along with the bandit, Hadley, and the midget El Niño—headed farther south.

AS USUAL, THE BANDIT entertained them as they went. Among many other stories of his onetime adventures, there were the stories of how he had once been a rich man: manager of one of the richest silver mines in southern Arizona. Whatever it was that had happened to change the course of his fate Douglas never knew—the bandit always skipped over that part of the story. He'd just sort of pause, sometimes marking the gap with a soft popping sound that he made with his mouth. Depending on how the story got told, sometimes it would seem to indicate one thing, and sometimes another, but always there came the point in the story when the bandit—*pop*—was obliged to depart from his home state, for which he was named, and his past glory, to which likewise (as the bandit would often lament appreciatively himself) he was never now likely to return.

THEY WERE CONTENT, FOR the most part, to get blown just as the wind blew, to move from job to job, and not to think much past the next meal, or the next place to lay their heads. And if there wasn't a next meal, or a place to lay their heads, well, that didn't trouble them much, either. Douglas still hoped (and in some small way, despite his fears, fully expected) that his path might cross, at some point or the other, with his father's. And so, even as they drifted farther and farther south following the rumor of work—always ahead of them, just out of reach—he continued to measure his progress and direction according to the relative distance he imagined between them.

Everywhere he could, he left his name and his next destination—if it was known—written in large letters across a scrap of paper, or whatever he could find, to be passed on to his father should anyone meet him. Because of this, by the time he returned to Washington again the next spring, there was a map of his travels that pointed straight down the center of the United States, hit the Gulf, and traveled back up again, so that if anyone had cared to they could have followed his trail and seen the pattern it made, though he himself had no knowledge of it until many years later, when he looked at a map for the first time and saw the great distance he had covered. Once he had even passed through Missouri at a point that was, he later realized, only a day or two's travel, at most, from his mother's door. Without knowing it, he had nearly broken the promise his father had made for them both by returning—however unwittingly—home.

THOUGH THEY HAD FOLLOWED the season and the rumor of work faithfully all that time, many weeks went by when they found nothing at all, and after a particularly long spell like that, the bandit—in proportion to his growing hunger—grew increasingly suspicious as to the reason they were continuously turned away. One night he told Douglas that the two of them had better make off on their own, as he doubted whether the midget and old Hadley were improving their lot any. He shook his head sadly as he said it. A man has got to make his own way in the world, he said. And he must harden his heart a little in order to do it.

This Douglas knew to be true. Every day they passed some poor soul on the road whom they were forced to walk right by. There was never enough, you see, to share on the road, and even if there was, by some miracle—if at camp one night, say, they were lucky enough to have at a stretch an extra helping of food in the pot—it was clear there was no point to sharing what was left with one man if they could not share it with every other man, too.

If, at times, this was lamented—either by themselves or the strangers they passed on the road—the bandit would supply the company with a simple lesson in economics, which ran along these lines: If the surplus, he would say (what was left over at the end of any meal, if they should be so lucky as to have any to spare) was measurable, and the deficit (that observed lack: the beggar next to them, for example, who clamored to be fed) was not, then it was evident the surplus was best banked—shored up. That it might grow upon and against its own worth, rather than be dispersed until all value was lost. There are (the bandit would always conclude) at least two things to be learned from this and kept in mind. One is that value is always reduced through division rather than multiplied. (Take—he would say—for example, when a loaf of bread is divided into two parts, so that one man gets one half and the other, the other. At the outset, though it may seem there is an outcome greater than if the loaf had stayed whole, it must be remembered that the loaf, once divided, *exists only in parts*. This fundamental principle has not, and cannot, be changed—no matter what immediate demand or desire has been momentarily satisfied.) The second law (the bandit said) is that value—though it cannot, perhaps, be measured—always exists, nevertheless, in the possibility of both its accrual and dispersion. (It is possible, therefore—the bandit explained—that two halves of one loaf of bread *could* equal, on certain, rare occasions, more than one loaf of bread as a whole, *if* the potential for earning, making, or stealing *another* loaf of bread once the bread is divided—two men now fed, instead of just one—is greater proportionately than it would be feeding one man alone.)

And so all of these lessons were spinning around in Douglas's head the night the bandit suggested they part company from the midget and Hadley and make their own way, and later he would not have been able to say what decision he and the bandit would have come to had they been required to. He would not have been able to say rightly whether he would have accepted, in the end, the crude calculations of the bandit, though he suspected at their root a gross inaccuracy: something he could neither figure nor describe, but of which he felt deadly certain all the same. Because, in the end, they were not faced with making the decision at all: it was El Niño who left *them*—in order to rejoin a traveling circus, which had made him an offer (he said) he simply couldn't refuse. This, despite the fact that he had sworn on many occasions—in front of them all—that he would sooner be churned into the dirt of a tobacco field, or tumble off a ladder and be buried a free man in the wide open, than be trampled under the foot of an elephant; that is, die—in the circus—as the property of another man.

He left at night, just after they had dispensed to him (in honor of his departure—which, now that the decision to part did not rest solely on their shoulders, they honestly regretted) the greater portion of the meal. Taking with him, with his small, deft fingers, from the lining of Hadley's coat, three whole silver dollars—the existence of which neither the bandit nor Douglas had ever suspected. In order that he might report his grievance the next morning, Hadley first had to admit, of course, to the hidden coins having existed at all, and once this was divulged, the bandit and Douglas were torn as to how to feel about the whole thing. They were furious with Hadley, first of all, for having kept his secret from them—then at the midget for having discovered it ahead of them. But they also felt relieved: it was, in the end, another man's self-interest, and not their own, that had been revealed in this way, and—finally—they were visited by doubt that the three dollars to which Hadley referred had ever existed at all.

And not even a circus to join, Hadley (whom Douglas and the bandit did not, in the end, forsake) would grumble after that, time and again.

No, it was he who forsook them, too. One day when they were preparing, as they had been for some weeks, to follow the rumor of planting jobs farther north, Hadley announced he would just as soon, that morning, stay behind. As he said it he had in his eye the same look Cecil had had in his when he'd offered up his portion of the meal, so Douglas knew there was no point arguing. It was the sort of look a plant gets when it settles itself into new soil. They respected that, and did not ask any questions, and the next day, when they left him—the bandit and Douglas alone now, just as the bandit had once wished—as they waved over their shoulders at Hadley and made their way down the road—he stood straight as a stalk in the breeze, shifting only very slightly, and they knew it would not be in this lifetime when, if ever, they saw him again.

—

IT WAS LATE MAY BEFORE DOUGLAS AND THE BANDIT MANAGED TO work their way up to Washington again, to where Waters's men had gathered, for a second season now, in the government camps outside the city. As in the previous spring, the camps had been appointed comfortably enough; they were greeted with hot coffee, an army cot, and—best of all—the promise of three square meals a day. Nothing tasted sweeter—nor, Douglas figured, was ever likely to—than that first hot meal, which was served up to him and the bandit immediately upon their arrival. They hadn't had a full meal like that in coming on two weeks.

The bandit gritted his teeth, but sure enough he ate and drank his share—it was, of course, the only logical thing to do. That night, though, lying in the army barracks, he whispered to Douglas: They're trying to buy us out, don't you see that, kid? We've each got a ticket in our pocket worth near a thousand dollars. Some of us more! And still they think they can buy us off with a cup of coffee!

He whistled through his teeth and propped himself up on an elbow, peering at Douglas through the dim light that streamed in from a lamp in the yard.

It ain't right, he said, I swear it. If your daddy was still alive, I can bet—

But Douglas did not wait to find out what he would bet, and later he could not explain even to himself what happened next, except to say that something sprang loose inside him as the bandit said those words.

The next thing he knew, he had the bandit by the ears and a knee to his throat.

What did you say? It was his own voice that spoke.

The bandit, his eyes wild, tried to answer but could not, because Douglas was pressing against the bony parts of his throat with his knee.

It was a pleasure to feel how fragile it was. To feel the way those bones connected to the bandit's lungs, and his lungs to his brain, and his brain to his heart . . . and how all of that connected in that moment to Douglas's own knee, which was, in turn . . . part of a great and complex system about which he knew very little, but was nonetheless part. There could be no doubt, though—despite what existed beyond him, which he did not understand—of the way the pressure of his knee on the bandit's throat corresponded to the bandit's inability to speak or breathe. This correspondence was still further proven a moment later when Douglas partially released the pressure from the bandit's throat and, as a direct result, the bandit began to splutter and speak.

Forgive me, he said.

Douglas rolled off of him and the bandit sprang up, spitting and coughing, while Douglas watched—wondering what had come over him.

Then, for the first time, he understood. Or rather, he felt—in his body—what he had witnessed two years before, the night he had first seen the Indian, John. The violence that had overtaken the Indian that night, which had seemed so mysterious to him then and had since troubled him— as all things do that one suspects one will never understand—was not a thing, he realized at last, to be finally comprehended. And, indeed, even in that moment it was not quite accurate to say that he understood the Indian's violence—but instead that it was a thing he recognized, suddenly, as his own.

The bandit had stopped coughing by then and was settling into sleep. Overcome with remorse, Douglas reached out; he touched him lightly on his thin shoulder.

I'm sorry, he said.

It was true. He had never felt more sorry for anything in all of his life. But the bandit just stared back at him blankly, and Douglas realized he did not even recall what had taken place.

What? the bandit said. A crooked smile on his face.

Douglas shook his head.

Nothing, he said. Let's both go to sleep.

But he could not sleep. He lay awake and for the second time in his life attempted to pray to whatever was still holy in that darkness, that he could rid himself of whatever it was that had, that night, made its home in his body. He felt its presence at that very moment burning in him, and the more he concentrated on ridding himself of whatever it was that burned there, the more it burned. The more he told himself he was not to blame—that it was not actually resident in him, that he could not truly imagine killing a man—the more the images of that death, that thing that he could not imagine, lodged in his brain. The more he resisted them, the more they came, and the more they came, the more there rose in him a pleasure at their arriving there in stubborn opposition to his own demands. He told himself, more and more insistently, that it was not *truly pleasure* that he felt then, in their arrival; that the slight chill that rippled through him as each subsequent image appeared before him— which he himself brought into being before his own eyes—was instead a horror at discovering that which was inconceivable inside him. That it was due only to the great confusion caused by that discovery that he mistook the feeling that came over him then for the thrill of pleasure.

But the more he insisted upon this, the more he allowed for a logical correspondence between the two emotions to take shape in his mind, and the more certain he was that the feeling was indeed, if not pleasure itself, then so closely akin to it, it was useless to make any distinction. He lay there thinking this, with the fire burning in his stomach so fiercely that even his skin began to burn. He wanted badly to scream; to scrape at his skin until he tore from it whatever fire burned there inside. It was all he could do not to, and the longer he resisted it, the clearer it became to him how it is that men go mad.

It was not, he realized, by allowing the images that at any time appeared before them in their minds—what was *not real*—to get mixed up with what was, but by *refusing* those images; by attempting to pre- serve some sense of distance from them.

We are all mad (Douglas thought), but most of us know how to get along anyway, and he did not know then whether he wanted to get along or not. If letting all the ugly things into his heart and mind and all the possibilities of ugliness within himself and everyone else was the way to get along. But he did not want to be like the mad people he encountered sometimes on the road, who did not have a true companion in all the world, even in themselves, and then he felt deeply ashamed of his recent cruelty to the bandit, who was his only friend: how he had been ready, just a moment before, to destroy even that: and he resolved, then, that he would not go mad, and finally—after firmly settling on this decision in his mind—he slept.

—

JUST AS BEFORE, THEY DID NOT KEEP THEIR PROMISE: NOT TO LEAVE Washington again until they'd exchanged their tickets for the money they were due. As soon as the first good opportunity for work came up, only three weeks later, they took it and were gone. The job didn't promise, as far as Douglas could tell, to be much better, or different, from any of the jobs offered the previous year, which the bandit had scorned, but after shuffling in line for three weeks as though they did not carry the promise of nearly a thousand dollars in their front shirt pockets and were just like any other men, out of work—any money they'd made already spent on liquor or food—they accepted the first government offer that came along.

The job was in Florida; a project which, they were told, could last two, maybe even three years. Those who signed on now would see their pay increase several times over before the project was through. The idea of it alone beat chasing down jobs the length and breadth of the eastern states—even the bandit could see that.

They were shipped first to Fort Jefferson, on the island of Dry Tortugas—then on to the Upper Keys. Fort Jefferson served as a prison, just as it had many years before (most famously it had once housed Samuel Mudd and the rest of the Lincoln conspirators). More than once that first summer the bandit and Douglas had cause to joke to themselves that, though they had been shipped off to prison, by a stroke of luck they had landed in hell.

But it wasn't all bad. Even when there wasn't any work, which there

often was not, they were always fed. There wasn't any rhyme or reason
to it, it seemed—when there was work and when there wasn't. It wasn't
like farmwork that way, when the thing needed doing until it didn't anymore. Sometimes they'd be working on a stretch of road and when they
had got it laid out halfway to nowhere, the foreman would come in and
say, Stone says put a hold on this, and everything would stop. If a man
had a shovelful of dirt he would drop it and sit down on it wherever it lay
and say, I'll put a hold on this, sure, and maybe a week, maybe more,
would go by 'til there was approval to move the road ahead a few more
miles, and no one knew why, and everyone grumbled, Do they want this
damn road or not? but mostly it was good to have the work when it came
and to hold off when it did not.

By November there were somewhere near seven hundred men spread
between the three camps that spanned two keys—Windley Key to the
north, where Douglas and the bandit had been stationed, and then two
camps on Matecumbe Key, just to the south. Though they all continued
to get fed—and in fact as a direct consequence of it—it wasn't long
before the sewers were full to overflowing, and the whole island reeked
of veteran shit when the wind was blowing in any direction except
directly offshore. By the middle of the month the conditions got so bad
the men wrote letters of complaint, which they sent to Washington to be
published in the *B.E.F. News*. But nothing was done about it and the
fumes got worse—so toxic sometimes that the men tore off the bottoms
of their shirts to use as masks while they worked.

By December—the job stalled, going on three weeks—pretty much
everyone was of the opinion that the whole thing, from the beginning,
had been nothing but a hoax; whoever believed, they said, there was any
possibility of turning that godforsaken swamp into a tourist paradise
was either a con man or a fool. It was clear, just looking around—at the
half-built road that stretched out toward nowhere along that little spit of
an island overflowing with shit—that there never had been nor would be
any real work or anything else on those islands, and so it could only be
true that, as the word went around now, the government had only one
thing in mind when it shipped them all down there, and that was to get

the Bonus Army—or whatever was left of it—as far away from Washington as it possibly could.

But when they complained, they didn't get much sympathy—even, or especially, from the BEF. P. C. Farrell, who wrote an "island report" regularly for the *B.E.F. News*, got a note back one day from a veteran in Washington asking him to please not send in any more articles about "vacationers" down in Florida. As far as anyone else was concerned, those who had landed the jobs down South were living high on the government hog. Perhaps, having "got away from it all," Farrell was told, he had lost touch with the fact that in the rest of the country there was a Depression on. Farrell got boiling mad at that and wrote back, but no more of his reports were ever published, and he received no reply.

But then the Patman Bill, which demanded immediate and full payment of the bonus, passed through the House again, with a resounding majority. Getting past the Senate, and the President himself, who—it was well known—had promised to veto the bill, was another matter. But this did not stop the veterans from feeling—just as they had back in '32—that genuine progress had indeed been made. The day Douglas and the bandit heard the news—it was a Sunday—they hitched a ride down to Key West in order to have a drink and celebrate a little at Josie Russell's Bar. That was where most of them went when they got the least chance. With a dollar in your pocket you could stay all afternoon, if you drank slow. Sit there underneath the portrait of General Custer and admire what a sad son of a bitch he looked—like he'd never stepped foot out of a painting in his whole life—and feel like a real man yourself for a while. Glad that if history was as flat and stuck-up as General Custer looked to be, you didn't have any part of it. That you were instead part of the living, breathing world—even if it smelled like shit most of the time. At least you were a real human being, you thought, and it felt good to think it, and feel that way, even if it was only on account of the rum in your veins.

It was good to be drunk. It was good to be drunk and alive for a while. Whenever he felt that way, anyway, Douglas wouldn't have traded it in for anything in the world, not even getting painted up on a wall or written into a book. And indeed there was always the chance of that at Josie's, because every day the writer Ernest Hemingway, who had a house down on that key, would be in the bar, and when they'd had enough to drink some of the men would call out to him: Are you going to write me into one of your books? And sometimes he promised he would.

He sat at the back, a little crowd always around him, but sometimes he didn't speak to them, or to anyone at all, but instead would only scribble away in the notebook he carried, and when he finally looked up again, he would say that, sure, he was going to write all of them up in a book one day.

You better play it straight, the bandit said to him once. Write it down like it is—don't make any of us ugly or dumb, except for the ones that is, and the writer said that he always played it straight, and the men nodded.

On the day the Patman Bill passed, the writer was at the bar when Douglas and the bandit arrived, and by the time Douglas could edge his way to the counter to order a drink, he found the writer had already paid. He was so surprised he accepted the drink and didn't even say thanks.

What's your name, son? the writer asked, and when Douglas told him, he said he had seen him before and often wondered to himself why a young man like him had come down to work on a job with a bunch of old men. So Douglas told him how he had signed up with the bandit and how even though he hadn't been to France, he had been a proud member of the Bonus Army since 1932 on account of his father, who had fought in the war. He felt in his shirt pocket for the bonus ticket and it pleased him to feel it there, and to tell someone, especially the writer, who he knew had driven an ambulance during the war, and won several medals—and especially on that day, when the Patman Bill had just passed through the House—about his father, and what he was doing there, at that very moment, in Josie Russell's Bar. He felt proud to be among those men, some of whom were twice his age. To have remained with them, tramping back and forth to Washington, first with the Cadons and then with the bandit, when he might have gone his own way just as easily, and perhaps squared for himself a better deal out of it somehow. He knew that if he had done that, that when he went to cash in his father's bonus for him, though he might still have the ticket that said exactly what they were owed, he would have cheated both of them somehow. Plus, at the beginning, the Keys jobs had been coveted—and not just by veterans. They promised work and plenty of it; who wasn't in the market for that?

Julius Stone, who managed the project, swore it was only a matter of time once the highways got built before the money started pouring in. There would be no end to the work then, he said.

Key West was the example he used when anyone doubted him. It was—he reminded them—hardly recognizable to anyone who'd known it before he and his troops had arrived! And sure enough, the tourists flooded in. This was a thorn in the side of the writer, as he himself had, in the process, turned into one of Stone's tourist attractions. After he had caught all the stray dogs and cats and run them out of town, whitewashed the buildings, and burned all the trash and litter on the beaches and streets, Stone had drawn up a map of the island that marked—among other points of interest—the precise location of the writer's house. Then he issued it to the tourist board. Soon the writer could expect on any given day a stream of curious passersby looking in at him from the street. Sometimes they would come right up on his front lawn and peer in through the windows of his house while he was trying to work, or sleep, or any other number of things that a man tries to do in the privacy of his home. He'd built a wall around the yard almost at once, but the people disregarded the wall, because (the writer explained) once a thing is written in a book, and the book is sold, the people who buy the book think that everything the book contains, including its author, belongs to them. To get away from all that, the writer would come regularly, every day at three, to Josie Russell's Bar and bring his notebook and tell his stories and listen to the veterans', and complain about the government and reminisce about the days before anyone dreamt of intervening with the "natural order of things"—not caring, or at least not blaming the veterans particularly, for the fact that they were employed to alter that very thing. It was well known among them, however, that he hated the President and the New

Deal and everything that had come from it with a passion, and from time to time he would let loose about it, so that everyone would know what exactly he thought of the President of the United States. That paralytic demagogue, he would say—which was something Douglas never understood until the bandit explained to him that it was sort of like a Fascist with no legs.

The bandit was often educating Douglas like that, which was something he appreciated, though sometimes the explanations he gave did not make things any clearer than they had been before. Like the time when, after they first signed up for the job in the Keys, they learned that a man they knew from the government camp had been turned down for the same job and sent to work in another camp instead. He was mad about it, and said, They save all the best jobs for the white boys. This had surprised Douglas, because he hadn't known until then that the man, Ben Stokes was his name, wasn't a white boy himself. They were keeping all the work camps segregated, even though everyone got along just fine, and so that was how Douglas found out Ben Stokes was a Negro, because he went to a Negro camp, and because he was bitter about all the choice jobs going to white folks.

When Douglas asked the bandit if Ben was a Negro, the bandit laughed and said, Sure!

Douglas said, What? And the bandit said again, Sure, you ain't never seen a nigger don't look like a nigger before?

When Douglas said he had not, the bandit said, Well, how do you know you haven't if you already said you wouldn't know if you saw him? and Douglas said that was precisely the point. But by that time the bandit was no longer interested and Douglas did not get any more information out of him, and often afterward he would look at a white man and wonder if he was really a white man, or look at a black man and wonder if there was any possibility he was actually white. It was more difficult to imagine that a black man could be a white man than the other way around, he found, because it did always seem conceivable that with a white man he had failed to detect some element of blackness in his skin, which had such gradations to it, and less likely that he might mistake blackness for white, and so, though he decided that this was unlikely, he was not prepared to rule the possibility out entirely. And sometimes he thought of Ben Stokes afterward and wondered how he was faring in the Negro camp and if there were really less opportunities for Negroes than for white folks, because it was just as hard to imagine how there could be less opportunities for any man than there were in the Upper Keys as it was to imagine a black man that was white. But it was clear that nothing was as it appeared to be and that his estimation of anything and understanding of it were almost certain to be false, and that there existed a great deal more complexity and contradiction to any thing than ever met the eye.

IT WAS NOT LONG after the news of the Patman Bill that the men on Windley Key began to talk of a strike. In February, a small battle raged between the veterans and the camp officials, and even though most of the organizers of the strike were soon driven out of the camp—they headed back to Washington to continue their protest there—and there was a growing concern among the men that the whole project (which ran at the best of times only in fits and starts) would be abandoned, and the labor they had done before the strike would remain unpaid, not one of them lifted a finger to lengthen the highway and the tourists got no nearer for the entire month of February.

One of the veterans, a real southern gentleman (or so, at least, he would have you believe)—name of Spencer Ford—was one of the organizers who stayed on. At the end of February he even managed to get a sit-down with the camp commanders, and the night before it was to take place he called a general meeting to compose a list of grievances he planned to bring to the management's attention the very next day. Number one was sanitation, of course—but then once they got going nearly everything needed improving, and the men started shouting all at once until Spencer Ford held his hand up, like he was accustomed to being listened to, and sure enough the men quieted down, and Ford said, I am drawing up a list of only our most pressing concerns, gentlemen.

So they decided on three main points for Ford to discuss with the camp commanders the next day, but neither Ford nor the three men who accompanied him to represent the veterans' affairs ever returned to report on how their demands were received, so they never did know. It was rumored the four had been shipped off to Fort Jefferson, though some said they had only been sent back to Miami, from which point they were encouraged to "make their own way"—anywhere but back to Windley Key—and still others said they knew for certain they had been taken into international waters and drowned.

Whatever the case, neither Ford nor any of his men were heard from again, and the veterans' situation did not improve. There was continued talk, after that, of heading back to Washington—of remaining there, this time, and no mistake, until the bonus was paid—but everyone, including Douglas and the bandit, when they talked of leaving, talked of leaving "after the next paycheck," in order to ensure they had something with which to start the journey. But that day was always, at any given point, at least two weeks away, because as soon as any paycheck arrived it would be the next paycheck that would decide them and the paycheck that came was spent, at least in significant part, drinking at Josie Russell's Bar.

—

BEFORE THEY KNEW IT, IT WAS JULY, AND ROYAL ROBERTSON—THAT charismatic veteran from California (who, it was rumored, had once been a star on the silver screen—though no one could ever actually claim to having seen him in the pictures)—had moved his troops into Washington, establishing himself and his followers in a vacant lot off Pennsylvania Avenue. It was like 1932 all over again! With this encouragement, half a dozen men did go—taking whatever was left of their last paycheck, if there was any left over at all. But most of them—Douglas and the bandit among them—stayed on through the brutal heat of that summer, and so were still there on the first of September, 1935, when the hurricane hit.

..

THE NEXT DAY BEING Labor Day, most everyone was drunk the night before the storm. They sat together in the small tavern on Windley Key, drinking what was left to drink and leaning from their chairs as though they hadn't a care in the world.

Many of them, like Douglas and the bandit, were still there at six o'clock in the morning, when the roof blew off.

A general confusion erupted then. Men rounded up vehicles in order to head to Key West—but there weren't many. Word came that a train was on its way—but hours passed and the train never arrived. Soon they had no choice but to give up on the train; to turn their attention instead— too late—to whatever they had on hand. As the winds picked up to a frightening speed in the early afternoon, some of the men began to dig trenches in the dirt just like the ones that had saved them on so many occasions before, back in France.

Like all terrible things, it arrived, when it did, all of a sudden—as though without warning. There was nothing to do but brace them- selves against it. But even that was not a thing they *did*, it was just a thing that happened. It seemed to Douglas as if the whole world had suddenly been swept out from under him. At first he could see nothing at all, so it was a relief when he managed to catch sight of the bandit. He could make out only a dim shadow on account of the direction and force of the storm, but he knew it was the bandit. Leaning there, into the wind—his body turned toward Douglas, though he did not seem to see him. It took another several seconds before Douglas understood why. The bandit's face, left exposed, had (Douglas realized only now, with horror) been completely torn off by the wind, which was by then whipping the sand from the beach with the force of a thousand tiny grenades. Douglas may have screamed at the sight, but he could not be certain. It is possible it was only the wind that he heard, which he mistook as his voice—or equally that it was his voice that he mistook for the wind. He looked around for shelter, his hands shielding his face and his eyes. The mess house did not exist any longer. Nothing existed.

Once, he looked back, toward where the bandit remained, and though he could still make out the outline of his shadow, he no longer recognized him. It was a great mystery what kept him riveted there.

He ran, and did not stop until he reached the last stretch of road, built just before the storm. It ran adjacent to the railroad and a small trestle bridge, which spanned a small estuary emptying off into marshland. Somehow Douglas managed to wedge himself underneath the bridge, and only then—protected by the overhang—was he able to remove his hands from his eyes. What he saw, he did not immediately comprehend: it was the ocean. Raised on its back, like a great horse on hind legs, and moving steadily toward him.

How it was that he managed to brace himself against the wooden ties of the railway bridge; how it was that he remained there, as the ocean crashed over him—crushing his bones with its weight—he would never know. At the time, indeed, he couldn't be certain if he was alive or dead, and even after the wave passed he remained braced against a force that no longer existed except in his memory of its having been.

Four times the ocean surged and plunged and crushed him beneath it, and four times he managed, somehow, to hold on. But it was not— he knew then, and always after—according to his own will he was sustained. It was according to some other force, hardly proper to him—the same, perhaps, that had threatened at one time to crush the bandit's throat—that he remained, clinging to the underside of a trestle bridge, fourteen feet in the air, as the waves beat against him, and huge ugly crabs fell with the weight of stones, and then continued their slow unthinking course over his body just as naturally as though he were not still suspended above it but lay already at the bottom of the sea. They crept in through the tears and folds of his clothes, locating whatever warmth existed, close to the skin. Later—no; he would be unable to account for it. How it was he'd managed to hold on all that time. Because, even years afterward, when he thought of it, he wished he could have drowned. That he could have had his flesh torn from his face and fingers and been laid out to dry like the swollen bodies he found the next morning, splayed on the beach or suspended from trees. Their clothes torn from them, their skin blasted. That he would not have been among those few who remained. Roaming about, without speaking, looking among the ruins for other survivors—and not recognizing, equally, when he met them, the living and the dead.

VI.

Sutton

ON THE WARPATH. WASHINGTON, D.C., WINTER 1936—
WITH A BRIEF DETOUR TO NEW YORK CITY, 1928—NEW
YORK CITY, SUMMER 1936—VARIOUS LOCATIONS IN THE
SOUTH, SOUTHWEST, AND MIDDLE WEST OF THE UNITED
STATES, 1937—NEW YORK CITY, 1937–1941—LONDON,
1942—THE HAGUE, GUADALCANAL, GUAM, MAKIN ISLAND,
1943—NEW YORK CITY, CASSINO VALLEY, ROME, 1944—
BERLIN, DACHAU, 1945.

In January 1936, when the Bonus Bill finally passed, Sutton had been working for just over three months at the *Washington Evening Star*. She put her name in for the story, even though she knew she didn't stand a chance of covering it. Jim Dalling, editor in chief, had already made that much clear: he was never going to send her, or any woman, for that matter, he said, to cover the news on the streets. The *Star* was not the *Los Angeles Examiner*, and had no need of the sort of journalism propagated by the likes of William Randolph Hearst, say, or any of his "sob sisters."

Well, she was no "sob sister," Sutton had told Dalling. He would find that out sooner or later if he was willing to give her a try. Dalling had just chuckled and shuffled the papers on his desk, marking the end of their interview.

I like that, he had told her. A woman with spirit; a woman with grit. Yes, I would not be surprised, he said, if you are invited to Mondays at the White House very soon.

Sutton was still working copy for the "women's pages" then, but if she was lucky, Dalling told her when she was hired, she stood a decent chance of becoming one of "Eleanor's girls"—allowed to attend the First Lady's weekly press conferences. Still, she put her name in for "street" jobs from time to time anyway—just to let Dalling know that he could always change his mind.

Even when, three days later, the President vetoed the bill, the verdict—which had easily passed through the Senate—was never in doubt. Roosevelt's veto was purely symbolic—intended only in order to save face after his having so staunchly opposed the motion for so long. He managed to look unwavering and resolute and, in the end, still got credit for passing the bill.

Within a week the bonus checks were being mailed out all over the country—the average payment somewhere in the vicinity of $550.

Once again, Sutton suggested a story. It would be from the "women's angle," she said. What did it mean to the families who had waited so long to receive their check? To the women who had been left behind when their men marched off, first to France, and then to Washington, after the war? What did it feel like, after such a long wait, for the bonus to actually arrive? But by the time Dalling got around to seriously considering her proposal, even Sutton recognized it was too late—the whole thing more or less forgotten. What remained of it was only the taint on Hoover's career from the riot of '32, and the more recent scandal surrounding FDR's "rehabilitation" projects after, just that past September, hundreds of veterans had been drowned off the Florida Keys.

For six months there had been a call to investigate the disaster from the VFW, the American Legion, and a spattering of citizen groups, but the Roosevelt administration held it off; the official stance was that the veterans' deaths had been an act of God.

"Everyone makes mistakes," it was decided in a government meeting directly following the disaster. "But not everyone makes hurricanes. It may be ignorance and error in judgment on the part of the government but it is not a crime, and to measure the ignorance and the errors in judgment of the government or any one man against the ignorance and the errors of judgment of nature, is to measure a single grain of sand against the bed of an ocean."

Still, the taint on Roosevelt's career did not go away overnight. He continued to be criticized for the "mistakes," however relative in the cosmic scheme, his administration had made. Most notably, this criticism came from Massachusetts Representative Edith Nourse Rogers, who had been elected to her husband's seat in Congress in 1926 and had promptly become the self-appointed protector and champion of disabled veterans. She insisted loudly that the truth about the veterans killed in the Labor Day hurricane was being systematically withheld, and after being twice refused a direct audience with the President, she further complained that a "reign of terror" existed in Washington, and that ordinary employees of the government were afraid to "express themselves."

Finally, in March, six months after the disaster, several hearings were called in order to address the issue of compensation. It was a whitewash—an undisguised attempt to "clean up" the mess that had, since the hurricane, refused to go away. Rogers was well aware of this, but could do nothing but hound witnesses and argue bitingly with the chairman of the investigation, John Elliott Rankin—and Wright Patman, also on the committee, who still maintained the "act of God" position. Patman called for a "point of order" whenever Rogers mentioned anything that deviated from the agreed-upon New Deal script.

Sutton put her name in to cover this story, too. This was certainly, she insisted in her note to Dalling, a "women's issue"—belonging next to the exposés on cosmetics companies and decorating tips. Again she was refused.

She went to the hearing anyway. There was, after all—she realized—nothing to stop her.

When Rogers asked Ivan R. Tannehil—the assistant chief of the Weather Bureau's forecasting service at the time of the hurricane—if, according to his professional knowledge and opinion, he would have chosen Islamorada as a place to send veterans for rehabilitation, Rankin almost leapt from his seat, invoked a point of order, and accused Rogers of "embarrassing the witness." Sutton scribbled all this down and more, then went home and typed up a piece. She turned it in to Dalling early the next morning, but Dalling told her that the story had "already run."

Not in the "women's pages," she said.

This is not a woman's story, he said.

He did not find Sutton's "spirit" as amusing this time as he had before. Finally, though, to her surprise, her story did run—and not in the "women's pages," either, but on page three of the national news. The delay had in fact proved opportune because on June 1, Rogers had come back with one last swing when the bill for relief of the hurricane veterans finally came to a vote. She accused Rankin of refusing to call key witnesses, and of withholding anything that suggested a contradiction to the preestablished "act of God" theory.

The government, and everyone seated here today, knows, she said, that though what occurred in Florida may well have been an act of God, the responsibility for those men's lives was *not* God's, but our own—all of us gathered here today. These responsibilities were not carried out.

The Relief Bill passed and even those who had championed the "act of God" position throughout the proceedings were glad that something had been done—enough at any rate to quiet Rogers.

It wasn't until 1941, five years later, that Sutton ran across any mention of the Bonus Army again. She was working "on the street" by then, for the *New York Herald Tribune*, when she caught wind of the story. Someone had come across what they claimed to be one of Eddie Gosnell's famous photographs of Hushka and Carlson—the two men killed in the July '32 riot—photographs that had later mysteriously disappeared. Gosnell himself had been found dead in a rented room in an apparent suicide back in '33—an event that had at the time caused quite a stir, though very little of it got into the press. None of the veterans believed that Gosnell's death was a suicide. It was rumored, instead, that he had made some powerful enemies leading up to, and then directly following, the publication (some weeks after the riots) of the photographs he'd taken of the two dead men. Why—it was wondered aloud—had it taken so long for the photographs to appear? What had stopped Gosnell from printing them right away?

Whatever the pressure had been, it was later suspected to have ended Gosnell's life. After some disagreement and a consultation with two ex-wives, Gosnell (which was discovered not to be his real name) had been buried with full military honors in Arlington Cemetery under the name of Edward Steinkraus. An investigation into the affair had been led by the right-wing Khaki Shirts, but even the angriest veterans seemed resigned to the fact that it would come to nothing— and it did. Not only had the photographs disappeared, but all record of them had as well. The last known word on the subject was an exchange that took place between Gosnell and an unknown caller, shortly before Gosnell's death, in which he reportedly exclaimed, "Tell him I'll see him in hell!"

But now, suddenly, nearly nine years later, a disabled veteran from Ohio named Jim Bradley claimed to be in possession of one of the Gosnell photographs—not the ones that had originally been published, but one that, instead, had never made it to press. Sutton followed up on the story right away. She even traveled up to Boston to meet with Bradley— but no one but her seemed the slightest bit interested. It had already been five years since the Bonus Bill had passed, and now there was a new war on. Besides, as was pointed out to her several times, there was no proof that the photograph was actually Gosnell's—or even that the men in the photograph were Hushka and Carlson.

It was true that Jim Bradley's photograph had been so badly damaged it was difficult to clearly make out the faces of those it pictured—and indeed there were very few identifying features in the photograph at all that designated it as having been taken at the conflict on the twenty-eighth of July, 1932, and not any other day. But since when, Sutton had asked, did one require proof to run a story in the paper? Here was a man claiming to be in possession of one of Eddie Gosnell's photographs. *There* was the story. In all likelihood, a man had died on account of that photograph!

Still—the story never ran.

IT WAS ONLY NATURAL for Sutton to feel that way then; she had "given up representation," as almost everyone had "given up representation," just before the war. It was as liberating to give it up, she found, as it had been to first discover it. To learn, as a child—through the simple technique of shading—to lift simple objects from the page. It was remarkable: the way that little empty square in the left-hand corner of each apple she drew into the margins of her school notebook (the one part of the drawing that she had not, and would not, touch) was what in the end rendered the image whole. She had felt, she remembered, an almost irrepressible joy as the apples had rained down on her page—each one marked by a simple caricature of light in its upper left-hand corner.

It was this same joy that she felt in the realization—so many years later, when she encountered the "painterly realisms" of Malevich; the glorious abstractions of the Delaunays, or Fernand Léger—that it was not the apple, but in fact, precisely, what the apple *was not* (what, that is, of the apple remained stubbornly beyond her power even to perceive, let alone re-create on the page) that allowed it to be reproduced as it was—or at least as it seemed. If it was, in this way, only through the acknowledgment (an actual *physical allowance* within the space of the represented object) of the limitations of the eye that an object might be brought suddenly—miraculously—to form, was it not probable that to realize anything in its truest sense, one was obliged not to reproduce what was at any time visible to the eye, but instead what escaped it entirely? Further: if "reality"—what appeared to the eye, and therefore to the mind—was based, in essence, on *what did not in fact exist at all*, how could it itself be based, in the end, on anything more than simple faith?

..

BUT PERHAPS SHE HAD discovered all of this much earlier, when she had stood in front of Pieter Brueghel the Elder's *Big Fish Eat Little Fish* on her first visit to the Metropolitan Museum, at the age of eight. It had been the first—and also the last—time she had been invited to accompany her mother on one of her "rests," to visit her Aunt Sylvia in New York.

Aunt Sylvia was three years older than her mother, and had never married. She was what her mother described, with great respect, as a "real working artist." An interior decorator, she had started her own business, which had even—though just barely—survived the crash of '29. Sutton would always remember it very vividly afterward, the way her mother and Sylvia had sat together, hip to hip, on Sylvia's chaise lounge, leaning into each other as they spoke—her mother's hand sometimes even pressed into the pocket Sylvia made of her own. She remembered her mother's expression as she spoke, in a whisper, so that though Sutton could observe them from a distance she could never hear what they said. It was a blank, beseeching look—as though the words she uttered, which seemed to stream from her all at once in a rush, were in fact one long extended question, to which there would, or could, be no reply. She recalled that if ever she approached, Sylvia would look up brightly, before folding Sutton, along with her mother, into a firm embrace. For a few moments, then, the three of them would be pressed together like that, and Sutton would feel almost perfectly happy—having found herself, in this way, in sudden proximity to the great mysteries that that intimacy, which more often excluded her, contained.

Everything, she realized, existed like that—in proximity to some great mystery; simultaneously both included and excluded from it, by the very fact of its being, or imagining itself to be, a complete and separate thing. It was one thing, in any case, to bring an apple to a "whole," and quite another to depict the way it existed in relation to everything else. How, that is, was the empty space, which was (as she had recently found) so necessary in order to constitute any image as a whole, to remain empty when it was set, necessarily, against an inconceivably vast array of *other* objects? How could it be both whole in itself and yet a part of what (when figured alongside or against what it was not) could only be understood as another, still *greater* whole? How, indeed, could one whole ever be any greater or lesser than any other?

ALL OF THIS SUTTON pondered as she regarded Brueghel's fish, puzzling over the way the smaller fish were overlaid in the strangest way on the larger. She did not understand, you see—at first—that the knife also figured in the drawing was being used to some end: to cut open the belly of the larger fish in order to reveal the smaller fish within. What hesitation in her own perception of the image, she wondered (when finally this became clear), had suspended the knife for a moment in her mind before it achieved, at last, its inevitable end?

It was only after she understood the knife in this way that she was able to turn her attention to the rest of the image. To notice a fish with legs, for example, as it made its way toward the leftmost limit of the frame; then, suddenly, overhead (how had she failed to notice it before?) a fish with wings! She nearly laughed out loud when she saw it. Not because she found the representation—a bird as a fish, or a fish as a man—to be humorous, but because it revealed a suppleness to form and its perception that she had not previously allowed. That she could look and see, for example, in the place of a fish (with legs) not *only* a man, but a fish *and* a man; that the image could be, that is, at the same time neither and both at once without either her eye or her mind needing necessarily to understand where the line had been drawn, was, she considered (though bewildering), a very great and powerful thing.

So absorbed by these thoughts had Sutton become, it was some time before she noticed that she had been left quite alone. For several whole minutes she gazed around the empty gallery, unsure of what to do. Then—she could not later explain it, even to herself—something shifted. The room extended—flattening itself, so that it stretched ahead of her suddenly in a single plane—then it righted itself again. It was, she realized (the way that the world at that or at any time appeared), like Brueghel's fish—a simple matter of perspective. She could stretch and flatten it at will; could see it as both fixed and

unfixed, as both separate and part of a greater whole. It was no surprise, then, to discover that she had, over the other images she
regarded—even the dark portraits in the colonial rooms—the same
power she had had over Brueghel. Inspired, she began to move from
one heavy frame to the next down the long gallery hall, and—first
concentrating on the lines that bound them there—she freed the subjects of the Metropolitan Museum one by one. She *willed them*—men,
women, babies, horses, even apples and flowers and skulls—to grow
legs and walk away!

By the time she was returned by a kind guard to the museum lobby,
her mother had grown so pale and distracted by fear that it appeared to
Sutton, at first, as though she herself had been transformed into a
museum statue. She barely responded to Sutton's exuberant account of
her revelations among the "prints and drawings," or, indeed, to the fact
of her having been returned at all. In the end, the excursion proved, for
her mother, so altogether unrestful that it was no surprise to anyone that
(though her mother continued to visit Aunt Sylvia often after that, at
least for several more years) Sutton never went along again.

As time went on, and—apace with her growing abstraction—Mary
Kelly's relations with her sister became increasingly strained, she began
to depart more often than not to the seaside resort of Fenwick, Delaware, rather than to New York. She took comfort in the proximity to the
ocean, which recalled her to her own early childhood—spent near the
Gulf of Mexico. She had often spoken to Sutton of those days, and whenever she could, she searched out signs and cues that might serve to transport her there. She would stop suddenly in the street, for example, when
a streetcar rushed by, putting her hand to her face as though to touch the
impression made by the wind. When she did this, Sutton knew it was the
great breezes that blew off the coast of Pensacola—which emptied themselves at that point into the Gulf—that her mother recalled. And for a
moment (so vividly and on so many occasions had her mother described
that landscape over the years), she almost believed that she, too, had
been transported to her mother's coast—though, in truth, her own
experience of the ocean had so far been limited to Fenwick and, once (on

that same ill-fated trip, when she was eight years old), to the dark industrial waves of Coney Island.

At the time, it had felt to Sutton as though her mother re-created that landscape just for her; it took her years to realize that it was instead for her mother's own sake that she so carefully maintained, through repeated description, her childhood memories. For her own sake that she slowly shaped each image—careful to maintain an empty space within each one, by which route she might be permitted to enter, once again. That perfect square of light, which was not a square of light, or indeed anything at all—but, for every image, only the agreed-upon indicator that there exists, beyond both the image itself and the perceiving eye, that which cannot be drawn.

DALLING WAS RIGHT. BEFORE long Sutton had become a regular at Eleanor Roosevelt's Monday press conferences. She would show up with the rest of the reporters—anywhere from twenty to thirty of them on any given day—and wait for the usher to enter, lift the red velvet rope, and release them up the front stairs. At the top of the stairs, in the private living area of the President and his wife, they would await the arrival of Eleanor herself. It was important, Sutton soon learned, to get to the front of the pack, because those who arrived first—snagging chairs up front—were the ones, more often than not, to get their questions heard. Oddly, it was the older ladies, Sutton noticed, rather than the young ones who were the real contenders—and she soon realized why. It was on account of their shoes. The old ladies wore flats rather than heels and so were more sure-footed on the stairs. When she discovered this, Sutton took to wearing flats, too— which she in any case preferred—and pretty soon she was seated in the front row with the feature writers when the First Lady entered the room.

Good morning, good morning, girls, she would say, going around to shake everyone's hands. That took upward of a half an hour, leaving them all only a little less than that to ask the questions they'd prepared. Even so, on her first Monday, Sutton had found it almost impossible to keep up. She had sat at the back of the room next to Martha Strayer from the *Daily News*; had watched (she remembered) in wonder as Martha's hand skittered across the page at twice the speed of her own, leaving a trail of mysterious, unintelligible symbols in its wake.

She went home that night and began to teach herself shorthand, and before long could keep up with Martha and just about anyone else in the room. But she wanted more than that. She wanted—more than anything else—to leave the *Evening Star*, Martha Strayer, and even Eleanor Roosevelt, forever behind.

To this end, she traveled to New York to visit Stanley Walker, the editor of the *Herald Tribune*. It would be far easier to persuade him, she thought, than it would be to persuade Dalling, to hire a woman onto his regular news team. He had hired Dorothy Thompson, after all—whose column "On the Record" was widely read, having become especially popular after her book *I Saw Hitler* had been published back in 1932. There was also Anne O'Hare at the *New York Times*—the *Trib*'s major competitor; she had just won a Pulitzer for her column "Abroad," and had also managed to secure interviews with Mussolini and Hitler. Her coolheaded assessments of current events were the furthest thing from Randolph Hearst's "sob sister" reports as you were ever likely to find.

But on her first trip to New York—June 1936—Sutton failed even to secure an interview with Walker. Undeterred, she returned the following month, and—though she once again failed to meet with Walker in person—left the office that day, in what felt like a miraculous stroke of divine luck, with a job.

—

SHE MOVED TO NEW YORK IN LATE JULY, WHERE SHE SHARED A FLAT WITH TWO other girls. One, Ann Grover, worked as a photographer for the *Trib*. The other—Ann's cousin, Paula—worked as a fashion model for Macy's Department Store. It was through Ann that Sutton first met Louis, who also worked part-time for the *Trib*. He was five years older than she— twenty-four that spring—and had the cool nonchalance of a person who was not afraid of the world. You would almost forget, looking at him, that he was rather ordinary-looking, with slightly irregular features—his nose rather too large, his eyes a little too closely set. It was something about how he held himself, the offhand gestures he made as he spoke, or the way that he looked at you—the cool, unabashed intensity of his stare—that in the time it took your eyes to settle on him—by the time, that is, that any distinguishing features had even been drawn into view—he had already convinced you that he was far more handsome, and probably more intelligent, than he actually was, or was ever likely to turn out to be.

Also, he liked her—and said so. She herself was not at all bad-looking, having some time ago grown into the features her mother had always wistfully lamented would have been better spent on a boy. Her high forehead and strong, pronounced chin were offset by wide lips and a deep indentation in her right cheek, which lent to her overall appearance a mischievous air—and the impression that, despite her serious manner, she might, at any moment, disarm you completely with a broad smile.

Even so (having never had much of an affinity for, or been terribly good at, games), before Louis came along she'd had very few of even the most casual flirtations. Because of this, Louis's frankness was a trait she both admired and appreciated—and one that, ever afterward, she would find absolutely irresistible.

IT WAS AN ALMOST unbearably humid afternoon late in August, the first time she accompanied Louis back to the small studio he rented near Tompkins Square. Inside was even more stifling than out. Because of it, Louis spent the first five minutes of their time alone together wrestling with the kitchen window, though it was obvious it couldn't be opened any farther than it already was. It pleased Sutton to see that even Louis must have felt it, then: whatever it was that had been building between them all afternoon. That he knew—in the end—how to behave, on account of it, no better than she.

Finally, Louis gave up on the window and offered Sutton a glass of water instead. He stood beside her while she drank it. She felt she could almost taste it now, whatever it was between them: that same element— slightly sweet, slightly metallic on the tongue—that she now tasted in the water, which, just a moment before, had been extracted from the tap and handed to her. For the briefest moment her fingers touching Louis's on the glass.

It was as though they existed, then—the two of them, in those moments—as moisture exists; suspended in the air. Just at that point of humidity that, in another moment, will turn it heavily to rain. It was in this precarious state that they moved together across the studio floor to the darkroom (a converted utility closet, where Louis also kept a small, untidy bed). Strung across the ceiling were a dozen or so prints Louis had recently made. Simple studies: A lightbulb. A balloon. Then one of a young man—turned, so that half of his body was drawn into sharp focus, while the other half was badly blurred. He presented each to her, explaining the process according to which he'd developed them; how, that is, as he'd done so, he'd adjusted the contrast between dark and light tones—dodging and burning when necessary, in order to achieve the overall effect.

It was not until they had come to the last print—a study of the underside of the George Washington Bridge—that Louis (having turned suddenly, in order to make his way back to the door) caused Sutton (still moving in the opposite direction) to collide into him without warning. With that, the pressure between them burst and any final lingering hesitation on his part, or hers, was (as everything was, in that moment) at last dissolved.

It happened that Louis's father—a small-claims lawyer from Sioux City, Iowa—was personal friends with Harry Hopkins, supervisor of the Federal Relief Administration: so that was how, the following spring—June 1937—they both landed jobs with the Farm Security Administration, better known as the FSA.

They drove south. Through Virginia and North Carolina. Then west, through Tennessee. Passed through Dry Fork and Danville; through Long View and Cherokee; through Pigeon Forge, Friendsville, Ellendale, Bells . . .

They would turn up at the local diners, order coffee and pie, and, after they had succeeded in obtaining the names and general whereabouts of a few tenant farms in the area, drive off to find them. Sometimes it took all afternoon, but nearly always they found their way somewhere. That was the easy part. Once they arrived, it was more difficult. More often than not the families refused to be photographed. They would shrug their shoulders and insist that it could be of no particular importance that anyone in the city "get a look" at *this*, or *that*— gesturing off as they said so, in the direction of the house or the yard, or even on occasion toward themselves. Sutton and Louis would have to argue that, just the opposite, it was exactly *"this"* or exactly *"that"* that, despite what they wanted, people needed to see. It was their job, they said, to see that they did.

When a thing isn't *seen*, they explained—especially in Washington—it's just as if, sometimes, it doesn't exist at all. But it was a difficult point to make because when they were asked anything specific—like who exactly would see their photographs, and what "real" things would be their direct result—their answers couldn't be anything but vague. They themselves had no idea where their photographs would go, or what impact they might have—if any. But for a while they had faith that they would indeed have an impact, and that any impact was genuine, and being genuine was good. They still believed, in other words, that it was possible to do what they'd been asked. To press into the frame of each photograph they took a corresponding reality—as though it were the responsibility not only of themselves, but of the page, to absorb the world in perfect ratio, one to one.

—

THEY DROVE ON. TO JONESBORO, ARKANSAS. WEST PLAINS, MISSOURI. To Ozark, Bolivar, Dunnegan, Stockton . . . And everywhere they went, especially as they drew near the Kansas border, Sutton looked for Arthur. For Douglas.

How she might recognize them if she saw them, she didn't know. After so much time had passed, she had only the most abstract image of either one of them left in her mind. And even that—when she tried to hunt after it—seemed nearly always to swim from her grasp. If she didn't think of it, there they would be: she was fairly haunted by them. But always, just as—sensing their presence—she turned toward them in an effort, at last, to finally apprehend them . . . they would, just as easily, be gone.

What did not leave her, what had never left her—even after all the years that had now passed in between—was the moment she had stood, *seeing but unseen*, opposite her brother and Arthur—Arthur nearly unrecognizable even then. His face scratched and bloodied—wearing, for some reason, another man's hat . . .

What did not leave her was the moment in which—as though impelled by some force beyond her—she raised her own hand toward that hat. And the knowledge that—though it had indeed seemed as though she'd been *impelled by some force, beyond her*—there had, in the end, been no one but she who had raised her hand; who had pointed at Arthur Sinclair and identified him, falsely, as the guilty man.

It was on a visit to Washington, just before her departure with Louis that spring, that Sutton had made her first—concerted—attempt to locate some record of Arthur Sinclair: a whole afternoon spent scanning through the courthouse register, searching for some evidence of his arrest back in 1932. She found none.

The clerk had shrugged when she finally worked up the nerve to inquire.

That was a busy afternoon, he said, when she mentioned the date. No question there'd be some came through and released without any record at all.

She returned the next day, this time taking out all the records from October 1932 through November 1934. She scanned through them slowly, one page at a time. It was tedious work, and after a while the names and dates began to all blur together so that she worried that even if Arthur's name *did* appear she wouldn't recognize it.

But then—suddenly (she need never have worried)—there it was. Trembling, distinct, and alone against a sea of other names, which, rather than distracting from it, served instead to set it apart. Beneath the typeset date, February 6, 1933, exactly what she had been looking for: the name *Arthur Sinclair*, and beside it, clearly marked in red, a single word: *Released*. She had not realized the extent of the relief she would feel until she felt it. Until she saw his name there, in legible letters, and that single word, indicating that he (and, accordingly, she herself) had been set free—and, indeed, some time ago.

She gazed at that name and its accompanying date for a long time. Then, very slowly, very deliberately, she closed the book and returned the stack to the clerk.

Had she found what she needed? he asked. Coolly—as though he hardly expected a reply.

Yes, she said. Yes, thank you, I have. She turned to go then—but something stopped her. No doubt her reply had surprised the clerk. She had seen it—she was nearly certain of it: something flicker behind his otherwise impassive gaze. After all, she considered, it must be very rare that—spending his days overseeing the consultation of so many years of dusty files—he might observe—indeed, have a hand in—the retrieval of some fragment, however minute and ultimately inconsequential, against that tide.

She turned back. There was really perhaps no one with whom it would be more fitting to share the news.

For some time, she told the clerk then, she had been concerned over the fate of a certain Arthur Sinclair—of whom she had not had any news since his incarceration back in 1932. It now seemed—she continued—that though she had yet to find any record of his having *actually been admitted*, it was clearly recorded that he had in fact been *released* from county jail, in February 1933.

But now the clerk appeared distracted. He blinked, and once again—unmistakably now—something flashed behind his eyes.

I know that name, he said. Twice more he blinked. Yes, I am almost certain of it. *Arthur Sinclair*. Again: blink. It wasn't so long ago I had an inquiry after *the very same man*. Yes, I am quite sure of it. Wait, will you? Wait here a moment.

He disappeared behind the stacks.

Anxiously, Sutton awaited his return. After a while she began to feel a little ill. She looked around for a place to sit down. There wasn't any.

Finally—nearly twenty minutes must have passed—the clerk returned, his thumb pressed among the pages of a book.

Yes, he said, it's here.

Now he laid the book open flat on the counter between them and jabbed at something on the page.

Yes, unmistakably: for the second time in one afternoon, there it was. *Arthur Sinclair.*

But what could it mean? Sutton looked at the name, then at the clerk, then back at the name blankly.

The *Missing Persons Bureau*, the clerk said. Arthur Sinclair has been listed in the book since—he squinted at the date: August 1932.

But— Sutton began. If the file was made *before* the recorded release, it must have simply been a matter of . . . she paused. Somehow—temporarily—*losing track* of him during that time; that *afterward*—

The clerk shook his head.

No, he said. It's indicated that the name has been reentered every year since, and I can quite clearly recall, myself—only last month, in fact—a young man once again making inquiries. Which is why—you see—the name, just now, so clearly rang a bell—

And the young man—Sutton interrupted. Do you recall his name? Would you have for him—perhaps—some forwarding address?

I'm afraid that's not at all my jurisdiction, the clerk said. You would have to contact the bureau, I suppose. With that, the light that had burned briefly in the clerk's eyes flickered, and went out.

Sutton telephoned the bureau, asking directly for the name and address of whatever person was responsible for reentering, year after year, Arthur Sinclair's name into the Missing Persons file.

She did not meet with any luck.

It's just, you see—she lied—I have some *pertinent information*, which I am sure would be quite useful, if—

This did not get her much further.

I'm sorry, miss—she was told. That is just simply not our policy. We are not at liberty to deal with these matters case by case. We must, for each, follow a standardized protocol; otherwise, as you must understand, we would put our clients—who put their every trust in us—at great personal risk.

Of course, Sutton said.

Then—nearly giving up: Look, she said. I admit I have no pertinent information about this case—none at all. In fact, it is just the opposite. It is purely a matter of personal importance. But, if . . .

Here she paused. She did not know how she might continue.

If—what? It was useless.

If I am able— she continued. But then her voice, which had grown thin, broke onto a disconcerted silence.

It is hardly policy, said the voice on the other end of the line, after a moment or two in which neither spoke. I'll see what I can do.

Two weeks later, Sutton received the name she had anticipated: Douglas Sinclair, and an address of a corps project in Boonsboro, Maryland. On her last day in New York, she posted a letter there—urging Douglas to contact her as soon as he reasonably could. Ashamed, for some reason, to provide him with her own father's address, she included Louis's father's address instead—promising that the letter would be forwarded on.

Three weeks after that, however, it was her own letter that arrived, general delivery, to Athens, Tennessee: unread. A scrawled note on the back indicated that, the project (a thorough reconstruction of the Washington Monument, which had, in more recent years, been allowed to crumble into disrepair) completed, the corps had dispersed, Douglas along with them—leaving behind him no forwarding address.

It was a bitter disappointment. As the fall wore on, a profound loneliness descended over Sutton, at times bordering on despair. The feeling was only accentuated by the vastness that stretched between the deserted towns she and Louis passed through, as they continued to make their way; now into the most windblown and uninhabited reaches of Oklahoma and West Texas.

And by another vastness. That which stretched—increasingly—between herself and Louis. Never once had she breathed a word to him about Douglas or Arthur, and neither had she spoken (except to offer the most basic account) of Alden or her parents. For Louis it was the same: a rare occasion that he talked—if ever he did—about the past. With them, instead, it was always the present: what, of it, they might be able to seize; or—at least for Louis, who had become thoroughly obsessed with F. W. H. Myers and his *Human Personality and Its Survival of Bodily Death*—the *distant* past. More and more, with the help of Myers, Louis had become convinced that—with the correct attention and time—he might recover all of his past lives. That they might—as simply as from a roll of film—be spun out one day in a long chain, where they had remained, all along, imprinted inside him.

To comfort herself on long drives—or in the evenings, while Louis read or slept—she wrote long letters to Alden in her head. First one way, then another, she described to him the events, as she recalled them now, immediately following his arrest.

For the first time. As best she could: her father's voice. His calm advice. How *"the truth"* had sounded to her then. In that room, and from his lips.

Most often, she would defend herself. *I did it for you!* Or feign innocence: *I hardly knew* what *I was doing, and still don't; how can we know?* On rarer occasions she would berate herself pitilessly for what she had done. How could she not—she would wonder—have pressed her father for some other solution? There *must*—she'd insist—have been *some other way* than such a willful abuse of justice—a *lie!*

But no—she had willingly complied. She had condemned an innocent man to a wrongful fate, without so much as a moment's hesitation—and for what? She was certain that Alden himself could see (as she could see quite clearly now) that *the truth* would not have had, for Alden, the same consequences it had had for the other man.

On still rarer occasions she lashed out at the Judge—or at Alden himself. How could they have put her—*a child*—in such a vile position? How could they have let her carry that burden all these years—alone?

No matter what version of the letter she wrote, however, she always closed it in more or less the same way: Did Alden also—she pressed—

find himself troubled by the past? And so piercingly, sometimes, that it no longer seemed like the past at all? Did he ever suspect—as she did—that the past did not ever really disappear? That everything remained, instead: haunting the present, forecasting the future, and rendering every effort, on account of it, utterly futile? Every outcome as inescapable as if it had already arrived?

Finally, she did write. An abbreviated version of the letters she wrote in her head, and something of a compromise between the various directions she had previously taken. She simply confessed. Recounting, as simply as she could, her complicity in the events that had led to Alden's release—and the arrest of Arthur Sinclair.

In closing, she sketched out, in a few words, what details she had managed to glean as to Arthur's and Douglas's present circumstances from the courthouse register, and very briefly inquired if he, like she, found himself troubled by the news.

AN ANSWER WAS A long time in coming, and in that time Sutton regretted bitterly having written at all. It would have been better, she thought—as she had long suspected—just to let the thing go.

Why had she been so bent on preserving the old demons? On dragging them up now, after so long—and not only for herself, now, but for Alden, as well? What possible motive could she have had for doing so? Perhaps, she considered regretfully, instead of a genuine desire to bridge the distance that had grown between them, it had been a desire instead—to punish him, somehow. A way of making sure that *Alden*, too, would be unable to forget—

Well, what purpose could that serve either of them now? Let alone—she reflected—anyone else? Douglas—or Arthur.

ALDEN'S REPLY CAME—WHEN at last it did—as a great relief. He wrote at length, and far more intimately than she herself had dared. But instead of responding to her confession, or reflecting directly on the news she had shared, he advised her to see the whole thing in an entirely different light. One thing (he reminded her) had, at least—through all of this—become clear. Arthur had been "released." Why not allow her-self to be?

At no point did Alden mention that he had in fact been aware of everything to which Sutton had recently confessed. He wrote only: *The world and its workings are much vaster than any of us can even begin to imag-ine.* Only: *Though we may be doomed to read things always and only accord-ing to our own, very limited point of views, that does not make the singularity of that perspective any more true.* He himself (he told Sutton) was begin-ning, at least, to understand things this way—ever since the death of his dear friend Emmett Henderson, who had lost his life fighting for the Spanish Republic just that past spring.

It was Emmett who had urged him, Alden wrote—just shortly before his own untimely end—that *one played, even within the context of one's own life, only a limited role.* To imagine it otherwise, Emmett had argued, was an error both in judgment and scale. And (contrary to what it might seem at the outset) to *truly* understand that this was so, and act accordingly, was an exacting—if not downright impossible—task; far more difficult than any pre-Copernican formulation: each man for himself and at the center of all things. It was only—counseled the doomed Emmett Henderson—by releasing oneself from what could only be the most illusory sense of an ultimate claim over one's own life, down to its smallest and most insignificant thought or deed (a compulsion, he'd observed wryly, that—in our present day culture—had become *downright pathological*), that one might actually begin to understand one's place in the world. And become, therefore, *more* rather than *less* capable of working toward some greater good.

He himself understood, of course (Alden continued), how the feel-ings Sutton mentioned arose. He himself had at one time—not so long before, and as mad as it sounds!—been convinced that in some small way he had even *become* Arthur Sinclair, so deeply and earnestly had he taken him, and his fate—unknown as it was—into his heart. The auda-city of this idea now simply astounded him. What a relief (Alden wrote), *more* than a relief, to be—finally—released from that delusion! To be just—what luck—*himself* again!

AFTER THAT, ALDEN AND Sutton kept up a vigorous correspondence. Sutton writing long descriptions of the towns they passed through—Waco, Shreveport, Vicksburg, Jackson—and the landscape, which, even as they left the desert behind and drove deep into the South, seemed to become (in accordance with her diminishing faith in her ability to press from, or against it, any "reality" at all) only emptier by the day. Alden returning—at her request—brief comic sketches of his life in Paris, and the people (mostly Americans, she was disappointed to learn!) he knew there. And, from time to time, a scrap of an almost indecipherable poem, which, in her next letter, she would ask him to parse (a request he could be counted on to ignore or refuse).

Still. And despite her relief that the past, in having at last been spoken, had become less the impassable object it had once been between them—and Alden's encouragement to leave it, simply and finally, behind—Sutton continued to expect, at every turn, around every bend, if not Douglas or Arthur Sinclair to actually *appear*, then . . . something. A hat, perhaps, she thought to herself sometimes—just to be cruel. The one distinguishing feature of either man she could, with any sort of certainty, recall.

—

LOUIS TOOK TO TAKING PHOTOGRAPHS AT MIDDAY; BLANCHING FROM them those details he might otherwise have captured in the milder light of the early morning or pre-dusk hours, and lending a slightly windswept quality to even the photographs that had been meticulously posed. He was particularly proud, for example, of a photograph entitled "Dust Storm," because, in actuality, it been taken on a very still day. Southern Oklahoma: his subjects—a father and three of his sons. They had posed patiently for him all afternoon, while Louis shouted orders like a general, made endless rearrangements, and shot through four rolls of film . . .

Hot and tired, Sutton had asked: How much is the truth worth if you insist on sacrificing reality to it every day?

As her own faith flagged, she was, perhaps, beginning to resent Louis's continued enthusiasm. (Though even he, as time wore on, began to agree: the more they persisted in their attempt to capture the "true," or the "real," the further away they seemed to get from anything at all.) Still, they tried. Staged shots, candid ones. Long exposures, short ones. And still, just as Sutton suspected, each, in the end, turned out the same. Nothing more than a photograph; flimsy and alterable as a word. How could she ever have expected anything else? A photograph was only, after all, an object like any other, meaning very little on its own. In fact, it seemed to Sutton that any photograph they took, or could take now, would require not only—like a word—a complete sentence, if not a whole book, to lend to it meaning, but a whole world; that it would require the entire state of Kansas or Oklahoma to stretch itself again just as it had in the moment it had first been "captured" on the page; for the dust to blow again through the flattened landscape; for the bodies of the people in the photograph, if there were any, to, once again, take on their proper dimensions and forms; for their thoughts to reach as far as they ever did into the invisible corners of their minds.

At the beginning, though, whenever she expressed this sort of doubt to Louis, he would only grind his teeth and swear.

Well, dammit! he would say. What do you expect? You'll go mad if you think you can draw the whole world, like that, on the head of a pin.

But he was just as guilty as she was in that regard—more so. If anyone was going to go mad, Sutton told him, it was him. A reporter, she said, drew lines whenever she could between what was "visible" and what was not; an artist attempted to push past those lines. It was only a madman, she said, who attempted to eliminate them entirely.

Louis had continued—more and more urgently, perhaps, as the weeks and then the months began to pass—to devote himself to his study of F. W. H. Myers. At night, camped out in the back of their 1931 Willys Knight (a gift from Louis's father), he read particularly persuasive sections of *Human Personality* to Sutton out loud—making it even more impossible than usual for her to sleep.

There existed, Myers and then Louis explained, continuities between the living world and the dead that had long been overlooked. How could she not see it, Louis wondered in genuine confusion, just as clearly as he? Photography, after all—he added after further reflection, in an argument all his own—was *direct evidence of Myers's claim!* Just *think of it*, he begged. How everything we've done—all our efforts to date (here he gestured loosely toward the back of the Willys Knight, where box upon box of as-yet-undeveloped film lay jumbled together in packing crates) sit spooled in darkness. And will continue to—he said—until, one day soon, with the correct application of water and light, they—*the past itself*—will rise again to meet us!

Why is it so hard to imagine? he would ask on other occasions, when Sutton laughed outright, or—afflicted suddenly, as she often was in his mad moments, with an almost asphyxiating boredom—turned impatiently away. If they are intent, he said, on science providing the answers only to the things we already know, then it isn't of any more use to us than religion! The surrealists, Louis argued further, had not gone far enough. They pursued their investigations the way they pursued everything else—as an approach, a pose. They plumbed the unconscious only for the purposes of surface ornamentation; they skated, in this way, Louis said, *right over the truth*, which—if they had only looked a bit deeper—they would have easily found. (Incidentally—it was by this logic that Louis defended the manipulations of the photographs he took—a photograph fails, he said, as everything fails, if you depend only on what is immediately apparent to the eye.)

It was not just conjecture, either, insisted Louis. Myers supplied "hard proof": dozens of transcripts of the communications he and his friends had conducted over the years with the dead. That this "proof" had been largely discredited or (worse) ignored by academic scientists—a fact Sutton often pointed out—did not bother Louis one bit. It was not because the research wasn't valid, he said; guided by the same principles as all modern science has been, ever since Aristotle woke up one day and discovered the universe *in particular*, and from there began to reason, then to extrapolate, and finally to dream! No, it was not science but politics that had clamped down on Myers's research—trivializing his efforts in the same way that, once, Galileo and Copernicus had been sidelined and condemned!

Think of it, said Louis. What Myers discovered threatens the very structure of our current state! If it were to actually get out, if we were suddenly to make *use* of these findings, in a broader and more systematic way, think what upheaval there would be; what final, total revolution! If Alexander the Great or Napoleon, say, suddenly reared up their mighty heads once more and gave counsel (or denied it) to Franco or Roosevelt! Think of it! Louis exclaimed. If Galileo came back and described for us, in detail—based *on his personal experience* beyond the grave—the music of the spheres, and Poincaré reported on relativity and the proper measure of infinity, and Goethe discussed his latest postmortal notions of the transmutation of the soul!

THE MORE DISTANCE THEY covered together—north again: Rock Hill, Summerfield, Lynchburg; then east, toward home—the more certain Sutton became that the problem was not, as it seemed to Louis, that nothing succeeded in going deep enough, but just the opposite: in not being able to pause anything for long enough that what existed at the surface could be properly seen. Perhaps Alden (she thought) was right after all. There existed at any moment much more than could ever possibly be witnessed, let alone understood, but that what escaped *was not hidden*. It might indeed even be quite evident, were we not so obsessed with looking for it in the wrong places. Sometimes she would take Louis's face in her hands so he could not turn away; look at him, very squarely, like that. And she would be sure—quite sure—in those moments, that he was wrong. That it was a mistake, a madness—in art as equally as love—to assume that the truth existed somewhere beyond or beneath the surface of things. Because the harder, the deeper, she looked into Louis's eyes, the less sure she was that she was seeing anything at all. When, on the other hand, she let her gaze rest on him only lightly—letting the spray of colors around his black pupils (they were ringed like small suns) dance in the light and the shifting focus of her own eyes—she felt it. A powerful surge of something in her, which she knew could be nothing other (as in that first moment of contact, when the two of them had burst like clouds in each other's arms) than purest love.

—

FOR SOME REASON, AS THE MONTHS PASSED, AND THEY BEGAN—INCREAS-ingly, and for very different reasons—to sense how ultimately "empty" the photographs they took were, or would soon turn out to be, they could no longer bear the thought of parting with them. They began to develop and, each month, send to Hopkins in Washington only a fraction of the film they shot over the same period. By the time, therefore—in late fall of 1937—they arrived back in New York, they'd amassed several crates' worth of "stolen" negatives. These they printed in a crumbling one-bedroom they rented on the Lower East Side before laboriously cutting each print into tiny pieces and arranging them according to light and shade on the living room floor.

When, for the first time, they stepped back to observe the result—their efforts of the last six months arranged around them in luminous abstract shapes; each appearing almost three-dimensional, as though collapsing in on itself like a dying sun—they were overcome (again, for their different reasons) with a strange mixture of devastating sadness and indescribable joy.

THANKS TO HOPKINS, WHO had personally recommended her, Sutton landed a job almost immediately upon her return to New York with Federal One. They started her off with the Writers' Project—the guidebook series, in copy—but within two months she was promoted to managing editor, everything from Maine to Maryland suddenly under her domain.

Louis had declined a similar offer. He spent his time running up everyone they knew, trying to get them a private show for their work. Finally, he managed it: at a small gallery owned by the Polish artist Franz Wilhelm—an old acquaintance of Louis's, who, it was rumored, was a direct descendant of Ferdinand I. In defiance of his own extraordinary size—he was as big as three men and had fingers like piano keys—Franz Wilhelm painted miniatures on fragments of pottery and glass, which were sometimes so small one needed a magnifying glass in order to see that anything had been painted on the surface at all.

He displayed his own work in an emptied shop front in Red Hook attached to an old factory building. There he collected art the way scientists collect rare specimens of insect or gemstone: the "factory" was a jumble of the work of every artist he had ever met, many of whom—as he bragged, unusually, when he showed Louis and Sutton the space—*no one had ever heard of.* But they didn't argue when Franz Wilhelm purchased two of their "exploding stars" to add to his collection.

Even with the patronage of Franz Wilhelm, however, and the absent-minded support of Louis's father, after only a few weeks their brief career sputtered to a halt. Finally, Louis admitted that he, too, would need, at least temporarily, to support himself by other means, and shortly after landed a job at *Life* magazine—which was just then becoming famous for its glossy photo spreads.

That was the beginning of 1938; Europe was boiling. At any moment war might break out. Sutton was loath to spend it—if and when it did—editing the "Major Points of Interest" sections of New Jersey or Maryland.

With this in mind, she went back to Walker at the *Herald Tribune* and asked for a job.

A real job, she said. I want to report from London, or Paris—or Berlin.

Walker laughed appreciatively and shook his head. So long as I live, he said, I won't be sending any woman overseas; you have my word on that.

But he gave her back her old job.

So she resigned from the Writers' Project, and a month later was called up to testify for Martin Dies. She should have seen it coming. The Dies Committee had been investigating "un-American activities" in Federal One projects for over two years, and was famous for tracking down just the right witnesses—those who, for one reason or another, had a bone to pick with Federal One or the WPA. Having abruptly quit the Writers' Project (where, indeed—having no Communist Party affiliation herself—she had found herself in the minority), she must have looked a likely candidate to Dies.

Just the year before, another former employee—the recently retired Edwin Banta—had aided Dies's personal crusade by testifying that thirteen of the fifteen supervisors of the New York section of the guidebook series were Communists. Lou Gody (Banta testified), who had been Sutton's supervisor, had never written a line of his own, and Mr. Kingman, of the Foreign Language Division, did not speak a single foreign language. All of this may have been true, as Sutton wrote to Alden—searching for advice on the issue—but as far as she was concerned, it spoke more than anything of the *dis*organization of the project than anything else. The thought that anyone in that office could have held a significant threat to the government—or anyone, for that matter—was laughable, she wrote.

Alden wrote back to say that, though he would be careful making any grand pronouncements (it was always impossible to know what you were looking at, after all, he said, when you really started looking at a thing), she should be just fine if she told them exactly what she knew. And who can tell—he added—perhaps she knew more than she thought; that her testimony would even do someone, somewhere, a little bit of good.

Despite this encouragement, Sutton wrote to the committee requesting she be excused from the hearing. It had only been a matter of months, she wrote, that she'd worked for the project: she knew of nothing untoward about either the project or the organization under question, and had nothing to report.

The idea of appearing in front of the committee frankly horrified her. The only employee whom she knew personally who had done so was Ralph De Sola—a former zookeeper from Miami. Unlike Banta, he had stayed on at the project even after his testimony—earning himself the nickname "Reptile" because of the way he continued to slink daily into his corner of the office in order to continue work on his pet projects: *Who's Who in the Zoo*, and *American Wildlife*. The last thing Sutton wanted was to align herself with De Sola. She wasn't a party member, but she certainly wasn't a "reptile," either.

DESPITE HER PERSONAL APPEAL, however, Sutton appeared in front of the Dies Committee—which consisted of Dies himself and a nervous-looking girl of about twenty, charged with the task of typing up the transcript of their exchange—in September 1938.

Let's get straight to the point, Dies had said, after Sutton had been directed, opposite him, to a straight-backed chair, and the typist, her fingers poised above the keys, had indicated with a worried nod that she was ready to begin. Were there, in your work with the Writers' Project, Dies said, and in particular in your role as editor of the state guidebook to New Jersey, any . . . *particular guidelines* about what should be included and not included in the text?

Sutton had badly wanted to appear aloof, to answer calmly and coolly, but right off the bat she stalled.

How could there not be? she asked. It seemed like a trick question. We could hardly include everything.

Enlighten me, Dies said—a smile playing at the corners of his lips, which looked chapped and dry.

The guidebooks are . . . intended—Sutton began, hesitatingly slow—to convey only the most basic information, sir. They are intended, you see, as . . . objectively as possible, to show—

Ah! Dies said, raising a hand in the air. *As objectively as possible*, you say. May I perhaps here inquire after the limits against which this effort of yours—to be *as objective as possible*—may have been pressed?

Again, Sutton hesitated. I can't say I know what you are getting at, sir, she said.

Dies cleared his throat and shifted his attention to a folder in front of him. Very casually, he began leafing through the pages the folder contained, as though he had forgotten the question himself.

Finally, he found what he was looking for.

Were you, or were you not, he asked, peering over the top of the sheet of paper he now held between them, responsible for the sentence in the New Jersey guide claiming that a certain factory—he glanced down, consulting the page—was, and I quote, "the biggest buyer of tear gas in the state"?

The chair felt suddenly very hard beneath her, and Sutton shifted uncomfortably. I can't quite recall, sir, she said.

Well, said Dies cheerfully, let's say for the moment that it is true—because I have it on record that it is so. Would you say that this was an . . . *objective* statement?

It was—Sutton said quietly, her voice tight in her throat—the information I was given.

What was that? Dies asked, though it was quite clear he'd heard.

Sutton cleared her throat and repeated her reply. Louder this time.

And did you—Dies shot back, satisfied—check that information against the facts available to you?

Now Sutton could feel her cheeks grow hot. They *were* the facts available to me, she said.

Dies sighed exaggeratedly. Miss Kelly, he said—as though all at once he had grown tired of the exercise. It is my duty to inform you that there is no record of the factory in question acquiring, let alone *using*, tear gas against strikers or anyone else. What, then, I wonder, was the purpose of including this claim in your "general interest" touristic guide to the state?

Sutton said nothing.

Let me stick a little closer to the point, continued Dies. We seem to be having a little difficulty understanding each other. Are you, or were you at any time, Miss Kelly, under the impression that the Federal Writers' Project, or the WPA more generally, had as its express purpose the intention to spread communism throughout the United States?

No, sir, Sutton said. It was hardly the express purpose—she began.

But a purpose, Dies said, leaning slightly forward in his chair, nevertheless?

Listen, Sutton said. She felt terribly impatient with the whole thing suddenly, and experienced a powerful urge to simply get up and walk out of the room. Would Dies follow her if she did? Would the girl? Her typewriter still rattling?

Listen, she said again. I don't see what the purpose of an inquiry is if you know exactly what you want to hear from the beginning.

Dies smiled. Ah, yes, he said. I do apologize. You were saying . . .

I was saying that . . . it was hardly the express purpose of the Writers' Project or any Federal One organization so far as I know to spread communism or any other political doctrine, in this country or abroad.

Dies nodded his head slowly. The typewriter rang. There was a slight pause then, as her inquisitor gazed upward, as though in deep contemplation of what she had just said. Then, in a changed tone, his voice suddenly bright, as though the two of them had just been introduced at a party by mutual friends, he asked: Have you, by chance, read—Miss Kelly—the essay by Mr. Richard Wright that was recently commissioned by your organization?

Sutton hadn't the slightest clue where this was leading. She had never had any association with the book *American Stuff*, in which Wright's essay had been included, and to which Dies now referred—it had gone to press before she'd landed the job. She knew of Wright only by reputation.

No, she said, I have not.

You are familiar, though, Dies said, with the writer and the collection in question?

Reluctantly, Sutton nodded. Dies nodded, too. Then, once more, he opened his folder, this time easily locating the page he sought.

I'd like to read you an excerpt, he said. I regret it very much, given the very particular . . . *quality* . . . of the piece, but I do think you'll understand, given the circumstances, and that it may indeed prove to . . . further our discussion. Here, now. He cleared his throat. Page forty-three.

When I was a bit slow in performing some duty, Dies read, *I was called a lazy black son of a bitch*. All right. Dies glanced briefly over his eyeglasses, licked his thumb, and turned the page.

Page forty-four (skipping just little ahead, he said). *If yuh say yuh didn't I'll rip yo' gut-string loose with this fuckin' bar, you black granny dodger. Yuh can't call a white man a liar 'n' get away with it, you black son of a bitch.*

Is that enough, Miss Kelly? Dies asked, snapping the folder shut. I'll say it is! Now I'm curious, Miss Kelly, if you actually find "literature" of this type to be in some way "rehabilitating"?

Sutton stared at him. What possible connection can my opinion, she asked after a heavy pause, of what you've read just now have to do with this discussion?

Oh, everything in the world! Dies said. Everything in the world! Are you—let me ask you this again—of the opinion that this sort of "literature"—the sort I've just read—holds some value for reader and listener? That it might enlighten us in some way? Enlarge our cultural tradition, or our minds?

I believe this discussion is over, Sutton said. I have nothing to report.

Dies raised an eyebrow, scribbled something furiously on the cover of the folder in front of him, then let the subject drop.

SUTTON DID NOT LET the subject drop quite so easily. She was working first-string news at the time, but kept after Walker for a feature piece on Dies, and before long—to her surprise—he relented. A week later, she followed Dies to Washington, where—having been forced at last to extend his investigation beyond the Federal One employees who had openly broken with the project—he interviewed Henry Alsberg, the project's director.

The interview was far less intimate than her own had been. The press was wild for it, and—to mark the occasion, as well as deflect some attention—Dies had invited the rest of the committee to join him this time. More usually (as Sutton knew from her personal experience) he roved the country, aside from the typist, alone.

Alsberg played his cards right. Right off the bat he managed to win sympathy from even the toughest critics of Federal One, and even Dies himself, by admitting to a onetime radicalism he had since, he promised, been cured of—thanks to a stint as editor for a collection of letters sent surreptitiously from a Russian gulag.

This was just the sort of stuff Dies wanted to hear.

There are certain things, Alsberg said, that once you learn you just can't turn away from. They haunt you; you give up all your old ideals. Everything becomes treacherous and confused, and you don't know what to believe anymore. After this happened to me, and I became staunchly anti-Communist—as I remain to this day—I can tell you one thing for sure. I suffered for it in America. I was blacklisted. I couldn't get any of my articles printed any more. Even today, I am considered a reactionary. I hadn't known how far the influence stretched before because I had been a part of it: that's how it goes.

But after this promising initial outburst, Alsberg seemed to have nothing more to say; certainly nothing to hang a case on. It was a tremendous blow for Dies. Now, even according to America's self-professed "arch-anti-Communist," as the newspapers had it, nothing was amiss with Federal One. Dies was heralded by the press—and even by some more outspoken members of the cabinet—as "the harbinger of American fascism"; it was recalled in editorials and government assemblies alike that Mussolini, too, had "risen to absolute and despotic power" after having organized a similar hunt for "Communists" in his own country. Same thing with Hitler. "We are deluding ourselves," the newspapers chimed, "if we believe that it is out of the question in this country that, after just such a scare as was recently drummed up by Hitler in Germany and is currently being drummed up by Dies and the rest over here, some man on horseback might also rise up in order to 'protect' us from the perceived danger."

But Dies was not easily discouraged. After the Federal One hearings, he hit the road, holding hearings in Chicago and Detroit. The teachers' union was investigated, along with every student group (to his credit, most turned out—just as he'd suspected—to be verifiable fronts for the CPUSA). Finally, he homed in on Hollywood; but there, for some reason, he cut his investigation short. Later, it was rumored that Dies had been paid off by the head of Paramount Pictures, Y. Frank Freeman; that he had been so flattered by his treatment there—all the stops had been pulled, the red carpets rolled out—that he entirely forgot why he had come.

The investigation had initially been launched on the strength of the testimony of John Leech, who, a month prior, claimed to have served as a recruiter for the Communist Party in Hollywood since 1936. He rattled off a dozen names for Dies to follow up with, among them Humphrey Bogart and Jimmy Cagney. But—unusually—after only a few weeks, Dies reported with confidence from Hollywood that nothing was awry. His official take on the situation (in sharp contrast to every other investigation he had so far pursued) was that "no man can be held accountable for what someone says about him"; the case was abruptly put to rest.

Not long after, Dies got into some trouble of his own when his investigations came in at cross-purposes with the newly revamped FBI. At the end of 1938 he was invited to the White House for an urgent chat with the President. Sutton heard about it later from her father, who was so galled by what he called Dies's "blatant insubordination" that it took nothing, hardly, to get him to speak freely on the subject.

I would have had him thrown out for a rogue years ago—the Judge complained—but for some reason the President's seen fit to go the absolute opposite direction. Invites him to the White House, you know. Calls him "Martin." Was absolutely at his most ingratiating.

You know you have to protect innocent people, "Martin," the President had said. You can't go around dragging in everyone and anyone that crosses your path.

Dies had, by all accounts, agreed wholeheartedly, grateful for the note the President had chosen to strike—considering the terrible mess he'd just made for the FBI.

Of course, he'd said quickly, I do understand. We had, for instance, as you may have heard, quite a bit of trouble awhile back with certain movie actors—but in those cases it was clear we had to be quite sensitive—

Quite right, the President had said. We all make mistakes. But these types—as I'm happy to hear you agree—must not be held up to the public as sympathizers, where it may simply be a matter of ignorance on their part.

Oh, yes, Dies returned. Like you, Mr. President, I am a very busy man. If we dragged every ignorant man in this country through the dirt, I can assure you there would hardly be time for anything else.

At that the President laughed good-naturedly—a response that confused Dies at first. He hadn't been joking. Soon afterward, however— as, later, Judge Kelly reported irreverently—the two parted on agreeable terms, shaking hands like old friends.

—

SUTTON HAD SCORED A MAJOR VICTORY IN SECURING THE DIES ASSIGN- ment, but when the Hollywood scandal fizzled, and, soon after, war erupted in earnest, she found herself no closer to convincing Walker to send her overseas.

From Paris, Alden's letters rang with a mixture of excitement and alarm. She anticipated them eagerly: keenly jealous, as she did not mind telling him, of his having, inadvertently, found himself "right in the midst of it all."

But then, without warning—just before France capitulated in June 1940—Alden's letters stopped abruptly. After that, the summer dragged endlessly as Sutton waited for any word from—or (she braced herself) of—Alden at all.

Finally, at the beginning of September, she received the briefest of letters. He was being held—Alden wrote—in a German prisoner-of- war camp, just south of Berlin. He said very little other than that, and nothing as to how he had ended up there—only promising that, all things considered, he was well, and further assuring her that, with a little luck, he'd be back in Paris before long.

IT WAS SHORTLY AFTER that, just after the first bombs rained down over London, that *Life* magazine offered to send Louis overseas. Sutton redoubled her efforts with Walker when she heard the news, and felt the sting of his refusal, when it came, even more acutely. Briefly, she consid- ered Louis's suggestion that she go along anyway—not bothering with the proper press credentials. But something stopped her. Almost everything else, she reflected, that she had so far accomplished in life, she owed to someone else's influence or authority. Her first job at the *Star*, for example, had been secured by the Judge; the job with the FSA and later the Writers' Project she owed to Louis, or at least the connections of his father. Perhaps it had become personal with Walker as well. She wanted badly to force from him something other than his by-now-familiar, rehearsed replies. That there were no "facilities" for women in the field was a particular favorite of his. She refused—she insisted on multiple occasions to him and to Louis—to have a lack of women's toilets keep her out of the war.

Once Louis was gone, however, she bitterly regretted her decision. She waited anxiously for any news of him, and in her own letters plied him with questions pertaining to every detail of his experience. In order, she said, that she might be better able to imagine it, and not feel, therefore, quite so far away from him, or from the war. His letters, however, when they came—at first fairly often, two or three in a week, then fewer and farther between—were disappointingly void of any details at all, save on the subject of his new acquaintance, the writer and philosopher P. D. Ouspensky—who, by a stroke of unimaginable luck (but there is in these matters, I am now quite certain, wrote Louis, *no such thing*), he had met almost immediately after his arrival in London.

AN ANTI-BOLSHEVIK, OUSPENSKY had appeared in all the fashionable occultist circles of Europe throughout the last decade. He had written *The Fourth Dimension*, and more recently *A New Model of the Universe*—two books that, after Myers's *Human Personality and Its Survival of Bodily Death*, Louis especially admired. He wrote enthusiastically after his first meeting with the author at a press conference held at Ground Zero that Ouspensky had been "an absolute delight," and assured Sutton needlessly (she had barely heard of Ouspensky, except from Louis himself) that "anything that might be said against the man in America is absolutely false." His understanding of the research conducted by Myers, not to mention the advancements he had himself made in the field, was more thorough, and far-reaching, than—Louis wrote—he'd once guessed.

"It is remarkable," he wrote Sutton a week after he and Ouspensky were first introduced, "to be offered, finally, something in which I can actually believe, rather than merely speculate about."

Indeed, many of Ouspensky's proposed "revisions" to Myers's approach struck Sutton as comparatively levelheaded. He held, for example, that the rumored "Messiah child"—conceived through channels Myers himself had opened to the unconscious world of the not-yet-born and the dead—was just another myth; created, like all religious and quasi-religious exercises, in order to explain away the imperfections within the lives of those who invented them or fell under their sway. A way, that is, for them to imagine that all the seeming trivialities (and infidelities) of their own lives were in fact serving some higher purpose; were part of a linear trajectory toward total redemption. That Myers's "Messiah" would one day turn out to be an ordinary man who, having been raised an only child in a quiet London suburb, was intent only on continuing to live his remarkably ordinary life, would not have surprised Ouspensky. For him, there never was any possibility of final redemption. Though every person was born and reborn ceaselessly upon the earth in a sort of incessant reincarnation—one that, unlike the Eastern philosophies, took place recurrently at exactly the same point in time and under the same circumstances. It was a process that (still more importantly) was not to be confused with the sort of nihilism inherent in a concept like Nietzsche's "eternal return." For Ouspensky, there was always a *perceivable progress* to be achieved through such multiple succession—if, that is, one was appropriately aware of the possibility of achieving it. With the correct discipline and training, Ouspensky urged, we might learn to uncover our past lives in such a way as to affect not only the present, but the past and the future as well. No, there was no final or total "redemption," in Ouspensky's opinion—only diligent hard work. Through which, eventually, we might pass out of the system entirely, having been absolved of everything but the most vital aspects of our human personality.

Ten years earlier, Ouspensky had enjoyed an immense following.

There were those who argued that he had single-handedly shaped the Russian avant-garde—which had, of course, shaped everything else. Of late, his star had dimmed. He had lamented as much to Louis. Most of his work was being carried on now by others—former followers who had all but forgotten him. He had managed to retain only a very small, but exceptionally loyal, coterie; most devotedly, perhaps, a young woman named Cécile, who—at just barely thirty—had made, according to Ouspensky, more progress in the field than anyone else he had ever had the pleasure to meet. She could recall not only small "flashes" of previous lives (the purview of most of Ouspensky's devotees), but could recount from them whole narrative sequences. "She does this," Louis explained to Sutton in one of his letters home, "with her eyes closed. Sometimes traces of other languages mix in. It's remarkable! Once, for example, a language no one present could understand was later identified (with the help of a local ethnographer) as an ancient Hopi dialect—a language Cécile herself, of course, would not have had the least opportunity to learn! The question of how any English woman born—recurrently—in Leicestershire in 1909 would have had the chance to pick up an ancient Hopi dialect is still to be worked out—but it certainly is an interesting one! Ouspensky has suggested it may have to do with what he calls 'static' information—excess data and energy a time-traveler picks up as she makes contact with, and learns to read, her own past. Whatever the case, it's apparent Cécile is on the verge of recalling much more than has ever been substantially recorded of a previous life through a living person—something that will very soon make all of Myers's experiments look like child's play."

ON AT LEAST ONE OCCASION, Louis had the tremendous luck of being asked to sit in on Ouspensky's "sessions" himself. Afterward he wrote glowingly that "all that has been said is absolutely true." He'd experienced, he reported to Sutton, the strangest sensation—quite impossible to describe. A sort of "vision," perhaps, of what he had assumed at the time was the future, but knew must actually be the past. And all the while, he was traveling, or seemed to be—it was the most uncanny thing—down a long, narrow staircase. He could see hardly anything at all along it, and the more he strained, the more the angle of the "vision" tilted so that whatever lay below remained, from that incredible vantage point, just beyond his line of sight. "I imagine," he wrote, "that with practice I may be able to train myself to see farther. It is just, as Ouspensky assures us, like learning to draw—or take a photograph. Not a question, that is, of learning the skill in itself (which is always secondary, and anyone can do), but of learning—in the first place—to see!

"I would not be sharing this with you," Louis continued—it was a letter dated the tenth of October, the height of the Blitz—"or at this troubling time be so inspired by its discovery, if I was not absolutely confident in the truth of these findings. Though, sadly, I do not feel hopeful that anything of significance can come of this in the public sphere for some time—given the deeply entrenched bias against anything that disrupts our persistent and obstinate reliance on the tropes of 'realism' and 'naturalism,' not only in art but in politics as well. I ask you, is it not true that every encounter—in art, in politics, and even in love—fails the moment it imagines the 'reality' it encounters as preexistent, fixed; capable of being simply transferred like a rubbing of a leaf or the inlaid inscription on a headstone to the page? The leaf, the page, the headstone, the words—all are concatenations of hard matter, existent within the visible world . . . but the work of every encounter—art, politics, and especially love!—should be, should it not?, to move *between* the material of this world and the material of another. There is, then, at the heart of every 'naturalistic' attempt at encounter, which accepts the simple appearance of things, a great error of judgment and perception. In short—a lie. Think of it! What a boon it has been to politicians to have us all suddenly develop an aesthetic appreciation of the gritty real! I feel that my work here—to catalogue and therefore to promote only misery and misfortune—is doing a great disservice not only to the present, but to the future as well! The photographs I'm taking now, for example, of the bombs; every one, as you can imagine, is so extremely overexposed as to render half the image entirely blank. What can result in a fragmentation of any present reality—dividing the world into mere surfaces, that is, of such and such dimension, overexposed and nearly blank of everything but the abstract play of shadow and light—but a future reality drawn from and against exactly those same lines?"

Shortly after, Sutton received an almost illegible message in slanted scrawl, unfamiliar to her, which recounted the events of an evening Louis had spent in the company of Ouspensky and a handful of other followers (Cécile—she noted—among them) trapped on the rooftop of Ouspensky's mansion in Virginia Water, about twenty miles from London.

"From there," Louis wrote, "we could see it all. That unearthly spectacle: London burning! But so removed were we from it up there, it seemed to be happening like it does in one of my visions—or like in a dream. The sort that, without any clear interruption of logic, seems to move backward rather than forward—proving itself as it goes.

"Soon enough, it became obvious I was not the only one who felt this way. I looked at Ouspensky and saw he had already begun traveling along those ill-used, back routes of the mind toward the distant past. It was the expression on his face that told me this was so—an expression I have seen on no living man but that I instantly recognized when I saw it as one I must have worn myself on the few occasions that I, too, had traveled that way. But then—I can hardly bring myself to write it. Suddenly—his face changed. He appeared to be physically jolted by something. Then he turned very pale. Even in the low light I could see the way his face blanched; how his eyes widened in confusion and fear. It was not the sort of jolt one might receive through the consideration of some psychological or intellectual dilemma—it was an actual, physical jolt, as though he had run into a wall. He looked around, first toward us—we, who sat, anxiously waiting for what he would say; for a sign, any sign at all, of what was to come. Then his eyes drifted past us. They scanned the horizon where London spat and popped and roared in the distance like a vision of hell.

"This—he said, finally—I cannot remember."

AFTER THAT, LOUIS'S LETTERS, which had slowed to one or two a month, stopped abruptly; Sutton's own letters went unanswered. On good days, she surmised that this sudden silence was only a sort of attempt to move their love (the one thing she had never once—since that first day in Louis's apartment—seriously questioned; even when first one distance, then another, intervened) finally past the "naturalism" on which it had so far been based. She tried to abandon her longing for some material trace of him as best she could; to train her mind instead toward some more abstract method of communication—but these sorts of exercises, whenever she attempted them, always left her cold.

Then, in February 1941, Sutton was distracted temporarily from her growing anxiety over Louis's prolonged silence. The Judge suffered a massive stroke, leaving him paralyzed—unable to speak. Directly, Sutton sent news to Alden, but by the time her letter arrived he had returned to Paris; the letter never reached him. His reply, when it finally came, therefore, never mentioned their father at all, and responded only to her previous letter about Louis's adventures with Ouspensky into the "beyond," which she had related to him.

"I am reminded," Alden wrote, "of that hideous tale of Wells's, do you know the one? *The Island of Doctor Moreau*. Moreau is a sort of alchemist—intent on remaking animals into human beings. He inflicts on them untold suffering in order, he says, to 'burn out all the animal' in them. When the experiment fails (he only manages in the end to lend his animals a very few human characteristics; at root, their natures remain unchanged), he is forced to admit that he has succeeded only in creating 'a problem' . . . 'I wanted,' he says, 'it was the only thing I wanted—to find the extreme limit of plasticity in a living thing.' Isn't this quest for immortality that Ouspensky and his lot are invested in a quest along these lines? To 'burn' from the human all his 'animal' tendencies—even the tendency toward death—in order for him to become . . . but, what? Something yet to be defined . . . Anyway, I wouldn't worry too much over him. These ideas have been fashionable for some time, and among plenty of people who are considered—mistakenly or not—quite sane. Wells himself, you know—and Gorky. Yeats, Eliot, and the rest. They were even at the root of the revolution in 1917. Have you heard, for example, of something they called *Bogostroitel'stvo?* It can be literally translated, I believe, into something like 'god-building.' Imagine! Having a whole revolution to do away with God just to build him up again!"

It was true, Alden went on, that the "god" imagined by "the Commissar of Enlightenment" employed by the Bolsheviks was humanity itself—but not as it could have been conceived of, then. It was, instead, a humanity of the future—a humanity purified; all its "animality" burned out.

"Gorky himself believed," he continued, "that the highest state of man would not be physical at all. Everything around us would, instead, at some future time, be transformed into a collective body of thought—a single, pure and inclusive, psychical energy. He reportedly had a few heated discussions over it with the poet Blok, who was horrified by Gorky's vision—protesting quite rightly that all the known laws of the universe contradicted it. According to trusted scientific accounts, the universe is, if anything, compressing. Everything pressing in, at every moment, more densely and solidly than ever before. It is my guess, therefore, that if we unite at all and in any form, it will be as a small asteroid firing at a distant planet. But that cannot be proved, and even if it could would not stop the majority of the world—regardless of their religion or creed, or lack thereof—from believing *nonetheless* in some sort of afterlife, thereby, in large and small ways, succeeding once again in undermining the present, and pitting us against one another and ourselves in the most inhuman ways. All in the name of a cause or a thought or an idea of a future that exceeds us. That, indeed, has no knowledge of our existence at all and probably in itself does not exist— or, if it does, does so at such a remote distance from any of our more pressing concerns as not to warrant any part in the discussion of our immediate affairs."

One thing to be said for Stalin on this point, according to Alden, was that it was he who was finally able to diminish the hold religion still played (through Lunacharsky's *Bogostroitel'stvo* movement) during Lenin's time. Even Lenin himself believed apparently that one day electricity would take the place of God. "Let the peasant pray to electricity," he said, "let him feel the power of the central authorities more than that of heaven!" Like Wells's dystopia, the idea—hardly straying very far from the overtly religious—was to deliver humanity from the clutches of nature; from the clutches, in essence, of *itself.*

It was in order to move closer to this goal that human beings themselves were liquefied: "the statistics," Alden wrote, "we heard rumored over the years are if anything too low an estimate to account for the sort of absolute death that was visited upon that country, and in the most unspeakable forms, according to those who have seen it with their own eyes. I have heard rumors of things I can hardly even bear to write down. From one man, who worked as a statistician, for example—they are very diligent there, as here, about keeping good records—I've heard it is general policy for the hands of those prisoners who had frozen to death to be chopped off, in order that their fingerprints might be used for the files. Someone else recently told me of her employment fabricating loaves of bread out of plaster of Paris during the famine of 1933. Do you remember the optimistic accounts of the Soviet state we read at that time? The confident reports that rumors of hunger, and worse, had all been fabricated by the Americans? And this woman was fashioning bread out of plaster, displaying it for all the journalists who trooped through the idyllic villages of the 'beautiful and fertile Ukraine' to see! Ah, the plastic arts! The endless malleability of the human mind!

"There was the case, for example, of the parapsychologist Vladimir Mikhailovich Bekhterev, whose research into the scientific basis for the immortality of the soul had begun during the reign of the tsars, and continued under Lenin. In fact, on several occasions, Bekhterev had acted as Lenin's personal psychologist. The purpose of this life, he said, was to develop the human spirit in such a way as to actually effect a change upon the species—a sort of Darwinian 'All-Spirit' or 'Overman.' Where, previously, humanity had been bound to those limitations imposed by personal flaws and inhibitions, by uncoordinated desires, it was possible—Bekhterev (like Ouspensky, after him) claimed—to systematically surpass those limitations. Electricity would not merely replace God; man himself would become electricity! As it was—and this was a viewpoint he presciently maintained, well before the days of the revolution—humans were not directed by conscious choices but instead by the mechanics of chance, which played them for toys or ill-fitted machines, destroying or creating things willy-nilly around them based on nothing more than the associative power of suggestion. Whole civilizations had been built, then crumbled and fallen, in just this way—to say nothing of individual lives. And indeed, Bekhterev's own life was destroyed according to just such a whim.

"After Lenin's death he was invited to the Kremlin in order to meet with Stalin—presumably over the question of whether or not it should be permitted to publish Freud's work in Russia: Stalin was opposed to the idea; Trotsky supported it. Bekhterev had voiced his doubts as to the scientific basis of psychoanalysis even as he pursued it—he always hoped to move beyond it, into the physiological. Perhaps it was indeed in order to discuss this issue that Bekhterev was invited to Stalin's quarters on that day in 1927, or perhaps it was that Stalin wished for the sort of consultation Bekhterev had provided for Lenin in his final days. Whatever the reason for the visit, Bekhterev's opinion of it was clearly recorded by his colleagues. 'Diagnosis is clear,' he reported afterward: 'typical case of heavy paranoia.'

"The next day Bekhterev was found dead, his body swiftly cremated. His eldest son was executed, his wife sent to a prison camp, and the rest of his children to the state orphanages. Soon afterward, his name was removed from his books and manuscripts, and his research was burned.

"That," wrote Alden, "was the judgment visited upon Bekhterev."

—

MARY KELLY HAD ALREADY LONG SINCE DEPARTED BY THEN—LATE November 1941—for her last, permanent "rest" holiday, at St. Elizabeth's Hospital, just outside the city. She spent her days peacefully, looking out over the Potomac River from her second-story room, and contemplating the days during the Civil War when the grounds had still been used to house large animals brought back by the Smithsonian Institute from South America, Africa, and the Philippines. Sutton visited when she could, but it was not often—and even when she did, her mother hardly knew her. It was as if she had been plunged into a deeper memory—one that extended far beyond the Gulf Coast of her childhood. One that reached back, finally, to the sub-Saharan plains of East Africa and the humid jungles of southern Campeche: the respective origins of her imaginary animals, which grazed the hospital lawns. She would chatter endlessly about the details of her own feeding and bathing rituals as she stared—past Sutton—out the window; as though her daughter, barely recognizable to her, were only the slightest imperfection on the otherwise unblemished hospital glass.

Visiting Judge Kelly, it was just the opposite. Though he could no longer speak, he remained as alert—as much "the Judge" as he ever had been. Sutton could feel it: the way he continued to peer out from behind the paralyzing hold his body had on him with the same fierceness she remembered from her childhood. This power—abstracted from any ability to actually wield it—made him at once both more terrifying and more sympathetic. As they sat together in the Judge's study (where, throughout that final year, he remained: propped up with blankets and pillows in his usual chair, his chapped and swollen feet resting on a low ottoman and his blank gaze riveted toward his own open window, which watched the street), Sutton felt that, perhaps—for the first time—they understood each other.

She rarely spoke during her visits—though Germaine, who had stayed on at the house all that time, reminded her often that she must.

He understands everything, she said. There's no mistaking it, he absolutely does.

But when Sutton did attempt to speak in his presence, her words always came out thick and strange. More than that—they felt extraneous, and perhaps a bit unfair. If her father and she were finally going to confront each other after all this time, it should at least—she thought—be on the same terms. No more than in her professional career did she want to be considered at any advantage.

The only time she spoke, therefore, was to give him news of Alden—and that came very rarely. Even when it did, there was never much to report. Thanks to the efforts of an American friend, he'd been repatriated; was back in Paris now. He did not think it possible, or at any rate advisable, to return to the United States due both to the delicate situation in France and his various responsibilities to those who had arranged his release—the details of which he never made clear. There were difficulties, of course, he admitted, owing to food shortages and the constraining effects of the occupation and the war, but these difficulties were common to all, and, if anything—he always insisted in closing—he was faring better than most.

It was only when Sutton spoke out loud—of Alden—that her father's eyes would darken and burn, and, forgetting himself, he would make an effort to speak. Then, cowed by failure, he would retreat once more into silence—his eyes flashing with an anger that had, over the years, been refined to such a point that it had, anyway, become too pure, too powerful for words.

FINALLY, ON THE THIRD of December, 1941— just days before the attack on Pearl Harbor signaled the United States' entry into the war—Sutton received a telegram from Germaine in New York. The Judge was dead. She traveled back to Washington that night in order to make the final arrangements for the burial, and her father's estate. And so she was there—in her father's house, in his study, in fact (his bed had been moved there, under the window), which had once seemed so impenetrable, when it was announced that the United States had entered the war. She had waited so long to hear that announcement, convinced she would feel just as she had in its anticipation: filled, in equal parts, with excitement and relief. So it was a surprise to find—sitting with Germaine at the edge of her father's bed after it had been stripped of its linens and every trace of his presence, which had once been so overpowering—how simply and terribly sad she felt then, and how empty the President's voice sounded to her in that moment, as it echoed through the room, promising "absolute victory."

Less than six months later—due to the sudden dearth of male reporters, what with the war on—Walker's concerns over the lack of women's "facilities" at the front, which had been plaguing him for years, were briefly forgotten, and it was agreed that Sutton would be sent overseas.

Nearly six more months passed before she managed to secure all the proper press credentials and arrangements could be made. Finally, though, on the eighth of December, 1942, she shipped out along with over ten thousand American troops, to Gourock, on Scotland's southwest shore. From there she was to travel to Lowestoft, where she'd be sent on to Holland in a week. That left (as she had been careful to arrange) just enough time to see Louis, to whom—through a mutual contact, Shep Stewart, another foreign correspondent at *Life* magazine—she'd finally managed to get word.

So, they met. The week before Christmas. At a shabby restaurant, suggested by Louis, in Lambeth, where holiday decorations had been strung up on the lampposts—contrasting strangely with the ruined streets. Sutton arrived before Louis did, and ordered a glass of red wine, with which she hoped to still her nerves.

Her fingers trembled as she lifted the glass. What if he didn't come? She felt a sudden, visceral panic shudder through her at the thought.

But then—there he was. Looking exactly as he always had; what had she expected? Still—it was surprising. How absolutely . . . *himself* he was. All the unnecessary details of his particular human existence, which she had forgotten, apparent again: the lines on his face (had they deepened? Not significantly, if so), the wrinkles in his clothing, the way he nodded his head ever so slightly, apologetically, with each step—a nervous motion that belied his otherwise confident pose.

Sutton did not rise to greet him. She could not. He leaned in, therefore, to kiss her on the cheek.

He would have written, he said, after he had settled across from her and ordered scotch and soda. But then . . . He paused. Shifted in his seat; ran his fingers through his hair.

Do you remember . . . Again he paused. Cécile? The student of Ouspensky's? The one—

Yes, Sutton said.

—who could remember whole episodes of her past lives, when for the rest of us they come only in the briefest of flashes? The one who spoke in French, Russian, Old English, and—once—in an ancient Hopi dialect, which would have gone unrecognized except for the fortuitous discovery of a local ethnologist who had, in the early 1920s, spent time studying the American Indians of the Southwest?

Yes, Sutton said. Yes. I remember.

Louis raised his glass to his lips with one hand and with the other, once again, ran his fingers through his hair.

She had, he explained, become pregnant. The child was his. Though it was difficult for both of them, he knew (he said) that Sutton would understand. There were certain responsibilities that were (weren't they?) quite simply . . . impossible to avoid. Even, therefore, after the war ended, he'd resolved to stay on.

Sutton had become light-headed from the wine, which she'd drunk too quickly. At first all she could think to say was: The end of the war? Is this something that you—or *Cécile* (she pronounced the name with heavy emphasis on the accented first syllable) have foreseen?

He shook his head and laughed self-consciously. Oh, no, he said. It's the past Cécile can see most clearly, not the future, and I myself have only the briefest of revelations—even of the past. No, no—again he shook his head. I base my prediction instead, he said, smiling, on what I read this morning in the *Daily Telegraph*.

Oh, Sutton said, and put down her drink, which she had drained. You know, don't you, you shouldn't believe everything you read.

Louis laughed good-naturedly, and stirred the ice in his drink, which was melting fast. Mechanically, Sutton reached for her hat and umbrella, which she had leaned on the back of her chair. Louis half raised himself, but she waved him away.

No, no, she said. I'm quite all right.

I'm—I'm sorry, he said.

No, no need, Sutton said, preparing herself to depart. Absolutely no need.

Where her hands had trembled, they were steady now. She felt devastatingly calm.

Perhaps, she said—clutching her umbrella tightly in one hand as she rose and made for the door—we should not have not given up so easily. The Messiah will be arriving after all. And somewhat sooner than expected.

—

SUTTON WAS LESS THAN A MONTH IN THE HAGUE BEFORE BEING REAS-signed, along with three other American journalists (two of them women) to the South Pacific. At first she was desperately disappointed. She had hoped she might be transferred to Paris—or at least (because even during the height of the war, *everyone* wanted Paris) stay on in Europe. She could not help but suspect that, even from afar, Walker was doing whatever he could to keep her, and the other female journalists, from the heart of the war.

When she landed in Guadalcanal, however, at the end of January 1943—right in the midst of the Watchtower campaign—she had to admit that this was far from the case.

SIX WEEKS LATER SHE was posted to Guam, which—after the sound-and-light show of Guadalcanal—proved relatively quiet. At least for her. The fighting was taking place just a few miles away, but she was not permitted anywhere near it. Instead, she spent most of her time at head-quarters—a dingy hotel in Honiara—typing up the reports of the other correspondents and wiring them back to Washington. It was there that she received word that her mother had died—"peacefully," Germaine wrote, "in her sleep." (In a hurried addendum she reported that "prob-able cause of death" could be owed to a bungling of prescription files, and the unfortunate oversight of a night nurse—later dismissed for her mistake.)

It was hard to feel anything. She had, after all, lost her mother many years before—that day when she was eight years old and stood in front of Brueghel the Elder's *Big Fish Little Fish*, and discovered the absolute relativity, and mutability, of perception. Thinking of that, she felt sad, but mostly what she felt—as she sat out on the balcony at the hotel in Honiara and listened to the explosions from the direction of Henderson

Field—was vague relief. She could not help but hope—and she did, so fervently in those moments that, briefly, it bordered on firm belief—that her mother had been returned, in death, to whatever native island from which she'd come; that life, which had for so long held her captive, had been shaken from her as easily as if it had been a dream.

She wrote to Alden in Paris, and tried to convey something of all of this, what she felt just then—a mixture of sadness, relief, and the stirrings perhaps for the first time of something else, something more; for which she did not, in the end, have a word, and so failed utterly to understand. (Was it faith? Was that even possible, she wondered, when one had lost, long ago, any sense that there was anything in which to believe?)

But Alden's reply when it came was almost as incomprehensible to her as the small poem that accompanied it—she could make no sense of it at all. He mentioned their mother only in passing, spending the rest of the brief note (as had become usual with him) recounting the trivial details of his daily rambles; sketches of places that seemed to her of scant significance; people whom even he didn't know.

After that, their letters tapered to a minimum, and though Sutton missed the correspondence, she did not blame Alden particularly for his cryptic replies; it was only natural, she reasoned, that their letters should have become, over the passing months, increasingly strained. Even she had begun to find, more lately, when at last she *did* sit down to write, that she had, after all (especially after the censors had been taken into consideration), very little to say.

IN APRIL, SHE WAS transferred again. To Makin Island this time, though nothing much was happening there. There was always the chance, she was told, that it might, and—sure enough—by June the Japanese had moved nearly five thousand troops to the islands of Betio and Tarawa, directly to the south. Still—no one made a move. It rained, and Sutton wired in every day that there was nothing to report. That lasted all through the summer and fall of that year—'til nearly the end of November. Then, on the twentieth of that month, just before dawn, sixty-six

U.S. destroyers, thirty-six transport ships, twelve battleships, and just as many cruisers emerged on the horizon.

The Japanese opened fire; the *Colorado* and the *Maryland* immediately countered with their own. One of the American shells found its mark, opening a key entryway into the lagoon.

The plan had been to land Marines on the north of the island, but they soon found (though they now had a point of entrance) that the boats couldn't clear the reef. They bided their time, waiting for the tide to change, but, according to later reports, the ocean just "sat there." It was weird. Everything—the ocean itself—was at a standstill.

What they hadn't known, and so had been unable to account for in their approach, was that when the moon was in its last quarter, it exerted hardly any pull on the water just north of Tarawa Beach at all. Soon there were Marines stranded everywhere—still on the boats, or else stuck on reefs, their vehicles swamped and taking on water. By the end of the day, only one tank was still functioning properly. Still, they had somehow managed to cut Japanese communication lines, forcing Commander Keiji Shibazaki to abandon his post. He readied his men and prepared to move farther south—but before he could do so, a naval high explosive detonated just outside the command post, and he and most of his men were killed. After that, things started to go a little better for the Americans, and three days later they held the island.

"Cleanup" continued up and down the beaches for another week. When the last pockets of resistance were cleared out, only one Japanese officer and sixteen enlisted men—the only ones willing to surrender—remained alive. American casualties were disastrous as well: upward of three thousand.

The numbers set off a furor in Washington. How could a tiny island in the South Pacific possibly be worth the lives of three thousand American men? General Holland M. Smith, commander of the V Amphibious Corps, did nothing to dampen the public's growing concern when, after touring the beaches one day toward the end of the battle, he compared the scale of the loss he witnessed there to Pickett's Charge.

Sutton saw nothing of the battle itself, of course, until it was over—

but then she saw plenty. On the twenty-fourth of November, just after the worst of the fighting had ended, she traveled back to the United States aboard the hospital ship *Solace*. At first she went among the men, interviewing those who could still speak about their experiences in "the largest single operation ever launched in the Pacific," but after a while she stopped asking questions or writing anything down. Later, when Walker asked her about a story on the *Solace* voyage, she said there wasn't any.

How's that? he asked.

Sutton had shrugged. I wasn't on assignment, she reminded him— that was just my ticket home. But who knows—maybe I'll write about it someday, she told him.

She knew, though, that if she ever did, it wouldn't be for him.

So, Walker said. Had enough? He was grinning at her.

Sutton shook her head.

—

YOU WOULD THINK THAT THE WAR WOULD HAVE PREOCCUPIED ALL OF her thoughts, so she would hardly have had a moment to think about Louis in all that time—but just the opposite was the case. She found that, in fact, she had nothing but time on her hands to think back over everything that had happened between them; to retrace the chiasmic route of their correspondence, which she knew practically by heart; to count the days 'til the arrival of the Messiah (as she ever afterward referred to the child in her mind); to wonder wryly when she might begin to see the signs that he was indeed living among them, on earth . . .

She chastised herself endlessly for it, willing her thoughts to find for themselves some different course—but without fail they found their way patiently back to that same tired groove, each time as if they (and therefore she herself, she could only suppose) somehow imagined there was some way she might *think her way out*. That if she approached the thing (the great tear in her heart, which not even the war could distract from or repair) from the right direction—if she managed to surprise it somehow from an unexpected angle—it might just . . . go away. That Louis would be returned to her; that everything would go back to the way it had been. The problem was, she considered: it never really had been anything much at all. Not, at least, anything solid enough (nor even, for the most part, she was forced to admit, *desirable* enough) that, with her rational mind, she could ever really *will* its return. Yet still, whenever she was not completely vigilant, her heart slid back there every time, and her mind followed.

Sometimes she would manage to convince herself that it was not really Louis she longed for. Perhaps, she reasoned, he stood for something else—something larger. Her father's or her mother's death; her worry over Alden; the outcome of the war. But mostly, as she could not help but be aware, it was—the pattern of her thought, and the system to her grieving—a very small, very personal, and very limited spiral.

And she had plenty of time to dwell within it—especially after she returned from the Pacific. Once more, it took nearly six months before she was dispatched again. New York, empty of Louis, was nearly unbearable; she could not remember a time she had ever felt so alone.

It came as a tremendous relief, therefore, when, in mid-April, she was posted to Italy—just before the Allies attacked the Gustav Line. That was the first time she got anywhere near the front—which served to get her mind off Louis anyway. That, and Lieutenant Frank Jenson—a shy young redhead from Washington State.

She was just about to go out flying with Jenson one afternoon when he got a radio call to go out on a mission instead. A rocket gun—what Jenson called a screaming meemie—had been holding up an infantry division; Jenson's job was to spot it, then radio in its coordinates back home.

Nothing too special, he said. I should be back before lunch—I'll take you up then.

How 'bout I come along now? Sutton asked.

Jenson hesitated, then shrugged. The captain—Benelli—a skinny man of about forty with a nose and eyes like a hawk, balked at the idea, though.

Girls can't go out on missions, he said.

They can if you take them, Sutton replied—to which Benelli laughed loudly.

All right, he said. Come on.

IT WAS AMAZING, ONCE they got some height, to look down from above and see how the pattern-bombing tracks, which always looked so chaotic from the ground, seemed as regular as though they had been drawn with a ruler and compass. As though there were some bigger picture in mind—and if they could only just pan out a little farther, they might at last be able to make out what it was.

Sutton took pictures until her hands went numb. Then she tucked them into her coat to warm them and asked Jenson how long it would be until they got to the front—and how they would know when they got there.

Oh, that's easy, Benelli said. It's when you stop seeing stars on things.

She looked below and saw that the jeeps and trucks and landed aircraft were all marked with a white star, clearly visible from the air.

The best way to tell, Jenson put in, is actually the bridges. When you see trestle bridges like those, he said, pointing, you know you're in friendly territory—those are bridges built by our own engineers. When you start seeing blown-out bridges, you're in no-man's-land: the last thing the Germans do is blow up their bridges. If they haven't been rebuilt yet it's because the territory's still too hot—gotta wait awhile. The first intact bridge you see after that? That's when you know you're in Jerry land.

THEY HAD JUST CRESTED the hills surrounding the Cassino Valley. Below them, the highway wound its way through the mountains. Then, in another moment, the whole Cassino corridor opened up below them, the valley glistening with shell holes made by the guns of both sides. It had recently rained and the holes had been filled with water; these glinted in the sun, nearly blinding them. Sutton leaned out again and looked back to where, from their own territory, the distant muzzle flashes of guns blinked on and off like fireflies. They dipped down toward the highway where wrecked tanks were strewn across a bend in the road; beyond that were the demolished bridges. Benelli phoned in the coordinates of these, and Sutton continued to take pictures.

Then—suddenly—the airplane seemed to buck under them, and there was a sound like a freight train passing. Benelli swore.

High explosives, he said.

Then he swore again.

Dammit. We've got troops down there.

Jenson pointed the nose of the airplane up, and they flew—leaving the turbulent air, and the men (impossible to imagine within it) behind. Ahead of them was an open stretch, split by a road with no one on it; then, at the far end of the road, was an arched bridge. It looked like no one had set foot on it in a hundred years.

Here we are, Benelli said. Jerry country.

Again, Jenson tipped the nose of the plane up and they rose higher.

Keep your eyes peeled, he said.

Once we spot that meemie, Benelli said, we can go home.

But just then they heard something: a faint crackling sound, like grease popping.

We're being shot at, Jenson said.

Spandau, said Benelli.

Again, Jenson tipped the nose of the plane, and they rose.

Spandau only has a range of twenty-four-hundred feet, Benelli explained to Sutton. He turned to Jenson. And we're at what?

Thirty-two hundred, Jenson said.

Sutton saw that his knuckles were white on the controls.

Benelli gave one of his laughs. *Hoo-hooo!* he yelled. You got that? he asked Sutton, turning around now to face her. D'ye get all that?

She leaned out again, but without really looking this time. The air was numbingly cold. She could hardly feel her fingers and so didn't even know if she was taking pictures anymore. She pointed her camera back toward the earth and just held it there.

Hoo-hoooo! yelled Benelli again.

When she couldn't bear it any longer, Sutton leaned back in, and tucked her hands into the pockets of her thin coat to warm them.

Shortly after, Jenson turned the aircraft around, and they headed home.

THE ALLIES TOOK ROME. Then, beyond that, Florence—closing in on the Gothic Line. Then came Omaha Beach, and the U.S. invasion of Saipan in the Marianas. In July, the Soviets captured Minsk, and by August Paris was free.

Sutton spent the fall and winter of that year reporting from Rome; then, in March 1945, she was dispatched to western Poland to follow the Russian and American forces as they advanced, in a final push, on Berlin.

—

SHE HERSELF DROVE INTO BERLIN ON FRIDAY, APRIL 27, 1945 (THE same day, as they later learned, that Mussolini attempted to escape to Spain). In a Russian jeep, with the British journalist Walt Kinsey, their driver—an American, Sergeant Gene Dobbs—and another female journalist, Frieda Westin—from St. Paul, Minnesota—who had spent most of the war in the South Pacific, and couldn't believe she had found herself "right in the middle of it all," and just in time.

It was a wonder they ever arrived. They lost their bearings as they approached the city and pretty soon it seemed like there were no longer any coordinates at all. Sergeant Dobbs, at the wheel, was as white as a sheet as, from behind, Kinsey shouted at him whatever conflicting thought or direction occurred to him in a nearly incomprehensible language all his own, as though speaking in tongues. Each moment a new emotion would occur to him—anger first, at being driven out into the middle of the German wilderness to die, then embarrassment at not being personally able to deliver them from the situation, and finally the sudden inspiration that he might do so after all.

Sutton had never been to Berlin before but the extent to which she did not recognize it when, finally, they did arrive, went beyond the features of the city itself—or what, of the city, remained. The Russians had reached Berlin several days before; now they galloped through the streets with such mad and vengeant joy that it was as though the entire city were adrift, "run off the map." It was not any longer even properly victory that was being celebrated, but something larger, more total. Everything had been overturned. Quite literally. German goods spilled from carts, which had been left abandoned in the streets when the Russians arrived. Russian tanks drove right over them and everything else in their path. Shop doors hung on their hinges, their contents spilled into the street—anything worth taking had already been taken, and long ago. Every woman had been raped; every building had been blasted or burned. Still, the Russians continued to bombard the city, and the air was thick with smoke. Because of this, even once they'd arrived they had an awful job finding their way. Also, the German signs had already been replaced with their Russian equivalents and, as they had not a single word of Russian between them, they were at a complete loss to decipher them. Finally, Frieda had the idea to take out their American flag, and that was how they got to the command post where the Russians were expecting them. Frieda and Sutton waved the flag out the vehicle and repeated to incredulous inquisitors who passed that yes, they were indeed "*Amerikanski.*" This at first caused even more trouble—the crowd closed in on them in a burst of such unconstrained excitement that they weren't able, after that, to budge a single inch, until Kinsey got out of the vehicle and physically cleared a path.

When, at last, they did manage to reach their destination, their reception was the same. Every time Sutton turned around there was a Russian officer who wanted to shake her hand, and once she had turned around enough times, they wanted to shake her hand again, so there never seemed to be any end to it. Then the toasts began, and there seemed to be no end to them, either. Sutton raised her glass with the rest, repeating what she understood to be the Russian equivalent of "Cheers!" It was many hours before she realized she was simply mispronouncing—like everyone else—the name of the President of the United States.

"Trrrruman!" Again and again came the shout. There were toasts as well, of course, to the "late, great Rrrroosevelt," to Stalin, to Churchill, to American women, to Russian women, to the Red Army, the American Army, the Soviet tank, and the American jeep. While Mussolini and his wife spent the night in Mezzegra awaiting execution, and Hitler awaited his own death, which would take place three days later, below the garden of *Reichskanzlei*, Sutton—along with Frieda Westin, Walt Kinsey, and Gene Dobbs—was entertained in Berlin to the sound of the continued bombing of the city's interior and the shouts of the Russians, who were exacting their revenge on the city with indescribable joy. This was for Stalingrad—that was for Sevastopol!

THE GERMANS HAD DISAPPEARED. It was as though there was not a German left in the city. Those who could manage it had indeed fled; otherwise, they hid indoors. No army was so feared as the Russians', and for precisely the reason that—as the guards-major announced with solemnity that evening—every single officer of his staff had lost his family to the Germans. That, he said, was the secret of their extraordinary success—and the fall of Berlin. And let us see if it is not true—the guards-major said—if, for this very reason, in fifty or one hundred years we are not still fighting this very same war.

THE NEXT DAY HITLER would learn that a surrender had been proposed and declined. He would order Himmler arrested and Fegelein shot. The Russians would fight on in the streets. It would, therefore, be nearly impossible for the jeep (Dobbs again at the wheel) to penetrate the city center—though by midafternoon they did manage, somehow, to get within fifteen blocks of Wilhelmstrasse.

There were snipers everywhere—on rooftops, firing up from the sewers. It was madness to try to get any closer, but Frieda was intent on it. Her eyes shone, and with her blond hair and fresh good looks she looked like a midwestern Joan of Arc, ready to lead them, triumphantly, into certain death, and beyond. Sutton had learned to recognize it, by that time: the look she caught that afternoon in Frieda's eye. It was always surprising where it would come from and when, but one thing was sure, it was always terrifying when it did come. There was something rather than aggressive, defensive about it, as though parts of the brain were already shutting down. The eyes took on a dull glow, and death was suddenly not death as measured against life; the two blended and became one, as things do in a dream. So that there was no death any longer—even as you spoke the word; even as it reared its ugly head, and stood directly facing you. There they were, fifteen blocks from Wilhelmstrasse, being urged on by Frieda Westin as though in a dream.

At the wheel, Gene Dobbs was getting pale again—but even so, he didn't want, any more than the rest of them, to turn back. Perhaps because, as Sutton reflected later, when you are in the midst of a battle like that, every moment that you don't die is, in fact, a very ordinary moment. Nothing speeds up or slows down; time does not recoil, ready to spring, or stretch itself so thin as to come nearly to breaking. It just proceeds at its ordinary pace, and so the moment in which it becomes absolutely necessary to retreat never seems—until perhaps it is far too late—to actually arrive. Instead, it seems (just the opposite) even more urgently necessary to keep moving forward. Just as when, years before, Sutton had traveled down all those long empty highways through Oklahoma and West Texas with Louis and it would get to seem as though they were hardly traveling, or at least getting any nearer, to anyplace at all. As they sped along, her foot would get heavier and heavier on account of it, until finally Louis, beside her, would realize with a jolt and say, For Christ's sake, slow down. It was always hard to slow down; to recover a more moderate pace. And just so, it was nearly impossible for them on that day, fifteen blocks from Wilhelmstrasse, to turn back; to retrace their steps as nearly as they could, in order to avoid the battles they'd so recently skirted. Of course, by then new ones had broken out so it was the same thing coming as going—except this time Sutton noticed more Germans, dead or dying on the streets.

The Russians were clearing one block at a time, and they did so efficiently. Though it seemed, more often than not, as though no order existed at all: first one block would be cleared, then another—and the German dead continued to pile. Once, when they passed three Germans—a woman and two young boys—standing beside a row of dead German soldiers, the woman pointed at their flag, which, once again, they had stuck out the side of the window, and inquired in heavily accented English when they might be able to expect the Americans.

Coolly, Frieda replied in German: The Americans will not be arriving, she said. Berlin belongs to the Russians. The woman took a faltering step back, and they continued on—Frieda clenching her end of the flag a little tighter so that it became taut and flapped vigorously in the wind. Sutton could tell what a thrill it had given her to be able to say that a moment before—in her decent German—thinking all the while, no doubt, of the guards-major, who, it was obvious, she had fallen madly in love with the night before.

WHEN THEY RETURNED TO the command post there was a party in full swing, though it was barely noon. Once again, they were served cheese and fish on fine dark bread, and the vodka flowed. They danced, the guards-major and his handpicked staff of bereaved officers swinging Frieda and Sutton effortlessly around the room. "Love and Kisses" by Paul Whiteman played. Then Duke Ellington's "Take the 'A' Train." From time to time, Gene Dobbs cut in apologetically, while Kinsey in the corner started another round of toasts. To Trrrrruman! To Stalin! To Russian vodka and American jazz!

While the Russians advanced on Wilhelmstrasse; while Mussolini dangled by a meat hook in Milan; while the Scottish Division, preparing to cross the Elbe, piped "The Mist Covered Mountains" and "The Piper of Drummond"; and right there in Berlin, Eva Braun in the Führerbunker made the final preparations for her wedding day.

A WEEK LATER—IN WHAT would be her last assignment—Sutton flew to Dachau, in order to talk with a Polish doctor, who himself had spent the last eleven months of the war as a prisoner there. When she met him, he was busy treating a young Hungarian Jew named Petér Aleksei, who had survived the last death transport from Buchenwald. Outside the barbed-wire gates there were fifty boxcars filled with those on the same transport who had not survived; for the last week the American Army had been forcing the Dachau civilians to bury the dead. When Petér Aleksei was discovered alive, and informed of the fact, he did not believe it at first. He kept insisting: Everyone is dead.

But you, he was told, are alive!

He only shook his head in disbelief.

Now he sat, stripped to the waist, wearing his prison pants and a pair of unlaced boots. The doctor had waved to Sutton when she came in, indicating a chair in the corner in which she might sit. A little light had pooled on the floor by her feet, which also slanted across the patient's naked torso. It was a wonder it did not fall right through him, as though he were made out of glass.

The doctor put a stethoscope to the patient's chest and asked him to breathe. He did so. There was a slow rattle in his throat, but he didn't cough. He held the breath for several seconds, then let it out in cautious bursts. He stared ahead at the doctor, as though waiting to be told to breathe again.

In four weeks, the doctor told his patient. You'll see. You will be a young man again.

Then he dismissed him, and turned to Sutton. Yes, he said, he is one of the lucky ones. He is young enough that his body will heal—and when the body heals, the mind, and then the soul, nearly always follow. Humans are endlessly adaptable—that is what I've learned here, more than anything else. More than any of the other animals: I would attribute it to our ability to reason. If an animal is displaced, or if he encounters a change in his environment—he will die. The doctor shrugged. It is a natural defense system.

It is—he continued then, after a reflective pause—a common assumption that natural life is built to continue; that it is driven to continue, against all odds—but I do not believe that this is so. The living

organism protects itself when it is threatened by shutting down. Rodents
eat their young. This is an attempt to protect the living body from pain
and uncomfortable change. Human beings, however—they have the
capacity to reason through almost endless amounts of change; they
approach it gradually, intellectually, you see—they even attempt to
exploit it to their own ends. It is *reason*, not biological life, that strives to
promote itself. Life works *against* reason, but reason always prevails. At
the end of the world, when it comes, it will be because reason has tri-
umphed finally above all else. You see, he said. It almost succeeded here.

He took off his glasses and squinted into the light, which had narrowed by then into a single point on the floor. For several moments he
gazed at this point without speaking, before—abruptly recollecting Sutton's presence, and the reason for it—he turned toward her and addressed
her once more.

Yes, he said. There have certainly been some unusual experiments
here. For instance, he said—now taking his glasses and rubbing them on
his thin shirt—the Germans were interested to learn how long it would
be possible for an aviator to go without breathing oxygen; that is, how
high it would be possible for him to fly in the air. So they had a closed box
and put a prisoner inside, then pumped from it all the oxygen very slowly,
to see at what point the prisoners would die. It never took longer than
fifteen minutes. So it was discovered that no one can live above thirty-six
thousand feet in altitude. That's the absolute limit. After that, there is
simply not enough oxygen for the human body to endure.

Another experiment took place in water. How long could a body survive in cold water? they wanted to know. This could also be useful for
pilots. They wanted to find out how long a human body could survive if
it were shot down over the English Channel, for example, or the North
Sea. In waters such as those found in the North Sea during winter, it was
discovered that a body can resist no longer than sixty-five minutes before
falling unconscious—it could, however, be resuscitated for up to three
hours. This sort of experiment was always reserved for new arrivals:
those prisoners whose health had not already been compromised. When
the victims were resuscitated, they were given three days' rest and then

used in the experiment a second—even a third time. I am not sure I have heard of any prisoner being much use any longer than that.

Another experiment, performed mainly on Polish priests—because there was such a large number of them—involved injecting streptococcus germs between the muscle and bone of the upper thigh. Although only thirty-one deaths resulted from this experiment, those who did die did so after many months of suffering. Often they underwent numerous operations in their last days, in order to discover at what late stage it might still be possible for a man to be saved.

The answer? He could not.

—

ON THE TWENTY-THIRD OF MAY, 1945, SUTTON, ALONG WITH SIX OR seven American prisoners of war, left Dachau for New York in a C-47. Gene Dobbs was with her, too. And Hans Feldman, a reporter for the *Chicago Tribune*. Frieda was already in San Francisco by then, covering the United Nations conference, and Kinsey was in Berlin—still toasting to the health, no doubt, of President Truman. Nobody looked out the window, or spoke, when they lifted off; nobody looked down, or thought about the relative distance between houses, or fences, or borders, when the plane rose and all below them began to seem suddenly small and far away.

No, it wasn't until they had reached cruising altitude and were flying across the English Channel that anyone looked down, and there was something fitting in that, Sutton thought, when she herself looked finally, because there was nothing to see, and no way to distinguish, from that limited vantage point, the difference, any longer, between the water and sky.

VII.

Alden

CRACKING THE CODE. EMMETT'S ROOM, PARIS, 1936—
DETOUR TO ELIZABETHTOWN, KENTUCKY, AND
BARCELONA, SPAIN, 1937—DICK'S APARTMENT, PARIS,
1937—BRIEF DETOURS TO DICK'S "PLUSH" MENTAL
INSTITUTION, UPSTATE NEW YORK, 1945, AND CHAMONIX,
FRANCE, 1934—JACK AND PAIGE'S APARTMENT, PARIS,
CHARTRES CATHEDRAL, EN ROUTE TO STALAG VIII-A,
GERMANY, 1940—DETOUR TO PREFECT'S RESIDENCE AND
GERMAN HEADQUARTERS, CHARTRES, 1940—JACK AND
PAIGE'S APARTMENT, PARIS, 1941—DETOUR TO STALAG
VIII-A, 1940–1941—LUXEMBOURG GARDENS, ALDEN'S
ROOM, MARCELLO'S BAR, FRANZ ECKELMANN'S HOUSE,
PARIS, 1943–1944.

O f all of them, it was only Emmett who spoke of joining when the
first international volunteers for the war in Spain began to be
deployed in the fall of 1936. He did not immediately do so, or even take any
definitive steps toward doing so, but he spoke of it so boldly, and with such

assurance, that this did nothing to shake anyone's faith that he would. If things had gone somewhat differently and he had never gone to the war at all and been blown there into a thousand irrecoverable parts, perhaps they all still would have believed that he had. Perhaps they would have continued to listen to his stories and believe him resolutely when he spoke in his commanding tone of the sorry state of the Parti Communiste, and the radical split that would soon cause—he predicted—the downfall of the entire party, if not Europe as they currently knew it, and perhaps the whole of the Western world.

It was toward—he would warn them—not the radical right nor the radical left, but (he could almost see it, he said, glistening before them) the dark center in the middle they were ultimately bound . . . And all the time, as he spoke—propped comfortably on one elbow in his narrow rented room near the Jardin Atlantique on the Boulevard Pasteur—they might have easily been convinced that he was actually off fighting foreign wars, which they themselves could not entirely support or understand.

By the time he met Emmett, Alden could no longer imagine how any man might come to believe, with conviction, in anything, or speak with authority on any subject at all—but this only heightened his appreciation of those who did. He listened to Emmett with an admiration that bordered on devotion; savoring the flash of his eyes, for example, as he spoke of the Falangists and, in the same breath, of Léon Blum's Matignon Agreements—which had taken the place (he lamented) of global revolution. It was this same bright light that must have flared, Alden later imagined, if briefly, in Emmett's eyes as he was killed in the Barcelona riots of May 1937, his body sent back to be buried in his home state of Kentucky. The youngest of four generations of Emmett Hendersons— the first of which had died during the War of Independence, at the Battle of Brandywine. It was a proud history, the details of which Emmett had recounted to Alden so many times that he could almost picture him: resting up there in the Elizabethtown cemetery, all of the blue grasses of Kentucky gently saluting him with their continuous, casual wave. He could picture his mother, dressed in her Sunday best—still trim and retaining all the necessary indicators of a former beauty, so that even if it had not actually managed to be preserved, it was still understood from the traces of it that remained. Picture her walking up the hill in the late morning sun; slowly, on account of her heels, which got stuck in the soft grass and had to be carefully extracted with every step. Picture her arms, full of flowers, which in a moment she would distribute to each of the Henderson graves—careful to lay the bouquet not beneath the name of the man, but beneath the name of the woman: *"wife of," "beloved daughter to,"* because, as she insisted on many occasions (in her slow drawl that indicated she belonged farther south), it was the women who suffered the most.

Estaline Henderson, née Boutte, had in fact come from Louisiana at the age of twenty-two after having fallen in love with a Navy man, who was shortly thereafter to become Emmett's father. Emmett himself had hardly mentioned his father, and so it is difficult to place him in the story, or comprehend the specific brand of suffering that was Emmett's mother's own, and made her so particularly sensitive to the suffering of all women. Perhaps he is in the car, even now, as Mrs. Henderson extracts herself with every step from the soft dirt of the cemetery grounds and makes her way to the graves of her husband's ancestors—also, of course, the ancestors of her departed son. Perhaps he is in the car, with his hat on—a cigarette wedged partway out the window in order that its smoke might not ruin the upholstery. Waiting, letting the car idle, being comforted by the noise of the engine. (Evidence of the automobile's rumbling appetite, which his weekly attempt to satisfy, in turn, satisfies him. Yes, it pleases him deeply, somehow: the insatiability of his vehicle; that constant reminder that everything—even the most modern machinery—comes at a cost.) Waiting, while his wife steps into and then out of the soft Kentucky dirt, with flowers for the women who—as she reminds him so often in her soft Louisiana drawl—*have suffered the most.* (It is always unclear as she says it whether the suffering she refers to occurred most notably while the husband was still alive or after he was dead.) Waiting, interminably, letting the car idle, letting the powerful throat of its engine soothe him by reminding him of the tremendous cost of being alive in the world, while his wife trudges, also interminably, through the churchyard, wearing a rutted path to the graves of her illustrious, inherited dead—no closer to understanding the sudden demise of her son than she was when she first received the letter informing her that his body, or what was left of it, would (from a location she had until that time not yet heard of) be returned.

BECAUSE EMMETT WAS THE only person with whom Alden had shared anything of his own history—on a cool summer evening, which he would always remember later, in which they had walked home together from Dick's place, along the Canal Saint-Martin—relating to him, in a sudden burst, everything from the disappearance of Elizabeth Gregory and the tragic early death of Joe Hodge to the professor's onetime confidence in him: his prediction that he himself would one day be a great man. He spoke of the Indian, John, of his explosive, inglorious end, and finally of Arthur: of the shameful role he, Alden, had also played in that man's fate—a fate that (though he had no idea what it was) he now felt quite certain had become hopelessly entangled with his own. He had even—he admitted to Emmett that night—somehow managed to get his kid sister embroiled in the mess, and ever since, they had hardly spoken. She most certainly blamed him for all of it— and quite rightly, too. Though perhaps, after all, it was best that she kept her distance now—because (he hesitated, wondering what he could actually bring himself to say out loud). Well, he had gone this far. He was beginning—he continued—to get the distinct impression that everything he touched, every person he loved, would—was bound to; it was only a matter of time—give way, crumble, explode, or otherwise disappear. That despite (and perhaps in direct proportion to) any attempt of his to assert against those greater and more noble ambitions of chance and time some proper force of his own, the more that great wheel—on which those ambitions were hung—turned blithely against him; not as though merely ignorant of his deepest desires and intentions, but as though actually *conspiring against him* . . .

And all the while as Alden spoke, Emmett nodded and nodded his head, as if all of this were quite reasonable, and he had known it all along. So that, when Alden was finished—when, at last, he had nothing left to say—and though Emmett, still thoughtfully nodding his head, did not yet respond, he felt that something had been lifted.

The effect of it made him feel almost giddy; he even began to laugh.

You probably think I'm a madman, he said to Emmett then.

Emmett shook his head. On the contrary, he observed, it was all quite natural that Alden should feel as he did. Everything *did* eventually—he said—give way, crumble, explode, or otherwise disappear— just as well, and at a similar frequency to, in its various ways, its having come into being at all. Everything *did* (every moment, every thought, every whim or desire), as Alden would have it, get *rolled over* or *under*, by and through the very possibility of its approach; of its having been extracted from, cast (even if only in the imagination) as something separate from the wheel. It was, perhaps, then, not a matter so much of *reinventing* the wheel, so to speak (he chuckled here—softly, to himself), but of allowing it a scope and course vaster than is, at any time, perceivable to the eye.

Would you not after all agree, Emmett continued seriously, that in detecting a pattern of "the great wheel's" approach *in direct proportion and relation to your own life,* you risk severely limiting not only your perception of its path, but—as a more or less direct consequence—your own? You may entirely fail to see, that is, the manner in which what you claim to acknowledge as far larger and more powerful than yourself actually *is* that way: something over which you have no possibility of control and within whose ambit you play only a minimal part. Is it not, perhaps, then, more likely, Emmett asked—now turning for the first time to face Alden—that you have, of late, developed a false sense of responsibility over that which exists beyond your control, precisely in an effort to *control it?* He laughed. You must know, he added, that for fate and fortune to be rendered powerless, broken of "all the spokes and fellies from her wheel," one must only cease, at last, to count "the spokes and fellies . . ."

Now it was Alden's turn to nod and nod, and so relieved and comforted by Emmett's words did he feel that, for a brief but beautiful moment he could actually see how it all fit together, just like Emmett said that it did—but at such a remove that, even as he *saw* it, he knew he would never understand it, and even that became, in that moment, a strange comfort. Was *conscience*—in either sense: *to be*, or *to have*—simply a matter of locating a recognizable pattern between things? A forcing of circumstances into a shape that, if Emmett was correct, could at best be considered figurative, provisional—abstract? Sustainable only within, and according to, the intensely personal light lent by an individual mind?

Yes. Certainly. There must be (Emmett was right) something larger, outside and beyond all that; something that did not bend or conform to such a limited perspective—but shaped it all the same. And if this was so—well, then, *conscience itself* could only be considered a reaction to, *a figurative expression of*, that which existed beyond its control. One did not, indeed, suffer the "slings and arrows of outrageous fortune"; nor could one, through simple opposition, end them. They existed beyond all allegory; every possible appeal.

So relieved was Alden to have been able to arrive in this way, with the help of his friend, at such a new and redeeming understanding not only of his own past, but of all things, that even when—not long after—Emmett, too, disappeared, he managed (almost successfully) to resist grieving the loss in personal terms. Though he often found it hard, and at times even felt that same cold flicker of doubt—a creeping suspicion of the way the great wheel continued to grind itself, as though *deliberately* against him—he, for the most part, succeeded in looking at the event as yet a further reminder that what Emmett had said was true. One understood very little of one's own life, Alden reminded himself—let alone any other's. Perhaps it had even been fortuitous, in some small way, that he had managed to bequeath to Emmett his past, and just when he did.

It was high time to be rid of it.

It was in this spirit that Alden gathered what belongings he could from the drawers of Emmett's narrow room, and sent what he found, as a final gesture, to Emmett's mother. The room had by that time been taken over by an acquaintance of Emmett's from his single semester at Yale—an Egyptologist, intent on resurrecting Champollion's English rival, Thomas Young, as the true interpreter of the Rosetta stone. Perhaps due to his respect for history, and the potential intelligibility of even its most indecipherable clues, he had left Emmett's stacks of papers untouched in the closets and drawers. When Alden leafed through them for the first time he was unsure, at first, what it was he'd discovered. It appeared to be a sort of freehand journal interrupted by quotidian lists: things to do, items to buy, acquaintances to call on—and so forth. Upon closer examination, however, he saw that it was in fact the first draft of a novel, based loosely on the events of Emmett's real life. It was Alden's own appearance within these pages that had caused him, at first, to mistake the work as a personal diary. But because he could not recall the events described or the words that either pertained or were attributed to him—except for the telltale entrance of key elements of his own story: those details he had shared with Emmett as the two of them had walked home from Dick's house together that night along the Canal Saint-Martin—he was forced to reassess. Now, leafing back through the disorderly sheaves of the manuscript, he noticed that the first mention of his name was accompanied by a note: "Change name," the note said. In the margins two alternatives were scrawled: "Randall? Barney?"

What a strange feeling came over him then, as he transformed suddenly into an unknowable character before his own eyes—and on account only of the slight pressure applied by his dead friend's pen! That he could have become for Emmett a Randall—even a Barney! That all of the material of his own life, which he had so painfully unburdened, could be disassembled and rearranged to make what even he could see would have been the strangest of fictions! That even the smallest details of himself could have been altered in any imaginable way. That his hair, for example, could have prematurely grayed; that he could have developed a slight twitch in his right eye from an injury that had never actually been inflicted upon him; that all of these things could have taken place in the extraordinary alchemy of the imagination. It was astonishing! To think that all that time in the months before Emmett's death, and unbeknown to any of them, he had been reassembling everything around him—even the small, personal details of their own lives—into something entirely his own. Even more strange was the realization that the person Alden had been (not the character, half sketched, on the page, but the disparate parts of himself, which had floated around in Emmett's mind and had constituted for him a—if shifting and changeable—"whole") was gone. The "he" that he was, or would have become for Emmett, was now irrevocably lost. And if "he" was gone, had he ever existed at all? He who, even in the manuscript itself, had diffused into the disparate parts of the text—remaining ultimately exterior to it, unexplained: the character underdeveloped, the story—wherever it had been going—forever destinationless now, existing only in fragments, and interrupted by long lists, which Alden had at first mistaken for a quotidian accounting of daily life.

Gradually, he understood the lists for what they were: short bursts of inspiration its author was no longer able to contain within the slow progression of sentences on the page. Lists of place names, or objects, or other words without seeming destination or source, trailed each other in a sudden brainstorm, as in the following example, down the center of the page:

Gray owl seen through window.
Memory of St. John, as related by . . .
Piccadilly Circus Story
Rebecca?
If I had my wits and your age . . .
Unstoppable
"The Captain's Daughter"
Mother-Electra scene
Dancing figure
Lunch with Jude/Marc Anthony
Suspended constructions in space

What mystery! To consider in what way these baffling inventories might have one day emerged in full sentences, as communicable histories on the page! To reflect on the ways that Alden himself might have one day traced the patterns of his own life within it.

As it was, there were only these fragments, forever isolate now, detached from meaning—like reels of film doomed to retain whatever had been darkly inscribed there without once, even briefly, having been brought, flickeringly, to form. And what was memory, after all, but that dark chamber? It would be only by chance that one day you stumbled upon one—looking, no doubt, for something else. Only by chance that a slight misstep would set all the reels at once unraveling; whole sections of them suddenly glinting in the available light.

THIS WAS NO DOUBT the experience of Mrs. Henderson, who would, without warning, be overtaken by extreme vertigo, like the first warning of a migraine headache coming on, and have to sit down; have to pause in whatever she was doing—sometimes at the most inopportune moments—and shake her head vigorously for a while as if trying to get something as pervasive and material as water from her brain. She told Alden this in a letter she wrote, in response to his own, in the months following Emmett's death. She would, she said, be "overcome," all of a sudden, by the "senselessness" of it all. It would happen at the oddest moments. When she was, for all intents and purposes, thinking of nothing at all. (The mind could—it was devastating for the heart to learn, she wrote—continue to run along its usual course, as if it had not been, and never would be, interrupted at all.)

Poor Mrs. Henderson. Every week with her flowers. The women's names on the ancestors' graves. And then Emmett's, and no woman's name there . . . But it was then that it hit her. It was she—she, Estaline Henderson, née Boutte—who had, for this life, and now for this death, suffered the most. Alden hoped she took back with her on account of it a single flower. That she carried it away from the cemetery and that it was a small comfort to her as she made her way, picking her high heels with every step out of the dirt, back to the car. Just the smallest of comforts—

that she was, from that graveyard, taking something away. Something that could be hers alone; that she could watch slowly decompose in its jar, and would provide for her—that slow, organic deterioration, as first the flower wilted, then lost its color, then finally began to fester in the glass—some small relief.

But she never told Alden she did this, if she did. Alden had only the one letter, in which she thanked him for the belongings he had returned to her—the letters, the knit gloves, the photographs, a handmade ashtray whose origins he was unfamiliar with—just the few things that it seemed conceivable to fit into the international mail. She described her weekly pilgrimage to the Henderson graves and in some detail recounted the illustrious deaths of each of the members familiar to her. Then, without a clear transition, so that at first Alden was unsure whether it had been made at all, or whether they were still in the realm of the ancient, illustrious Henderson dead, she expressed her despair over Emmett's death.

She would have liked, she said—later, when the line had been more clearly drawn—to understand it as a sort of a punishment, meted out by an unkind god, but her despair had now plunged her past the possibility of taking even this small comfort, which assumed a larger justice and design. Instead, she concluded that Emmett had lost his life as anyone loses their life—as the result of a cruel and unaccountable accident. "There is a senselessness to everything," she concluded that section of her letter. Then: "I will never be able to look the world in the eye again. I used to spend quite a bit of time, you see, gazing out my back window." "The view there stretches out past the town limits—it is quite pretty country out this way. But now I don't have the heart to do it. I keep my eyes down when I'm in the kitchen, so I don't have to catch sight of that view."

A few paragraphs on, she continued (her last reference to the Henderson cemetery and its valiant dead): "It used to even bring me a certain satisfaction. I would go up to the cemetery and look around there, too. It was a peaceful place and, though it's hard to imagine all of the suffering those men and women had to go through, it all makes a certain sort of sense—them being buried like that, underneath the soil of the country they were fighting for. Even though, of course, you know—we lost. The Henderson graves are Confederate graves, and the South never really had a fair chance. But that all seems to make sense, too, in a certain way, now. Maybe it's just that so many years have gone by, or that none of those men were really ever—*mine*. Now I sit up near Emmett's grave and there isn't any sense at all anymore for me up there. I know that you have told me in your very kind letter that he had a 'strong and coura-geous belief' in what he was fighting for over there, but I can tell you that I have known my son all his life. He wrote letters—not very often—but he did, and never once did he mention this war. Maybe it mattered to him in a certain way, but not in a really important way—enough to die for. No matter how little you write, or how private, or grown up you become, or how much you feel that she won't or cannot understand, you simply don't believe in something, *not enough to die for it*, if you haven't even written about it once to your mother. You should remember that. I know you say you have no intention of fighting in this war, or any other, but I would ask you to remember those words, if you can. It seems that it is a very complicated world now, far more so than it was when I was a girl. That there are far less—boundaries, in a certain way, that separate men from their deaths than there once were. That's the senselessness of it, as far as I can tell. It's even strange, I'll admit this to you, to have my son back here in his own soil again. Sometimes I think I'd almost rather have him buried over there, far away, because whatever it is that killed him has nothing to do with me, or with this place. And whatever border he was fighting for is not one drawn on this ground, or as far as I can tell anywhere on earth. And the worst part is—the senselessness of his grave seems to spread itself out all around me, so that now none of the other graves make any sense either. Now there don't seem to be any borders or boundaries at all, and I don't know half the time—and this is why I keep my head down in the kitchen, so I don't look up and have to see that view: all those hills and the trees out there stretching off into the dis-tance, which is in itself even a lie—what the difference is between the dead and the living, or why drawing that line seems to matter so much."

When Alden got to the end of the letter, he went back to the beginning, and read again the descriptions of the Henderson war dead with which it had begun: the number of battles each had fought in, the medals received, the number of wounds that had been inflicted—recovered from, or not—even the number of attendees at the Henderson funerals in that part of the country where the Henderson men's courage and sacrifice had long been a source of pride. As he read it all a second time, it resounded on a very different note, which he thoroughly failed to understand. The deep sincerity that he had first detected in the words was clearly mixed—he saw now—with a fatal cynicism. The two could not be extracted from each other, and yet neither could they be understood as one. Alden himself was still at that time both too sincere and already too cynical to see that he was either one, or to understand, as Emmett's mother did, the ways that the two were irresolvably joined—so that there was no more boundary between them than there was between the living and dead.

You have to get very, very close to death—as Emmett's mother did then—to really see it like that. That is, to really see the way, as Emmett's mother implied she herself had seen—sitting up on the Henderson burial plot at the edge of town, her muddied heels crossed, her head bent, trying not to look around at a view that stretched as far as the eye could see in glorious, irresponsible blues and browns—the way the dead and the living were indeed all mixed up together. So that as she stared at the graves of the long-dead ancestors of her son, the boundaries that had once been fixed in her mind—not only between nations and other allegiances, not only between the suffering of women and the suffering of men, but even between her own fixed position above and those below— began to blur to such an extent that she had to push very hard against the rock beside her, push hard enough to make the knuckles and the ends of her fingers turn white, in order to gain some assurance of the durability of the things of this world, and remind herself that she was still alive.

Once this was, again, reaffirmed, Alden imagined (though this she did not recount) she would make her way again down the slope, very slowly, extracting the talons of her shoes, which sought to dig themselves farther and farther into the earth with every step, and return to her living room—driven there perhaps by the indistinct figure (amounting for the purposes of this retelling really to just a cigarette out the window, a turned-down collar, a hat) of her husband, who, waving the lingering smoke from the car as he witnessed her approach, nodded silently as she slid into the leather seat beside him, and gunned the motor, which had not ceased muttering all that time. And all evening, reestablished within the comfort of her living room, with the familiar photographs on the walls, the never-used china in the cupboards (inherited from her grandmother, on the English side), and the porcelain figurines, which she collected—twenty-nine of the thirty-one replicas presently available of the presidents of the United States (she was only missing Franklin Pierce and hadn't bothered with F. Delano yet, either, and for good reason)—she would drink gin and listen to the radio and call out occasionally into the vast reaches of the house small remarks about whatever it was she heard on the news—just for the exercise of comprehending the distance between herself and the rest of the world.

—

AFTER EMMETT WAS GONE THEY WOULD GATHER AT DICK'S PLACE IN the eleventh—near to where, just off the Boulevard Richard-Lenoir, the Canal Saint-Martin plunges beneath a treed median in order to continue its journey underground. Carol had not yet left Dick, and Jack and Paige were together, too—not yet dispersed as they soon would be (he rather farther away than she). Like Alden, Jack worked at the embassy—though much higher up. How he managed it was a mystery to all of them; he was the least diplomatic man any of them had ever met. He would often joke about it himself as he happily enumerated his latest gaffes. It was no doubt that his extraordinary tactlessness, if it did not contribute to misunderstandings and grievances in the public sphere, led at the very least to the great unhappiness that was his marriage. More often than not, when Paige and Jack were together, Paige would sit there on the sofa, her fat lower lip jutted out, looking like she was going to cry, while Jack—one thigh swung over the other—leaned as far away from her as he could and talked sideways to whoever was within range. You could tell even her presence there beside him got under his skin, and before too long he would get up and begin prowling the room. He was like a cat—he always knew who in any given crowd didn't like him, just on instinct, and would immediately approach, cornering them for an entire evening, in order to share his views on the latest topic, while his wife continued to sit alone in the corner, batting back tears from her big, beautiful eyes.

The poet Maurice Bonheur would be there, too: their only real "French connection," as they called him. Everything they did delighted him. So *Américain*! he would say about the simplest and most inconsequential things, when no one else but him could see why. Then he would get that look on his face, and they would know he was storing whatever it was that had struck him so particularly away for a poem.

He would last the war. Later, indeed, when everyone else had left Paris, he would be Alden's only friend. They would meet on the Boulevard Saint-Michel and he would read to Alden the long poems he continued to write, and once would even do him the disservice of suggesting that with his own small, cryptic poems he was really onto something.

Then there was Dick. He, too, would remain through the war—in the ambulance service. The two of them, Dick and Alden, would uphold a dwindling friendship, Dick distancing himself more and more, then finally going mad. He would stop eating and all the hair would fall out of his head, and after the war would be rescued by his mother, a Spanish princess, and taken to a well-reputed mental institution in upstate New York, where, as far as anyone knows, he remains.

Later, when Alden himself had returned to the States, he would think of him—about how interesting it would be to visit him, if he could ever get up the nerve and secure the permission to go. Imagine it! The madman and the condemned. They could talk about the old days. About that evening—just shortly after Emmett died—that had ended with Dick catching Jack with a back-fist to the eye, and making him bleed. About the way that Paige had sat there the whole time, watching, with the same irritatingly beautiful look on her face she always wore. He would ask Dick why he had chosen to go completely mad, or if he had—and if he had, if he was glad that he had, and what it was like. He would ask him if there were certain signs by which he knew he was going mad before or when he did. If maybe there were signs the rest of them could have picked up on, too—even all those years ago. That is, if there were certain clues that, if they went back even to that night they could have picked out and put together with other little clues and in the end formed some sort of picture of the way things would go. If they could have foreseen Dick himself, skeletal and hairless, emerging from his apartment after the war carried by two orderlies—his mother following behind, her face pinched, as though composing herself for the benefit of some observer to the scene, though there wasn't any. Just Alden, standing at the bottom of the stairs next to the poet Maurice Bonheur. Maurice sort of glancing over at him from time to time with that look on his face, as if to say, *I'm here, I'm here*, and he, with a rising panic, wanting to shout at him, *Goddammit, I know!*

Alden would have liked to ask Dick if he sometimes felt that way, too. How excruciating it was to be sitting around with a bunch of people who kept reminding you they were still there. *Well, we're all still here, and that's something.* As if that were really something! To exist! He'd like to ask Dick if maybe that was what drove him crazy in the end—everyone so pleased simply to exist. If that was maybe why he wanted to disappear, why he had stockpiled rations in his third-floor apartment off the Boulevard Richard-Lenoir (which, unlike most of them, who lived only in a few rooms, was really—on account of the Spanish princess—an *apartment*, with a grand dining room and high ceilings and doors that swung out onto little balconies overlooking the street) until he had constructed a barricade, which the authorities actually had to destroy in order to be able even to get past the front door. Even standing outside with Maurice Bonheur, Alden could hear the great clatter of tins falling and then rolling around on the hardwood inside, and neither of them had the least clue what it was until afterward, when one of the policemen explained.

Alden would have liked, he thought, to sit down with Dick now, maybe hold his hand. The way he pictured it, Dick's hand would be as thin and cold-looking as it had been the day he was first taken from his apartment (though, with any luck, being housed now in such a plush institution, he had managed to fill out a bit again), but either way Alden thought he would like to hold his hand, and ask, Do you still agree with what you said then? That evening, so many years ago now—what seems like centuries—when I read a portion of Emmett's mother's letter out loud? And if he had any trouble recollecting, Alden would say: That bit, you know, about how there was a certain "senselessness" to everything. You said—do you remember now?—that that was wrong. It *did* make sense, you said. All of it. There was a gleam in your eye, as I recall it—maybe that was a bit of madness in you, already then. You said that, of course, it was a shame about Emmett's mother, and an even greater shame about Emmett himself, but there was a greater system in play than just the relation between mothers and sons, and certainly than between individual nations and men. If we expected Emmett's mother to see the sense in it, or even to see it ourselves, then we certainly weren't looking at the thing from the right direction. But she got one thing right, you said. There *are* no boundaries—no boundaries at all; and that—*that* (didn't we see it now? you asked) was what Emmett was fighting for! Further, you suggested—and now there was that gleam more than ever in your eye, though everyone had begun to shift in their seats and Carol had got up to get more wine, rubbing her neck, because she always got physically sore when you talked this way—that if all those old soldiers, all of the dead relatives Emmett was buried beside now, could crawl out from their graves—if they could get up and dust themselves off—they would have been fighting beside Emmett, too, because they, of all people—they who had been dead for so many years and to whom all things had become gloriously relative—wouldn't have known or cared anymore what they were fighting for, or for whom.

As gloriously relative, Alden had reflected at the time, as it had been for Emmett himself; at least as he had expressed it in the last letter Alden ever received from him (which he had not passed on to Emmett's mother or shown to Dick or to anyone, but kept for himself). It had been written on the fifth of May, 1937, shortly after the street fighting in Barcelona had begun. He had dived for cover down a narrow alleyway—surprising a POUM fellow also seeking cover there. The fellow swore loudly when he saw Emmett—in English. It turned out, Emmett explained, the fellow was a Brit. Instead of shooting at each other, then, the two swapped cigarettes and stories, and discovered that for some months they had both been considering swapping sides, too. The POUM fellow thought it might be better to join the International Brigade, because he was sick and tired of wallowing in the mud at a distance of over a thousand yards from the enemy—unable to approach any closer because they didn't have any weapons. He grumbled that until this "play-fighting" in the streets had erupted a few days before he had been inclined to believe there wasn't really a war going on in Spain at all—that it had all just been made up as a serial fiction for the *News Chronicle*. Emmett had joined the International Brigade himself six months before but it was becoming clear, he said, that the Soviets were deliberately sabotaging their revolutionary hopes in order to maintain diplomatic relations with Britain and France. He'd rather be fighting with the anarchists, he said—who at least believed in something.

In those moments, talking with the POUM fellow, and all during the time that led up to his death a few days later when he was caught in the crossfire (and who knew which bullets finally entered him first, and from what side?), what struck him more than anything else, he wrote (he, who had railed against Blum, and denied that the thing even existed as a possibility in the hearts of men!), was the absolute *neutrality* of all those who were fighting—or supposed to be fighting—in Spain. A sense of utter futility had descended over the whole affair. He had seen it happen himself, he wrote. Had watched as, over the course of the six short months he had spent in the country, its citizens had gone from behaving in good proletariat fashion (both men and women, dressed in overalls, addressed you as "comrade" and performed military drills in the streets) to behaving just as they always had. Gradually, the expensive restaurants were reopened. The rich people inside and the poor people out. It was not, Emmett wrote, that anything had changed—first one way and then back—from the beginning, the whole thing had been a sham! Now all anyone wanted was for everything to get back to "normal," and as quickly as possible. It was absolutely despicable, Emmett wrote, how shortsighted we remain—*insist* on remaining—as a human race. The words on the lips of the rich as well as the poor—and even on those of the English bloke he had enjoyed a cigarette with while they dodged bullets together from their respective sides—regarded the "natural order" of things: that pervasive belief among everyone alike—the rich, the poor, the Fascists, Republicans, even the anarchists—that there existed some sort of natural state to which we might be able to return. That it was more "natural" somehow that the rich should eat in expensive restaurants—a thing inscribed in the blood, which no amount of marching around in overalls could change!

It was unbelievable, wrote Emmett in that (what would be his last) letter, that there should be, especially here, where even the war itself was the purest of fictions, a faith in anything being "natural" at all. How could they not also see how everything was, instead, contrived ahead of time—prearranged? Just as (he had once read) in ancient Mesopotamia whole battles had once been orchestrated in order to entertain the rich. They'd appeared to the guests as genuine contests of strength and chance, but in the ring every move was accounted for, and all the players knew from the beginning how it would end: the losing team ceremonially beheaded in front of the admiring crowd. Think of it! Emmett had written. Playing a perfectly choreographed game as if there were another outcome at the end than having your head cleanly removed by the opposing team, but knowing there was not!

You needn't—he continued wryly—stretch your imagination very far.

It was the resignation inherent in this last line that inspired in Alden the slightest tremor of instinctive fear, or knowledge—whatever it was—that Emmett's death had not been so purely accidental as his mother later claimed. He was prepared, however—so confused by the line that separated what one intended and what one did not had he become by that time—to understand this last comment, with which

Emmett concluded his letter, as the most banal and everyday of prophecies. The sort we make, or could make, at any moment: there not being, ultimately, very many outcomes to this life, or too many variations, when you think about it, of when or how it will end.

WHILE ALDEN WAS LOSING himself in these reflections that evening—just after Emmett's death, while they were all gathered, as usual, at Dick's place, and Dick had said what he said about everything making sense after all—Jack had launched into a discussion of neutrality, and somewhere along the way the conversation had taken a turn. Later, he was told that it had to do, in particular, with the Stavisky affair, which the poet Maurice Bonheur had brought up by way of something Dick had said—before sitting back again, amused as ever, to watch both Dick and Jack (now anything but neutral) circle each other, while he exclaimed out loud, Oh-ho-ho! So—*Américain*! But even had he known this, by the time Alden's attention had been recalled, he had no way of entering into the conversation—or of understanding why Dick especially was suddenly beside himself with fury.

Then Carol came in, still rubbing her neck, and holding on to a plate of American crackers; just as she did so, and before any of them—perhaps even Dick himself—knew it was coming, he had pounced on Jack with such force that, even with how much bigger he was, Jack was immediately knocked toward Paige on the couch, who—with her quick reflexes, which had only been quickened over the course of her close association with Jack—had already sprung effortlessly out of the way.

There they were, then: Dick and Jack scuffling on the floor, Alden to one side, Paige to the other, Maurice Bonheur perched on an ottoman, looking on with delight. And Carol. Still hovering with the crackers at the door and rubbing her neck. The struggle went on for some time without either Dick or Jack doing any damage to the other, or sustaining any, but then finally Dick broke free of the hold Jack had on him and succeeded in making genuine contact—planting a powerful back-fist directly under Jack's right eye. Jack roared. Then came another loud crash. The dinner plate filled with American crackers had hit Dick squarely in the middle of the back, so that in another moment the crackers, the plate, and Dick himself went flying. Then all came to rest: the crackers and the plate smashing into pieces upon contact with the floor.

Dick stood up, off balance. He touched his hand to his back, and started to say something, but no one paid him any attention. Even Carol shifted her gaze—bored—to where Jack was rolling on the floor, holding his eye.

—

SERGE ALEXANDRE STAVISKY, FOR THOSE WHO NO LONGER RECALL the affair, had been found dead in Chamonix on the eighth of January, 1934—a gun wound in his side. Among other questions that persisted even many years later, there was the question (memorably touched upon that night by the poet Maurice Bonheur) of whether, as the official reports of the crime would have it, he had inflicted this wound on himself, or if he had died at the hands of the police—who by that time had been after Stavisky (or, as he was better known, "Le Beau Sacha") for many years. It was more popular to assume (because it was also much more likely) that the police had killed him—but fourteen of twenty-two newspapers that reported the incident went with the official report: the death was ruled a suicide. Even with the forensic evidence, which described a distance the bullet would have had to travel far greater than the length of one man's arm. The only concessions that were made to the discrepancy within official reports were sardonic allusions to what became known as Le Beau Sacha's "long arm."

For many years before the incident at Chamonix, Serge Stavisky kept busy selling inflated, worthless bonds, which—for some reason, never fully explained—even after the first whiffs of scandal, people continued to buy. Among his most famous exploits was a pawnshop run on the surety of an emerald necklace purported to have belonged to the late Empress of Germany—a necklace which turned out to have been made out of glass. But how Stavisky managed to operate his

business for so long without getting caught, or losing the greater portion of his devoted clientele, is really only a small mystery. He had a
keen eye for business and in a short period of time had contacts and
partnerships with some of the most influential people in all of France—
those who, quite simply, could not afford to be embarrassed. If he was
threatened, Stavisky simply bought off the would-be whistle-blower—
or someone very close to him—with the threat of exposing their own
involvement in a scheme they could only have known from the beginning was not entirely as it appeared. Stavisky's favorite method of settling accounts with the media, for instance (who sought at various
times to endanger his integrity), was to buy large advertising blocks in
the paper—in order to continue to promote, of course, his own false
bonds. The real mystery of the Stavisky affair, then as now, was that
it was considered a mystery at all—as if Le Beau Sacha were a sort of
bogeyman, an aberration of a system that would otherwise have
destroyed him.

This was, quite simply—as Dick had once, disastrously, attempted to
argue with Jack and Maurice Bonheur—not the case.

IN 1927, SEVEN WHOLE years before Stavisky was finally brought to his
grisly end, he was arrested. The trial, however, was "systematically"
postponed. His bail was raised nineteen times; people with injurious stories to report no longer knew anything of the affair; a judge who claimed
he had "secret documents" (which would, he promised, finally lay the
whole thing to rest) was found dead, his head cleanly removed at the
throat.

After that, there were no more documents, let alone secrets of any
kind. The case was dismissed.

It wasn't, then, until 1934 that Stavisky, after fleeing to Chamonix,
picked up a gun at the end of a very long arm and shot himself. There
then proceeded a general overhaul of the government ministers, many of
whom were far too close for comfort to the nasty little affair. The right
wing accused the left of murdering Stavisky in order to protect their
own. In an effort to reestablish their integrity, Police Chief Jean Chappe

was dismissed, further inciting the ire of the right, and directly causing the right-wing uprising of February 6, 1934—perhaps the most blatant abuse of police power the country had ever known.

All of this on the price of a glass necklace.

AFTER THAT, NO ONE seemed to know the man. Even, or especially, Stavisky's well-positioned friends (the friends he had so conscientiously made precisely because they were so dependable in their continued refusal to embarrass themselves). If presented with a photograph, they could not recognize him. There was no paper trail of anyone having any involvement with him at all. The fake bonds, the advertising contracts, the business luncheons—these were all now otherwise accounted for. So *that* was the great mystery, in the end: the way Le Beau Sacha had been absorbed into his own story. That he disappeared, having taken on—like the Empress's jewels—only the most imaginary value.

As in the de Maupassant story of the same theme: the one about the poor woman, who borrows a beautiful diamond necklace from a wealthy friend, which, over the course of the evening she wears it, is either stolen or lost. She is, of course, forced to replace it, and at such tremendous cost that she and her husband spend the rest of their days indebted to the hockshop broker. Perhaps you remember by now (or, if you do not, will have guessed) that the story ends only after our unfortunate heroine encounters the woman from whom she borrowed the necklace and discovers that (though that woman is now, unwittingly, the proprietor of a genuine diamond necklace) the original had been made out of glass.

We are always, perhaps—as the poet Maurice Bonheur would later reflect to Alden, at the height of the war—as in this story, fooled twice. But not as the story would have it: as though we existed outside the story's frame and were able, therefore, to observe ourselves—our fortunes and misfortunes, whatever they may be—from that fixed distance. No, on the contrary. We exist very much within the story's folds. We are (the poet said) both women at once; on the one hand, believing, and paying, for what is in fact worth nothing at all, and on the other hand—unknowingly, unwittingly—proprietors of that which is worth inestimably more than we ever could have guessed.

—

THEN—AS IT ALWAYS HAPPENS, WITHOUT ANY SEEMING PROGRESSION by which they might later have accounted for its passing—four years went by.

IT WAS THE SUMMER of 1940; the tenth of June of that year, to be exact. A day in which—watching from the window of Jack and Paige's second-story apartment as the clouds of an impending summer storm darkened the streets—Alden waited. For what, he could never later be sure. Most Americans he knew had left the city some months before. He himself had received an urgent telegram from the Judge at the beginning of January, when things began to look increasingly grim, insisting that he immediately resign his post and return home.

Will make all arrangements, the telegram had assured him. *Return on first available flight.*

Alden had let the telegram sit unanswered on the window ledge of his seventh-floor flat; then—very carefully one morning—he tipped it over the side, watching as it skittered down the gleaming metal roof and was lost.

IT WAS ANOTHER WEEK before he sent a terse reply—stating simply that, as he could see no immediate reason for it, he had no intention of returning home.

Sutton had applauded the decision. "You must tell me absolutely everything," she insisted, every time she wrote.

What he *didn't* tell her was how often, now that the war had actually arrived, he regretted his decision. How often he thought wistfully after the Judge's telegram—churned into mud by then, no doubt, in a neighboring courtyard somewhere.

FOR WEEKS, JACK HAD been dead set on joining what was left of the French Army. They were still holding the line, just south of Chartres: Why didn't Alden come along?

Well, for one thing there was the notice from the embassy indicating that, if the Germans took Paris (as there was now every indication they would), both he *and* Jack would be expected to report to the office in Vichy—where U.S. Ambassador William C. Bullitt planned to immediately reconvene.

Then there was Paige's sister, who had been telephoning every day, urging all of them to join her in Châteaudun.

Jack had scoffed at that idea. Sit out the war! he'd said, shaking his head in amusement and disbelief. You wouldn't catch me dead! But he had not yet left to join the army, and Paige had not yet left to join her sister in Châteaudun. As usual, their conflicted impulses and desires held them in check. Even as the sirens screamed and the Stukas fell, and the people rushed, in every imaginable direction, into the street, they only continued to wait. Alden—having nothing to propel him, naturally, in one direction over any other—waited with them, feeling only (as he later recalled it) a sort of dull alarm, akin to boredom.

All day they remained, smoking cigarettes, sipping vermouth (everything else having long ago been emptied), and watching out the window as the street roiled below. It was stinking hot. Paige wore only a light chemise over a pair of slacks she had rolled to the knee and it was possible to see, beneath it, her very large brown nipples.

This is absolute madness, she said, for at least the fifteenth time that hour. If it wasn't for the two of you I would be well out of this.

Carol had already left, back to Ohio, by then. In response, Dick had barricaded himself (though not yet literally) inside.

Oh, it's my fault? roared Jack in reply. It's still a free country, he said—though (he checked his watch with a dramatic flick of his wrist) I wouldn't wait too much longer now—

From there the fight escalated, until Paige wound up poised above Jack, wielding the nearly empty bottle of vermouth. His hands grasped around her thin wrists, Jack held her off easily, but still, it was Paige who seemed to maintain the upper hand, and in the end it was she who came out victorious. Alden did not recall later how the decision was made. The bottle was replaced on the kitchen table, a few scattered things were packed into bags; they were on their way.

JACK HAD HIS ARIÈS, which he was very proud of, and they climbed in and revved the motor and began the slow push out of the city. They never got up any real speed, but they didn't stop, either—if they had, they would have become hopelessly bogged down and never would have got started again.

Everyone wanted a ride. They held up baskets of clothes or dishes, or sometimes, rarely, fistfuls of damp banknotes in offering.

Américain! they shouted. It was always a mystery to them how the French always knew, but they did. Even at thirty miles an hour, or perhaps because of it, they knew: *S'il vous plait!* they cried. But they didn't stop, and once they left the city limits they made good progress—arriving at Chartres just before dusk.

—

ANYONE WHO HAS EVER APPROACHED THAT CITY WILL REMEMBER THE two spires of the Notre-Dame; the way they rise up from the surrounding fields, as if from the very center of the earth. Everything else seems to spread from those two points in the landscape, flat and empty. It's strange how that is: how the eye, when it fixes on something—just as it fixes on it, and indeed *in order* to do so—causes everything else to fall away. That the central point toward which the eye is drawn, whatever it is, in this way both creates and eliminates the landscape. Alden was thinking about that. About how, if he ever wrote a poem again, something he had not done in a long time, he would try to write something that expressed that idea in some way.

How would it be possible to re-create it, he thought: the authority with which, in a single breath, the landscape absolved itself of mystery and assembled itself around the soaring spires of the Notre-Dame?

A brief, unsettling lull between air strikes overhead only added to the effect. For a few moments, as they drew near the city, there was just the hum of the car and the low strain of the vehicles in front and behind them as they rolled, in a long train, through the ancient gates.

Yes, how would it ever be possible to describe it? In a way that would not, that is, be just a transfusion of images, which (in accordance with the dimming of memory) could only ever, at best, be representative of— therefore, auxiliary to—the thing that it was? As Alden contemplated this, turning it about in his brain—the way that one might move finally *past* representation in a poem, if such a thing were possible, or if it could only be a matter of something like *active intent*? . . . of, that is, the *desire* to achieve such a thing, while the actual image or object was forced to remain forever absent from the page—another low rumble erupted from somewhere in the vicinity of the city center, as they continued their slow approach. This time the noise came as though from below them, rather than above—as though the earth had begun to crack open; as though in another moment, if they had looked down, they would have seen the ground open and yawning below them, and would have had no choice but to plunge below.

ONLY THEN DID THEY realize that the city was on fire. They smelled it first, but then, as they parked the car and made their way along the river toward the cathedral, where Alden was sincerely hoping to find the Canon Delaporte, with whom he had a casual acquaintance, they saw it, too. A dull red glow across the line of the horizon.

Alden knew the canon because of Emmett. It had been just before he'd left for Spain that the two of them had gone to Chartres to meet him—the leading authority on the cathedral's stained glass. They had gone to view the pieces and hear what was known of their history. They spent hours in the church together, sketching the windows so they would remember them. Alden still had those sketches somewhere in his notebooks. He had an idea of someday starting a great poem cycle that would be somehow based on their meticulous structure: part music, part story, part science, part light. Now he thought about those notebooks in his abandoned Paris flat—he had not thought to take them with him—and wondered whether he would ever see them again. He found himself curiously ambivalent to the thought that he might not. It seemed an appropriate sacrifice. In fact, he hoped desperately in that moment that they might be destroyed utterly, in order that he himself might be spared. If—he pledged—he was indeed spared, he would start all over again; something truly beautiful this time. And though he felt a little doubtful and guilty about what, in the scheme of things, seemed a very cheap bargain, he did not know what else to ask for, or to offer in return, and by that time they were very near the church anyway, so he put the thing out of his mind and began to worry instead that the canon would have already fled the city, or that he might not recognize him—or care to help, even if he did—and any number of other small doubts and apprehensions also passed through his mind.

When at last they reached them, they found the cathedral doors open but no one inside. The great arch of the ceiling as they entered struck Alden as far higher and the inside vaster and emptier than he remembered. This, he soon realized, could be attributed to the fact that where the stained glass had once been, only air now blew through the tall arched frames. On one of the gaping ledges a bird nested. The pews were still set up toward the back, but the labyrinth in the center of the cathedral had been cleared, and their footsteps echoed as they crossed it, resounding louder than they otherwise might have because of how empty the church—with the removal of the stained glass—had become.

It was their luck that, just before they reached the back stairs, which led down to the crypt, they met the Canon Delaporte himself. He did not seem particularly surprised to see them, but neither did Alden detect any flicker of recognition—even when he introduced himself, reminding him of their acquaintance. In any case, the canon nodded solemnly when Alden spoke, and invited them to follow.

In the crypt, thirty or so other refugees—including four postmen, who, like Jack, were intent on joining the French forces outside the city—had already gathered. The space was indeed, as the canon had warned, cramped, owing not only to the large number of refugees, but to the nearly one thousand packing boxes in which, as they soon learned, the great cathedral windows had been packed away for safekeeping—just as they had been during the aerial bombardments of 1918. Canon Delaporte had supervised the removal of the glass himself on that occasion, and for a second time had, he told them, preemptively ordered the removal of the glass in early 1939. Not one piece had been damaged in the process and the canon fully expected them to survive another war.

Dusk had long since settled, but down in the crypt everything was timeless and strange. Soon after they arrived, Jack departed in the company of three of the postmen in order to help collect food from the center —as well as to find out what he could about the location of the French troops, which he and the postmen intended to join the next day. Most of the shops in the city had been abandoned by then, their windows and doors blasted, so that finding provisions to bring back to the crypt was a simple matter of locating a vendor whose stocks had not been picked over too thoroughly by everyone else. But, only minutes after Jack and the postmen had left the crypt, the sirens again began to wail. Paige gave out a startled cry when she heard them, to which Alden responded by pressing his hand into hers.

He'll be all right, he said—too quickly. It would have been better if he'd paused a moment as if he'd really thought about it, he realized, too late.

Jack did not return until many hours later. When he did, the postmen were not with him, and when he was asked about their whereabouts Jack only shook his head. He was pale as a ghost and clutched his arm tightly to his chest, not speaking. A full minute must have passed before finally he said: I'm hit. Then he just stood there, as before, staring around. There did not seem to be any blood.

Let's take a look.

He held stubbornly on to his arm and wouldn't let anyone touch it. That night, because there didn't seem to be anything else to do, they left him alone. But by morning his eyes were rolling up in his head when he tried to look at anything straight, and finally he let the canon near. When the canon touched him on the arm, Jack screamed. It seemed improbable that a person could make so much noise. Especially down there in the crypt, where the air had become so rarefied and thin, his voice boomed out around them like it was ten or twelve men screaming instead of just one.

Hush, said the canon. Get some iodine.

We have none.

Some rum.

There's none.

Jack continued to scream. Finally, the canon managed to pry out the object that had been lodged in Jack's arm, cleaned the wound as best he could, then wrapped it up in a piece of clean white cloth. He held up the object for Jack to examine.

La coupable. It was a twisted piece of metal, no bigger than his thumb. Jack held out his workable hand and the canon handed the object to him.

Later in the evening, with the help of some wine—the one thing of which they had plenty—Jack was feeling better and he told them of the confusion he had witnessed above. The two hotels, he said, were packed to overflowing. There must have been hundreds of people in the streets—camped out at the door to the Hôtel de France because there was no more room inside—shouting for those they had lost. Cows, pigs, and horses grazed aimlessly through the streets. There was still fierce competition for the loot that had not yet gone bad in the shops—and for some of it that had. One had to be quick, as it was all being snatched up by semi-organized gangs in order either to be distributed or sold. One man, posing as the manager of the Hôtel de France (the actual manager had abandoned the city some days before), was busy selling the entire contents of the wine cellar at twenty francs per bottle.

War, said Jack, when he reported this, is the great equalizer. For twenty francs, one might have enjoyed everything from the finest cognac to the most undrinkable table wine tonight.

AMONG THOSE WHO, IN the chaos, had fled the city was the bishop himself. The prefect, Moulin, showed up at the cathedral to share the news with the canon shortly after Jack's return.

The coward, he said. The rogue. Everyone is abandoning the city. Imagine. The senior doctor leaps into his car yesterday saying, Every man for himself. The bishop does not surprise me—but the doctor? With the hospitals the way they are, he said, full to overflowing? It is unforgivable.

—

THE NEXT MORNING JACK LEFT WITH THE REMAINING POSTMAN TO join the French troops directly south of the city. Alden went along.

It was nightfall before they found any sign of them: a ratty, disorganized unit of something less than fifty men. If they had not insisted upon it, no one would have believed they were still at war.

A day later—the twelfth of June—the air sirens stopped working and there was no warning except the bombs themselves as they rained down on the city. For two days, then, with orders neither to advance nor to retreat, they watched from a distance as the city burned. Finally, the dark clouds, which had threatened for as many days—indistinguishable, above them, from the billowing clouds of smoke that rose from the burning city—broke, and a thunder and lightning storm drenched the fields.

It was not until the sixteenth of June—the Germans just on the horizon—that they finally fled. For days there had been talk among the men of heading south, toward Spain (indeed, many French soldiers had already departed in that direction), but that was the direction from which the German troops were also arriving—it seemed like walking into a trap. It was Gilles Dupuis, from Bourgogne, a small man with a closely trimmed mustache and a nervous tic, which made his eye flutter when he spoke, who proposed heading west instead. Crossing over into Switzerland at Lebetain—a border area he said he knew well. Jack was too weak to go along. He held his side, which was beginning to stink under the bandage he refused to change, and said to Alden, You'll do fine without me. I bet the Germans ain't half as bad as hoofing it to Switzerland or Spain. So Alden went. Traveling west with Gilles and three other French soldiers, camping in the open air, and listening to the rattle of artillery fire in the distance as the Germans, behind them, slowly closed in.

IT WASN'T UNTIL LATER, after he had returned to Paris, that he learned what had happened in Chartres. About how the prefect had stood alone, in full uniform, in the courtyard of his private residence when the German general drove up to the yard. How the general had asked him to approach, and how the prefect had refused. He would agree to the terms of surrender, he said, only from within his official residence. The general turned abruptly to his companion, said something in German, and drove on.

The prefect changed quickly, then, into civilian clothes and walked the short distance into the city. There were Germans everywhere. The chief occupation of most seemed to be employing the labor of French refugees in collecting whatever was left from inside the abandoned shops.

The first person the prefect recognized was a French baker, whom he had long suspected as a German spy, arm in arm with a German soldier. The prefect greeted the two, giving the baker a cold stare.

Hello, Prefect, the baker said. This German officer is most eager to see the great cathedral of which he has heard so much.

The two continued on.

Toward noon, the prefect returned to his residence, where he was told that two German officers requested an immediate audience. He dressed quickly and invited them into his office. There, he was asked to follow the officers to their headquarters at the Hôtel de France, which had recently been commandeered from the opportunists and refugees. Having no choice, the prefect accompanied the officers to the hotel, where he was kept waiting under armed guard for the general. But the general never appeared. After several hours passed, the same two officers who had invited him to the hotel arrived again to inform the prefect that retreating French soldiers had raped and massacred French women and children just outside the city.

Impossible, said the prefect.

One might think, said one of the officers. And if these were ordinary French soldiers I would be inclined to agree with you. We have, he told the prefect, the utmost respect for . . . most of your units. You see—the officer leaned in, adopting a more conciliatory tone—these were *Negro troops*, he explained. So, you see, the situation is, although unfortunate, in fact not at all surprising.

He then pushed a piece of paper across the table toward the prefect. It was a protocol, detailing the events the officer had just described. Politely, the prefect was asked to sign.

He refused. He knew for a fact that the Senegalese troops who now stood accused of this egregious crime had been massacred—shot down, unarmed, by the approaching German forces; his signature was all that was needed to legitimize their murder. The prefect couldn't decide, in that moment, what was more disgusting: that the thing had occurred at all, or that the attempt being made now to cover it up was so flimsy and apparent that even the German officers seemed to be enjoying the pure mockery of it all.

He would not sign. He would rather be shot.

But he wasn't shot. Instead, he was dragged out into the courtyard of the hotel, where German soldiers took turns beating him. His screams could be heard by the refugees who pressed against the gate to watch; the Germans did not turn them away. The prefect could not tell how long it lasted, but by the time the beating stopped it was dusk, and so he estimated it had lasted seven hours. He was then put into a German car and driven out to look at the "evidence": nine bodies of women and children stretched out side by side on the dirt floor of an unused barn. Their features, the ones that remained, had already begun to soften, and there was an incredible stench in the air. Even a quick glance would tell you that the dead were victims of an air raid, not a ground massacre. What a sick joke. The prefect almost laughed. Or rather, his breath came out all at once in a rush. He was not sure what it was until he found himself bent over double, vomiting up the remains of the lunch that had been prepared for him many hours before.

He imagined the German guards laughing at him behind their blank expressions, which betrayed nothing.

This is a joke, he said, when he had recovered himself. These are the victims of an air raid. They have been dead at least four days.

You think so? said one of the officers. Still, his face did not change. I think he needs a closer look. Should we give him a closer look? he asked.

The prefect was taken to a shed behind the barn and shut in with the bottom half of a woman's corpse, severed just above the waist.

This, too, the German officers insisted, was the work of the colonial troops.

You should not have underestimated the viciousness of your own army, said the first officer before shutting the shed door and leaving the prefect in blackness, with just the company of a woman's truncated body—and, of course, the smell.

He must have passed out for a bit, and that was a relief, but when he came to, he was being dragged from the shed to the barn, where, again, he was beaten. Finally, around one o'clock in the morning he was driven back into town.

Since you love Negroes so much, said one of the officers, we thought you might like to sleep with one. They locked him into the hospital gate-keeper's lodge, which was serving as a prison, with a Senegalese soldier who had been so badly beaten he could not open his mouth to speak.

The prefect let his emotions overcome him. He worried that if the officers returned again he would no longer be able to resist—in that case, who knew what he would sign? He looked around the room. Only the very faintest of light crept in from beneath the door, but a shard of clear glass, glittering within it, caught his eye. He picked up the glass and turned it over in his hand for some time, thinking. Then he jabbed at his throat, under the chin.

At first nothing happened. He wondered if he had the conviction to even make himself bleed. It was not that he was afraid, he told himself. It was just that the task required more energy of him than he actually had. But once he broke the skin it was easier. He worked at the cut he had made until the blood spurted, covering his hands, and finally making his neck too wet and slippery to cut any deeper. He had hardly felt it. Once you decide to do something, he thought to himself—it just happens. The idea thrilled him and for a moment he felt ecstatically happy. The blood spurted from his neck like a stuck faucet. He called out and a guard arrived, then swore in German. It was a word the prefect understood, and the last thing he remembered before he passed out.

SINCE THEY WERE ALREADY on the hospital grounds it was not long before the prefect's injuries were treated, first by the German army doctor, and then by Captain Foubert, the French military dentist, who stitched up the wound, which was not in fact all that deep, and had not touched a major artery. The prefect was driven back to his private residence that night and nothing more was made of the event. Within a few weeks he had healed completely and reassumed his duties under the Vichy government—though it was rumored, Paige told Alden later—he had soon afterward given up or otherwise been relieved of his post, and was now secretly working for the French Resistance.

After working as a puppet for Vichy? Hardly likely, Alden said.

You think so? asked Paige. Don't you remember how he was the night he came into the *cathédrale* (she had an aggravating habit of even while speaking English pronouncing French words with an exaggerated accent), remember how angry he was at the bishop and the doctor for deserting? I thought he was very brave.

—

FOR THREE DAYS AND NIGHTS, ALDEN, GILLES, AND THREE OTHER French soldiers picked their way over the open country, heading west. When they could travel no farther, they camped in the open air, listening to the Stukas as they screamed overhead. Every time a bomb exploded nearby, Alden closed his eyes. The noise would seem to cut everything away—to obliterate, for a moment, even a trace of a thought in his brain so that it always took him several seconds afterward to realize he was still alive.

It was a relief to be captured. Once they were marching toward Orléans he knew with certainty he was alive. Every moment brought that fact keenly to his attention, in largest part owing to the excruciating pain in his feet, where they had been torn by his shoes. He did not have any properly issued army gear. Most of what he had was borrowed from the dead soldiers they had passed, fleeing from Chartres.

It was not until they arrived a full day and night later at Orléans that they were given anything to eat—a thin gruel and a corner of stale bread. As the food touched Alden's stomach it came up again. Gilles scowled at him in disgust and he felt deeply ashamed for having wasted the food another man might have enjoyed.

The camp was full to overflowing. There was not enough food, and the barracks, as well as the latrines, had long ago reached capacity. Prisoners slept in the open air, amid the stench of feces that spilled out into the prison yard. One after another Alden's companions fell ill. Gilles became so weak that at last he was taken to the infirmary. Before he left he promised Alden that, once he returned, they would escape together. He was familiar with that region, he told Alden. Much more so than were any of the Germans. But before Gilles had a chance to return they were transported to a prisoner-of-war camp far away from the country that Gilles knew so well.

FINALLY, IN FEBRUARY 1941, after nearly seven months spent at Stalag III-A, just south of Berlin, Alden's release was arranged. Who could have imagined it would be to the beautiful, sad-eyed Paige he would owe his freedom and, with little doubt, therefore—such as they were—the rest of his days? She had returned to Paris immediately after the capitulation, rather than staying on with her sister at Châteaudun. There, very rapidly, and with tremendous initial success, she began to cultivate what would soon prove a valuable connection with a young German officer— who had connections, in turn, to the OKW (the German defense office then operating in Paris). It was in this way that Paige managed, finally, to track down both Alden and Jack, and arrange for Alden's release. Jack, they would soon learn, had been "released" some time prior—he had died from blood poisoning outside Chartres, mere hours before the arrival of the Germans.

But when Alden first returned to Paris they did not know this yet, and in fact, through some sort of mistake in internal communication, it was *Jack* whom Paige expected when she went to the station on the thirteenth of February, 1941. It was a surprise to both of them, therefore, when Alden arrived in Paris that evening alone—disembarking at Montparnasse.

FOR THE FIRST MONTH after his return, Alden kept Paige company in the apartment she had shared with Jack in the seventh, near the École Militaire. He would have preferred to have returned to his own small flat, though it was dismal compared to the apartment Paige kept, even empty (all the furniture had been taken by the Germans), but the building had been sold and the new owner had no knowledge of the previous one. The few belongings he had left there, including the notebook in which he had once sketched the stained-glass windows of Chartres, were just as lost to him, therefore, as he had once so fervently hoped.

So he stayed on with Paige, until it became unbearable to do so any longer, and just as he had back in Chartres, he promised her repeatedly that Jack would also be returning soon. They weren't going to keep the cooperative French, he said, let alone the Americans, for very long. Why should they? We aren't even at war, he reminded her. He said this because he believed it, but also because it produced a desirable result. Her face would relax suddenly and she would extend her hand toward him, willing him to take it in his own. He had no choice but to obey. It was odd: to be, on the one hand, the object of intense regret (that he had arrived in the place of Jack was something, he knew, she could not help but blame him for) and, on the other, of desire (that he was *not* who she had expected him to be was, he prided himself, not entirely to her disadvantage).

Won't your officer be jealous? he asked her on a few occasions, just to watch her squirm.

But she was not really ashamed. Not yet.

Soon, though, neither one could bear the strain of it any longer, and Alden found a place to live, on the Rue Auguste-Compte, not far from the Luxembourg Gardens and the OKW office, where, thanks to Paige's intervention in his affairs, he was now employed. Thankfully, it was not until after he had relocated that Paige received word about Jack. Quite naturally, she was beside herself—but, though Alden felt sorry for her being left alone like that, he honestly felt she was better off. A more tactless man than himself might have reminded her that, after all, neither one of them could ever stand the other.

—

AT FIRST ALDEN'S RESPONSIBILITIES AT THE OKW OFFICE WERE MINimal, consisting in the main of mind-numbing tasks, the purpose of which usually escaped him. He would spend an entire week sorting through stacks of American newspapers, say, in order to circle every mention of the Führer or Operation Barbarossa—creating a patchwork pattern of red ink across each page that nobody would ever bother to consult. But then, in March, the German military intelligence organization, Abwehr, captured a Dutch agent and managed to crack the coded messages being sent back and forth between Holland, Britain, and France. After this, the department was chiefly involved in capturing Dutch agents, sending false messages to Britain, and decoding the messages the Brits continued to send in reply. Alden's job in all of this was (along with continuing to sift through mountains of newsprint for seemingly no purpose at all) to create credible messages in English that could then be translated by Abwehr into stolen code. Now, you will likely hear that the Brits knew their agents had been compromised almost from the start, and that the information Abwehr received and decoded in response to Alden's own messages were themselves (though also "credible") false. At the time, this did not seem to be the case—though indeed it may have been. Whatever the reason for it, the information Abwehr received from the Brits never did seem to further the German intelligence effort in any significant way—a point Alden would later have cause to emphasize.

AFTER PAIGE AND ALDEN did not see each other anymore, and Jack was dead, and Carol gone, and Dick had begun (quite literally now, though they did not yet know it) to build his barricade, Maurice Bonheur was Alden's only friend. They would meet on the Boulevard Saint-Michel after work (Maurice worked as a museum guard at the Cluny and wrote his long poems on the backs of the maps to the medieval collections, because paper was so hard to come by) and Maurice would read Alden bits of the poems he had written, and from time to time, when he could no longer resist the temptation, Alden would read one or two of his own—based on the material he was all that time gathering from the American newspapers. You see, it was thanks to the time Alden had spent on his seemingly innocuous first assignment for the OKW that he had been able to make some significant intelligence gains of his own: an obvious pattern had begun to emerge within the pages he trolled daily for the most benign references—which could not have, in themselves, indicated anything at all. At first he had no means of understanding his discovery; he simply copied the pattern he'd found, puzzling over it in the evenings in the privacy of his rented room. As the material accumulated he became more cautious, however. How could he have explained, should anyone have thought to question him, a notebook quickly beginning to fill with—albeit as yet uncracked—code? The code would—Alden was sure of it—already be familiar, and thus instantly recognizable, to the OKW agents, as it could only, he reasoned (embedded as it was within American newsprint), be the work of German spies. It was then that he hit on the idea of disguising the information as small poems; of rearranging the words so they made sense according to each new piece's individual structure. He was always careful, of course, to keep—on a separate sheet of paper—an accompanying key to each new poem he produced. In order, of course, that he might be able to easily reassemble the code when, at last, he was able to crack it.

As the months passed, however, this secondary code—by which he disguised the first—became so increasingly complicated that Alden began to regret that more and more of his time was spent only further codifying the already coded information he found, rather than getting any nearer to deciphering it. But in any case, because the effort—as the weeks and then the months passed—began increasingly to consume him, it gave him great pleasure to share his "poems," on the few occasions he did, with Maurice Bonheur.

Once or twice (though he was careful never to divulge the true nature or potential import of the work, and always presented them as though he himself were their single author) he even intimated that they had been made up, at least in part, of rearranged code. The poems, he lied, were constructed out of *British* code words, which Alden had implemented according to their original, rather than their intended, meaning—rearranging them in order that they made sense on the page in a very different—indeed, far more obvious—way than they had within the context of their original form (the significance of which Abwehr had, by that time, already revealed).

Alden was onto something, Maurice said. Something potentially— he raised an eloquent left eyebrow—*revolutionary*. Had not the world, from the beginning of time, seemed set on a path of further and further fragmentation, so that soon meaning would exist only in the most minute and unassimilable parts? Just think of it, he said: the priests and politicians; the scientists—even the poets—everyone intent on moving away from any direct adherence between meaning and form; from the singular, pronounceable, literal word . . . And here Alden was doing the opposite!

Alden was flattered, and said so, but really, he said, he had achieved his results only by respecting the inherent sense of the code itself— which, he reminded his friend, was, by necessity, constrained by much stricter rules even than spoken language. It was only by breaking these rules, Alden explained, that he was able to reintroduce to the language of the code some sort of recognizable meaning. Though it might appear, therefore, at first glance (as Maurice had suggested) that he was translating nonsensical code into sensible language, in fact he was, in many respects, doing just the opposite. It was only a matter—as usual—of the way that you looked at the thing.

Maurice Bonheur agreed and said that no doubt Alden was quite right, but either way, he said, the thing was revolutionary. Maybe not— he admitted—in the sense of its *never having previously occurred*, but at least in the sense that the work had begun to inhabit the very *revolution* according to which meaning was produced—moving as it did between sense and nonsense, then back again.

But this did not add up, either, Alden said, after taking a minute to think on it. It was not *meaning* itself that moved back and forth, but their *apprehension* of it. Sense was, after all, not integral to the thing, but something only later applied in order that it might be apprehended at all.

You are right again, said Maurice, because he was always agreeable; it is not any particular meaning, or any particular form through which meaning is apprehended that is revolutionary, but *revolution itself*. The fact, he said—by now he had become quite excited—that there is *movement*, and because of that a *rhythm* by which meaning moves, repeatedly, from sense to nonsense, then back again. We apprehend something, he said, after all, only in contrast to what, in another moment, it is not; that is to say, we attribute to it a value only to the extent we understand it as a possibility of what it not yet, or no longer, is.

All of this may seem quite self-evident, the poet added, but I myself never considered the matter to any great extent until, by a terrific stroke of luck (though I would have hardly called it one at the time), I came to know the composer Olivier Messiaen—whose work I am sure you know, at least by reputation; he seems to be causing quite a stir in Paris these days. Indeed, the poet reflected after a pause, I do not know if I would be alive today if it were not for him. And with that, he began to tell Alden the extraordinary story of how it was that, while imprisoned in Lower Silesia over the long winter of 1940–1941, he had come to know the great composer, and witness the debut performance of his now-famous *Quartet for the End of Time.*

—

IT OFTEN HAPPENED—THE POET SAID—THAT THE COMPOSER AND I would be posted together on guard duty at night, so it was during that time, more than any other—in which we kept watch, together, over what I recall now as a nearly subterranean darkness—that we came to know each other in the end. Side by side in the middle of the night—attempting, with the ebb and flow of our voices, to keep the darkness at bay—we spoke of a great many things. Sometimes of his music; more specifically, of his *Quartet*—which, all that fall and into the winter, he labored to complete. These were the moments I cherished best. Perhaps, in part, because they came fewest and farther between. More often the composer spoke of his indomitable faith—which he refused, even then, to have shaken—and more often still of his wife and son back in Paris, whom he worried over constantly and greatly missed. He was always sure to inquire politely after my own troubles, as well—and these I gratefully unburdened upon him. But while he listened thoughtfully, he never offered even a single word of commiseration or advice. Then, after some time had passed between us in silence, he would himself begin to speak—on a subject that at first seemed to have very little, if anything at all, to do with our previous discussion or the subject at hand. But after a while (sometimes a whole day would pass, the poet said, sometimes more), I would realize the composer had, in the words he had spoken, provided me with an answer to a question I had not known myself, until that moment, I had posed.

One early morning, for example, just before dawn, after I had unburdened myself to the composer and afterward we had sat in silence for some time together, watching the reflected light of the dimming moon, three-quarters full, dance across the prison yard, he told me the following story, which has often, since, been of great comfort to me.

..

WHEN HE WAS A BOY, the composer said, he often visited the Sainte-Chapelle Cathedral in Paris, and looked at the light as it streamed, in bright colors, through the stained-glass windows there. One day he felt an extraordinary feeling flood through him as he stood looking at the pattern the light made on the glass, and in that moment he knew (how he knew, he could never later be sure—but he did): he was a musician.

Perhaps it is because of this, said the composer to me then, that I still see notes as though they are color, and why it is still their color—or rather, the relationship that exists within each note of music, as between glass and light—more than their sound that I want to be able to play. He paused. Then looked at me directly. Do you think that is something I will be able to do?

The question startled me and I did not know immediately how to reply.

Yes, I said, after only the slightest hesitation, which I hoped he hadn't noticed. Of course. In fact, I continued (I was not averse to flattery), I think many of your best works have already accomplished this great feat.

The composer continued to regard me steadily, an amused half smile playing at his lips.

Ah, he said, so you are familiar with my work?

I nodded. Everyone in Paris—I said—is familiar with your work.

At this the composer laughed happily and laid his hand on my shoulder. I am honored, he said, by your remark, and by your confidence in me, but—you are wrong. I cannot—it is not possible—to even come close to what I, a boy of ten, standing in front of the great windows of Sainte-Chapelle, set out to do. I know that, and you, a poet, must know it, too. But I must, I believe—as you must—at least *try*. At least do my best to keep in sight that very great thing with which I was confronted as a child; which inspired in me the desire—more than that, *the firm belief*—that I might respond in kind.

Just then the first glow of dawn appeared at the far eastern edge of the horizon, and as if in unison, the first bird called.

Aha! said the composer, as if it proved his point. He announces the opening pitch like a conductor. Now the rest will join in!

Very soon, it was true: the sky erupted in song.

BEFORE LONG, HOWEVER, THE conversation would come around again, as it always naturally seemed to do, to the composer's wife, Claire, and his son, Pascal, a boy of only three. His wife was not well, you see, and had not been for some time—ever since, in the early years of their marriage, she had suffered several miscarriages. Her sadness and anxiety—the composer said—only increased with each loss. Soon it became so severe that not even the eventual birth of their son could abate it. To the contrary. So strange and unknowable are the pathways of the human heart, Claire's sadness seemed only to deepen after the child arrived. She hardly slept at night. She became distracted and irritable; she no longer desired the composer's touch—would even flinch away from him when, at night, in an attempt to comfort both her and himself, he drew near. Soon the composer began to worry not only over the safety of his wife, but of his child as well. Once, the composer recalled, Claire had even returned home without their son; she had simply forgotten him. Left him alone in his pram while out for a walk in a nearby garden. She had stood in the doorway, clutching her purse as though her life depended on it, and meanwhile her own son had been abandoned several blocks away!

When the composer realized what had happened, he fled down three flights of stairs and out into the street. His heart pounded as though it were a separate thing in his chest, having nothing to do with him. In fact, those few moments—before he arrived at the park and saw the carriage, standing just as his wife had left it, his son still sleeping inside—he hardly remembered at all. It was not until he had collapsed beside the carriage, his head resting heavily on the body of his son, his own body wracked with violent sobs, that he became aware again of where he was, and what had occurred—as well as what could have, but had not. All the possibilities of the things that could and could not happen to a person in their life—all the various joys and sufferings, and the sufferings that were contingent on the joys, and the joys that were contingent on the sufferings, and so on—came crashing down on him. It was under the weight of this sudden burden that the composer sobbed. His son stirred and woke then, and when he did, he, too, began to cry, and many minutes must have passed that way—the two of them sobbing together—before the composer finally lifted his head and returned home with his child.

It was not until much later that he was visited by anger. It was an unfamiliar emotion, and it surprised him when it came, later that evening, in a sudden wave.

What were you thinking? he asked, turning toward his wife—his hand raised suddenly, as if of its own accord, ready to strike. It did not come to rest on her, or on anything at all—it only remained suspended in the air, confused suddenly by the force of its own, conflicted desire.

That is not only your son, he shouted. He is not a burden that is yours alone—to carry or abandon according to wish and whim!

His wife said nothing—but shuddered, as though the composer's hand had indeed descended and shaken her roughly. When he saw that, the composer, too, was shaken; he dropped his hand and looked at it as though it belonged to someone else. Everything, it seemed, belonged to someone or something else, and was only connected to him by the most haphazard of strings. How was one to act upon these things? How was one to believe, not only in the things themselves but in the way they were connected—not only to him, but to God? To a greater rhythm—outside his immediate comprehension, but that he knew to exist nevertheless? Yes, of this much he was sure. He had, unmistakably, heard it himself. But these moments, he had to admit, were rare. In any case, he made a solemn promise to himself in that moment that he would never again allow himself to be visited by anger, and he stuck to this promise.

Instead, a constant, invasive worry began to infect him—an anxiety he could not rid himself of, even when he was in the same room with Claire and the child. Even when Claire was in one of her rare moods in which it seemed she had not been altered by her troubles at all; that she was the same woman he had married, and for whom he had written many of his best pieces, which she had once played passionately for him herself on the violin.

WHEN THE WAR CAME, the composer was deployed to the front, but—on account of his poor eyesight—was excused from combat. He worked as a machinist instead. But he was as poor a machinist as he would have been a soldier, and finally he was relieved of his duties and reassigned to Verdun—this time as an orderly. It was there, at Verdun—just before the war broke out in earnest: May 8, 1940—that he first made the acquaintance of the cellist Étienne Pasquier (one of the famous Pasquier brothers' trio, you know, the poet said), the company commander, and Henri Akoka, a clarinetist from the Orchestre National de la Radio.

How the whole world was with us then! the composer had exclaimed one night, as—continued the poet—we sat, shivering together, outside. Do you remember it? How everyone thought, then, that—with only a little help from the Brits—the war would soon be won? Or (he chuckled softly to himself) almost everyone, that is. Some of us knew better. Henri, of course, was one of these. Hitler will never negotiate, he told us—even then. We've been wasting our time—and now, when he's prepared for a real fight, we've got nothing to give. If France had only listened—

But here another soldier had cut in. To whom? he asked, his voice thick with scorn. To *Trotsky?* (It was well known among the men stationed at Verdun that the clarinetist was a Communist, as well as a Jew.) What makes you think if your hero rose up like Hitler and took over France the situation would be any different than it is for us now?

Yes, there is the matter of religious freedom, the composer said—though he rarely involved himself in political concerns.

Religion again! the clarinetist replied. Just—even for a moment—think on it! "Blessed are the poor," "The meek shall inherit the earth." Is this not, the clarinetist asked, addressing the small crowd that by then had gathered, evidently the most blatant propaganda, employed only in order to keep us from thinking and acting for ourselves? He took a deep breath and turned to the composer: The entire structure of your religion, he said, more slowly now, is designed specifically to render you *complicit* in your own subjugation by those who could not dream of asking any more of you than what you yourself have willingly submitted to. That you should wait until you are dead for your reward! It's a preposterous proposal. I, for one, am not willing to wait that long!

The murmur of the crowd, which had been growing while the clarinetist spoke, reached its peak just before he broke off, so that in another moment (because it was, in fact, only a single word that passed among them) it could be clearly heard.

Jew, said the crowd, as the clarinetist concluded his appeal.

After that, there was only a long note of silence.

Well, isn't that right? a young man said, finally. Aren't you a Jew?

It was not an accusation—his face was blank and unconcerned.

I'm a Communist, Akoka said—*and* I'm a Jew. I have no country—and yet, at the same time, *this*—he lit a cigarette and spread his arm wide, gesturing with the burning end past the barbed wire and low barracks that stretched off into the distance—is my country, and my people are all people. They are *you*, he said—looking up pointedly at the men still assembled before him—and *you*, and *you*.

But the attention of the crowd had shifted, and soon they began to disperse.

You shouldn't smoke, the composer said, finally.

Akoka shrugged his shoulders and sighed.

Anyway, what am I saying? he asked, winking at Pasquier, who had been listening to all of this with amusement nearby. I have forgotten with whom I am speaking. *Here* is a real radical, he said. The musician—Olivier Messiaen!

The composer didn't smile—but you could tell he was pleased. You know I have never advocated revolution, Henri, he said.

That's ridiculous! the clarinetist replied. Have you listened to your own music? Every note of it calls for revolution!

They both laughed. But then the composer cleared his throat and looked seriously at the younger man. Truly, he said. You shouldn't smoke. Save your cigarette rations and trade them for food; you'll last longer.

..

THAT EVENING, HENRI BROUGHT out his clarinet and began to play. As usual, everyone who heard him—including the composer—was instantly transfixed. They sat listening—unmoving—as around them the light dimmed and darkness began, in ever-lengthening shadows, to throw itself at their feet.

By the time the clarinetist put down his instrument, it had become quite dark.

You know, the composer said, as they made their way together across the short yard to the barracks that night, I am writing a piece especially for you—for the solo clarinet. You have inspired me.

BUT THE NEXT DAY the war was upon them in earnest. It began with a warning—the same warning they had been given for each of the countless drills they'd performed during the long months of their training. Then the bombs rained down—their sirens curiously discordant with the sound of their explosions. From time to time, they could hear Pasquier shouting at his scattered forces from what seemed like very far away.

Fire! Men, fire! he roared. Get those guns in the air! Get those bastards out of the sky! But there was nothing to shoot at. There was nothing to do but dive for cover, and the composer did.

Where's our air force? someone yelled.

Alone, kneeling on the ground, his face dug into the mud, the composer imagined he was dying. He wondered at how different it was than he'd thought. He'd always imagined it would be peaceful—that the discordance he had for some time now sought to convey in his music had to do with the discordance of life interrupted by death, by time, not by its absence. But here, in the absence of everything, there was still only discordance and noise.

Finally, the smoke from the bombs cleared. In the space of less than an hour, the world around them had been utterly transformed. The sounds and smells of death were everywhere. Men staggered alone or in groups of two or three, leaning against one another on the roads and in the fields, some carrying their own limbs with them as they went. The

composer's first thought—after he realized that he himself had survived—was to go in search of the young Henri. He found him: looking
out across the devastated landscape, and clutching in one hand, not his
gun (which had been lost somewhere, irrecoverably, in the debris), but
his clarinet.

PASQUIER CALLED FOR HIS men to regroup. Their company, they soon
saw, had been reduced by roughly half. There was nothing to do, Pasquier informed them—his voice, usually brisk and confident, now suddenly tight with fear—except to try to recover what they had.

The composer groped over the bodies of the men in the field and carried those not already past saving into the makeshift hospital. He distributed iodine, bandages, and morphine to some, and to others, in the grip
of a pain so absolute he knew without thinking that it would be impossible to deliver them from it, he made only the sign of the cross.

At night they crouched together. Men covered the ends of their
cigarettes with their hands to avoid detection from the air. The
worst, they felt, as they waited for the combat to erupt again, was
still to come. Belgium had already fallen. At Dunkirk, the British
abandoned their weapons and withdrew. The Germans easily broke
through the Maginot Line; they had taken Ardennes, and were at
that very moment moving north toward Verdun. Everywhere the
skies were German.

We are beaten, said the clarinetist, still gripping his clarinet.

Pasquier only nodded.

There is nothing left to bomb; the British have gone home. It's over.

ON SUNDAY, THE CHURCH bells—as ignorant to the plight of man as the
sound of the birds—rang; as usual, the composer went to mass alone.
When he approached the church, he saw that a bomb had ripped off a
portion of its roof. Though at first he was horrified to see the damage,
standing there among the congregation in the open air he found he felt
even closer to God. The destruction with which they had been visited
had, he saw, also made room for light to pour, suddenly, in.

Inspired, he asked if he might play the organ after mass, and the request was granted. Encumbered by his rifle, gas mask, helmet, and bandolier, he approached the organ, leaning his rifle and his mask against it—not bothering to remove his helmet or bandolier. He began to play and, very slowly as he did so, the notes he played sounded more and more surely like the notes that needed to be played. He wondered if this was because it was so, or if in playing them that way he had made it so—and what the difference was. Then the air raid sirens rang out, interrupting the composition of both his thoughts and the song. The composer flew down the stairs of the choir loft, grabbing his gas mask on the way, but forgetting his rifle. He returned for the rifle but as he reached for it he instantly regretted it, thinking: What use do I have for a rifle? Then he ran back, bombs exploding around him, to rejoin the rest of his unit, who had been crouched all that time, miserably, underground.

What the hell were you thinking? asked Pasquier, when he arrived. We thought you were dead.

The composer only shook his head. His ears rang with the deafening screech and roar of the bombs.

Later, they picked their way among the debris. Men's bodies, in whole or in part, were scattered among the wreckage. Abandoned rifles, canteens, packs, and photographs blew about like fallen leaves. All the real leaves had been burned from the trees so that only their charred stalks remained—pointing, like crooked fingers, uselessly toward the sky.

Now the composer knew why his father had never spoken to him of the Great War.

THEY MARCHED. TOWARD WHAT? Everywhere it was the same. Overturned tanks and trucks, bombed-out artillery vehicles and gun carriers, the abandoned bodies of men. There was no time to stop to bury the dead. The Nazis were advancing, leveling everything as they went. In their wake were only the skeletons of buildings: flattened, burned, still smoldering. A parade of refugees staggered from the ashes. Mothers carried children, children carried one another. Everywhere overturned carts and spilled suitcases indicated the interrupted journeys of men and women now nowhere to be seen. They combed through the ruins shamelessly for food or ammunition, but found nothing. They woke to the scream of Stukas, and headed south along what had once been the Maginot Line. Broken, it was only what it was—an essay at form that it did not, could not, hold. They kept their eyes trained when they could toward no-man's-land, where the drone of military planes and bombs reminded them it was only a matter of time before the Germans arrived and they would surrender.

Finally, the shout went up. It was Pasquier. No more grenades! We are out of ammunition, men! Then, the final admission of defeat: Abandon any souvenirs! If the Germans catch you with anything of theirs—medals, rifles, or anything else—you will be shot on sight!

We will be shot on sight anyway, someone shouted back.

No grenades, no rifle, even, the composer said, looking with sad affection at his young friend Henri. And yet—you still have your clarinet.

Yes, returned the clarinetist, his eyes trained on the distance.

Just at that moment, they heard it: the barking dogs of the approaching Nazi soldiers.

THEY SCATTERED. PASQUIER, THE clarinetist, and the composer took shelter together in an abandoned building, which had been partially demolished. Without eating, hardly sleeping, they remained there for nearly four days.

Outside, they could hear the Nazi soldiers as they passed through, and once the sound of Frenchmen whom the composer urged them to join.

Pasquier refused. They are pro-Nazi French, he told the composer.

How can you tell?

Pasquier frowned. Better to wait, he said, and the clarinetist agreed.

The composer shook his head in disbelief.

Well, what did you think? asked the clarinetist, suddenly annoyed. Did you think there was a clear line that separated things—good from bad, German from French, Catholic from Jew? Is that what your religion teaches you?

Of course not, the composer replied.

Listen, said Pasquier. Be quiet, both of you.

They listened and did not hear anything but the distant rattle of guns. But then they heard what Pasquier had heard. The crunch of gravel and charred wood underfoot. Someone was just outside their building—perhaps he had already overheard everything they had said! Their hearts began to beat so loudly they nearly drowned out the sound they listened for, but finally they heard the footsteps again—this time in retreat. It was the sound of a man who did not want to draw attention to himself, his movements deliberate and slow. After a stretch of a minute or more Pasquier rose to the small window and peered out.

What do you see? asked the composer, his eyes wide with fear.

We've got to get out of here, Pasquier said.

They waited until night, and then they moved. Pasquier first, then the composer. The clarinetist took up the rear. They had made it nearly across the field to the cover of the woods—from which point they might have disappeared in any direction—when, behind them, there was the sudden roar of an engine. In no time, a German truck was upon them, its spotlight swinging, and again there was the sound of dogs in the distance.

Oh, dear God, said the composer. What now?

We surrender, Pasquier said. But he was still running, and did not turn as he spoke so the words were difficult to hear.

What? the composer shouted.

We surrender, Pasquier said again.

This time the musician heard—and so did the clarinetist.

What? the clarinetist said, overtaking the composer effortlessly and falling into step with Pasquier. The edge of the woods was only meters away—they could not afford to stop. Still, they could not help wondering: If they were going to be caught, was it better to meet their enemy head-on, or with their backs turned toward him in flight? It certainly seemed better, in any case, to face an enemy head-on. Yet there was nothing any of them could do to stop running.

Well, said Pasquier, can you think of anything else?

No! shouted the clarinetist. But I will not surrender. Don't you know what Germans do to Jews?

The same thing they do with anyone who doesn't cooperate, said Pasquier. So where does that leave us?

Death comes for us all, chanted the composer.

Pasquier put his hands to his ears. Enough! he shouted.

Not today, agreed the clarinetist.

Well, then? asked Pasquier.

All right, said the clarinetist, without letting up his pace. I'll surrender. But I promise that before any one of us knows it—you, me, or the Germans themselves—I will escape.

Yes, said Pasquier, slowing finally, and causing the others to draw up behind. Of course.

The composer drew out his handkerchief from the pocket of his pants. It looked unbearably white as he took it out, neatly unfolded it, and tied it to Pasquier's bayonet. They all nearly cried at the sight of it. How white it had kept! How perfectly folded it had remained in his pocket, among them, all of that time!

THE GERMANS APPROACHED. THE dogs yanked toward them on their chains, their teeth bared. From time to time, one of the dogs got near enough to snap its teeth on air within inches of the men. The soldiers held torches so their faces were lit by a strange glow. It seemed as though their heads were not even connected to their bodies. Because of this, the composer had the horrible thought that these were the dead men (whose heads, still lodged inside their helmets, had been cleanly disconnected at the throat) they had recently seen on the road. But then the light changed slightly, or it did not. Perhaps it was something else that changed. Perhaps in that moment the composer's fear, which could not support itself any longer, gave way, and it was because of this that he saw the men differently: they were just, suddenly, men. Boys, really. The clarinetist's age, or younger. Their eyes twitching with tiredness as they gazed back at them.

One of the German soldiers spoke French, though with such a heavy accent it was some time before the composer realized the sounds the soldier uttered was a language at all. But then, suddenly, Pasquier was prying the composer's rifle from his hands.

Let go, he hissed. The composer let go. It was only then that he made sense of the command of the German soldier who was speaking to them in his garbled French: Drop your weapons! Hands up. On your helmets! Let's go!

The composer looked around. All three had dropped their weapons by then, but the shouts continued. All three had their hands on their heads.

Finally, the French-speaking soldier approached Henri, who—his hands on his head—still clutched his clarinet.

Drop it! the soldier yelled.

The young clarinetist extended his instrument out as far away from his body and the body of the approaching soldier as possible, but he did not drop it.

This is not a weapon, he said slowly. It is a clarinet.

There was a pause as the approaching soldier examined the instrument now suspended at an oblique angle between himself and the Frenchman, then he turned toward the other soldiers, said something in German, and laughed. Then they collected the rifles from the ground and, without roughness, led the musicians back the way they had come.

So—they were alive. For that brief time—following the German guards across the same field that, just moments ago, they had fled in terror—the composer did not care, because of this simple fact, where he was headed, or with whom. After all, the men who led them away were just ordinary men. He could almost laugh! He felt no pain, and feared nothing.

IN THE MORNING, THEY stopped briefly at the German military headquarters and were given a piece of bread. They had not had anything to eat in five days. The composer ate half of what he was given and stuck the rest in his pocket, but later it was found by a German soldier, who ground it into the dirt at his feet.

Thief, he said. Do you know what we do with thieves? But he did not shoot.

All morning, the composer expected it. He would feel a slight change in the pressure of the air as the wind shifted and think it was a bullet. He became so attuned to the shifts in the quality and pressure of the wind, he hardly heard the commands of the officers or the more ordinary sounds of the men speaking softly to one another, or the crunching of their boots on the gravel as they marched. It was amazing to hear all the sounds that existed below what he ordinarily heard, and he marveled that he had not heard them before and regretted that it was the imminent approach of his own death that had, at last, so finely tuned his ear. He prayed to God that he would survive and made a solemn promise to both himself and to God that if he should survive he would listen even more carefully than he had before. That he would try to hear every sound God had created in this world—or (he corrected himself modestly) as many as God granted that he should.

They marched on.

The composer quickly lost track of the days, and of their direction.

They marched. Past the destroyed villages where the faces of the people stared back at them in contempt and shame. In every face they read the single word, which echoed in their own minds as they passed (though the word itself was left, except once, unspoken). Every face they saw—every burned-out home, every homemade cross, hastily fashioned, on the side of the road—seemed to say it.

Traitor.

It looked as though the countryside they traveled through had survived not only weeks but decades of war. According to one German soldier—it had. After twenty-six years, he said (though he himself could have been barely as old), France has finally fallen. A long war, indeed, but what was destined has finally occurred.

So, the Great War the composer's father had fought was at an end—but there was no victory. It was impossible to imagine any deliverance from the destruction that surrounded them on every side. The composer looked, but he did not recognize even the earth itself. It was as though they had been overtaken—all of them: the Germans, the French, all of them—by another force altogether, which, being equally distant from every faith and creed he could imagine, he now struggled to understand how it was not equally distant from God.

ONE MORNING THE COMPOSER refused to rise.

I cannot go on, he said. I am sorry for my wife, for my son, and for myself, because I have grown to love you all, but I can no longer continue.

Don't be ridiculous, said Pasquier. It is not a choice.

See for yourself, said the composer, motioning toward his feet that stretched before him, naked of the rags they were usually wrapped in. They were swollen, black in places. The clarinetist looked and then looked away.

Clean them as best you can and wrap them again, he said. We don't have much time.

When they were ready to march, the composer was standing, supported by the clarinetist, and that was the way—three days later—they finally arrived at the transit camp, which was already overflowing with other French prisoners. When they reached the gates, they could see that the camp spread before them for many miles in every direction—as big as a city, as big as Paris even! They had heard that many soldiers had been captured, but they'd had no idea—until that moment—the extent of their defeat.

A German officer seemed to read the composer's mind as he entered the gates. He spoke French, poorly.

You know how many of you Frenchies we've caught? he asked.

No one said anything.

I'm asking you a question, he said.

Pasquier volunteered. How many?

One million at least, said the officer. Some say nearly two. Either way you cut it—that's a lot of Frenchies. Now, what are we going to do with you?

It did not at first sound like a question but Pasquier was watching the officer's expression and saw after a moment that it was, so he asked hurriedly: Monsieur—what?

Well, that we don't know! the officer said. He began to chuckle. We thought everything through so carefully but that, he said. We hardly expected you to give in so quickly, and all at once like this. Now what are we going to do with you all?

He walked away, still chuckling.

THERE WAS NOT ENOUGH food and water, and soon the stench from the latrines became unbearable. Weeks went by, and though several thousand men were trucked out to their next station, the three musicians remained in the transit camp as the rations continued to dwindle. When the trucks left with men inside, going somewhere—anywhere —else, the three musicians were especially lonesome. But Pasquier warned them: Don't wish too hard. It is no better where those men are going. It certainly isn't home.

There is no home to return to, lamented Henri. Imagine! Nazis goose-stepping along the streets of Paris!

By that time the rumor that Jewish families were being deported from Paris had reached them; the clarinetist had grown increasingly concerned.

But you are French, the composer had said to Henri, when they'd first heard the news.

You think that will save you now? asked the man who had delivered it to them. Look at the rest of us.

THE COMPOSER SPENT HIS time reading his Bible and *The Imitation of Christ*, which he had managed to keep with him, and worked steadily on his composition. Soon he had even finished the solo piece he had promised the clarinetist, and offered it proudly to the young musician.

You, he said, will be the first clarinetist ever to play this new work!

The clarinetist graciously accepted.

Several days later, however, he returned the music to the composer.

I am sorry, he said, but I am never going to get this. I can't play like this—without any time signature, or really any structure at all! I believe it is genius, truly. But I am not the man to do it.

What? said the composer. Genuinely surprised. Where is your invincible revolutionary spirit?

Try it again, said Pasquier. He took the sheet music and held it open in his hands. The clarinetist picked up his instrument again, putting it to his lips.

He began to play. Hesitatingly at first—then with more certainty. The composer beamed with pride. Pasquier's hands, holding the sheet music, shook. After a while, the clarinetist began to feel it, too. He relaxed, and the notes flowed still more surely—they did not even seem to be coming from him after a while, but from somewhere—

Cut out that racket! came a growl nearby.

The clarinetist, startled, stopped playing.

Pasquier, still entranced by what he had just heard, was equally surprised. What? You don't like music? he asked.

Sure I like music, the man who had interrupted said. But that's not music!

Oh, but it *is*, the clarinetist said, laughing. Otherwise, he added—winking at the composer, who was still beaming with pride—how would I be able to play it?

BUT HE WAS RIGHT, the composer told me—months later, as we sat together on guard duty one night. It *was* a racket! I got the idea for the piece from the sound of the locomotives that rattle through the camp; from the incessant drone of the vehicles and the *clickety-clack* of the wheels on the rails as they pass. No matter how hard I tried, I could not make the sound align itself to any regular beat or measure—and it was then that I realized. All the things of this world, from which we make music, are not bound by time at all. They are utterly free! It is only we who seek to restrict things into units of measure; we who conceive of the symmetry that is both order and war. Everything—when the ear is trained to hear it—is free; everything is noise, and finally, everything is music! Even the birds (the composer continued) speak a language they cannot truly utter—a language of which, that is, their voices are only the smallest part. Is that not what makes their music great? It is clear and precise both in its register and voice, and yet—it says nothing! Even we humans—who understand so little—understand that when we truly listen.

THEN ONE DAY THE three musicians found themselves—without knowing where they were bound—on one of the trucks headed out of the transit camp. They arrived first in Nancy; there, they were marched to the rail yard and ordered into cattle cars.

The cars were so full it was impossible for all of the prisoners to lie or even sit down at once. A rotation was soon organized so that they sat and stood according to a fixed schedule overseen by an aging French officer. From time to time (which could not help but be irregular, there being no watches among them and only the smallest glint of sun that streamed into the closed car), the officer would bark out, Switch, and everyone would follow his command.

Before too long, however, the composer was no longer able to rise when the command came, and Pasquier pleaded that he might be allowed to remain seated—an amendment that required someone else give up his turn. After only a moment's hesitation, the clarinetist volunteered, and so the composer remained seated for the duration of the journey.

Even when the car stopped in a switchyard, the prisoners were ordered to remain inside the cars, and were not allowed to relieve themselves or obtain food or water. By that time, the composer was delirious, slipping in and out of consciousness. Sometimes he managed to rouse himself and utter a few unintelligible words, but hardly any sound emerged when he did, and he was forced to lie back down again, exhausted and confused.

FINALLY, THE TRAIN STOPPED and the door was rolled back. The sun shone in too brightly, temporarily blinding the passengers inside.

What town is this?

Görlitz, said a German soldier. This is home for you boys now.

The composer, confused by the light, tried to stand, but fell. Pasquier caught him in his arms. This man needs a hospital, he said.

He went to speak to the German who had just addressed them and, when he returned, said to the composer: When we get to the prison you will go directly to a hospital.

All right, said the composer. But you needn't worry about me. I know that God is still watching over me—that he is still taking care of me, in his way.

The clarinetist spat. I am glad you and I do not share a God, then, he said.

Oh, but we do, Henri! the composer said dreamily.

Perhaps we do, the clarinetist said. After all, mine is a vengeful God, and this is nothing if not vengeance.

ALONE IN THE HOSPITAL, the composer continued to drift in and out of consciousness. He listened to the sound of the train whistles, the church bells, and, of course, the birds. When he grew stronger he read his Bible. Particularly the tenth chapter of the Book of Apocalypse, in which an immense angel stretches a prism of color and light that encircles all things, and says: There shall be no more Time.

What did this mean? the composer wondered.

He prayed for understanding.

—

THOUGH WE HAD BEEN ON THE SAME TRANSFER (CONTINUED THE POET Maurice Bonheur), it was not, on account of his illness, until five weeks later that I first met the composer. By that time, I had already come to know Étienne Pasquier and Henri Akoka—both of whom had been assigned bunks near my own—and so of course I had heard many stories.

Upon his return, the composer was installed on the empty lower bunk beneath me. The clarinetist slept opposite, and Pasquier farther along. That left the bunk directly above the clarinetist empty.

Who sleeps there? the composer had asked on his first night in the barracks.

The clarinetist shrugged. Poor man tried to escape the first night we got here. They gunned him down on the wire.

The composer let out a low whistle. I guess that has given you some food for thought about trying to escape yourself, he said to the clarinetist. I beg you, Henri, promise me you'll never try.

Food for thought, yes, the clarinetist replied. But I cannot promise what you ask.

Henri, you are a Jew! exclaimed Pasquier.

The clarinetist hit his hand on his head as though this were something he had quite honestly forgotten.

Seriously, said the composer gravely. It is better you are here with us, a French soldier, than on your own, a Jew.

Well, there is plenty of time now to worry about all of this, the clarinetist said, grinning at the composer—now that you are alive again. Honestly, we were so worried! Then, after a little pause, he continued in a more thoughtful tone. I cannot say why I would wish life upon anyone anymore, but there is something in me that will not give it up—the idea, I mean, that to be alive in the world is, in itself, good.

Because, said the composer, it is so.

No one else spoke, and after that the darkness seemed to settle in around them more completely—interrupted only periodically by the searchlight as it swung its wide beam around the yard in a steady rhythm, like the beat of a slow heart. How could anything, the composer may have wondered (as, that night, I wondered myself—and ever after), ever be revealed by that light? Given the fact that it came so briefly, and that even when it did, it did not interrogate the darkness, but only, for a single moment, obliterated it entirely before allowing everything to fall back into darkness again?

THE NEXT DAY, THE clarinetist received word that his father had been arrested and deported from Paris. They had no address for him, his sister wrote, and from what they heard now, it was unlikely he would be returning anytime soon.

The stubborn fool! the clarinetist said when he read the news. He didn't believe it when he was told to go south, to the unoccupied regions! He said: I am a veteran of the Great War! A Frenchman! They cannot possibly touch me!

So now you know it is serious, Pasquier said.

The clarinetist shook his head. My father is an old man, he replied. The risk he took was not a risk at all. It was simply to be an old man. To be fixed in his mind. To refuse to see that things had changed so drastically from the way that he imagined.

That is a mistake it is possible for all of us to make, said Pasquier.

The composer said nothing. He only nodded, looking on.

SHORTLY AFTER THAT, THE violinist Jean Le Boulaire arrived. He was assigned the bunk above the composer, which had for some time been left empty.

Within minutes of arriving, he spotted Henri's clarinet, where it lay on the lower bunk, opposite him.

I lost my violin in Dunkirk, he informed us.

You play? asked the composer, sitting up.

Le Boulaire nodded.

Ah! the composer said. A clarinetist, a violinist, a pianist, and a cellist. All we need now are a violin, a cello, and a piano! We've got the clarinet. You, he said—pointing to me—you can write our first review!

Everyone laughed but the composer. And indeed, as the weeks wore on, the composer slowly began to realize what had seemed to us, at first, only an impossible dream—thanks always to the help of the sympathetic German guard, Brüll. Brüll had already arranged for the composer to be excused from the drudgery of camp chores and afforded the privilege of working each day on his *Quartet* instead—undisturbed, in the lavatory. Yes—the lavatory. And what a privilege, indeed! It was the one place in the camp a man could hope to steal even a moment alone.

Brüll's parents—as one day he confided in the composer—had been Catholics, and he himself had always been drawn to the music of the church. Because of this, he hated to think of the composer—a Catholic and a musician—as a prisoner. But after all (he admitted), there was very little of the war he understood.

So it is natural, the composer had replied, that we come together through music. Music is the one thing that everyone understands.

But not everyone, the German said shyly, understands your music. I have heard it called dissonant. He paused. Even ugly. I do not find it so myself, of course, he added quickly. But it just goes to show you that we do not always agree—even about the simplest things.

THEN ONE DAY, IN early October, a violin appeared during our absence on Le Boulaire's bed.

It is a miracle, the composer said, his eyes dancing. But we knew, of course, it was not providence alone we had to thank.

THE NEXT TIME I saw Brüll, however, several days after the appearance of the violin, he looked anything but the benevolent miracle-maker the composer now fully believed him to be. I was on my way with Pasquier to the mess hall when he approached, his face flushed with anger.

What are you thinking? he hissed at us.

What do you mean? Pasquier asked.

You know what, Brüll said. He glared at Pasquier. I suggest you find those missing spoons, he said. They are becoming suspicious, you know—and their suspicions always lead somewhere. I would hate it if it led them to you. Or, worse—to the composer.

Pasquier nodded. I could tell, then—the way his face went suddenly pale—that he was not as innocent as he had first appeared.

What was that? I asked, after Brüll had gone. Pasquier shook his head. Then he picked up his pace so that by the time we arrived at the mess hall I was several steps behind, and we did not share a table during the meal.

My heart raced, attempting to make sense of what I had heard. I felt torn between, on the one hand, concern for Henri and Pasquier, and anger, on the other, that I had not been let in on any escape plan—if that was what this was about.

Did they think I was like the composer? That I lived only in my head? Did they think I enjoyed living as we did, cooped up, more like animals than men?

They could not possibly think that! But as soon as I concluded this to myself, and resolved that I was just as prepared as any other man to risk my life for my own freedom and for what I believed, I felt a cold chill in my belly, and I knew that I was glad I was ignorant of this or any other plan.

AFTER THAT, I BEGAN to notice the dirt under Henri's fingernails, and then I didn't know how I had failed to notice before. Or the way he disappeared at night. How, I wondered, had I ever slept so soundly so as not to notice that he slipped away after the first guard duty returned, only to arrive back just before dawn?

It was not long after Brüll's warning that the composer confronted the young musician.

Henri, he said one evening, do you realize that Paris is fourteen hundred kilometers away?

Yes, answered the clarinetist, without hesitation—but Switzerland is a mere nine hundred.

The composer smiled sadly. I only pray for you, he said, that you will be delivered to safety—but in my heart, I have to admit, I grieve a little. Who will play the clarinet?

EVERY MORNING, THE CLARINETIST was back in his bunk before dawn, and over the next few weeks, the sound of the clarinet and the violin became as familiar as the sounds of the feet of the guards or the clattering of the engines of the trucks as they rolled past the prison gates. Then—by another miracle—toward the end of October, Pasquier was given permission to drive into Görlitz, accompanied by Brüll.

They returned with a cello. A chair was dragged out of the mess hall and placed in the middle of the exercise yard, where Pasquier was invited to play. He played for nearly an hour: Saint-Saëns's "The Swan" from *The Carnival of the Animals*, Bach's suites for solo cello, and Schubert's *Ave Maria*. When finally he laid down his bow, there was a strange stillness in the air and some of the men hid their faces on account of the tears, which had sprung, unbidden, to their eyes.

Now all that was missing was a piano. The composer worked more and more furiously—in the lavatory during "working hours," of course, but at every other time of day, too. He would stay up late into the night, reading and rereading his score by the dull glow of a candle (another gift from Brüll), sometimes long after the clarinetist had slipped away. Because, just as furiously as the composer worked, the clarinetist worked as well.

The German guards were no less busy. They crawled around underneath the barracks looking for signs of the digging. We would hear them at night below us, and we knew it was them and not our own men, because they made so much noise and didn't care who heard.

By then the composer had been giving inspired lectures in the theater barracks for more than three weeks. These were attended not only by French, Polish, and Czech prisoners, but sometimes even by the German guards. Brüll, of course, was always in attendance as the composer instructed us on nonretrogradeable rhythms, melismas, and Wagner's leitmotifs. We listened, every one of us, entranced not so much by the words, but by the reverence with which the composer spoke.

Imagine, if you will, he said one day, that the universe once comprised a single beat. And before that: eternity. And after it? Again, eternity. Before and after, the composer said—to conceive of that is to conceive of the beginning of time. So now close your eyes. Imagine a second beat. Almost immediately following the first, which was the single beat of the universe. This second beat, prolonged by the silence that follows it, will be longer than the first. A new number, a new duration.

This, the composer said, is the beginning of rhythm. It does not arise from the division of time, but rather can be considered . . . an *extension*, a duration *in* time. And what is the space of this extension or duration— but life itself?

Just at this moment, Pasquier burst into the room.

Olivier! he cried. Come quickly!

The composer followed Pasquier out to the yard—his devoted students, myself among them, were not far behind. There, just beyond the prison gates, we were greeted by a third miracle: a piano was being unloaded from the back of an army truck by two German guards.

Truly, God is great, said the composer.

BUT THE NEXT MORNING, when dawn arrived, the clarinetist did not. At roll call, when his name was pronounced by the German guard on duty, no answer came.

We were careful not to look at one another, and I tried not even to think because every thought tended toward the clarinetist, and resolved itself either in envy (imagine! I thought. At that very moment the clarinetist was a free man!) or despair (in my heart, I could not believe that it was so).

It was not. Less than a week later we heard that Henri had been captured. A few days after that he was returned to his bunk. He had been badly beaten. Now he slept solidly through the night—interrupted only briefly by the shouts of Le Boulaire. Since his arrival, Le Boulaire had suffered from recurrent nightmares, waking himself—as well as the rest of us—sometimes several times each night. The composer would speak: Jean, Jean, it is only a dream, it is only a dream, and the violinist would shudder and go back to sleep, but often the rest of us would not—disquieted by the anguish and fear we had heard in the shouts of Le Boulaire, who we knew otherwise as a calm and peaceful man.

What do you dream? the composer asked him one day.

Le Boulaire shook his head.

I don't know any longer what I dream and what I remember, or, of what I remember, what memories are my own. When I was a child in the

Great War, I lived for many years at the orphanage because my father could not take care of me and my mother had died. I remember that before my father returned I watched the men come home from the front—their faces disfigured, their bodies torn. I would have nightmares that my own father returned and I didn't recognize him. Then one day he did return. Of course I recognized him right away—but he did not recognize me, for he was blind. He had the most vivid memories of the war, though, and when, on Sundays, I was permitted to visit him, he would tell me stories that would make my blood run cold, and always in the most colorful detail. Now when I dream, I see those same images—those same details and vibrant colors.

FOR SOME REASON, AFTER the return of the clarinetist, Le Boulaire's nightmares got worse.

Shhhh . . . shhhh . . . it is only a dream, the composer would warn. Do not wake Henri, he needs his rest.

But it was not long before Henri was his usual self again—stronger than all of us. He even delighted in recounting the tale of his escape.

In the day we hid, he said, and at night we walked. Over five hundred and fifty kilometers—in the sleet and snow. Imagine! We were only twenty kilometers from the Czech border when we were captured. That close!

ONE NIGHT, THE VIOLINIST had a particularly violent dream. When finally we managed to drag him from sleep, he appeared confused, as though he didn't know us.

Everything is all right. You are here, safe, among friends, the composer said.

Later that same night we were woken by a siren and ordered into the driving rain. A radio had been found in one of the barracks and the Germans were eager to punish all of us for the offense. After a while I could no longer feel my feet, they were so numb with cold, and I thought I would fall in the mud. Somehow, I remained standing. Then, at the first light of dawn, we heard five shots ring out in the Czech and Polish camps. You French, said a German officer strolling between our lines as the rain continued to beat down, have been cooperative so far, and we appreciate that. But, he said—and gestured into the distance, in the direction from which the shots had come—the same is in store for you, if that should change.

Finally we were allowed back inside, where we massaged our feet and legs until the feeling returned to them. As usual, it was painful at first, and during that time I always wished they might have instead remained numb.

I can't take very much more of this, said Le Boulaire as he massaged his own feet. From the expression on his face I could tell the feeling was starting to return to him, too, and that he was regretting it.

If I had the composer's faith, he said. If I could pray at night and sing when all around me is nothing but misery and pain, then it would be different, but I have no faith and there is nothing to live for.

He began to cry silently. His shoulders, which I could tell had once been broad and strong, shook up and down.

Hush, the composer said.

But Le Boulaire would not be comforted. He turned violently toward the composer.

Your stubborn faith, he said. The way you pray at night! The words you use and the sound of your voice, when I am gripped in fear of what each night will bring—let alone each day. It's horrible! I hear your voice and I begin to doubt myself—my own doubt, even. I hate you for it.

THE DEBUT OF THE composer's *Quartet* was set for St. Nicholas's Day, and as it drew near he worked even more furiously to prepare. He hardly ate anymore, or slept.

Olivier, you must eat, warned Pasquier. Otherwise you will faint away onstage before we finish the first movement.

No, no! said the composer. I feel stronger than ever. But everyone could see that he did not.

I must confess, he told me one night as we stood watch together, I can no longer bring myself to eat. You see, when I do manage to fall asleep these days, my hunger results in the most incredible dreams. They are more like visions than dreams, and I can't help but look forward to them. I like to pretend I am being visited by angels!

Le Boulaire's nightmares, on the other hand—over the weeks the musicians worked (almost as feverishly as the composer himself) to prepare for the debut—became less frequent. By the middle of December, they had almost ceased entirely. I believe it is the music, he said one morning, after a night he had slept through. It is doing me wonders.

But does it ever trouble you—asked the clarinetist, who had overheard—what they say?

And what do they say? asked Le Boulaire.

You know what! the clarinetist said. But the look on Le Boulaire's face clearly indicated he did not. That we are allowed, the clarinetist said, these . . . *privileges* . . . our music, the composer's lectures, entertainment every Saturday night . . . because it looks good for the Germans in Paris that way. Does it ever occur to you, he asked—his voice deepening—that in this sense we are actually working *for* the Germans?

Music has no part in questions of war, snapped the composer, who had his head buried in his notebook and until that moment had not appeared to be listening. It cannot be used against anyone, he said. In music we praise God, and nothing—he paused—*nobody*, he said, emphasizing the word—else.

We have been over this a thousand times, the clarinetist said. God is an instrument of the state. And now—he shrugged—so are we.

Don't say that! the composer said, snapping his notebook closed and turning to stare at the clarinetist.

Not saying it won't change it if it's true.

If it's true, put in Le Boulaire. But we cannot be certain that it is. The Germans like the performances just as much as we do. I would say that word does not get to Paris very often, if at all—who would want to report that German officers are enjoying the entertainment of their prisoners because they themselves cannot carry a tune?

..

AT LAST IT WAS the night of the performance. The musicians assembled themselves with their instruments onstage, while the prisoners, fighting for position at the door, waited for the German officers to arrive—after which point they would be free to crowd in behind.

There was almost twice the regular turnout that night, and when at last the men burst into the room there was hardly any room left even to stand.

Pasquier and Le Boulaire tuned their instruments, Henri blew through his clarinet, and the composer, standing at the head of the stage, quietly surveyed the scene. It was indeed, he saw—his eyes scanning the crowd—his most international audience yet!

What you are about to hear, he said—after the musicians had laid down their instruments, indicating they were ready to begin—is an *apocalypse*, in the true sense of the word. A revelation. A music without time, but performed within time, because . . . for now—his voice trembled with emotion; he had waited for this moment, after all, for so long! For now, he said again—his eyes, for a brief moment, coming to rest on Brüll, seated in the front row—it is all we have.

AND THAT, CONCLUDED MAURICE Bonheur, was how I witnessed the debut performance of the *Quartet for the End of Time*—it really is an extraordinary piece.

Alden nodded. And does it manage to do what it claims?

Maurice Bonheur shook his head. That is not the right question, he said.

Their glasses had long ago been drained, but no one had disturbed them, and the street was quiet—the light on the boulevard just beginning to dim. Maurice waved for the check, paid, and was just about to go, when Alden stopped him.

Tell me, though, he said. How did you—and the composer—manage finally to arrange your release?

The poet shrugged. The guard Brüll, of course, he said. He arranged passes for Henri, Pasquier, Messiaen, and myself. Henri was stopped at the train depot, though, and detained. They said he was a

Jew. He told them: "I am uncircumcised" (his circumcision was done so poorly it is difficult to tell it has been done at all). He began to unbutton his pants, but the soldiers slammed him in the forehead with the butt of a gun and took him away. That was the last I saw of him, though I have since heard he's escaped. That he is even living in Paris again. And Le Boulaire—I am not sure what has become of him. Brüll could not arrange another pass.

And the composer, he is free to give concerts and teach at the conservatory? On the condition of . . . ?

Collaboration, of course, said Maurice Bonheur.

He winked at Alden then, but Alden glanced away—embarrassed, for some reason. It was difficult to read his meaning.

And did you write about it? Alden asked, to change the subject.

Sure, Maurice said. In the camp newspaper. *Lumignon.* A glowing review, of course! But I will write about it all again someday—when all of this is over, and I find the right words.

—

AFTER HIS RETURN TO PARIS, ALDEN'S DAYS SETTLED ONCE AGAIN into a regular rhythm of their own. He rescued an old bicycle from a tangled heap in the neglected courtyard of his new building on the Rue Auguste-Comte, and every day he rode to the OKW office at the Hôtel Lutetia on the Boulevard Raspail. At noon, he would leave the office and travel the short distance back to the Luxembourg Gardens, where he would spend his allotted hour walking in circles around the pond. Sometimes he would while the time away writing in his notebook brief sketches of the people or animals he saw come and go—or of the park itself, and the effects of the seasons as they began to roll slowly by. These he would later send to Sutton; she always appreciated that sort of thing, and it satisfied her somewhat in place of any "real" news—which, ever since the capitulation, he had been unable to send. Even if his letters managed to get through the censors, there was nothing he could reasonably tell her about his life these days; no way to explain the sort of work that he did, or for whom he did it, or why. He was keenly aware that anything he said now, even to Sutton (if it were indeed possible to communicate to her something of the delicate situation he found himself in), would only compromise his chances of, in the first place, hitting upon the key to the code he'd discovered. As well as of sending it, when at last he was able—undetected—abroad.

More than once, however, he took the risk of sending along a small fragment from his growing manuscript of twice-coded poems, which he had, until then, shared with no one—save on a handful of occasions with Maurice Bonheur. To his great relief, his poems cleared the censors easily—each, apparently, as incomprehensible to German intelligence as to Sutton, who responded with polite bewilderment every time. After three or four poems had been successfully transmitted in this way, Alden began to feel more confident that his plan, however unusual and difficult to arrange, could not fail to succeed; whenever, that is, he was finally able to put it into effect.

In the meantime, he continued his afternoon strolls around the Luxembourg Gardens at noon, writing short descriptions of and reflections on what he observed there, which he passed on to Sutton. It was only a short time before he came to recognize nearly every other pedestrian he saw during the hour he spent at the park. Having fixed his own steady pattern—arriving and departing from the garden at (necessarily) exactly the same hour each day—he found that the patterns of others soon became to him equally clear.

There was an old man, for instance, whom he wrote about to Sutton quite often, who set himself up each day next to the pond in order to paint the boats the children floated upon it. He must have started a new painting every day, and because Alden always observed him at midday, when he had barely begun, he never managed to see these paintings in anything but their beginning stages. Never once, that is, did he see the way the sail, billowing up from the empty hulls of the boats, actually took shape, or see the way the grass and the trees in the foreground, once the detail was filled in, might have balanced out the clouds, which (by the time Alden was forced to depart) would have just begun to bloom in the sky. And then one day, in the fall of 1943—he told Sutton—even that was gone. One day the artist simply did not appear, and then never again after that. Later (but this he did not share with Sutton), Alden learned from another regular—an aging widow, who, despite the dwindling rations, kept the ducks fed—that the artist had been a neighbor of hers: an Austrian Jew. He had a French father, she said, and was rather well connected with some higher-ups—French as well as Austrian army officials. For many years, therefore, he was able not only to avoid any trouble from the German authorities (he had all the "correct" papers, after all), he was able to arrange the "correct" papers for dozens of other foreign Jews. They would come at night; the widow would hear their muffled footsteps on the stairs. Some of them would leave again, but some of them would stay. She could hear them—scuffling like mice inside her walls. It was unsettling. She had not digested her food properly since before the war.

She knew what had happened as soon as she heard the first shout, the widow said. It could have been anything, but I heard a shout one night and I knew they had come. I should not have gone to the window to watch, but I did. I saw them take him. He wore his winter hat, and did not look up. And then behind him—the others. Seven of them. Seven! Imagine. I don't know how long they had been there. All along, living like mice inside the walls. I shouldn't have looked. I wish now I had not. That I didn't know for certain. People say it's difficult when people leave and don't come back. That it's difficult . . . not knowing. But I think that not knowing must not be as difficult as knowing. *Sans doute*, she said. That is the true burden.

And why . . . she paused, and threw a handful of crumbs to the ducks. They approached desperately, their wings askew. Why we make up mysteries, she said. We are so afraid to find out there are no mysteries at all.

IT WAS RIGHT ABOUT that time—shortly after, in the dwindling months of 1943, the painter disappeared and Alden could no longer pass the time watching him paint empty hulls on the water, or sketch his clouds into a foregroundless sky—that he met Marie-Claude. This, too, he kept to himself. He and Sutton wrote so rarely by then, anyway—and when they did, it was never easy and familiar, the way it had been before. She had become, he found—ever since their mother's death, perhaps (but nearly two full years had passed since then!), increasingly abstracted; her mind turned more and more toward the past. This was a habit (and he told her so) he quite simply couldn't abide.

Besides: he would have found it as difficult to describe or explain his love for Marie-Claude in those days as he would have anything else.

Although later Marie-Claude would tell him she had in fact been visiting the gardens at the same time each day for several months before making his acquaintance, it was difficult for Alden to imagine how—if that was so—such a long time had passed without their ever once crossing paths. They must have kept such a perfect pace with one another that at any given moment they were, by the central fountain, concealed from view. That whenever he paused, she paused, whenever she paused, he did, and so on. As improbable as it seems, it was the only way (he reasoned) that it could have happened. If he had looked at her even once—fleetingly, across the pond—he was certain he could not have failed to notice her, or had his blood thicken and beat at a quickened pace in his head. Because that was what did happen the first time he saw her, and she was even then at some distance from him, gazing out past the ducks on the water (who appeared for the moment calm and undisturbed, there being—the widow absent that day—nothing to desire). It was perhaps the sharpness of her gaze (though she did not appear to be looking at anything directly, but only very generally off, toward an unfixed point), more even than her startling beauty, that arrested his attention. It would have arrested anyone; that was the kind of beauty she had. The sort that cannot be described with any accuracy by a litany of adjectives or a description of specific features—though it would certainly give anyone pleasure to recall these, too. She was of a medium height, and fair, with a clear complexion rather unusual for fair women—almost olive in tone. Her thick, dark eyebrows lent themselves to the impression that her eyes, in contrast to her fair hair, were also dark—though on closer inspection one could see they were actually a pale green or gray—not really a color at all, in fact; more like the shade the painter had used for his clouds, in order to indicate that they were not to be mistaken for either water or air.

By the time Alden had come within range and could observe her more closely, she turned suddenly so that now instead of heading toward him she was walking in the same direction—counterclockwise around the outer garden path. She was a good twenty-five meters or more ahead of him, though, and because it seemed somehow gauche to hasten his step, he slackened it instead, and, rather than following the outer path in its most straightforward route, as he would have ordinarily done, he took the long, circuitous paths instead—dipping sometimes into the far corners of the park before reemerging on the main track once more. All this time he kept an eye on her as best he could—terrified she might not complete the circle and thus be lost to him forever. But she continued around the path, just as he had hoped, and soon was directly behind him. When he sensed her presence there (how attuned he was! He could almost feel the shape of it, and therefore the diminishing distance between them, as she continued to approach), he slackened his pace still more. Subtly—so it would not seem unnatural if he were to pick it up again as she fell in by his side. And before long, that was just what she did. As the distance closed between them, he quickened his pace infinitesimally—and they fell into step.

MARIE-CLAUDE WAS TWENTY-THREE YEARS old in the fall of 1943; she still lived with her parents on the Rue de Vaugirard, where she assisted her mother with the care of her elderly grandfather, Franz Eckelmann, who had once been a celebrated German chemist—most famous for preempting William Ramsay's discovery of noble gases (a feat for which he never received the credit he was due). He had come to Paris from Berlin in 1893 at the age of thirty and married a French girl, who had died shortly after their only daughter (Marie-Claude's mother, Marie-Thérèse) was born, so that—aside from the help of a few peripheral aunts on the child's mother's side—he was obliged to raise the girl more or less alone. During the Great War, he had been commissioned to work on the development of a powerful mustard gas, and it was his lengthy exposure to these chemicals that Marie-Thérèse now blamed on the deterioration of his mental faculties—although the more common opinion was that Franz Eckelmann had simply become old.

Marie-Claude's father, François Grenadier, had also been a professor of chemistry at the university where, after the Great War, Franz Eckelmann himself had been established. He had in fact inadvertently introduced Grenadier to his daughter one evening. If it were not for the birth of Marie-Claude, his complicity in the affair would have been something the chemist very much regretted, because—while Marie-Claude was still a young child—Grenadier abandoned the family to follow a celebrated American chemist, with a particular interest in the "development" of his younger male colleagues, back to the United States.

By the time Alden came to know Marie-Claude, she lived only with her mother and aging grandfather. Franz Eckelmann had lost most of his memory; he had, in effect, wound himself back to the earliest years of his childhood. For the most part, then, Franz Eckelmann lived in the same world in which he had lived in the Berlin of 1873, when he was ten years old.

FRANZ ECKELMANN'S FATHER HAD owned a small printing shop. On weekends and school holidays he had worked in the shop with his father and his sister, Marta—who was ten years older and still unmarried. Often, when they would return from the press, their hands stained black with ink, Franz Eckelmann's father would joke that they had indeed been "marked" by their trade. But he was not always so lighthearted. He was anxious for Marta to marry, so she could discontinue her work in the shop, and Franz was forbidden to go to school with the "mark" of his father's trade on his skin. It was for this reason that he was permitted to help only on weekdays and school holidays, and that once, when he had blotched his hands badly, he was kept home from school until the stain faded away. Of Marta, Franz Eckelmann's father demanded only the lightest tasks wherein she would run the least risk of staining her hands, and when she did stain them (as often she did), he would set her to scrubbing them in the sink for hours. It was very little use, however; only time itself would get rid of the stain, and it became a generally held belief in the household that Marta was deliberately setting about to stain her hands in order to absolve herself from the duty of marriage. Whether this was true or not would have been difficult to say. Marta never admitted as much, and a year later, when Franz was eleven years old, Marta did in fact marry. How she came to be betrothed to Oskar Schmidtt, three years her junior and the son of the butcher, who suffered from such debilitating shyness that he was always kept at the back of the shop, was a great mystery. But there was no reason to object to the arrangement, as odd as it was; the Schmidtts had a long-standing family-run business and could sufficiently provide for Marta and their three sons, who were afterward born in quick succession: Georg (named after Mr. Eckelmann), Reiner, and little Felix.

After that, it was just Franz and his parents who lived together above the print shop and just Franz who helped out his father, when he could. Marta had been "marked," after all, by a different fate.

It was the time directly preceding his sister's departure from the Eckelmann household that Franz now recalled in detail, casting all of the people who now surrounded him (his daughter, Marie-Thérèse, granddaughter, Marie-Claude, and later even Alden himself) as players, and, with resilient patience, converting the information of the world around him in 1943 so that it did not jar with the reality of seventy years prior. Marie-Thérèse performed the role of his mother, and Marie-Claude, his sister, Marta. Because Franz Eckelmann (who was for all intents and purposes, remember, only a boy of ten) saw his sister's departure from their family home as a personal betrayal, he would chide Marie-Claude endlessly for it. When, on occasion, she gently reminded her grandfather that she was not her Aunt Marta, whom she had never met, but his granddaughter, Marie-Claude, a look of such utter confusion would cross poor Franz Eckelmann's face that Marie-Claude would instantly regret having said anything at all. She would smooth the wisps of white hair, which still clung to his temples

over his gleaming skull (which, though it had lately fallen into disrepair, still concealed the mind of a genius), and say, It's all right, I'm
right here. I'll never leave you. And for a few minutes—until she was
needed elsewhere, to fetch tea, slippers, pick up the groceries, the mail,
or go (her one luxury) for her solitary spin around the Luxembourg
Gardens—all was as it should be in Franz Eckelmann's world. But
when she went away and returned—even for a short time, a span of a
few minutes only—the painful memory of Franz Eckelmann's aban-
donment would return once again and need to be, once again, and in
the same fashion, assuaged. Marie-Claude became adept at this, so
often did the scene repeat itself.

You see, for him, it is always the first time, she explained to Alden
on the first afternoon they fell into step together and turned several
circles around the pond in unison, before departing in their different
directions—she to her grandfather's house, and he to the OKW office
at the Hôtel Lutetia. Each time, Marie-Claude said to Alden, it is my
only chance. Over and over again, I have just that one—that single
chance.

AT FIRST FRANZ ECKELMANN had difficulty placing Alden within the
drama he had made of his earliest days. Though he obediently withdrew
his watery gaze from the facing window (the Eckelmann apartment was
on the second floor, so there was never anything on any occasion to see
there but the three facing walls of the neighboring buildings, their windows always blank and dark, but still Franz Eckelmann gazed with interest, as though he hoped to see something extraordinary there), his
expression did not at first seem to acknowledge Alden at all, or the introduction that had just then—by Marie-Claude—been made. He looked
at Alden in the same way that he had, just a moment before, gazed into
the empty courtyard. As if his face were only the face of an opposing
wall—his features the darkened windows that, at any moment, by some
flicker of light (Franz Eckelmann kept his eyes trained on him intently,
lest it be so), might reveal the contents of those unlit rooms. Might cast
in shadow a significant shape—the recognizable form of a man inside—

some proof, at last, that the world was indeed inhabited! A look of perplexed confusion followed: Franz Eckelmann's eyes narrowed in accusation and alarm. But this passed quickly; some light had indeed been cast, not from within Alden, but instead from somewhere deep within Franz Eckelmann himself.

Klein Felix, he said. And pressed his hand more firmly into Alden's own. Then another sentence followed this greeting in German, which Alden did not understand. Later, Marie-Claude translated it to him as: *You've grown tall.*

The strain that was evident on Franz Eckelmann's face at that moment no doubt corresponded to the stretch of almost a full generation that his recognition of Alden as his young nephew, Felix, entailed. But it was a strain, and an apparent confusion, that was evidently also mixed with pleasure. Alden did not at all mind being "Felix" in that room. It made him feel close to the old man, and thus, also, to Marie-Claude.

It was by powerful coincidence that several months later the real Felix arrived at Franz Eckelmann's door. In fact, he was not Eckelmann's nephew but his nephew's son, also named Felix—a young man of twenty-one who had been stationed near Forges-les-Bains, just about forty kilometers outside Paris. Whenever he could arrange it after that first visit, he would come into the city and call on his great-uncle, Franz Eckelmann, whom he had never before had the opportunity to meet, and his cousins, Marie-Thérèse and Marie-Claude. So there were two Felixes that came and went in the Eckelmann house, each interchangeable for old Franz Eckelmann, according to Marie-Claude. This made them laugh, for Alden and the German soldier could not have been more different. Though Alden was, by comparison, rather small in stature, he had always prided himself in having a full head of thick dark hair; the German's hair, so blond it was almost white, was already thinning noticeably at the crown. Also, when it came to personality, the German hardly had one. Marie-Claude reported back, whenever he visited and she took her obligatory stroll with him along the Boulevard Saint-Michel to the

Notre-Dame, that he was—as Alden had suspected—"just as stiff as he looks."

—

WHEN MARIE-CLAUDE WAS SIX YEARS OLD, THE OIL LAMP ON HER bedside table had been knocked from its stand, lighting her bed on fire while she slept. She had woken to heat and to smell, but not to pain. Her father, François Grenadier, awoke to the same smell and rushed into the room to find his daughter's bed ablaze with light. She was awake, her face frozen in the way that a much younger child's might be in the moment after a fall, when—unsure whether to laugh or to cry—the child awaits the response of those around her. Based on this early reaction to pain and other stimuli, it would seem that emotional responses of any kind are only an effect produced by another effect. And just so, it was not until Monsieur Grenadier actually entered his daughter's room—until he, with a look of horror that was itself both cause and effect, threw himself on his daughter's bed—that Marie-Claude screamed.

It was upon this scene that Marie-Thérèse entered—her husband's and daughter's faces (each reflecting the alarm of the other) illumin-ated by the flames, which still licked at the edges of the sheets where the weight of François Grenadier's body had not yet succeeded in smothering them. So gripped by horror was Grenadier himself in those moments, he failed to notice that he held his daughter's hand so tightly that one of its small bones was crushed. Indeed, this damage was dis-covered only several days later—on account of the more severe trauma suffered by the lower part of her body, where she had been badly burned.

Yes, it was fear and not reason that had propelled Monsieur Grena-dier. Though he had been trained as a chemist to respond to such emer-gency situations, he afterward claimed quite emphatically that at the moment he saw his daughter blazing in her bed every trace of prior knowledge escaped him. He had, he insisted, been quite empty of every thought and sensibility. At that moment, he said, it was as though he were hardly human.

What is it that makes us human, after all? he would ask whoever had assembled on that particular occasion. But, *nosce te ipsum*—"know thyself"? My dear gentlemen, I can assure you that I did not know anything at all at that moment—much less "myself."

But Monsieur Grenadier, someone would respond, it is clear to me that the knowledge you had already over your lifetime acquired—all the traits and conditions of your *being* human—your education and training, for example, your sensibilities and affections—were so far ingrained in you that you acted based on all of those factors *combined*. What appeared to you as *impulse* was in fact a very complex combination of causes that contributed, as they continue to contribute, to your very specific and accountable behaviors and reactions. Even now as we sit in this room, it is clear that though we do not carefully consider each gesture, each expression, or even—much to our listeners' disadvantage at times (a chuckle)—each word, they do not simply arise out of the ether. There is not simply: pain, simply: horror, simply: reaction, relief, or joy. All of these things are necessarily accounted for in a long chain of cause and effect whether or not we, at any given moment, can trace that lineage and speak for it with any confidence ourselves.

Well, I am only telling you how it *was*, Monsieur Grenadier would say. I understand your reasoning, dear sir, and sympathize with your assessment—it is no doubt astute. However, I equally cannot give over the notion that in those moments I suddenly found myself *outside of all categories* by which we ordinarily seek to judge and understand the actions and reactions of men.

But nonetheless, someone else would put in, you must admit that the course of action you followed was the correct one. It is quite simple to discuss the actions and reactions that exceed or fall short of what we commonly understand as "reasonable" when the result is one that neither exceeds nor falls short but instead corresponds directly with the effect we would most desire. Your daughter was saved! Your instinct—

whatever exempted you from your rational senses—transferred to an action that you would (had you had all of your senses in order) have equally arranged. Therefore, it is impossible to discuss either question, whether or not you actually found yourself outside your senses at all, and whether or not instinct or impulse in a sane man can truly be considered separate from his reason, without verging into the metaphysical.

Perhaps we should ask the wife, someone else would interject.

Ask the wife what? the wife would say, turning from her conversation at the opposite end of the room.

A toast! someone else would cry.

To impulse over reason!

What's this? a hunchbacked physicist would ask, blowing his nose. A gathering of monkeys?

No! the botanist would cry. Simply an artists' convention!

With that, the conversation would invariably turn to the company's divergent assumptions about, and reactions to, contemporary art, which they felt it was their duty to keep abreast of. Breton's *Poèmes Objets* were a favorite topic, and Marcel Duchamp—who had recently returned quietly to the art world after ten years of playing chess, and from whom everyone was wondering what they could expect next. The company was divisively split on their reactions to the works of these artists, and many other things.

I can't quite see what it's all about, Monsieur Girard, a physicist, would say, for example, regarding Breton. I wouldn't be at all surprised if after a time we discover that it's all been a childish prank; that one way or the other, like usual, we've been *had*.

Wait a minute, now—Monsieur Bernstein, the alienist, who had a great interest in matters of the subconscious, would say. How is one in a situation like this "had"?

Well, quite simply, Monsieur Girard would reply. If you buy a piece and go to the trouble of hanging it in your hall, and then it comes out later that the whole thing has been a complete joke—

But it is still seriously hanging in your hall, is it not? Bernstein would return seriously. Or even if not, even if it is only hanging there as a bit of a joke you have with yourself, what separates the seriousness with which you take that little joke from the prank of the artist who mocks you?

Are you not referring—I'm sorry to interrupt—someone else (a young man, who had not yet made a name for himself in any field) would pipe in—you seem to be referring only to the *cultural* response of the work, and not the work itself. You are thus considering, if I am not mistaken, and as per our previous conversation, the *effect* of the work on the viewing public and the faddish response we seem now to so *encourage* in the arts—serious art being sadly relegated to the academy. Isn't what needs, the young man would continue, on the contrary, to be discussed, the veritable *cause*; just like any good science, isn't that—the serious pursuit of *a cause*—also the true purpose and function of art?

—

MARIE-CLAUDE HAD BEEN SO BRUTALLY BURNED BY HER CHILDHOOD accident that, though in all other respects she recovered quickly, the skin of her lower left leg never healed. The first time Alden saw it—when, after months of serious attentions, she finally accompanied him to his little room on the Rue Auguste-Comte (once again on the seventh floor), and slowly, very slowly, he was permitted to undress her—he found the skin of this region of her body to be as smooth and raw and undeveloped as though it had never been touched. It was she who—before she permitted Alden to press on with the satisfactions of his own desires—lifted her skirt to reveal the damaged limb. As she did so, she looked neither at him nor at her own body, but toward the ceiling, as if in prayer. She hardly breathed in those moments. The muscles of her throat stood out, tense and distended, and Alden even thought he detected in the corners of her eyes two standing tears. They were not tears of sadness or self-pity, but instead of tremendous exertion—as the tears that might stand in one's eyes after being forced to hold a heavy object for a very long time, or strain in a singular direction against an opposing force. It was, that is, a purely physical strain Alden detected at that moment, and so it was with the attitude of one relieving another from a heavy physical burden that he approached her. No, there was nothing tender in their initial contact as he knelt and began to touch the damaged regions of her body, at first tentatively, with the tips of his fingers. Indeed, the skin was so smooth there that it hardly appeared to be human flesh at all—or to have anything to do with human beings (just as François Grenadier had argued for his own part in rescuing his daughter from the flames). It seemed, if it were possible, to be hardly object, even.

All this was apparent to Alden as his hands touched that skin, then as he leaned in to place his lips upon it, not—at first—with the tenderness of a kiss, but instead in the way that a child might test the frozen metal of a pole with his tongue. Lured, that is, not by any sense of his own exemption from physical laws, and neither from danger, but by the purest curiosity. It was with this most innocent of human sentiments that Alden approached the damaged regions of Marie-Claude's body, and relieved her, at least for the short time he held the limb in his own hands, of a physical burden he had not, until that time, had any knowledge of. There was nothing between them in those moments but a pure and perfect physicality, and with what relief did they relent to it! The relief a machine must feel, say, as it falls, for the first time, into the regular rhythms for which it has been made.

After that, Marie-Claude and Alden could not be separated long. The period of time before they had encountered one another (when Marie-Claude was still only an atmospheric pressure as Alden circled closer toward her along the garden's outer path, and no contact was certain) became increasingly difficult to imagine. But, just as between two objects drawn together by a magnetic pull, it would have been impossible to express their relation at that earlier time in terms of desire—at least for one another. As tempting as it might be, that is, to attribute the pull by which two people are eventually drawn together as the cause of contact once it has been made, it simply cannot be so. It simply cannot be toward any one person, or object in itself (still as yet unimagined, unknown) that another is driven—but toward *desire itself*. It must be, therefore, that the realization of any desire in actual contact is made possible only by its continued impossibility. In many

ways, Marie-Claude and Alden maintained—even as they fell into the
inevitable rhythms their contact produced—that impossibility. Even
when Alden sensed beneath him all the muscles of Marie-Claude's
body contract in a spasm of what he could only imagine to be the full-
est contact between her body and his own, something remained
between them: the physical objectness of their bodies, that greatest
impossibility of all. Even, that is, as he sensed the pleasure of her body
in his own, and as his own pleasure quickened and finally released
itself, so that the two pleasures became—for a brief moment—one, he
did not feel as though any contact had been made. It was as if he accompanied himself out to the furthest reach; that he was his own nerve
standing erect at its outermost end—that final, inherent limit every
body maintains in order, if nothing else, that it not absorb itself into
other bodies and other things. He would cling to Marie-Claude's perfectly shaped shoulders, refusing even when she began to adjust herself
beneath him (having realized, suddenly, that for some time now she
had been arranged uncomfortably) to release her, and it was as though
he were clinging not to her but to a body that had only referential
value. It was not that he did not love her—it was just that something
always remained between them that made it impossible for him to
actually feel he was not merely clinging to the outer and extraneous
regions of a body that would always remain to him unfamiliar and
unknown.

Well, perhaps he did not love her. He believed he did, but it was difficult to be sure—not ever having had any particular confidence in the
definition of the word, or any sense then or later of the correct and most
accurate proportions of what it was he either felt or did not feel in proximity to Marie-Claude as they—spent—lay like stilled locomotives in
each other's arms. As those arms became again what they had been all
along: mere physical facts, disentangling themselves from the contact
they had only, as if inadvertently, made.

IT WAS NO ACCIDENT, perhaps, that it was around this period of time, a
few months after he met Marie-Claude (by now having abandoned

their garden strolls, they would ritually mount the seven flights of stairs every afternoon, instead, to Alden's narrow flat, Marie-Claude in the lead) that the pattern Alden had some time ago detected in the American newspapers took on for him an even more unmistakable form. At first it was gradual. As a developing photograph: the details emerging slowly against a background that remains (necessarily) blurred and grayed. As he continued to scan the news daily, circling the names of major political figures and sites of battles that had already occurred, hunting for clues—something shifted. Now it was not just certain words and phrases that stood out for him—whole images began to appear before him in sharp relief.

And yet still he was no closer to understanding why—or detecting in them any meaning.

It became even more difficult after this for Alden to conceal what he found in such a way that whatever it was might easily (by another; at a time and location he might always remain ignorant of) be reconstituted in its original form. Even from the beginning it had never been a simple matter of rearranging coded words according to a pattern that could be repeated exactly the same way every time. It would (Alden was quite sure—especially given the environment in which he worked, and his colleagues' very particular expertise) take only a quick glance at something like that to know that *something* was up— then only a few concentrated hours after that, at most, before anyone who cared to would know exactly what was. If, however, it was never suspected that the words Alden assembled were code at all, it followed that the code itself would be that much more difficult to break. It was for this reason he had first hit—back in the spring of '41—on the idea of creating out of the material he discovered a series of original "poems." A decision he later had cause to regret—not only on account of how difficult each poem, in itself, was to achieve, but also on account of a further difficulty he hadn't even anticipated: for every poem he wrote he was additionally required to keep track of an appropriate "key." (In order to appear as a *genuine poem*, and not merely garbled code on the page, it was, of course, essential that whatever he wrote abide by a certain internal sense and logic, which could only continuously shift and change.)

As—two and a half years later—whole images began to appear to him, this process only became more complicated. He was now obliged to describe what he saw, but in such a way that whatever he described could *never be recognized*—except at the appropriate time and distance and with the appropriate key. It was Maurice Bonheur who (shortly after Alden met Marie-Claude, during that otherwise grim winter of 1944) inspired the idea he eventually settled upon: a system that would no longer rely on words at all.

Now, instead of scrambling the words or images he found, then "resurrecting" them according to a sense all their own, Alden began quite literally to dissect each word or image that he found piece by piece, until they did not resemble words or images at all but only a series of floating dashes and lines. These, too, required a key (they could only, of course, be reassembled according to an accompanying diagram) but, in all, it proved less complicated than his previous method, with less risk of betraying the work's true content and aim. Though Alden did not divulge to Maurice Bonheur the existence of these accompanying diagrams, or the actual origin of the words he disassembled on the page, the poet was nevertheless as enamored with the result—when, with modest pride, Alden showed a few of them to him—as he had been with his earlier efforts.

You have at last broken through! he exclaimed to Alden one afternoon when they met at their usual place on the Boulevard Saint-Michel. The false barrier that has for so long existed between the visual and written arts!

Though Alden was bound to the initial shape of the coded letters and phrases his process would conceal, the possibilities for their rearrangement were, indeed, nearly limitless, and the process in itself extremely liberating. Alden could not help but draw the comparison in his own mind to when, at the age of eleven, he had first learned how to steal. This comparison—when later Alden shared it with him—positively delighted Maurice Bonheur. Truly, Alden told the poet, the feeling that flooded through me then . . . it was—unrepeatable; but this came close. It was a feeling . . . but how can I describe it? Of absolute freedom—uncontainable joy. It happened, you see, almost completely by mistake: I simply failed to notice I still held the wrapped chocolate, which, with my very last penny, I had contemplated purchasing a moment before. Though I had decided against it—choosing to save the coin instead—I had neglected to replace the candy, and so still held it in hand as I approached the shop door. It was not too late! Not at all! I could have simply put the chocolate back in place on the counter where it belonged, or alternatively sought, in the depths of my pocket, that ultimate coin, and given it up. But I did neither. And it was that moment of brief but total awareness of the digression I had not yet but was just about to make, as I willfully closed my hand around the chocolate and walked out the door into the afternoon sun, that resulted in that pure, unrepeatable feeling of perfect freedom, and indescribable joy.

As Alden and the poet Maurice Bonheur contemplated this, across the distance of an ocean and nearly twenty years, they agreed that it was, after all, only a very simple revelation that Alden had stumbled upon: that the logic by which the world seemed to be governed was in fact only the loosest of codes—one that could easily be pushed aside, slipped through, or rearranged. It was not that Alden had "escaped," even momentarily, the system to which he was otherwise bound; his was not, that is—on either occasion—a revelation of gaps, or of holes he might first discover, then slip through. It was instead a sudden realization of the way in which he was a part of—and therefore responsible for, at least to a certain degree—the system itself. That (the possibilities within each moment being effectively endless) it was up to him at every turn; that he was, and would remain, the crucial interpreter of what would continue to prove an ultimately unfixable code.

IN HIS ENTHUSIASM FOR what they began to refer to as Alden's "pictograms," Maurice Bonheur even managed to arrange a small show at the house of the painter Emil Gabor. It was an opportunity, Maurice encouraged him, to destroy the divide once and for all—not only between the visual and literary arts now, but between *all* the arts; it was an opportunity Alden simply couldn't refuse. If he had, perhaps he would still have some trace of the work with him still.

As it was, the gallery space was raided by the police and the work confiscated. It was rumored that the show had been sabotaged—that someone had tipped off someone else that Gabor was a homosexual (a fact, if it was one, of which Maurice Bonheur swore to Alden later he'd been innocent). Alden was grateful he was never himself questioned regarding the affair, or his association with Gabor (which had after all been limited to a single exchange), and Maurice Bonheur apologized profusely for having gotten them into such a fix, the repercussions of which might have been far more serious than they were.

At any rate, the pictograms were gone. Having fulfilled their greatest promise: abstracting themselves, finally, to such a degree that, except for Alden's occasional, brief, memory of them, they completely disappeared. He was left with only the diagrams, according to which—if they still existed—the pictograms might have been reassembled. Of course, lacking any referent now, the diagrams were as useless to him as the instructions to a model airplane would be to a child missing all component parts. And though to this day he retains the manuscript within which he so carefully transcribed the hidden code of German spies, this information (whatever it was), too, has been abstracted to such a degree that it might as well have disappeared: the war is over. Before he was able to unravel the code.

—

BUT AT ONE TIME, THERE WAS NO END IN SIGHT. EVEN WHEN THERE was talk of it, no one any longer believed in "an end" at all—or not, at least, the way they had at the beginning. And yet somehow there was no rhythm to fall into anymore. The threat of being drawn, unwittingly or not, into the kind of fix the poet Maurice Bonheur had so narrowly avoided drawing them both into due to his association with the painter Emil Gabor continued to grow as the Germans (with the grip of a

drowning man) tightened their hold on the city. Not even the top officials at Abwehr or the OKW believed themselves to be truly safe. And
there was good reason, too, for them to be afraid—though Alden would
not learn of it until February 1944, when Canaris was dismissed and it
came out that he (a German admiral who had headed Abwehr since 1935)
had been working against the state for years. He had even obstructed the
September 1943 plot to kidnap Pope Pius XII, and himself had plotted to
kill Hitler.

If, Alden would later lament, he had known there existed such dissent
within the Germans' own ranks, perhaps he would not have been so
afraid! Perhaps he would even have had the nerve to enlist the help of
Canaris's men in cracking the code he had stumbled upon, rather than
only further burying it in his "manuscript," or, later, his "pictograms,"
and being lured by the possibility (all but promised to him by his friend
Maurice Bonheur) of artistic innovation and glory into showing his work
at the studio of an obscure painter who would shortly disappear. Had he
had some inkling of the potential support he might have had within the
ranks of those against whom he was trying to protect himself, perhaps—
Alden would later suggest—they might have been able to crack the code
as early as 1942, and circumvented half the war!

But it was useless to speculate about all of this after the fact. Even
he could see that. He had known nothing, and believed himself to be
acting utterly alone. Not only did he fear his own double-dealings
would be at any moment suspicioned and revealed, he feared that his
past associations with known Communists—Emmett Henderson, for
example (though he had been dead for several years), and the American party (though all of his involvement with them had been officially
deleted from the record since 1935 when he had gone "underground")—would resurface somehow. He tried to assuage his fears on
both counts by reminding himself that the Germans did not look too
deeply into things. That they were, for the most part, content to look
for and connect only the most obvious signs and symbols that existed
(already known) on the surface.

Despite this, he grew increasingly anxious, and the more anxious he became, the more complex and abstract his "recoding" strategies—as the pictograms attested—became. It was always a relief, come evening, to absorb himself in the absolute physicality of Marie-Claude's body, and his own. But the more he began to rely on the relief he felt—growing in him as he climbed the seven flights of stairs behind Marie-Claude, then exploding in a rush as he fell into her arms—the more abstract it became, and very soon he was no longer able to differentiate it from that most dangerous and abstract emotion of all, which, as everyone knows—is love.

What is most beautiful, after all, about love is also what makes it so terrifying: the sensation—as Alden reflected later—of having entrusted yourself into an unknown, as yet unimaginable world, which you are not certain is solid or will hold. It may be that the parts from which it's been made—those things, whatever they may have at one time been, that first convinced you of the fact that love existed at all; that appeared to you, at first, so real, so dazzlingly bright—turn out on further examination to have vanished years before. That the dizzying glow according to which you had been for so long drawn on, and which, during that time, kept you buoyed, afloat, was merely the reflection of that long-extinguished light. Just as the mind, which allows from a distance the glow of stars it knows may have vanished long ago, and does not quickly resort to extinguishing them in the eye (as it would extinguish, say, an apparition of a man, which turns out not to be a man at all, but instead the leaning post of a fence in semidarkness or the limbs of a tree), so the mind, in love, can sustain the shape of that which it knows may only be rendered visible by some long-extinguished source, which is not made up of matter at all, but exists only in the long delay between matter and reflected light.

It is within this realm, thought Alden, that the mind and the heart, in love, may freely wander—among a dazzling brilliance of stars, concerning which the mind no longer thinks to ask how long, how much, and the heart no longer thinks to ask how bright, how vast— but only looks and wonders. It is, Alden further reflected, one of the great mysteries, perhaps—given the remoteness of this realm, and the momentum that must be built up in the heart or mind that has loosed itself from the restrictive bonds of reality to float freely in that kinder atmosphere (in which one hardly has to breathe! In which one can either hold one's breath interminably, or otherwise travel with one's own supply, breathing into a closed-circuit system of one's own creation!)—why it is that one finally falters there. Why the gaps begin to show—not merely as distances between the stars but as great and gaping holes in an uninhabitable atmosphere. Perhaps it is just that the governing properties, from which one thought to be released, never in fact do leave hold. That even at a great distance from the earth, or perhaps especially there, one is obliged to obey simple, physical laws. A man cannot, of course, sustain himself on his breath alone, or not, at least, for very long—he will begin to slowly poison himself. It is easy to imagine why it is often, therefore, with a degree of horror that (choking finally at the limit of a long-soured supply of air) he surveys his surroundings, finds them unforgiving, and returns to the less dazzling, but more durable, surface of the earth.

Perhaps it is, then, a simple question of gravity. As dull and ultimately uninhabitable as the earth itself can often seem, there is, perhaps, no other place more hospitable beyond—and so it is to the earth that we are constantly obliged to return. It was always, though, and each time equally, Alden thought, the greatest imaginable defeat to do so—to, as if instinctually, arrive again, gasping; to acknowledge that, by some atmospheric trick, the earth persists as the only environment a man is readily adapted to, and so must, more or less, remain.

It was along this course, at any rate, that Alden's love for Marie-Claude ran. At first he considered that his old paranoia might simply be returning; that his sudden reluctance in love might be owed only to a lingering fear of exposing Marie-Claude to the destructive power he once believed to be the purview of his affections . . . But then he thought back to Emmett Henderson, now long buried, and the great wheel, which continued (he reminded himself) to roll steadily along its invisible course, well beyond his own powers of perception and control, and tried, as best he could, to push the thought from his mind. And despite these first holes beginning to show—not to mention Alden's continued doubt as to the prudence (for his own sake, if not for hers) of dragging the affair on any longer—he could not tear himself away.

Often, when the two of them parted (Marie-Claude reminding him gently that she would soon be obliged to return, to feed Franz Eckelmann and reposition him from his chair by the window to his bed by the stove) Alden would feel torn between begging her, on the one hand, never to leave him (not even, or especially, to return to Franz Eckelmann) and, on the other, turning away in disgust. He would play through the various imagined outcomes of these responses in his mind until he was quite sick of either course that lay open to him, and—when he had sufficiently contented himself that no solution existed and no decision could be made—he would take his leave from her in as neutral a fashion as he could. With a sinking heart, he would follow her down the stairs and wander alone to the brasserie on the corner, owned by the one-legged Italian, Marcello—from which point, some hours later, he would not mind so much the lonely route he would be obliged to take—coolly, disastrously, drunk—back to his solitary room, up seven flights of stairs.

It occurred to him, then—as he lay there at night in his bed, alone—that if he just managed to sustain this neutrality long enough the decision would be made, in any case, for him—and certainly not in his favor. He was not blind: he saw very clearly that in Marie-Claude lay what was perhaps his only real chance at happiness. What was happiness, after all, but the simple acceptance of chance: Marie-Claude's steps as she traveled around the Luxembourg Gardens one afternoon, happening, for a brief moment, to perfectly align with his own? What was it but the *choice*, to enter into chance events, and all the moments of one's own life, as one enters into words—allowing that (though they are not, and never can be, *the thing itself*) they are at least a decent representation, and from time to time may even come to stand in for that very thing?

But still, he could do nothing to disrupt the supreme neutrality with which he prepared himself in those days to accept what could only, he reasoned, be a decidedly unhappy fate. It even began, after a while (especially after the mishap with Gabor), to affect his pursuit of the code he'd discovered—the key to which had so long eluded him. He continued to painstakingly record the pattern that appeared to him, but by now it had become for him a simple habit; he hardly strained any longer—as he had once done so ardently—to read into it any meaning at all. You might imagine his surprise, then, when there suddenly arrived—and around precisely the same time he ceased to expect it—if not the ultimate key with which he might have finally unlocked the code in its entirety, at least a veritable clue, which, once he had discovered it, did not need to be deciphered or abstracted in any way. Its meaning existed at the very surface; he recognized it at once!

So, too, did the German intelligence officers. But that was the beauty of it. Their "surface" was, and would remain to the end, very different from the one that had appeared so recognizably to him. So that was the trick! he thought. Of course. Like the very best art, the ultimate code must imitate nature to such a degree that the line between where the one ends and the other begins quite naturally begins to fall away. Rather than there appearing at the surface a single, fixed meaning—immediately identifiable to everyone, and in exactly the same way—the meaning of the code must exist (in the way that it always, most naturally, does) according to a shifting spectrum—contingent always on the particular moment and set of circumstances in which it is perceived. And rather than the code's true value (concealed within itself) existing so finally at odds with its representation as to be accessible only to a very few, every person who happens upon it would discover its value at once—each according to his own perspective.

So it was, in any case, when the body of a British Marines officer washed up on the beach just south of Bayonne in early March 1944, and the Germans happily went about accepting what appeared to them most immediately (the body belonged, as all the papers and identification retrieved from it indicated, to a certain Lieutenant Colonel Joseph Gordon Rawlings), that Alden recognized another, far more profound, value to the incident.

The body did *not* belong to a British Marines officer at all. It belonged, instead, to Arthur Sinclair. It took Alden only one glance at the photograph to see this quite plainly. How Arthur had managed to end up in the guise of a "lieutenant colonel," washed up over four thousand miles away from home, was a question, to be sure, he did not know the answer to, but he knew without a doubt that it was the single clue he had been looking for, and that it signaled a change had occurred—or was just about to. For the first time in a long time he began to believe in "the end of the war."

THE SIGNIFICANCE OF THE retrieved body was not lost on German intelligence, either, of course. Little did they know, however—so close had "the end of the war" begun to feel for *them*, in March 1944—the way in which this particular piece of the puzzle, which seemed to have landed so gratuitously in their lap, would, rather than secure their ultimate victory, spell their defeat. Because Alden instantly recognized that the body of the "lieutenant colonel" was in fact the body of quite altogether another man, and held therefore altogether quite another meaning—he was already a step ahead of the rest of German intelligence. Though they took precautions, and followed what leads they could to reassure themselves of the "lieutenant colonel's" identity, and therefore of the validity of the documents he carried, their investigations inevitably hit an impasse, which Alden was at liberty to overstep. From the beginning, his own attention and energies were directed instead to the question of *why* a false body, carrying what were therefore unquestionably false documents, had been employed in the service of the British Marines. It goes without saying—and later, he would make a point of emphasizing it— that this was a question he kept to himself.

SUCH ELABORATE INTELLIGENCE HOAXES were not at all unheard of. Alden knew for a fact that they had been, on several other occasions, attempted by the Allies (and on several occasions—this was how he knew of them, after all—they had been foiled). It was with curiosity and delight that he now watched the Germans assess the bogus documents they found on the "lieutenant colonel's" person—outlining plans of an Allied attack, which only he could know they never had any intentions of making—and come no closer to discovering the manner or extent to which they had already been fooled.

There is, you see, the inherent impossibility, just as in mathematics, not of any truth being recognized, or expressed as such, but of its being expressed within the same system that has been designed to expose it. Because, you see, as Alden insisted later, the Germans—though at times obtuse—were certainly not stupid. Indeed, he couldn't fault them in the very thorough investigation they subsequently carried out. It never ceased to astound him (he said), the artistry that went into the whole affair! Here was a man constructed by Allied intelligence—a complete and utter fiction!—and yet there was no loose end for the Germans to catch hold of, no irregularity in the details on which the story snagged.

"Lieutenant Colonel Joseph Gordon Rawlings" carried with him not only the crucial documents that revealed the false plans of attack designed to fatally upset the German offensive (plans which, despite their false-ness, succeeded in their stated aim), but letters from his "mother" and "wife" in Hampshire—both of whom, when they were contacted by undercover German agents, claimed, indeed, to be the bereaved next of kin to this "lieutenant colonel," who never in fact existed at all! Even a receipt for a guesthouse in London that was found on the "lieutenant colonel," when the guesthouse records were looked into, was verified by the neat signature of a certain "lieutenant colonel" next to the date indi-cated on the receipt itself. The "lieutenant colonel" was a fiction con-structed so carefully, and with such minute attention to detail, that he aligned perfectly with the known and established "facts" of the world he was invented to alter. At least from the perspective of the Germans.

But you see, that was the whole thing! The success of it lay in a care-ful consideration of perspective: what it would be possible to make the Germans believe. As Alden would later attest, every cover operation rests on this principle: on a compromise, that is, between the ideal cover and what the enemy will actually believe. In many cases, the best strat-egy was simply to tell the truth—only then to give some indication that it could no longer be trusted. It was of utmost importance that, whatever this indication was, the enemy would notice it—but that it would never prove *so* noticeable he might actually recognize it as such. The other crucial element was that the information at any point accessible to the enemy be—at least for the most part—information with which he was already familiar: the average mind, after all, is only prepared to understand, let alone accept, that which contains a large percentage of what it already knows. You have to think about that very deeply: What sort of background and assumptions might a person have—a person just like you, but on the opposite end of things, who is presented with the same situation? What will matter to him? You have to think about what questions he would ask and give him the answers that would satisfy not you, but *him*.

PERHAPS IF SUCCESS HAD not already, for the Germans, been so flavorfully on the tongue, things would have turned out differently. The documents retrieved from the "lieutenant colonel," even once his identity was no longer in question, might have been treated with more circumspection and concern. But there is, in victory, or in its expectancy, a tendency—even more than usual—to read things at face value. And so, as far as Alden was aware, once the veracity of the "lieutenant colonel's" identity was confirmed, there was very little circumspection over the documents he carried with him. There was no apparent code to decipher, no trick to the document at all—which was of course the first thing you would think would raise questions among the security department; but it did not. So assured of their own success were they, the Germans quite readily accepted the blunders of their adversaries as simple error. But there was another, larger error that escaped them, and that was the one they had already made.

THE DAYS PASSED AND Alden spoke to no one—not even to the poet Maurice Bonheur (their friendship had anyway cooled after their misadventure with Emil Gabor). He still saw Marie-Claude, but his sustained neutrality in the affair had, just as he'd suspected, begun to take its toll, and there was, each time she took her leave, an increased terseness in her gesture and tone. Alden knew it was only a matter of time before an ultimate terseness would conclude their relations, and with them every chance of his personal happiness. It was not without regret that, over the course of the winter and spring of 1944, he watched those chances slowly diminish until finally (though he and Marie-Claude continued their at least several times weekly ascent and descent up and down seven flights of stairs) they ceased to exist at all.

He grew accustomed, instead, to his private evenings—in which, after Marie-Claude's departure, if she had indeed come, he drank steadily at Marcello's bar. Though he considered this time "private" and appreciated it as such, he was never alone at Marcello's. Far from it. The bar was always filled with men, nearly all of whom were veterans, and in some way incapacitated; some more obviously than others. Most (like Marcello himself) were missing limbs, but there was also a blind man, an epileptic, and—the strangest case—an attractive young Bretagne man, otherwise healthy, who, after the Battle of Oran off the Algerian coast, had developed a bad case of Tourette's. Intermittently, he would let out a bark, like a dog—an affliction that rendered him more or less useless as a Vichy soldier. He had been returned to Paris and now worked in the mailroom, where he was free to bark as much as he wished while sorting through the piles of letters returned from his comrades at the front who were no longer receiving any mail.

On a few occasions, when a new patron entered the bar, heard the unfortunate sounds the young man made, and answered with a bark of his own, Marcello—who looked after all of his regular patrons like a devoted don—would turn on the offender, and, with his one expressive eye (the left side of his face had been permanently frozen by a botched surgery that had once sought to repair a demolished cheekbone), communicate so much information that only once as far as Alden was ever aware was he required to do any further explaining. It was not long before all of Marcello's patrons, not just the regulars, learned to accept the young man's eccentricity.

It was among this company that Alden spent most evenings, overhearing the spattered stories of those men returned from the front, and the whispered rumors of the end of the war. And it was among this company that he celebrated the end of the war when it did come, as if by a miracle, in early August of that year, 1944.

He recalled later the blank looks on the faces of the administrative staff at the Hôtel Lutetia. The closed doors, the periodic slamming of telephones; from time to time a raised voice. Aside from that, and considering the sudden, extreme reversal of circumstances with which they were all confronted, it was amazing how calm everyone remained. All through that day the German tanks rolled through the streets, papers were burned, and finally—the office was closed.

The streets, as Alden walked home that evening, were unspeakably quiet—a stark contrast to the noise that greeted him as he arrived at Marcello's bar, where Marcello—teetering on his single leg—was keeping up marvelously with the almost constant demand for champagne and wine.

At first it was difficult to get any news at all. There was just a dull roar, everyone speaking at once—not caring if they were speaking or being spoken to, or what was said, or if anyone heard. Alden spent most of the night shouting back and forth with a soldier recently returned from Algeria, where he had been blinded by the detonation of a fuel-air bomb. The soldier recalled for Alden those first days of blindness in a hospital in Algiers. When they first brought him in from the field, he said, they had just received news that Benny Goodman was dead. All night long he heard the news repeated, over and over, and the sound of it seemed to echo more resoundingly because he couldn't see. And if you could only imagine the darkness: it was worse than blackness, he said. Did Alden know that? That blindness was not actually black, but gray? It was, the blind man said, just a dimness, which kept everything at such a distance, impossible to diminish, that whatever suggested itself to the eye (as things did, almost continuously) was doomed to remain forever unattainable, unknown. He himself, he assured Alden, had not known this until he had gone blind! One supposed—he continued—one could only suppose—that in time he would become accustomed to the relative distance and aloofness of image and form and not tire himself out anymore in the search of it. That he would establish instead a new system of interpretation that made sense of shapes not according to the forms the inner eye would have them become (as though they might correspond to the images he had for so long been accustomed to), but in terms that corresponded to the very absent shape the eye sought. That filled in the value of that shape through logical equation, much the way that an x (though it in no way serves to solve the problem) still manages to balance two terms of a mathematical equation by providing the possibility of agreement between them. But this was not yet so, he said, and even now—did Alden realize it?—Alden was himself only a dim shape the soldier was, in his mind's eye, searching after. Did he realize that even now, in regarding Alden as he spoke, the blind man was under constant strain, because of the way that Alden failed to correspond to his own possibility? That he was but an apparition, an imbalanced equation, not the resolution—leave that to the mathematicians!—but just the x of which the soldier would always now be constantly in search? And all of this was no less the case, the blind man said, but more so, on that first night of his blindness, in the hospital in Algiers, when he learned that Benny Goodman was dead. Even with how the news was repeated over and over again, he was so unsure of everything on account of his blindness that every time he heard it, it was as if for the first time. Benny Goodman must have died over one hundred and fifty times that night, the blind man said, and each time it struck him anew as a most unconscionable loss. He had, you see, up until that point, even through the worst of the war, been able to maintain a sense that there existed, beyond his immediate experience, a stable outside world unaffected by war, where all was still promised; now he realized, with a shudder, every time he heard the news, that that promise itself was not infallible. Benny Goodman was dead!

Of course, later, the blind man said, they would learn that Benny Goodman was alive and well, living in New York. His death had been only a rumor—its source unknown. He should have been suspicious, of course. It was not uncommon for such rumors to spread, and indeed, it would have been impossible to count the number of celebrities who had died and been resurrected again during the war. It was almost as though the rumors generated themselves for the sake of the comfort and relief of learning, eventually, that Benny Goodman, or Ingrid Bergman, or Bing

Crosby, or Vera Lynn, were indeed alive and well—untouched by war. And even in the course of the conversation Alden sustained with the blind soldier, which was repeatedly interrupted by the profound blasphemies uttered by Marcello at the bar as he poured from what appeared to have been, against all expectation, all that time, an unlimited supply of wine, the blind man's words—*Benny Goodman is dead*—were picked up and circulated, so that in among the chorus of celebration there was a new note—one of alarm and genuine sorrow, but also a certain appreciation. The words gave shape to an injustice of particular dimensions, which could be immediately shared and understood. And so, though at first when the blind soldier heard the rumor he himself had inadvertently resurrected echoed back to him, he had shouted, *Benny Goodman vit! Il vit toujours!*, after a while he gave up—in any case, his words made no impression now. The single phrase, *Benny Goodman is dead*, continued to mix in, and for a while lend shape, to the dull roar of the crowd—punctuating it with sudden bursts, if not of truth, then of intelligible meaning. Soon everyone seemed to be chanting it, and finally even Alden and the blind man joined in—as at last they, too, began to understand its place there.

—

IN ALL OF THE CONFUSION THAT AFTERNOON, ALDEN HAD ENTIRELY forgotten his appointment to meet Marie-Claude—and then the next day, and the next, when he *did* go to meet her, she failed to appear. Three days passed, and each day that she failed to appear at the usual hour, Alden's heart beat with greater insistency and longing. He *willed* her to come—but she did not. Finally, when he could bear it no longer, and heedless of snipers who still peppered the streets with occasional fire, he picked up his bicycle and went flying, all the way to Franz Eckelmann's flat on the Rue de Vaugirard.

WHO IS IT?

It was Marie-Thérèse who asked from behind the closed door.

Alden informed her, but the door did not immediately open.

I'm looking for Marie-Claude, Alden said, though this was something that would have been immediately clear.

The door opened a crack. Marie-Thérèse peered out—Alden could see just a single sharp cheekbone as it gave way to an angular jaw. The rest of her face was either obscured by the thick door or fell into shadow.

She isn't in, Marie-Thérèse said. Her voice sounded strangely mechanical and cold.

Alden said he would wait.

No—no, Marie-Thérèse said. Now her voice broke and trembled on the word. No, she said again. You mustn't do that.

Her words—something in the way her voice had trembled on them (a timbre that was far more forbidding than the cold, mechanical sound that had echoed within it just moments before)—filled Alden, suddenly, with agonizing dread. It was a feeling not unlike absolute desire; that point at which it becomes a physical thing; pressing with such maddening force from within that at last the body can no longer bear the pressure, and—

I must see her! Alden said, attempting to push past Marie-Thérèse at the door. But Marie-Thérèse, with surprising strength, held it firm. Still, he had managed to wedge himself partway into the door frame and so now could see Marie-Thérèse more clearly—could see, glowing there, in her eyes—it was unmistakable—a hatred that bordered on madness.

He was so startled he almost withdrew his position. But he did not.

Let me see her, he said—though now his own voice trembled.

No.

Listen— Alden said, but he discovered, suddenly, that he had nothing to say. No words with which to defend himself. He had been terribly amiss, it was true. He realized it in a wave. But all that—he had never felt more certain of anything before in his life—would change now! He felt it deeply: a firm resolve, which he could not possibly explain to Marie-Thérèse. If he could only—

He plunged into the dark hall. Once he decided to, it was easy. Marie-Thérèse's weight gave easily away.

You can't see her, she won't be seen, she called out after him—but by that time he was already well past her, heading toward the darkened room where Franz Eckelmann, as usual, gazed out the window toward the empty courtyard where nothing, as far as he was concerned, had changed in seventy years.

When Alden entered the room, the old man's face clouded with the first signs of confusion as he attempted to make sense of his unexpected guest—but Alden did not pause long enough for him to do so, continuing on down the long hall, which led, he knew (though he had never ventured there), to Marie-Claude's room. In the long period of time before she allowed him to sleep with her, he could not help but keep its doorway in view, at least peripherally, on each of his visits to the house— imagining the clandestine space where as a child she had caught fire, and within which she had always slept alone, perfect and (except for the flame and her father's hands, which had, once, descended upon her in order to extinguish them) untouched.

It was through this doorway he burst, and there saw, as he knew that he would, Marie-Claude. He could not say later, even with the state he found her in, that it was not still a relief to see her. The abstract fear and longing that had driven him through the house was much worse than anything real, though it was indeed terrible what he saw, and if he had not known that no other possibility existed but that the body that lay on the bed before him in Marie-Claude's room (that sacred space into which, at last, he had penetrated, which he knew to be hers alone) was indeed Marie-Claude's, he would not have recognized her.

Her face was scratched, raw in places, and both eyes had been swollen shut. Her thick, beautiful hair had been clumsily shaved and still stuck out in matted tufts, gleaming with congealed blood and medical ointment. Alden had come to an abrupt halt just inside the door, and he stood there—dazed—breathing in the air, which smelled strongly of antiseptic and another smell—slightly sweet—like diabetic urine.

His hesitation had given Marie-Thérèse, who had been following him closely behind, the opportunity to pass, so that now she stood facing him at the head of the bed. He looked at her and did not speak. She did not speak, either, but only stared at him. Then something flickered. He saw, for an instant, that same recognition he had seen in Franz Eckelmann's eye as all at once all the disparate, conflicting signals he received from the world around him clicked and, for at least a brief moment, he understood his place in it. It was with this look that—each time the old man saw him—he made sense of Alden's presence by recognizing him all over again as his nephew, Felix. And then—*that was it*. In a flash, Alden saw it, too. It was *he*—the *real Felix*—who was responsible for all of this. It was for *him* that Marie-Claude suffered now.

Marie-Thérèse must have seen by the changed expression on his face that he at last understood. She nodded. Then turned, ushering him back through the door and into the dark hallway from which they'd come. Alden obeyed—he had no choice—but, also, he was no longer opposed to doing so.

When she closed the door behind them and they walked together into the dim light of the next room, where Franz Eckelmann waited, as he perpetually did, for the world to assemble itself around him in accordance with some sort of recognizable meaning, and she paused and turned to face him, Alden could see that, though there remained in her eye a trace of the cold glow he had first detected there, there was something else now, too. Perhaps she hoped she wouldn't need to hate him.

What—? he began, though he knew now. How foolish they had been! Who—? He began again.

Marie-Thérèse burst into sobs.

Who? she cried. Her own schoolmates even! I used to watch them playing together—happily in the street!

Why, oh, why had it not occurred to him? For three days as he had waited anxiously for Marie-Claude to arrive, attempting to calm his nerves at Marcello's bar, he had overheard rumors of the punishments already being meted out to those, among others, who had been cooperating with the Germans—if not in any official capacity, then in the bedroom. The collaborators themselves, and other "war profiteers," had begun being rounded up by the French police and gangs before the Germans had even left the city. There were public beatings and executions;

day and night, police vans trolled the streets, delivering collaborators to Fresnes Prison in Val-de-Marne, and La Santé. It was no wonder Alden's nerves were so exceedingly on edge; that he kept a low profile; that he spent nearly every one of his waking hours drinking, slowly, but nonetheless deliberately, in Marcello's bar. Really, though (and over the course of those three days he repeated these words often to himself, like a prayer), he had nothing to worry about. He was American—first of all. And if that wasn't enough: he'd spent time in a German prison camp—having risked his life fighting for France. His work for the Germans? He had been forced into it; absolutely anyone would be sensible to that. There had been no other way.

And if that still wasn't enough? There was the "lieutenant colonel." Whose true identity he had, all that time—and for good reason—kept to himself.

And there was the manuscript. Even if (Alden told himself, again and again) the code remained uncracked; even if his efforts had ultimately led him no closer to solving the puzzle as it first revealed itself to him than in the moment it had—his intentions, at least, had been good, and . . . he had been close. The poor girls he saw beaten on the streets, their clothes stripped, their heads shaved—what did they have with which to defend themselves or their intentions? These "horizontal collaborators," as they were sometimes called, were (it was said) *no less traitors*—and should not be permitted to get off easily. Alden had thought immediately of Paige, when he'd heard—but she was American, too, and anyway safe by then with her sister, in Châteaudun. Why had it not occurred to him that Marie-Claude would be vulnerable? Caring day after day for the old German, Franz Eckelmann, German blood flowing in her veins, seen, no doubt, on the arm of the real Felix, her cousin, who from time to time came to call?

How dare he! Alden was filled with sudden disgust at the clumsiness of it all. How her own cousin had exposed her to this outrage—and where was he now? Had he fled? Like everyone else? Alden hoped sincerely that wherever he was he felt every bruise and burn on Marie-Claude's body.

I didn't think— Alden said. Of course. *Felix*, he said. They would not think to make the distinction that . . . well, he is only her *cousin*; that it was not a matter—

Marie-Thérèse had covered her face with her hands, but now she looked up at Alden, surprised.

Oh, no, she said. It wasn't *him* . . . But here she paused.

Alden waited.

Well, he said. What then? The vague thought that Marie-Claude had been seen with other German soldiers—that she had even had "horizontal" relations with them—flashed into his mind like a hot flame, but it was quickly dampened. Impossible.

Don't you understand? Marie-Thérèse asked him slowly, still staring at him with a blank expression of surprise and disbelief.

He must not have replied. There was a strange feeling in his throat like something was trying to catch at it, but there was nothing to hold on to, and whatever it was kept slipping away.

Don't you understand? she asked again. She stood there shaking her head, waiting for him to reply, but he did not.

Alden, she said, finally. It's . . . Her voice trembled again as it had at the door. *It's you.*

He shook his head. There was indeed nothing to hold on to. He felt he was not made out of flesh and blood, but only the absence of where flesh and blood once imagined itself to be. He could see himself as if from above. And Marie-Thérèse, too, Marie-Claude's mother. The way she looked at him, almost curiously now, all hatred dissolved; her face concerned, her hands fluttering like two pale birds.

Alden, she whispered. You must be careful; they will be looking for you now. And you must— she added. You must—Alden—do you promise me?—never come here again.

Her voice broke.

Alden nodded his head and somehow managed, with the help of Marie-Thérèse, who led the way, to navigate his way to the door. She opened it; the sun streamed in, temporarily blinding them.

Tell her, he said . . . But just at that moment whatever had been attempting to catch in his throat caught, and there was no way for him to open his mouth again, or utter any sound at all, and that was a great mercy, because he did not know what—even if he could speak—he would say.

He turned, and exited onto the street.

VIII.

Sutton comes. Twice a day to the door. She stands there, hovering for a while, as though she has something to say, but can't bring herself to say it. When she does speak, it is always the same thing that she says. She admonishes him, for example, for his poor eating habits when she takes up a tray of food he's left out for her, more often than not untouched, or for not resting properly, or for straining his eyes. It is very dim in the room, there being only an empty ceiling hook where, if it were the last century, a chandelier might have hung. The only light comes from a small lamp on the desk, which casts—even when he remembers to light it—only a very limited glow.

He rarely remembers. Even when, each time she enters, he picks up a book kept open nearby, and for this very purpose—burying his nose in it the instant he hears her at the door. He suspects she knows the book is only a ruse—especially if she enters the room after it has already been plunged (the lamp still unlit) into darkness—but she uses it as her own. It provides her with an excuse to linger awhile longer, as she fusses with the light—turning it on, then adjusting it, so that it illuminates the still-unread page. Only then does she disappear again down the hall.

As soon as her footsteps fade, he shuts the book and switches off the lamp again.

Sometimes she comes with papers for him to sign, or with information on doctor appointments, and from time to time she shuttles him herself to the hospital in their father's old Hupmobile and sits beside him, flipping through magazines in the waiting room.

And they wait. She snaps the pages deliberately: *snap snap snap*, as regular as the ticking of a clock, and doesn't say anything until his name is called. It is as if she is waiting for this cue—which indicates that the time in which to say anything is already gone.

You must remember, she warns him, just as he is obliged to rise and follow the starched white nurse into the cavernous hall, the more information you can give him—here she pauses; the word even before she says it rings out ridiculous and false—*the better*, she finishes. Apologetic now.

He nods.

ALL RIGHT, THE ANALYST says as he enters, indicating a chair adjacent to his own where Alden should sit. It is, after all, the only unoccupied chair. It is hard-backed and upright. Funny. He always imagined he might be allowed to recline.

Let's go back, the analyst says. And with that—as though no time has passed between this visit and the last—they begin where their previous session left off.

You were saying, the analyst says, that . . . this certain photograph; that the man pictured was immediately recognizable to you. Did there ever enter into your mind any . . . doubt? At any time, did you consider the possibility that the man who appeared to you might in fact *be* the man he, and everyone else in the position to have an opinion on the matter, affirmed?

No, Alden says. There was never any doubt.

The analyst nods, and glances down at his notes, which are open before him. It seems very odd, he says slowly, scratching his head and seeming to genuinely puzzle over whatever he has found on the page. Does it not indeed, he says, looking up again, and leaning forward in his chair, seem odd that a man convicted of a crime in 1932, sentenced to a five-year prison term, but released *the very next year*, might show up *eleven* years later disguised as a dead British officer whose records are all perfectly intact?

Yes, says Alden, returning the analyst's gaze. It strikes me as very odd, indeed.

Again the analyst nods. He says nothing for a little while. He only continues to regard Alden. Watching, as he can only suppose, for any signs that might indicate—what, exactly?

Alden tries very hard not to blink, and he wonders, given the harsh glare of the fluorescent light overhead and the overlong time to which he has now been exposed to it, if his pupils are retracting slightly, and if they are, if that might be read as a sign. But there is no way of knowing this. As hard as he tries, he cannot detect any manner in which to be certain if his pupil is expanding or retracting, and he only tries to remain calm and still, and not to blink, for as long as he can.

Finally, the analyst drops his gaze and leans back in his chair.

You see, he says, the curious thing is that your own report of your activities during 1932 through to the present day does not always correspond with the official record. He glances down again at his file, and shuffles through a few pages before returning his gaze.

You see, there are records here of your employment with the *Washington Post*, then of a short stint at Internal Affairs—but there is nothing to indicate the sort of *extracurricular* involvement to which you allude. I can assure you the government has a vested interest in keeping track of such involvement, and is able to do so with an accuracy that may surprise even you. I am not saying, the analyst continues carefully, that your recollections are . . . false, exactly. It is only pertinent to consider—given the emerging pattern that can be observed in your account—that you do have a certain . . . history . . . of experiencing events somewhat sideways to their—

But this is all simply ridiculous—Alden can't help but put in, a little more hastily than he would have liked. He tries, whenever possible, to keep his responses and reactions to a controlled minimum. Need I remind you that my *extracurricular*, as you say, dealings with the Communist Party were kept under strict confidence for the express purpose of their remaining strictly *off the record*?

The analyst strokes his heavy jaw and shifts in his chair.

Does it not strike you, he says, in an altered tone—his voice suddenly deep, almost conspiratorial—as somewhat *odd* that it is only now, when the charges that have been brought against you are so much greater than they ever would have been had you actually been brought to task for your earlier involvement in the party's business and the—he waves his hand—the Bonus Army affair—that these phantoms from the past should suddenly appear? And that it is precisely on the basis of these phantoms that you are presently seeking to exonerate yourself from the *current* charge?

Now this is simply outrageous! Alden cries. I am not, he says—tempering his tone, and employing everything in his power to keep his voice steady and controlled—attempting to exonerate myself in any way! It is—he hesitates, but only slightly—just the opposite. I am most guilty, he says. Only not of the crime of which I'm accused.

The analyst nods and nods. Then he bends to his file and writes something down. For several minutes all Alden can hear is his pen scratching away at the page—it is an irritating sound. That, and the electric whirr of the light overhead.

Finally, the analyst lays his pen aside.

It is clear to me, he says—his tone apologetic now—that regardless of your personal culpability in the previous affair, real or imagined, what we are faced with *today* is a simple confusion between events of the future and events of the past. You see, the analyst continues, the mistake most analysts make in these sorts of cases—and which I am not prepared to make in yours—is to fail to realize that for certain patients, such as yourself, Mr. Kelly, with what we might call an *improperly elongated* sense of time, the past and future can seem to occur as if simultaneously. It is possible, you see—that is to say, it *does* happen—that things become in a patient's mind, especially after difficult periods of stress, so confused that the boundaries that would normally separate different experiences or events are erased. Two things—something heard, or imagined, or seen—become overlaid in the mind with another, in this case earlier, episode.

Think of a dream—the analyst says, becoming suddenly animated—where a single person may represent two or more people at the same time, or two disparate events of the day—each one in itself quite solid—can recombine to engender the strangest of fictions. When it comes to *interpretation*, we find ourselves, just as with a dream, in very tricky territory indeed. The dream imagination, you see, almost always prefers a different image than the object to which it corresponds—*as long as*, that is, it is capable of expressing some particular *aspect* of the object the imagination would like to represent.

It may be that the fixed form in which objects or events appear to us in the waking world is too simplistic—that the dream imagination attempts to express them more truly by deconstructing and rearranging the images it experiences and the information it receives. The problem lies in the fact that what results from this effort most often appears to us, in our waking life, as utter nonsense!

To make matters worse, the dreamer very rarely paints any picture in an exhaustive or methodical manner. Instead, he will offer only the broadest strokes, and we are never privy to a finished image but instead only to brief glimpses into an ongoing act of free association. Not only that (and here we may come to the root of the thing), the images (even as they remain incomplete) are not content to *remain* images. The dreamer is almost certainly compelled to interact with them, to turn them from mere information—lines drawn cursorily on the canvas of his mind—into some sort of dramatic act or deed. If a dreamer, for example, encounters a lake, he is liable to enter it. He will at least wet his feet, if he does not go any farther—the water may even threaten to drown him. Or perhaps a boat will appear. If it does, he will certainly board it. Finally, the compulsion of the dream to conjure up what has been systematically repressed by the dreamer runs directly counter to the dream's compulsion to repress any disturbing impulses that might interrupt the dream and thus disturb the dreamer, further complicating things.

Now, it would not surprise me, Mr. Kelly, the analyst says, eyeing Alden sharply over the width of the desk, if in your case we are faced with just this sort of situation, where the guilt and anxiety regarding your *current* situation (which cannot help but cast itself apprehensively forward, toward a far deeper anxiety—vis-à-vis the "ultimate punishment" with which you are now faced) has been absorbed, adapted, and finally expressed, through what we can only reasonably understand today as a "demonic" resurrection of the past. In short, Mr. Kelly, it is my recommendation that—as you are unfit at the present time to act as your own witness—

Alden has been drifting—for some time only half listening to what the analyst is saying—but now he is jarred to full attention.

Unfit?

Yes, Mr. Kelly, the analyst replies. I am sure you will agree—perhaps with some proper rest and treatment, you may once again regain the . . . perspective, and perhaps even more importantly the . . . *resilience of spirit* needed in order to undergo these sorts of procedures, which, as I am sure you must understand, can prove quite grueling.

I assure you, Alden says, I am quite fit.

Again, Mr. Kelly, the analyst insists, I must impress upon you—there's a certain procedural code with these sorts of measures, which you would be required to obey. They are quite adamant, of course, that every word that is spoken for the record is the truth and can be verified without—

I assure you, I am quite fit!

Perhaps—yes. After some rest. But for now, my recommendation will remain—

If it is a matter of the outcome, Alden says, I can assure you—it makes no difference to me. I am prepared simply to recount—so help me—the whole truth, and nothing but, and have the ax fall, so to speak, as it may!

The analyst clears his throat. He has already closed his file, and now has begun to rise.

This is not, he says, leaning over the table and extending his hand, about what you would feel prepared to do or not, but about what is advisable—and permissible—in the court of law. And now, if you'll excuse me, he continues—then pauses. He drops his hand, which Alden has not taken in his own, and shakes it a little, as though he has touched something soiled.

But he has touched nothing.

Alden stares ahead—remaining as calm and still as he possibly can. He tries not even to blink.

Our time is up, the analyst says.

—

DESPITE THE ANALYST'S EFFORTS, HOWEVER—WHICH, ALL ALONG, AS Alden could not fail to realize, have been thinly disguised as Sutton's own (it is she, in any case, who pays the hourly rate, and who, as Alden reflects to himself, can say what the cost is to take official leave of your senses these days?)—the trial is set to go forward as previously arranged. He can't help but feel a little smug when Sutton delivers the news.

So I'm "fit," after all, he says. If not yet, perhaps, enough to have actually *committed* the crimes to which I've confessed, at least enough to account for the ones I have not.

There is—Sutton insists—still a fair chance; you must not think, she says, there is not. With the help of the analyst's recommendation we might manage (she pauses) to significantly . . . *lighten* the sentence. Yes, she tells him, still a reasonable chance.

He repeats this silently to himself. A reasonable chance. That he might, after all, live—like his mother—to a respectable middle age, gazing out on the Potomac River from a comfortable private room at St. Elizabeth's Hospital . . .

In as indifferent a tone as he can muster, he begs her not to press the issue.

And indeed, as the days and then the weeks begin to pass, Sutton mentions chance—along with almost everything else—less and less. It is now, as she also must be beginning to see, only a matter of time.

MEANWHILE, OUT OF IDLE curiosity sometimes, Alden wonders what sort of price has been put on his head—but he has never inquired. He is grateful to be allowed to remain at home, and supposes, in any case, their father must have left Sutton quite a sizable sum. It is some solace, at any rate, to think so. To have the assurance, at least, that after all of this is done, *she*, at least, can stay on at the house. Never have to marry, if she does not wish to. Even give up the "women's pages." (Now that the men have returned, it is, as she often laments, the only thing open to her—just as it was before the war.) There is something pleasurable in the thought of it, though he feels a little guilty to go so far as to think it. To keep her—if only in his imagination—in this way separate, apart; to suppose that, after he is gone, she, too, may abstract herself from the world of other living women and men; that she, too, may desist, finally, in any attempt to stall the flow of time, and the changes it inevitably brings. May instead absorb herself—or be absorbed—only in its continuous flow.

You know, she says—it is the evening before the trial. She is paused, in her usual way, with a dinner tray, by the door. I tried—I tried very hard—

This is not the usual, rehearsed script they perform nightly with each other. Alden does not want a scene—now, or the next day—but, still, he is interested in what she will say.

She continues. To find him, she says.

Who? he asks.

Arthur, she says.

Of course. Alden knows all of this—he does not feel as though they have to go over all of it again.

Listen—he says. Listen, Sutton. The thing is out of our hands.

She shakes her head. No, but you see—and now there is something in her voice that catches him. He trembles for a moment with it. What is it, he wonders, that she—that anyone—could have left to say?

I did manage—she continues—some time ago. To locate Douglas. I didn't tell you, I'm sorry. I don't know why.

Douglas, he says.

Yes, she says. And then she tells him all about how he survived the war. He was even made corporal, she says, after the Battle of Overloon. About how he lives in St. Louis now, married to a nurse whom he met overseas—a student at the university. About how he had been working out in Arizona when he first heard the news, back in '36, that the Bonus Bill had finally passed. That he took his father's bonus, which he had kept all those years folded inside his shirt pocket, down to the local Veterans' Bureau, and filled out the form so that he might finally make good on it.

The clerk stopped him.

Well, what's that, sonny? he said. You don't look hardly old enough to have fought in the war, how old are you now—fourteen?

He was not much more—sixteen that September.

No, sir, Douglas said. This is my daddy's bonus. I was given it for safekeeping, and wherever he is, if he's still among the living, and even, or especially, if he ain't, I know for certain he'd want nothing more in this world than for me to cash it in and bring whatever it's worth to my momma—and that is what I'm planning to do.

Well, son, the clerk told him—unable to resist a smile. Now, see, it doesn't quite work like that. If'n this is your daddy's bonus, it's going to have to be him to cash it. When's the last time you saw your daddy, now—and how did it happen he left you his ticket?

So Douglas told the clerk at the Veterans' Bureau all about how he had lost his father in the summer of 1932, and how ever since he had followed the Bonus Army, returning to Washington every year, three years running, each time expecting to find his father there. Or otherwise somewhere on the road. He knew his daddy would not have given up and gone home until he got his bonus, as he had made a solemn promise to that effect, and so had Douglas himself.

He told the clerk about how he had traveled up and down the eastern coast he didn't know how many times, and how he had had countless adventures, and met a great many men, some of them good and some of them bad, and finally how he had nearly been drowned just that previous fall out on Windley Key during the Labor Day hurricane. He had only afterward made his way west, he said—where he was lucky enough to find work on the Corps project where he was currently employed.

The clerk took all this in, nodded solemnly, and said, son, I would sure like to see you and your momma get what you're due. I don't mean to upset you none by what I'm about to say, but you see, now, if'n there *is* the possibility your daddy is no longer among the living, you know that money would go straight to your momma and you. If you can't find where your daddy is currently residing, might be a chance you can find out where he died—sometimes, as strange as it sounds, it's a lot harder to track down a living man than it is to track down the dead.

So Douglas Sinclair thanked the clerk and, once more, went in search of his father. But his efforts looking for a dead man proved no more fruitful than his previous efforts looking for a living one, and after a while the war came, and he transferred his father's bonus into the inside shirt pocket of his uniform, and he would, he told Sutton later, be amiss not to grant that it served to protect him there, because on many occasions he believed by rights he should have died. That there was no reason over any other that he did not become, in the great deserts of North Africa, for example, even before he was shipped north to Holland to the Battle of Overloon, particular again—just one more grain of sand that had no knowledge of the way that it was, or might still be, connected to the rest of all the things that there were in the world. But he did not, and still to this day, he told Sutton, he believes that some promise had, indeed, been kept. That same promise he himself had kept for so many years nearest to his heart had proved—though it now had nothing to measure itself against, and had become, even for him, only the greatest of abstractions—to be a thing of value nonetheless.

It was, he further reported to Sutton, by peculiar coincidence that just before he was to ship out he met his father's old friend Chet Oke once again—in Newport News, Virginia. Chet was at that time preparing to be shipped out, too—an officer, this time; his second war. I believe he was bound once again for France, Douglas said, but at that time, as now, every place and every mission sounded the same to me, and I do not recall any of the details that might now make it easier for me to place him, or to discover what sort of a time he had there, and what the chances are that he would still be living today.

It was during that brief encounter that Chet informed Douglas of the last occasion he had seen his father. It was just before he was set to be transferred from the city jail to Lorton Reformatory, in Fairfax County, Virginia: February 6, 1933—the only recorded date that anyone had yet been able to find. There had been no reference, alongside this date, of Arthur's having been transferred to another facility—Lorton Reformatory or any other—or indeed any further record of him at all. But it is certain that Chet did indeed see Arthur one more time, because it was during this visit that he was entrusted with the letter he carried back to Douglas's mother, which she undoubtedly received.

It was, Chet told Douglas—by way of apology—Arthur's specific request on that last occasion he saw him that—if Chet was bound back to Kansas with a letter to his wife, as he pledged he was—he should not seek Douglas out, or ask him to follow. It was your father's wish, Chet said, that you might make your own way in the world and not be bound to the same fate he himself had been. Chet shook his head slowly, and said he was sorry—but, he said, he supposed now Douglas's father had been right. He looked at Douglas in his uniform and said that he looked all right, and that made Douglas feel proud, but also strange. He had spent so many years in the company of soldiers and he had not been one of them himself, and now he was.

After that, neither man had much to say. Chet said that if Douglas didn't get himself killed he would do right for himself in the end, and after Douglas returned the compliment, the two parted company, and it was just in time that they did, because Douglas had felt a pressure growing in his chest all the time they spoke, and when he had turned a corner, and Chet was no longer in sight, he had to lean his hands against his knees and rest there like that for a while, in order that he might catch his breath.

—

NOW, WITH SUTTON DEPARTED—WITHOUT LIGHTING THE LAMP THIS time; simply excusing herself, then retreating quietly down the hall— Alden is left quite alone. The light off, the book overturned on the table. It is, indeed, dark. Perhaps, he thinks, it will calm his nerves to smoke a little, though he has never made a particular habit of it. He shuffles about for a book of matches, but finds none. There must be some, though—somewhere. He jiggles the handle of the desk's top drawer. It sticks a little; then slides open.

Inside, he finds nothing but his father's old riding whip. It surprises him, at first. He almost jumps to touch it—as though he's touched something live. Funny. He'd almost forgotten it. The whip his father used to swish about in order to soothe his nerves, maddening everyone else in the house. *It helped him to think*, he had said.

Imagine, Alden thinks now. It's remained, all this time. Coiled in darkness.

HE TAKES IT OUT; feels the cool, soft leather against his hand. It's as thick as a cat's tail at the butt of it, then narrow at the end—as thin as a single blade of grass. Perhaps it will do, he thinks, in lieu of a cigarette, if he can't, in any case, light it. He gives it a try; flicking his wrist so the whip cuts up sharply. It stops short, though, and a moment later lands in a heap.

It's clumsy like that at first, but after a while he gets the hang of it, and there begins the familiar *swish swish*, which he remembers echoing from his father's end of the house—from the very same spot, come to think of it, where he now sits, attempting, just as his father once had, to calm his nerves; to sustain in his mind a single—

Yes, it does help some, he finds. His hand relaxes, adjusts to the motion—which steadies itself as if it, too, were a physical thing in his hand—and, just as it does so, the strangest sensation begins to flood through him. It is as if—the analyst is right—all his memories, regardless of their chronology or progression, return to him at once—and from all directions. Indeed, he is no longer certain if, as he sits in his father's chair and listens to the steady rhythm of the ancient riding whip as it cuts against the air, the memories are his own or someone else's; or if, indeed, they are the fantasies of some future man who takes his likeness and form and who, out of some perverse desire to repeat all of this from the beginning, takes up his life at the very point where he is obliged—

The poet Maurice Bonheur flashes suddenly to mind. The great composer to whom the poet—he'd once said—owed his life.

Imagine, if you will, that the universe comprised a single beat.

He had heard that, recently, even he—the illustrious composer—had come under some scrutiny for his actions (or lack thereof) during the war. It had not yet come, so far as he knew, to the point of outright *accusation*, but there were uncomfortable rumors afloat. *Did you hear?* people asked in hushed voices. That the comfortable conservatory position the composer won shortly after his return to Paris had been made available only months before by *a Jew*, in permanent exile now—in Poland, or beyond? So the composer himself had been a prisoner for a brief time; but had he not also been released—due to his connections, and in various capacities, *collaborations*, with the enemy?

Music, the composer had always insisted—like light refracted through the stained-glass windows at Chartres or Sainte-Chapelle—had nothing to do with questions of war, or even of men. It was his faith that this was true that had sustained him, after all—just as it later had the poet Maurice Bonheur—and Alden himself. Was it not according to this same faith, that . . . ?

But he cannot bring himself to finish the thought.

The whip slices the air.

The creation of a second beat. This (the composer had said) is the beginning of rhythm, which, arising not from any division, exists instead as extension . . . duration. In which all things, utterly free—

Yes. His father was right. It does—the steady rhythm of the thing—help a man think. He feels quite calm now, quite—altogether—unafraid. There is, after all, very little to be frightened of—if all exists, as it seems to him now very certainly that it must, all at once, in this—

Yes, he will tell the analyst if he should see him again. (Oh, he'll be there tomorrow, no doubt: to argue over the relative dimensions of time; to defend Alden's inability, under *current circumstances*, to measure himself—or anything else, therefore—against it.)

Yes, he will say. There may in fact be, in the flickering flashes that stream now like magic-lantern images before his eyes, an impulse to repeat what has already passed, in order to escape the inevitable moment in which—

Another low *swish*, like the sound of water underground.

Quite right, yes. It does help a man—and it is only natural it does. Having afforded him some measure along which, at least for a short while, he might be permitted to string his thoughts, only natural that there should also begin to appear to him some sort of end; according to which—

—An instinct, he will say. Inherent, perhaps, to all organic life. An attempt to retrieve *an earlier state of things*. Not from the consciously remembered past, but from some deeper and more remote realm. An instinct to plumb the depths, to regain what has been lost—what might still, what must, be inscribed within our every cell—

But here he falters—only very slightly:

What to hang it on? What to hang it on?

Ah. Yes.

—A state prior to all life; indeed, to all time. Yes, he will tell him. Yes. Accordingly. We shall be compelled to say that "the aim of all life is death," but we will also be compelled to say: Not for long. Not always. Because—just as diligently as we press toward it—we resist—and in doing so succeed in winning, indeed, what we can only regard as potential immortality—! And though we continue to submit ourselves—he will say—to the remorseless laws of nature, it is only because by doing so it is easier to bear our own deaths, and for that matter our own lives— or to consider that either one was or is not integral to itself but instead a chance that might have been escaped.

It may well be—*yes*—he will say—that this persistent belief in the internal necessity of dying is only another of those illusions that we have created "*um die Schwere des Daseins zu ertragen.*" To bear the burden of existence.

Yes.

Death may indeed be only a matter of expediency. A manifestation of the external conditions of life. Merely, that is—an adaptation. A foray into territory that has already been charted—as salmon spawn in pools they have never themselves frequented, but their ancestors once did, or birds migrate in perfect *V*'s to unknown destinations, guided by the intuition of previous generations; by a will to regain what is still sensed in the blood, or whatever it is that whistles through hollow bones.

Steady, now. One foot, the next. As always. Nothing to it.

Ha! Precisely!

Nothing at all to it, in the end.

And, ah—

Yes. From this perspective he can see more clearly still. Though the past—or is it, as was once suggested, the future?—still streams, and perhaps even more rapidly now before his eyes. It is easy enough to distract oneself; to forget that, even now, there are, as in all practical matters, still steps to be taken—few enough and simple—before, at last, the thing is arranged.

He tries, on account of it, to clear his mind; to—just for a moment, a single moment—clear it of everything but a single, empty frame. But each moment closes on itself as quickly as it comes. There is no time in which to enter—and yet, there is still the last, the final step. The *faux pas*. He must not—he will not falter; no, that is not a possibility now. There is no return—no. No earlier state of things. Everything exists at once—only now, and again now—so that even his own thoughts become suddenly unfamiliar to him. His own words—though he is certain enough he has heard them before; that he has even spoken them himself, perhaps even many times—yes, strange. Their syllables incoherent, suddenly, as though pronounced at increasing distances to one another—so that now the meaning begins to escape, and all is awash in a low, unconsonanted moan.

Yes, he will say. It is into this—last scattering of vowels—that they come. In every imaginable shape and color and creed.

At last. Ascending.

Behold! he will say: A white horse!

And the one sitting on it? With a countenance more in sorrow than in anger?

My father's spirit in arms.

Alas. Poor ghost . . .

If it is, indeed, thee, Father—answer me this. Why make of the night such a hideous darkness, and of us such fools? Why shake our dispositions in this way—and so horridly—with thoughts beyond the reaches of our souls?

He says nothing. And yet—it *is* he. It is.

Unquestionably, it is.

Why else—I ask you—would all the armies of heaven, arrayed in fine linen, also follow him on white horses?

Or from his mouth come a sharp sword with which to strike down the nations; which he will rule, from this day forward—just as those who came before him—with a rod of iron?

Acknowledgments

With gratitude to Olivier Messiaen's *Quartet for the End of Time*, and the many histories, personal narratives, and works of art that inspired this book; to my editors, Jill Bialosky and Nicole Winstanley, for their guidance and belief in this project; to my agent, Tracy Bohan, for her friendship and support; and to my husband, John, for being my first and most devoted reader, and my best friend.

Art Title Index

.

.

ing before a joint session of Congress to deliver a veto of the Patman Bonus Bill. This is the first time such action was taken by a
president, and marks a new high for presidential vetoes of the
veteran bonus legislation. Vice President Garner, seated left
under the flag, and speaker Joe Byrns, seem very impressed.

Harris & Ewing, photographer, May 22, 1935.

p. 200   CCC (Civilian Conservation Corps) boys at work, Prince
George's County, Maryland.

Carl Mydans, photographer, August 1935.

p. 201   The hands of Mrs. Andrew Ostermeyer, wife of a homesteader,
Woodbury County, Iowa.

Russell Lee, photographer, December 1936.

p. 202   Hurricane shelter under construction, Matecumbe Key, Florida.

Arthur Rothstein, photographer, January 1938.

p. 203   Family walking on highway, five children. Started from Idabel,
Oklahoma. Bound for Krebs, Oklahoma, in Pittsburg County.
In 1936 the father farmed on thirds and fourths at Eagleton,
Oklahoma, in McCurtain County. Was taken sick with pneu-
monia and lost farm. Unable to get work with Work Projects
Administration and refused county relief in county of fifteen
years' residence because of temporary residence in another
county after his illness.

Dorthea Lange, photographer, June 1938.

p. 204   Opens for business as usual. Washington, D.C., October 26,
1938. Despite President Roosevelt's rebuke of the House committee investigating un-American activities the day before,
Chairman Dies opened his committee room for further hearing
of witnesses.

Harris & Ewing, photographer, October 26, 1938.

Deviates, *published in 1955 by the Rand Corporation.*
The numbers were produced by an electronic "roulette
wheel," which, after ensuring the numbers and their pro-
gression contained absolutely no information, were then
transposed. The need for large quantities of random num-
bers began with electronic calculating machines, and the
Manhattan Project's development of the atomic bomb. As
the largest known source of random digits, the Rand book
has become a standard reference for engineers, statisti-
cians, gamblers, physicists, poll-takers, market analysts,
lottery administrators, and quality control engineers. The
New York Public Library had yet another take on the proj-
ect, originally filing it in its "Psychology" section.

p. 211   High school Victory Corps. Invading a field previously almost
exclusively masculine, this girl at Polytechnic High School,
Los Angeles, California, takes her radio and code instruction
seriously.

Alfred T. Palmer, photographer, September–October
1942.

p. 212   Argonis, Kansas. Crossing wheat fields along the Atchison,
Topeka, and Santa Fe Railroad between Wellington, Kansas,
and Waynoka, Oklahoma.

Jack Delano, photographer, March 1943.

p. 213   New York, New York. A soldier and his girlfriend dancing at
the Hurricane to the music of Duke Ellington.

Gordon Parks, photographer, April 1943.

p. 214   Female French collaborator having her head shaved during lib-
eration of Marseilles.

Carl Mydans, photographer, Time+Life Pictures—Getty
Images, December 31, 1943.

Sources and Inspirations

Quartet for the End of Time, by Oliver Messiaen.

The Doughboys, by Gary Mead (Overlook, 2000).

The Gulag Archipelago: 1918–1956, an Experiment in Literary Investigation I–II, by Aleksandr I. Solzhenitsyn. Translated by Thomas Whitney (Harper & Row, 1973).

Reds: McCarthyism in Twentieth-Century America, by Ted Morgan (Random House, 2003).

Macbeth, by William Shakespeare (Norton, 1997).

War, Women and the News: How Female Journalists Won the Battle to Cover World War II, by Catherine Gourley (Atheneum Books for Young Readers, 2007).

Let Us Now Praise Famous Men, by James Agee and Walker Evans (Houghton Mifflin, 1941).

"The Ethics of Living Jim Crow," by Richard Wright. From *American Stuff: WPA Writers' Anthology*, 1937.

Human Personality and Its Survival of Bodily Death, by F. W. H. Myers (University Books, 1961).

The Island of Dr. Moreau, by H. G. Wells (Dover, 1996).

The Immortalization Commission: Science and the Strange Quest to Cheat Death, by John Gray (Farrar, Straus and Giroux, 2011).

Reporting World War II, Part II: American Journalism, 1944–46, The Library of America. In particular: Martha Gellhorn's "Surely This

War Was Made to Abolish Dachau," from *Collier's*, June 23, 1945, and Virginia Irwin's "A Giant Whirlpool of Destruction," from *St. Louis Post-Dispatch*, May 9–11, 1945.

Homage to Catalonia, by George Orwell (Harcourt, Brace, 1952).

The Best Short Stories of Guy de Maupassant, by Guy de Maupassant (Airmont, 1968).

Suite Francaise, by Irene Nemirovsky (Vintage Canada, 2007).

Resistance and Betrayal: The Death and Life of the Greatest Hero of the French Resistance, by Patrick Marnham (Random House, 2000).

The Miracle of Stalag VIII-A—Beauty Beyond the Horror: Olivier Messiaen and the Quartet for the End of Time, by John William McMullen (Bird Brain Publishing, 2010).

Messiaen, by Robert Sherlaw Johnson (Omnibus Press, 2009).

Olivier Messiaen: Journalism 1935–1939. Collected and translated by Stephen Broad (Ashgate Press, 2012).

Messiaen Studies, edited by Robert Sholl (Cambridge University Press, 2007).

For the End of Time: The Story of the Messiaen Quartet, by Rebecca Rischin (Cornell, 2003).

The Man Who Never Was: World War II's Boldest Counter Intelligence Operation, by Ewen Montagu (Montagu Estate, 1952; Blue Jacket Books, 2001).

Beyond the Pleasure Principle, by Sigmund Freud (Broadview, 2011).

Hamlet, by William Shakespeare (Norton, 1997).

The Book of Revelation, verse 19. *The Holy Bible* (Thomas Nelson and Sons, 1952).